# STITCHES & TEETH DUET

# THE MONSTER OF HOTEL N°. 7

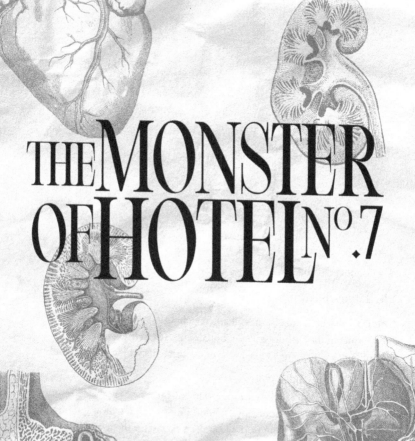

# THE MONSTER OF HOTEL Nº.7

## K.V. ROSE

# Author's Note

This is book one in the *Stitches & Teeth* duet. *The Monster* is a **dark romance** flirting with horror. Proceed with caution.

There are Frankenstein-esque elements throughout, but this is not a retelling.

While it is not required, reading my novella *Ambition* will acquaint you with characters mentioned throughout, as well as Writhe, the criminal organization Karia Ven and Sullen Rule both were born into.

As a little background information, **Writhe** is led by Mads Bentzen, the father of Von, whom is a friend to Karia. Lora Bentzen is Von's mother. Isadora Croft, another friend of Karia's, is dating Von. Her parents are Shella and Rig Croft.

**Stein Rule, Sullen's father, is the former leader of Writhe, and he stepped down and *vanished* several months before this story begins...**

*To each and every monster who held me in the night.*

# Playlist

Can be found on Spotify.

Take Aim - Sleep Token
Over Now - Post Malone
Antichrist - The 1975
BloodShakeTheEarthWhenItDrip - KAMAARA
I'd Do Anything - Baroness
This Won't Go Over Well - The Haunt
Whatever Lets You Cope - Black Foxes
Bloodbath - Polyphia, Chino Moreno
Will - Blacklit Canopy
Pigs - We Are PIGS
Hold Me Down - Halsey
skins - The Haunting
Strange Flower - Copeland
Be On Your Way - Daughter
33 "GOD" - Bon Iver
Move Me - Badflower
Drag Me into the Woods - Holy Fawn
Fortune Teller - Hippie Sabotage

*Playlist*

Love You to Death - Type O Negative
Tancevat - Molchat Doma
Sensation - (Crosses)
0% Angel - Mr. Kitty
Silent Season - Thousand Below
No Place Like You - Thousand Below
Never Too Late - Three Days Grace
Tear You Apart - She Wants Revenge
Hurricane - Dream on Dreamer
Dirt - Dream Drop
Push Me Away - OmenXIII, Palaye Royale
Jeepers Creepers - Slayloverboy
Sour Switchblade - Elite
War of Hearts - Ruelle
Sweet Dream - Bohnes, Underoath
The Perfect Girl - Mareux
HEARTBEAT - Isabel LaRosa
then i met her - EKKSTACY
Question...? - Taylor Swift
Ascensionism - Sleep Token
Sex Metal Barbie - In This Moment
All Over You - Live
The Day That I Ruined Your Life - Boston Manor
Is It Really You? - Sleep Token, Loathe
Far Away - Nickelback
JUDGEMENT NIGHT - HEALTH, Ghostmane, SIDEWALKS
& SKELETONS
i'm yours - Isabel LaRosa
Lightning Crashes - Live
Ice Cream Man - Tyga
Slow Down - Chase Atlantic
I Hate Everything About You - longlost

# ORGANIZATIONS OF ALEXANDRIA

NOT A COMPLETE LIST

FAMILY

## THE 6 UNSAINTS

SHADOWY

## CRUOR

REPORTS TO THE 6 & UNSAINTS

## WRITHE

OTHER

## VIPERA

# Chapter 1

## *Sullen*

*Dear Sullen,*

*I miss you on Ritual Drive. There is nothing but everything here and yet I dream only of you. It's pathetic and you would say so, wouldn't you?*

*But maybe not. You never said much.*

*Besides, when I'm restless from my own apathy, I let Cosmo drag his nails down my spine and kiss the scratches in his wake. We fuck, too, and he's good enough to make me come but...*

*I won't say it, what I want to. You'd roll your eyes and probably stop reading, if you even get these miserable, desperate letters.*

*I wish I could've told your mother when she was still alive that she must have known exactly who you would be before you were born, the way she had the most accurate name picked out for you.*

*You were boring and cruel and quiet and awful and I cannot get you out of my head.*

*I know I won't see you again. If Writhe couldn't find you, how could I?*

*But you'll appear in my dreams like a haunting nightmare and maybe one of these nights I'll have the courage to turn my back on you then, too.*

*You never cared for me—I know. You never cared for any of us.*

*But you were a familiar shadow, and do you know what it's like for your shadow to disappear?*

*No. Perhaps not. Maybe you were born without one.*

*Always unwillingly yours,*

*K. Ven*

I crinkle the letter in my fist and stare into the flames dancing in the fireplace of the sitting room inside Haunt Muren. Red and orange flicker alongside blue, and I imagine incinerating the white page with an anatomical header of hearts and brains stretched across the top. But Karia's sloping script is soothing in its own way, even if her words are not.

*Cosmo.*

I grip the page tighter, my short nails digging into the pad of my palm as I grind what's left of my teeth and effectively ruin her correspondence.

She could do better than Cosmo de Actis, a childhood friend of hers—I never had those—but she could do worse too, if I'm being objective.

It's impossible though.

Karia Waveria Ven is embedded under my skin like a bullet I can't remove. If she is dislodged, it'll be fatal.

I can't survive with her. And I can't live without her. But I've had to try and do the latter for the past two years. The lacerations along my skin are nothing compared to the gaping wound her absence leaves in my life.

And the most pathetic part is she was never really there *before*. We had no love affair. We exchanged few words. But she looked at me more than anyone ever did and... *Pathetic,* I know.

A creak sounds above my head, and I tip my chin up, heart thudding fast inside my chest, heat that has little to do with the fire expanding in every cell of my body. After twenty-three years of him, my nervous system has not adjusted to his nearness.

Stein is awake now, rising as he always does just after dawn.

That means my misery is only about to begin.

Karia wonders why I stay away. Why I never returned to Alexandria. I have heard of the many theories swarming the air there: Kidnapped for ransom, a brief escape to clear my head, I finally lost what little I had left of my mind. The night I walked out of my father's house on Ritual Drive when I was twenty-one, the speculation ran wild. Money was stacked upon my name as a performance from my father. A bounty offered for my safe return, then later, for even less. Scraps of my bones.

Two years ago now, almost exactly. Will be tomorrow. October second I went missing. The third is the day my new life started.

But I didn't do it willingly.

Stein needed a puppet.

*Now he pulls my strings.*

He only arrived to do so himself seven months ago, but in the interim, he had me acting for another; his guards.

But he cannot be everywhere always.

Tomorrow, Friday night, there is a gap for the first time in years, not only of his absence but a few of his more brutal men too. I know his schedule like I do the back of my eyelids. *October 2nd - Vancouver.* It's written in the ledger embossed with

3

snakes, the symbol of Writhe. One night only. I won't accompany him, and I won't be guarded inside this prison.

Finding Karia could be simple enough. Being who I am, there are many mouths willing to open and divulge what it is I want to know. Not from respect, but fear of Stein. If they only knew just how much he loathes me.

Regardless, I'm not sure I trust myself alone with her.

I didn't before my relocation, where I was kept inside a different tower in the same way. I watched her from the window of my room; we spoke in glances. She, like everyone on Ritual Drive, was frightened of me. And yet she rarely looked away.

I bow my head, pressing my scarred knuckles to my temple, her letter kept inside the cage of my hand.

I don't know why Stein delivers the epistles to me. Or perhaps it is just another form of torture. I know she places them in her mailbox, no address, and she understands how everyday tasks work in mysterious ways on Ritual Drive. But does she know I read each word?

One letter a month, sometimes less, and I have them all inside my pillowcase.

*Tomorrow night, I could find her.*

There is one place we might spend hours in alone.

Would she walk out alive though, when the sun rose?

I think of green light and test tubes and wet specimens, and my stomach hardens with sickness.

I am not sure I won't kill her.

I am not sure I can stay away.

# Chapter 2

## *Karia*

I stare at the double doors of the ballroom, intricate wood in deep blue, twisted with silver serpents, closed off to me. Inside, Von Bentzen and Isadora Croft and their parents discuss upcoming movements within Writhe, next assignments, ways to better deflect and conceal. My father is inside too, and my mother is at home, but I came to Hotel No. 7 because even though I am relegated to the outside, it feels better being near than far.

"Why do you give a fuck what's happening inside that room?" Cosmo de Actis's voice wisps against the shell of my ear and I straighten, my spine stiff as I ball my hands into fists at my side but don't turn my head to look at him.

"You came," I say instead, my voice hoarse.

"It's a Friday night in October, Alexandria is alive, and I knew you would be here wishing you were somewhere else." He speaks with that familiar lilt of amusement, so different from Sullen Rule in that way.

Both childhood friends; one—Sullen—inside Writhe, the clandestine organization my family is a part of, helping to keep guns and drugs and more nefarious crimes moving slowly and quietly through the city of Alexandria, North Carolina. The other—Cosmo—a boy who attended my private school and thus, we became close.

I've never wanted an in with Writhe; my parents have spoken in hushed voices about arranging my marriage and at the age of twenty-three, I think they would like it to happen soon. But I've heard nothing of my potential spouse and since Mads Bentzen—Von's father—just assumed leadership of Writhe as Stein Rule stepped down and vanished without a trace, just like his son, I don't think they have any immediate plans for me.

Sometimes I think I could fall into Cosmo's arms, but he is not involved in Writhe despite his nearness. It would give my parents no advantage to bind us.

"I want to be right here," I lie, tipping my chin up and taking in the sheer height of the doors in front of me, locked from the inside. I can hear nothing due to the thickness of the wood and the well-erected walls lined in blue damask wall-paper surrounding it.

"*Liar,*" Cosmo calls me out, his fingers bracketing my waist, cold fingertips on my bare skin, thanks to the red crop top I'm in. The words *half-mad* are splashed across the chest in black. It's how I feel, not knowing my place in this world. Never one for fighting like Isadora or cold command like Von. Writhe is wasted on someone like me.

I like shopping and fashion and film and luxury and maybe I am spoiled and stupid because of it, like Sullen once told me. One of the few times he spoke to me despite the fact we grew up on the same street and his father led Writhe and therefore, my own parents.

"What do I want, then, Cosmo, since you know me so well?" I fold my arms over my chest, and he squeezes my sides, making me squirm a little as I rock back in my white Vans. My spine grazes his solid core and I feel him dominating the space behind me. Shaved head, green eyes, olive white skin, that tilt of humor on his full lips he carries like an accessory; he is gorgeous.

But he couldn't be mine.

And he's...nice to me.

Kind.

Something may be broken inside my brain, but it makes me want him less. Being ignored by Sullen piqued my interest more. It still does, two years after he left.

"I think you want to explore," Cosmo says against my ear, then drops his mouth lower, his lips brushing my neck, exposed from the messy bun I threw my light blonde hair up in, strands still wet because I showered before I rode here with Isadora and Von in Isa's Jeep.

They gave me lingering looks as they left me on the outside. I could have demanded a seat at the table with my friends; my dad might give in. But I don't want one.

*I just want...*

"I think you want to find what it is you really desire," Cosmo speaks against my throat and goosebumps pebble over my arms, across my chest, down my exposed thighs.

His hands follow the path, fingertips gliding down my body before he pauses, picking at a loose thread from my ripped black denim skirt.

I let my eyes flutter closed as Cosmo plays with me. He is familiar. I could sink into him like it's nothing; let *him* sink into *me* as I have so many times in the past few months since letting Von go completely when he started dating Isadora. It would be easy, comforting, *hot.*

"Let's go to Septem and get a drink." He bands his arms around me then, pulling me back against his chest and hugging me from behind. "We're not spending an October Friday standing outside of rooms filled with people who don't want us inside of them."

# Chapter 3

## *Sullen*

I see her descend the curving staircase with him, his hand on the small of her back, palm pressed to her exposed spine.

They were far too easy to find, even if leaving Haunt Muren was physically laborious.

Writhe needs more discretion, but I suppose they don't count on my unique type of tenacity. And I *am* my father's son.

Inside my head, I imagine breaking the bones of Cosmo's fingers, snapping each one beneath his skin and leaving gaping space as they dangle uselessly from his metacarpals.

But despite the violence in my brain, *she* is smiling, cheeks lifting upward, her thin, petite nose in the air as white teeth flash and she reaches for a stray lock of blonde hair, paler than the rest, and tucks it behind her round ear. Leggy and lean and tan, she is probably everything Cosmo wants beneath him, and I know she's been in that exact position many times. I see things, even when I am not around. Haunt Muren is far, but there are grotesque ways for me to be near.

Cosmo hovers behind her like a protector, gray T-shirt over charcoal pants, his eyes lowering to her every few seconds as they head down the stairs together, soon to enter into Hotel No. 7's foyer.

The building is closed for "maintenance," so there are no bellhops or cleaning staff; no one mans Septem, the bar in the basement where these two plan to grab a drink together.

I know because I heard them.

She might have always looked for me when we were younger, when Ritual Drive was still home, but she wasn't the only one looking. She just rarely saw.

Even now, as I stand still and quiet and tucked away in the shadows of a silver gilded hall off the lobby, I am invisible to her while I stare. My hands are in the pockets of my black jeans, hoodie pushed over my head to cover the deep brown wavy strands, and aside from the necklace in silver tucked beneath my T-shirt, everything I'm wearing is the deepest shade of black.

They won't see me here because they aren't looking for me.

And as they reach the landing, then head further into the hotel to the out-of-the-way stairwell which will deposit them at Septem, neither flits their gaze to the shadows. Cosmo doesn't see the way my body stiffens as he slides his hand down her back and over the petite curve of her ass, palming her softly.

But even if he did look, he would have no idea of what's inside the purple vial pendant of my necklace. He couldn't know that the stopper forms an edge like a knife, so easy to prick a vein to place the poison that Stein Rule has used on me many times before.

A smile curves my lips, and it feels unusual.

I don't think I've performed the expression in years.

But tonight I'm back in Alexandria and I don't intend to waste another second staying away from the girl who has begged me in letters to come back to her. To the ghost of a connection we once had.

Will she like it when I see her in person?

When she realizes, despite our proximity and the passing we had at parties and rituals and on our childhood street and the ways she stared up at my bedroom window as she played with Cosmo and Von and Isadora and others, she doesn't really know me?

Tonight she'll know enough.

And I suppose I'll find out how well I like the sound of her screams.

# Chapter 4

## *Karia*

"I don't know how to mix drinks, but I can pour vodka into cranberry juice?" Cosmo offers his services with a grin as he stands behind the luxurious bar of Septem.

This place may be in a basement, but it's an immaculate one with high, arched ceilings and tones of silver and blue lights from inset lighting and battery-powered candles flickering along the edges of the bar top, gleaming in marbled black. The walls are exposed stone and the stool I'm perched atop is inlaid with smooth crystals that dance with the strange lighting every time I shift in my seat, my legs crossed so very properly like I'm not thinking of fucking Cosmo right now inside my head.

The scent of wild lavender and the old pages of a book linger down here, and in fact, deeper into the bar, a few steps down, there are leather couches facing a low table filled with volumes of obscure texts alongside empty champagne glasses and black dessert plates. I assume Writhe will descend here after their meeting in the ballroom and have a twisted little afterparty I may not want to witness, what, with my dad involved and all.

But for now, I only smile at Cosmo and nod my head as he gets to work behind the bar, pouring cranberry juice over ice, then a shot of vodka, all very haphazard and unofficial. I'd prefer a piña colada, but I don't think he's skilled enough for that.

He garnishes my drink with five cherries, and I laugh as he pushes it over to me with a smile.

I reach for the short glass immediately and our fingers brush. Lifting my blue eyes to his green ones, I bite down on my bottom lip and try not to think of Sullen Rule.

It always seemed to me he silently appeared more often when I was flirting with Cosmo. He wouldn't say anything if he happened down the street where I walked with my friends, but his silent, disturbing presence was enough to make me step a little away from de Actis.

Everyone hushed when he drew near.

The son of Writhe's leader, mysteries and rumors about him spread like a disease around our street, oozing as if from a wound.

It was strange to me that he was born the same year I was, and we had known each other our entire lives through our connection to Writhe, and yet I felt I was closer to Cosmo, whom I only met in high school, than I was Sullen.

In some ways.

In others, when he so much as looked at me on Ritual Drive, deep brown eyes glinting with pieces of amber, it was as if he could see into my soul.

And he never stared at the others in that way.

All the same, he became the butt of inside jokes; the monster and freakshow and isolated kid of our family's organization. Sometimes Von would tease that maybe my arranged marriage would be to him, a sacrifice for my duty to Writhe. Considering he rarely spoke to me, I think he would fight against an arrangement like that.

Because when he *did* speak to me, it wasn't very nice.

Once, at a Writhe meeting in which we were cloistered with the other kids inside a cathedral lobby, he told me I was stupid when I suggested we play truth or dare.

*"Then you come up with something," I snapped back to him, my heart galloping inside my chest as I stared at him watching me from a high-backed chair tucked into the shadows of the room.*

*He sat up straighter, gloved hands on his thighs, wearing long black sleeves and jeans. Every inch of him from the neck down was covered.*

*Everyone was silent, riveted by us.*

*He never spoke, and yet he had just antagonized me.*

*"No, let's do yours." His voice was low and rough, deep for our age—fourteen then. "I dare you to take my knife and drag it across one eye."*

*My breath caught in my throat.*

*Then Von cleared his own and said, "Anyway, moving on..." But he wouldn't address Sullen directly.*

*No one would.*

He was a psychopath, some said. He didn't speak, others claimed, although I knew that wasn't true. His father beat him, many whispered—I could believe it. His mother had committed suicide when we were both seven and everyone on the street heard the gunshot that night. Stein Rule was as quiet around me as his son and I sometimes wondered, when I was alone in bed and staring out my window toward his black, shuttered house across the street and two homes down, if Mercy Rule shot herself in the head because she was married to a man like him, and mother to a son like Sullen.

As I take a messy gulp from the vodka-cran Cosmo concocted, I guiltily marvel in my constant pipe dream and wonder if Sullen would ever show up to stop me from fucking my friend. Especially here, a familiar haunt of Writhe. But this silly fantasy has been inside my head since he vanished two years ago, and his father said there was no use looking for him despite the ransom money he offered up.

It didn't make sense though.

The highest-ranked member's son goes missing and Stein Rule's hollow face—so like his son's—and dark eyes betrayed nothing of worry anytime I saw him? He wasn't tearing the world down to get him back?

*Why?*

"Woah, slow down," Cosmo says with a laugh, and I realize I've sloshed vodka along my chin and tossed back three-fourths of the drink already, cherries bobbing around my lips.

I swallow hard, the sting pleasant and spiking in my belly as I set the glass down, then pluck out one cherry by its stem.

"Can you do anything with that?" Cosmo asks suggestively, his hands planted on the bar top between us as he stares at me with light green eyes.

I nip the sweet cherry off with my teeth and shake my head as his pupils dilate, watching me bite down on the garnish.

"Nope," I tell him honestly after I swallow. "But we both know what I can do to *you* with my tongue." My cheeks heat as I say it, but the alcohol has already made me brave because I don't look away.

I've slept with Von, before he was committed to Isa, and I've had sex with Cosmo many times, but that's where my count ends.

Of the two, only Cosmo knows the thing I really like, and it has nothing to do with my tongue.

He glances down as I set the cherry stem on the bar top and cup my hand around the ice-cold glass in front of me.

"Finish it," he says, his voice soft as he flicks his eyes up to mine. "Then another. And another. One more, maybe? When you're woozy, I'll set you down on the couch." He glances at the space with the table and books and plates. "When you're nodding off into unconsciousness, I'll have my hands all fucking over you."

I tighten my thighs, one knee still crossed atop the other, and my entire body grows hot. But he doesn't have to tell me twice.

I like to be touched when I'm out of it. Sleeping, drunk, drugged.

It's my thing.

Maybe I feel less guilty that way, since my parents always alluded to the fact they would decide my fate in terms of relationships, and there was a subtle hint that I should stay as pure as I could, not whore myself out and ruin my prospects, all of the usual indoctrination.

But if I'm incapable of fighting back or saying no, I'm not ruining anything, am I?

I finish the drink, the ice hitting my teeth then clinking together on the counter before Cosmo makes me another.

Then one more.

Three.

I have *three* in a row, on an empty stomach, only cherries in my belly.

Cosmo's stare grows more intense as I let him get me drunk and I slip a little on my bar stool, but only laugh it off.

It's just us here, in a cave of sorts, surrounded by blue light and dim shadows and bottles of expensive alcohol. Sullen won't come for me, but as Cosmo finally helps me off the stool, his arm around my shoulders, me leaning my weight into him as I stumble, maybe I can pretend for tonight the nightmare of my dreams is my present company instead.

Cosmo slides his arm off my back once I stand in front of the plush, black leather couch in the open room of the bar. My vision is a little blurry and if I squint, Cosmo is Sullen, although the latter is a few inches taller.

I remember that. The shadow he cast over me.

15

But when I sway on my feet, a giggle leaving my lips, and Cosmo pushes me harshly onto the cushions of the loveseat, it's easier to pretend.

It's how I imagine Sullen would touch me. Unattached, casually rough.

I want Cosmo to fuck me up.

*I want to see how Sullen feels.*

The two thoughts blur and I laugh again before Cosmo is in my face, his eyes flashing, but they look darker than his usual green.

My heart thumps wildly and I tip my head up, letting the sloppy strands of hair that fell from my bun slide away from my gaze.

Deep brown stares back at me.

A strangled breath leaves my lips, right before one single word.

*"Sullen?"*

Then the lights go out.

# Chapter 5

## *Karia*

"What?" Cosmo's voice is a whisper in the dark, harsher than I've ever heard from him. *"Sullen?"* He is close to my face, his breath dancing on my lips. "Why did you say his name? Why did you *scratch* me?" *What?* I didn't even touch him.

I shake my head, unseen. "Why are the lights out?" I counter his question with one of my own, blinking in the night dark of Septem. I don't hear the hum of the AC—still running everywhere in North Carolina—or the sound of the mini fridge behind the bar buzzing softly or...anything at all. I dig the heels of my hands against the thick leather edge of the sofa, curling my fingers around the material and squeezing. *"What's happening?"* The vodka has hit me, and everything is warm and pleasant but it's only a thin layer overtop the truth of fear strangled inside of my veins.

"Maybe the end of the world," Cosmo says cruelly, and I jump my eyes to his green ones, vivid in the dark. "I don't know, and I don't care. You didn't need to claw at me so deep, fuck. And *why did you say his name?*"

I frown, brows pulled together, shoulders tense; the eerie,

17

unnatural silence is like a spider down my spine as I sit up straighter and dart my gaze around the room. *I didn't touch you at all.* But I'm too scared to say that. "I thought I saw..." I trail off as I look to Cosmo once more. "It doesn't matter. Maybe we should go back up."

"Sullen hasn't been seen for two years," Cosmo continues, like he can't let this go. "Why the hell would he be here tonight? Have you been taking something, Karia? What the fuck is—"

A creak sounds, cutting him off. Not loud but hair-raising, unnatural in the gloom of Septem.

My breath hitches as I turn my head slowly, staring deeper into the shadows of the basement. There's a small corridor further in, leading to restrooms and a supply closet and not much else as far as I know.

I blink, straining my eyes to see through the near-total darkness we're drenched underneath. But in my focus, it's as if my limbs seem to sway from a calculated breeze despite the fact we are indoors. The vague shadow of the floor tilts in my line of vision and then beneath my feet. Everything is *off,* skewed, and I slump back against the couch, pressing my fingertips desperately into the leather as the temperature in the room plummets.

It is ice cold, or maybe that's only inside my brain, the way my body feels numb, and I am *frozen.* I can't blink, turn my head, move my tongue. It is clumsy in my mouth, swollen, and the floor falls away from my white Vans. I have no sense of my body occupying this room beneath the hotel.

My chest rises, rises, *rises.*

Then there's a thud.

Like a body dropping.

*Finality.*

Too close.

So close I should flinch, but it's as if my nerves have forgotten how.

There is something—*someone*—standing where Cosmo stood, but I know it is not him any longer.

On sensation alone, I recognize the former leader of Writhe's son. His presence has always chilled me, but something is more wrong now.

*Wrong and...worse.*

I didn't imagine him.

*I see you, whether you want me to or not.*

The thought feels strange in my head—bubbly, vacant—as unwillingly, my fingers and spine and the curve of my neck relax. I am collapsing against the couch. Sinking into helplessness. I have no choice in the matter.

*There was something in my drink.*

It comes to me quickly, being a child of Writhe.

*Someone drugged me.*

The thought is welcoming. Horrifying. Grotesque and sensual and frightening all at once.

*Sullen.*

"*Have you missed me?*" His voice is right *there,* deep and croaking, as if he never spoke, just like the rumors say.

A sharp intake of breath hovers between us before I feel strong arms beneath me and I am tilting, the couch is long gone, fallen away, and instead, I am being...carried.

I cannot pick up my limbs. My muscles do not work, my bones are sinewy rubber, snapped from a band, useless and dangling. I can breathe though, and the inhale through my nose brings the traces of darkened roses, earth, and sandalwood. I obsessed over this same scent each time he passed me on Ritual Drive, wearing a black hoodie, the same color pants, hands in his pockets, chin dipped, hood over his deep brown strands. Darkest eyes, flecks of amber lifting to me and framed by onyx lashes, his heavy bottom lip pushed out further than his top in a severe sort of pout.

I studied him in ways no one else did.

They were too busy casting judgment.

There was no room for inquiry where my other friends were concerned.

But I noticed things about him. I found his history in the way he began to wear black, high-collared shirts underneath his hoodie as we grew older, covering the column of his throat, all the way to the underside of his chin. He was always buried in fabric and yet... He was tall, strong, moving with a preternatural, wicked grace, like a boy who had been taught in violence how to remain a shadow. Never seen, rarely heard, forbidden, it seemed, from looking out.

Yet when he did, he only ever looked at me.

I took pride in it. Secretly, in stolen, quiet moments. When Von teased me about the arranged marriage to Sullen, I would pretend I loathed the idea, while on the inside I glowed with a sick, secretive pride.

But now, cradled in his embrace yet held at arm's length, sticky regret sludges through my veins as my pulse thumps quickly but weak, too feeble and frail to fight an agony like Sullen Rule.

I blink heavy lids, fear of falling into a forced sleep oozing through my bloodstream. *Stay awake. Don't dream. This is a nightmare you have to survive.*

My lips part, as if to speak, but when my eyes catch on the darkest gleam where Sullen's gaze should be, the words scratching up my throat stay stuck there.

He is moving, I realize, a rhythmic motion swaying my body as he walks softly, striding as he always did, a murderer slipping through locked doors.

The room is still darkest night.

There is no sound and yet the sensation of cotton in my ears grows thick. I want to tug at them, hear more clearly, swallow to pop my auditory canal, yet I can do nothing but latch onto the whites of Sullen's eyes. The circle of horrific sins contained inside of them.

And as he disappears into the corridor, toward the bathrooms, but further, deeper, into a hallway perhaps I did not know existed, my mind slips from wanting to move, scream, touch, run; to something far...worse.

*Where have you been?*

*What happened to you?*

*Who put the fear of being seen inside of you?*

*Which one ripped away your voice; your mother? Your father?*

*When did you ever think of me, two long years apart?*

He is staring at me as he moves, his fingertips digging into my hips, my shoulder blade, the way he's carrying me with my head resting against the crook of his elbow.

*He is looking back now.*

I should think of Cosmo. Wish to know he is okay, unhurt, safe. Still breathing.

*Think of the one who loves you.*

But Sullen is clawing into me, the same way he did when we passed like two ghosts in a graveyard years ago as children; him never seen and me rarely understood. We were never whole.

And I don't think of Cosmo.

I think maybe I would *let* this happen; Sullen carrying me into the dark. Perhaps, even if I could, I wouldn't fight him.

But now my choice is taken away, so I don't have to pretend.

I swear a smile curves his mouth, the glint of a few white teeth just visible in the dark, as if he knows precisely what it is I'm thinking.

"I can feel your pulse race through the back of your skull, on my arm." He speaks in that same strange tone, and it is as if he is tasting words for the first time in far too long. "Don't get excited, Little Sun. I will never bring you out of the dark now."

# Chapter 6

## *Sullen*

The room glows green. Test tubes and Mason jars line the walls, the lighting inset along the base of cabinets. It is not for decor. It contains not only light but air, chilling the subject, suspended in formaldehyde. There is half of a serpent stuffed inside one vessel, wicked patterns along his scales, the tail a sharp, dark point and the head...absent. Blood exists in vacutainers, a pattern of the tubes interspersed with other specimens in the room.

Each wall is filled, floor to high ceiling, the path to this secret of mine has no door. Instead, the escape is above my head. I have to climb each shelf carefully, past the lamb's eye floating in the highest-most jar, reach a hand for the groove that does not belong, set in the deep black ceiling.

Then I must climb up, and out, and move through the air ducts to the places I am supposed to exist within this hell. The rooms my father strangles me inside of on Ritual Drive.

Now, though, I simply survey each wall, listen to every wire humming to keep my collection of monsters cold. This is not strictly necessary, but I have become accustomed to the lowest of temperatures. I cannot leave them in less. Besides, Stein is obsessed with fire, *even on the hottest days. I cannot stand it. I can't abandon my creatures to sickly warmth.*

*Some I have found on the premises. Others I have acquired through different means, plotting deliveries around Stein's chaotic schedule.*

*They are the only ones who see me...if they have eyes to do so.*

*Even the maimed observe me.*

*What choice do they have?*

*I am their god.*

And it is not enough.

*I long for a different subject to worship me instead. I would crash each jar, empty every glass, swallow all of the slithery, slimy, sinister creatures caged in this room if I could only get a taste of her.*

*Sunshine hair, cerulean eyes; an unnatural blue. The way her pale pink lips slip into a hauntingly endearing frown when I am close. She stops speaking too, her breath catching in her throat. Even if she is beside de Actis, or Bentzen, or with one of her other, many friends, she becomes a frightened doll for me.*

*When I can't stay away, when I need to inhale her innocence—bitten with the scent of violets and cedar—I come to her on our street. Her pupils widen, edging out the sharp blue, and I watch her pulse flutter at her throat and her long legs put distance between herself and whoever her companion of the night is, and I can't help but want.*

*In the darkness of Ritual Drive, she is the everlasting, unattainable sun. I want to storm over her, cloak her in violent lightning and blackest clouds.*

*I desire little more than to smother that hope she carries with her always, getting her on her knees for me as I do it.*

*It is a cruel illusion, that longing for better than she has.*

*I know this to be true.*

*But even as I stand in my lab and my fingers clench inside the pocket of my hoodie, bandages and broken bones lancing bright and dull pain both up my wrists, I know I will never reach for her when we dance by one another.*

*I don't trust my own desire to keep her alive for more than one use.*

Hope.

*It is all I have.*

*Maybe one day I will recreate this room for her, away from the stifling, torturous evil of my father. I will have only one wall.*

*It will house pieces of her.*

*There are many properties my father owns, but only one I have enjoyed seeing her inside. A few times, but there was a moment she doesn't know exists; stolen and snatched like any slivers of melancholic joy are for me.*

*I watched her with Cosmo inside Hotel No. 7.*

*She did not move.*

*She did not speak.*

*Her arms dangled by her sides.*

*He did anything he wanted to her.*

*I pretended so well, to be inside of his skin and feel hers through his fingertips.*

*I did not kill him either, when it was all over, and that is a job well done.*

*I need it again.*

*I need it with her.*

*And this time, maybe far in the future when I come for her again, when I am no longer content to watch,* it will have to be real.

# Chapter 7

## *Karia*

The room is green. It glows with the color.

*"I know what you like,"* he whispers against my ear, my head in that woozy space between sleep and wake.

*Nothing makes sense.*

*The color is lit up around me. And the scent of something in the air that is sharp, strong; like apples but...wrong.*

"You think I left without knowing? Without watching? You think I didn't see what you let boys do to you in the dark?"

A cold hand splays over my low belly, fingertips pressing lightly against my bare skin.

*Bare.*

A hand.

*That voice.*

"Sullen." I mumble his name as I lie on my back, but my eyelids are so heavy, fluttering weakly to see verdant, lime, poison. So much *green.* And in between each blink, there are jars and bottles and vases and beakers.

This cannot be my reality.

Because Sullen Rule disappeared two years ago and he has never come back. Even if he did, why would he ever find *me?*

"You're the only one who ever spoke to me when we were children. I had to know why, you see."

My heart pounds loud and strong but I'm not anymore awake than I was.

So many poisons. So many drugs. My eyes fall closed. *I do not see, Sullen.*

The green burns behind my lids.

There is the sense of a shadow drawing close, then his breath is warm against my cheekbone, his voice dropped low. "I watched you from my room, not so close you'd see me if you ever looked up, but close enough to catch you laugh and smile and flirt on our street. Sunshine, but you'd tip your head over your shoulder too, glancing back. At *my* house." He slowly slides his hand lower, slipping his fingers over the bones along my hips.

There is nothing between us.

*Nothing.*

Alarm bells ring inside of my mind, crawling and scratching and embedding themselves into my brain, but my body does not react. I try to open my eyes and it is useless. Every part of me is heavy and tired and still.

"Rats and snakes and lifeless bats pinned by their wings. That was around me when I saw you. My bedroom's decor. I wasn't a place for you then. But sometimes I imagined it, when Stein was away. I wrapped my hand around myself and closed my eyes and it was you there. Kneeling for me. Waiting. No one ever touched me like I did myself, but in my head it wasn't me. And no one ever touched me... like you."

*"Sullen."* It comes out clumsy. I'm not sure I say it at all.

But he brushes his lips against my skin and goosebumps rise across my chest, and while my breasts feel full and heavy, something is very wrong.

"Do you shave? Are you bare?" He pulls at my lobe with his teeth, fingertips dancing over my low belly. "I don't want you to be. I want everything how it's meant."

My cheeks flame hot, and I'm not waxed but I do trim and I'm wondering if he'll love or hate it and I'm scared of wondering the wrong things because what does any of that matter when I don't know what he's going to do to me and—

*This is a dream.*

It's so clear to me, all at once.

*This is not real.*

I don't have time to play with the thought before my sleep continues, so vivid and borderline horrific with the sound of his voice.

"Let your knees fall to the side. Stop being so tense. You're as rigid as a corpse. I thought I gave you enough..." He kisses my ear then and his hand goes lower.

In my mind, my spine curves and arches off whatever soft surface I am lying upon, but in reality, I do not move as he flickers his touch over my pubic bone.

But no lower.

He is teasing me.

*I am dreaming. I am growing wet for him.*

"*Sullen,*" I try again because this is not real. There was no Cosmo. No meeting I was not invited to. There were no years in which I dreamt of the devil of Writhe. Or perhaps, the devil's only son. Worse than the father; he knows all the tricks.

His breath warms my mouth. He is looming over me now as his thumb draws circles on my low belly. The green lighting is dimmed behind my closed lids, blocked by his presence alone. "You cannot stop it, you know. *I never could.*"

I have no idea what he means, but there seems to be a world of sadness and grief and hatred for himself in those words.

Then he presses his palm flat, on my low belly, directly in

the center. The pressure is firm, nearly painful, as if he wants to squeeze my organs out.

"I wonder what I could make this do." He speaks as if I am an experiment. Not a person, only a body.

"*Sullen.*" My pulse is rapid now, but I still cannot see or move or scream. I try again, though, with my words. "Where did you go?" My breath hitches, my voice breaks. I do not know if I am being clear.

But he stops trying to crush me and instead lets his hand relax.

I greedily drink in air. I try to survive the dream despite the fact I am still rendered motionless.

Then I sense him move away, as if he is straightening, sitting up, but he doesn't stop touching me.

He is silent.

A soft hum moves through the green-tinted room. I do not know what it is; like a fan turned on low. But it disguises my heartbeats from my own ears.

"Sullen?" I can't stop saying it. It's like a prayer on my lips, a hope for the hopeless because this may be a dream, but Sullen Rule is always unreachable, in sleep or wakefulness.

This, though, is a moment I have craved.

Aloneness, with him. The ghost of Ritual Drive.

"Please don't go." It slips from my mouth like poison, viscous like honey, the way it oozes between us, unanswered.

My eyes feel heavy, pressure building behind the tight, shut lids, shame growing wet in the form of tears at my own pathetic desperation. It is getting harder to remember this isn't real as it slices through my nervous system like a scalpel.

*Why do I want you?*

My parents aren't evil. They are indoctrinated and we are obedient to the whims of Writhe, but I am not abused, mistreated. Neglected, perhaps, but I have Cosmo and Von and Isadora and the rest of them for that. I can buy anything I want on Mommy and Daddy's credit cards. I drive a BMW. I have more commas in my bank account than most people see in a lifetime.

Given to me.

Handed down.

I know Jimmy Choo and Gucci and Valentino and Burberry like the dearest friends.

*Why do I look for you around every corner? Imagine your unseen hands twisting and wringing out my body, forcing me to stare up into your pain.*

*It's there.*

*I sense it.*

*Let me drink it from your blood, Sullen Rule.*

"Something happened to me, you know." His voice claws through my euphoric, deranged thoughts. It sounds so real, and I am enthralled.

I lie still, even as he slips his hand from me.

His touch is gone.

I cannot move.

See.

Speak again.

But he continues and I don't cry for his absence yet. "Beautiful horrors. They are embedded in my skin, Karia Ven." The way he says my name is divine, full of wanting, *worship.*

*Tell me everything.*

*Rip it from your soul.*

*What did they do to you?*

Something shifts. A movement in the air. A specter of steps.

The green is gone.

Yawning darkness takes its place.

I shiver, tremble, I cannot stop it.

Then the whisper of a blanket, it is unfurled over my naked body. A gust of air, the settling of deliciously soft cloth on my skin, starting at my chest, grazing over my tummy, my hips, lightest and last on my legs, my feet.

I am covered. A pre-burial, perhaps?

"Do you want to know who did it to me?" His voice is lower. Scratchy, rough. *Distorted.* "*Who made me this?*"

I hold my breath.

I want to wake up now.

Everything feels worse as I lie here motionless, useless, helpless.

*I want to wake up, please.*

Then he is closer.

*I don't want to die yet.*

Gone one heartbeat, there the next.

His mouth is over mine.

His teeth scrape my lips, awkward and detached and animalistic in the brief motion of bright pain.

Then he says, a garbled, eerie hiss, "*You.*"

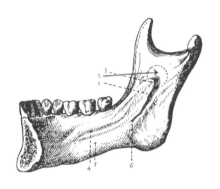

Karia,

I don't know why you write me.
I don't know why you enjoy torturing us both.
There is nothing for me to say to you.
I only think of you all the time.
I only want to bite you so hard you bleed.
I only want to bracket you in glass, taxidermy of the worst kind.
I only want...

# Chapter 8

## *Sullen*

S tein is away. We have guards, but they avert their eyes when they see me coming, so long as they know I am simply walking the street. It didn't used to be that way. Before, they would hurt me, too. Restrain me, hit me; a few were brave enough to land a kick at my head once or twice. I always ended up seeing stars and sometimes, throwing up blood. Never did I make it out of the house, no matter how invisible I tried to be.

I couldn't collect animals then.

Now, though, I'm eighteen and I can't leave my room without getting fully dressed or else my seams start to show.

The guards must believe even I have had enough.

I slip out into the night, glancing once over my shoulder as I always do when Stein is allegedly away for business. If he catches me, I might not have legs to leave on anymore. I doubt the guards keep my secret, but by the time he arrives back, he already has a new punishment in mind and anything I did in his absence, I pay for dearly.

For now, the looming, dark bricks, and gleaming, glittering windows—lit by security lighting in the expansive front yard—are all I see. Dark curtains beyond each pane, the circular fountain with *a pair of stone gargoyles, they both watch me in silent judgment, but they cannot reach me here. Water pleasantly fills the large gray basin and it's the only sound in my ears aside from the crickets; the auditory sensations are enough to convince anyone that while this house may look Gothic, everything is beautiful and calm and serene inside.*

*It could not be further from the truth. But the three garage bays are closed, silent, and the paved driveway stretches ahead of me along with hours of stolen October night, until sunrise.*

*It doesn't take long for me to reach Ritual Drive. Our entrance lane is one of the shortest along our street; it is how I can see* her *from my bedroom tower.*

*And she is out here now, unless she has skipped inside one of her friends' homes; I watched her walking beside Cosmo under the light of the full moon.*

*My heart thumps fast in my chest as I head east, the direction she was going in her short, white shirt and even shorter black skirt.*

*I am eager and alive in the fresh air, the cool chill of early fall dancing over my cheekbones, whispering across my lips. It feels* pleasant *here, away from my dungeon of a room and the glow of the lab. And the idea of catching up to her coming near...it has the numbness of tingles shooting through my veins.*

*I blink in the shadow of the night; there are few streetlights on Ritual Drive, considering we are all trying to hide who and what we really are. But the wind catches on her beautiful laughter at the same moment I spot her in Cosmo's arms; her long, blonde strands hang in pale sheets as he spins her beneath the closest lamp post, her chin tilted up, throat exposed as she lets him twirl her round and round. He is dressed in jeans, an orange shirt, and the color is contrasted with her white and black outfit in a way that momentarily mesmerizes me. So much of her skin is visible, too; long, tanned legs, the planes of her stomach, the arch of her neck.*

*I stop breathing for a moment as she laughs louder, a brash,* noisy sound, and Cosmo slows his movements; neither of them have seen me yet.

I keep my head bowed beneath my black hoodie, gloved hands in the pocket. Despite the cool temperatures, I feel the clammy stickiness of sweat along the back of my neck, thanks to the high-collar shirt beneath my top layer, the black jeans, and thick black socks under my high-tops. They help with the lacerations on the bottom of my feet.

A burst of wild anger erupts through my brain as I think of it; the way she is so free and exposed, and I am imprisoned from wounds even when I have managed to escape.

I stalk toward them faster but on quiet steps as Cosmo slowly drops her to her feet and keeps his arm around her shoulders to steady her. She is shorter than him, and therefore I am far taller than her. I could snatch her off this street and hide her in my shadow and not even Cosmo would be able to find her again.

But when I am so close I can see the frilly white tops of her socks and the goosebumps on the back of her thighs, I do not grab her like I'd love to.

I am scared of what I would do to her; if she became parts of a jar inside my lab, what fun would that be? She couldn't speak to me, laugh in my presence, tell me everything about her spoiled little life.

But I am also terrified to see her recoil from me if I did something less rash and tried to begin a crooked friendship. I do not know how to have those; I've never called anyone 'friend' in my life. And if she somehow agreed to be mine, what would I do after? I have never touched someone intimately. I have never kissed, even, despite Maude's imaginary offer.

I am experienced in violence and horrors, and I can take a beating, but I am a virgin in every other way.

The last time I was hugged was eleven years ago, by my mom, the night before she...

I shake my head, clenching my jaw tight as I stop walking, eyes closed.

My pulse is beating against the inside of my brain, and I feel as if I may explode. Scream at the top of my lungs and beg for her to see me, touch me, talk to me.

But if I did, Stein would kill me over the embarrassment and perhaps before he even got home to do it, the look of disgust and dismissal in her eyes might slaughter me first.

"Sullen?"

My eyes snap open, my entire body tense as she calls out my name as if she's spoken it many times before.

Cosmo hangs one step back, no longer touching her, and she has her fingers in the ends of her hair, like she is clutching a blanket, other hand in a fist at her side.

Her deep blue eyes are so vivid in the night and the black lashes framing them so long, looking at her face is better than any type of scientific experiment I could conduct in my lab. Any removal of blood from roadkill, slice of a snake's scale. Any macabre invention I could create, she surpasses it all. She would be better than any doll, any toy.

She is...so pretty.

There is a small crease between her light brown brows, and her pink lips are parted as she stares at me, waiting for me to speak. I feel Cosmo glaring my way and I can sense his tense body, like he will beat me to death if I come closer to her.

I don't move, but as the silence stretches between us, she takes a step toward me.

"Karia—"

She silences Cosmo's protest with a wave of her hand, letting her hair slip between her fingers as she does, her eyes flashing as she looks at me, but I know it's directed toward him.

"Sullen?" she whispers again. "Do you...want to walk with us?" Her voice is rough, like she is scared, and her hand is still lifted to keep Cosmo quiet.

I glance at him and find green eyes glaring at me, his entire body radiating hostility.

*I take a quick breath as I look to her again.*

*I open my mouth.*

No, I only want to walk with *you.*

*That is what I want to say, but nothing comes. My mouth stays mute and my eyes on her and I want to cross the two feet between us but she is still now and if she saw the scars along my body and the worse things under my skin, she might...*

*I turn around.*

*I don't walk away, though, but I can't look at her.*

*She is perfect in every way and there is nothing I can give her. I would only trap her, dissect her, keep her, kill her.*

"Wait, don't go." *Her voice is still so hoarse, low and quiet and scared.*

*I close my eyes and inhale the October air.*

*Sweat drips along my spine.*

I don't want to go, but I don't know how to stay.

*I can't say that, either. I can't say anything.*

*I...can't.*

*I have to go home.*

*Stein is right, I know. I don't belong out here. No one will understand me, and they will only laugh and if she ever truly saw me for who and what I am, she would scream. She would run.*

*I can't have this little piece of sun in my life unless she is dead, a body in a jar, and I am not brave enough for that.*

*Not yet.*

# Chapter 9

## *Karia*

"I never hurt you." I find my voice again as he begins to tuck me in underneath the light, soft sheet. He starts at my shoulders, pressing the fabric around me, stuffing it beneath my arms, elbows, wrists. Methodically, he does the same to my hips, thighs, calves, feet. Cotton tight around my naked body, his shadow hovering over my face, the sting of my lips from his half-bite the realest thing about this moment.

My eyes flutter behind closed lids but I can't even turn my head, let alone see. My mouth is dry, and my lips feel clumsy, and everything is so very *heavy*.

"I never..." I trail off because I cannot continue. It is taking too much effort to simply *breathe,* let alone speak or reason or explain to him.

He touches my temple, smoothing back my hair from my face. There is leather on his fingers now; *gloves.* He wore those too, as he grew older, although he tried to hide that he did, with his hands pushed into the pocket of his hoodie.

Unlike his twisted kiss from before, his touch now is gentle. Almost *hesitant.* He loops my strands behind my ear, skimming over the tip of my cartilage, sending cold shivers down my throat, my back, across my chest, tightening my nipples into hard, heavy points.

Then he rests one hand along my cheekbone, cradling my face softly.

I want to say something, ask a question, understand where I am, if this is reality, or if I can hold onto the illusion of a dream.

His breath is over my mouth as he leans in, and I catch the scent of nothing. He is not chewing gum or eating mints, it doesn't seem as if he has just brushed his teeth, but his breath is clean and absent of anything. There is, however, the aroma of wilting roses and damp earth around him. It is divine in its unholiness and as I inhale him, comfort and danger both spark inside of my chest, pushing my pulse to that of a frightened rabbit's.

"Oh, that is not true," he says, voice so throaty, it sounds inhuman.

I feel my eyes move beneath my lids, wishing desperately to *see,* but I can't. Since he seemed to have flipped a light switch, even the green is gone, and there is only gloom around us.

His thumb strokes over my bottom lip, his touch light and scarce. I taste the leather of his glove, like new shoes and thick smoke. I've never consumed either, but I imagine if I had, it would be like this.

"I didn't." A sliver of relief pulses through me when I can speak again. "I...looked for you. I invited you. I always wanted to talk to you."

Aggressively, more sure, he presses his thumb to the center of my mouth, over both lips, like he wants to sew them closed. He pulls back; I can sense the cold air shift around him. "The first time Stein saw me watching you from my window, he flayed the flesh along my bicep and pushed a candy wrapper inside before he stitched it over. He laughed as he pressed his latex-gloved hand along my arm, listening to the crinkle. 'Peach chews,' he said, and I realized he was sucking on the one that came from the wrapper under my skin."

Revulsion is a visceral reaction in my body. My stomach tightens and a wave of sickness—hot and sticky—washes over me. I cannot stop myself from parting my lips, a dry wretch coming up my throat, the sound audible over the hum of a fan inside the room.

But Sullen's finger is there, and he pushes it inside my mouth, pressing down on my tongue, the taste of leather thick and soft and unnatural along my tastebuds.

My stomach swirls with nausea but I don't heave again as he then moves his finger to the underside of my top teeth, dragging it slowly along the grooves of my molars. My mouth begins to water, saliva dripping from the corner of my lips, and I am not breathing.

"Does that disgust you?" he asks quietly, and I cannot imagine how he is positioned around me. If he is sitting in a chair adjacent to this table I seem to be on, or if he is standing. But the way he touches me, with such hesitant ease, makes me believe whatever pose he is in is comfortable for him. He slides his finger over my teeth now, along the sides, across the front two, my top lip pushed out a little with his invasive exam. "Because if you think *that* is bad, Little Sun... If I extracted *this* tooth," he pushes his gloved finger beneath the sharpness of my canine, "right here, without anesthetic, you would understand a small fraction of what it means to be *his* child."

Fear like I have never known shoots through every corner of my body. Fear and sympathy and a desire to comfort him; they all contort and confuse inside my brain.

"*Why?*" I can't help it, and the word is muddled from my mouth. When I speak it, my lips close briefly around his finger.

I hear his sharp intake of breath and I don't know what it's from until a second later when he says, "Do that again," in a calm, hoarse voice. Before I can ask what, he adds, "Suck on my finger. Use your teeth."

I am breathing with my mouth open, spit running out the corners of my lips, and I want to tell him no and I want to ask why Stein Rule hated him so much and I want to scream but before I can do any of that, he seems to stand or straighten, the way the shadow of him moves behind my closed lids.

Then his other hand is pressing harshly against my low belly, over the sheet, and my ab muscles contract as I heave again, around his finger still in my mouth. The pressure on my abdomen is full and painful and deep and he says very clearly but so raspy, "I am trying to control myself with you and it is incredibly difficult. Please, do as I say, Karia."

I don't think. I am no longer sure I am dreaming, but if there is a chance I'm not, I would like to survive this. I close my lips around his finger, which takes more effort than it should, like my muscles are still sleeping, hovering on the border of wakefulness. I let my teeth catch softly around the bones, the sensation of the leather soft and spongy beneath them.

He lets up on the pressure along my stomach, although he does not move his hand away.

I hear him breathing; it is loud, over the fan in the background. He sounds frightened, but he hasn't told me to stop and in fact, he presses his finger further into my mouth, touching the back of my tongue.

"Bite down," he says, a low rasp.

I close my mouth just above what I think is the last knuckle of his finger.

*"Harder."* It is a command laced with desire.

Heat flares inside of me, sweat forming along the back of my neck, but I do as he said. I do not wish to hurt him, though, and inside my head, I see his father sucking on candy after he abused his son, laughing through it all.

That pressure becomes fuller behind my eyes.

Then, as I bite on his finger pushed to the very back of my throat, I can... *blink.*

There is a hazy vision of *him,* lit by the softest green glow I couldn't sense through my lids before. Perhaps he only turned the verdant lights down instead of off.

Dark eyes, brown with a fleck of amber. A hood over his short, dark strands. The high black collar covering his throat.

His plush lips parted as if in ecstasy.

He is standing over me. There are high ceilings, jars atop them, but I focus on nothing but him.

Until he sees me watching.

He snatches his hand from my mouth so violently, my canines scrape along his glove and my breath hitches as he places his hand over my eyes, the feel of my own saliva wet and warm against my skin just above my brows.

"I did not get the dosages correct," he says, muttering as if to himself. "I did not. I messed it up. You shouldn't be awake. You shouldn't see—"

"I'm so sorry he hurt you, Sullen." I speak while I can, my lips trembling as I try to clench my fingers into fists at my side. I am regaining some control, but I want to be subtle. I pretend this is real, in the case my death wouldn't be something I could wake up from. And that means I cannot let him know I am able to feel and move again. "Your dad is—"

His hand comes to my throat.

He squeezes the sides, *hard.*

My voice leaves me, and he is speaking over my mouth again, palm keeping my vision dark.

*"He is not my dad."* The words are animalistic, breathy, and guttural. His fingertips close tighter around my neck with each one.

"I'm sorry, I just meant... You deserve better." When I speak, I can feel my own breath reflecting back to me because of his closeness. Everything is muffled with his hand at my throat.

"You deserve so much better. Where have you been? Where did you go? Let me wake up so I can see you and talk to you and—"

"No. *No.* No, I've done this all wrong." He releases me all at once, both hands, and when I blink again, clearing my vision, I see him turn his back to me, broad with wide shoulders beneath his hoodie.

I cast my eyes downward, trying to decipher what he's doing, but before I can spot more than a sterile-looking steel table, he is facing me, and there is a syringe between his fingers, his thumb on the plunger.

He must see the fear in my eyes, the way I jerk my head back, twisting away from him, because he *changes*.

"Shh, shh," he says so softly, bowing his head, his features barely visible with the hood. He has high cheekbones, hollow cheeks, full lips, minimal, dark stubble along his defined jawline. But he is coming close to me with the needle and the nearness obscures some of what I can see beneath his hood. I focus on the barrel of the syringe, clear liquid inside. Panic makes my pulse race and a surge of adrenaline shoots through my body, but I can still only close my fingers into fists.

I try to kick out with my legs but manage just a flutter of one toe before he grabs my face, fingers along my jaw, and turns my head away from him, like he doesn't want me to watch what it is he's going to do to me.

Then I see it.

What is inside one of the many jars in this room.

*No.*

There is a white rabbit floating in what must be formaldehyde, pink eyes looking at me, its fluffy body bent and compressed to fit inside the large vessel.

"*No,*" I say it out loud this time, trembling along the table.

I try to kick again, and this time I manage it, the sheet slipping lower on my body, exposing my breasts.

Sullen grips my face harder and he makes some strange noise in the back of his throat. A groan, maybe.

I feel cold air along my chest, my heart racing in my ribcage.

Then something sharp pricks along my nipple.

I freeze.

Close my eyes tight, so I don't see the rabbit as I dig my nails into my palms, but I can't seem to lift my arms. When I desperately kick again, the sheet slips lower, exposing my abdomen.

I am half bared to him, of my own doing.

"Does this hurt?" he asks quietly, still gripping my face, keeping it turned away from him.

I do not know precisely what he means until I feel it once more.

Another prick along my nipple.

Tears form behind my eyes.

"What are you doing?" I whisper, feeling the warmth of my own silent crying streaking down my face. "What are you doing to me?"

He doesn't answer, but I sense him shift.

Then something warm and wet is along my breast, closing over my nipple, and he is *sucking* on it. *Me.*

A whimper leaves my throat as his teeth scrape over my flesh.

He lifts his head an inch and cold air tingles along my skin where he had me in his mouth. "You are...divine, Karia." He tugs my nipple between his teeth, and I cry out, my spine arching from the table. It doesn't hurt so much as it is overwhelming, and I don't know where the needle is and I'm terrified of where he will put it and what it will do to me.

"Please let me see you," I whisper, even as I keep my eyes closed, his hand still forcing me to look away from him. *"Please."*

He bites at me once more, this time his teeth close around the flesh of my breast, then he lifts his head and abruptly pulls my face toward him.

I flash open my eyes.

"Do you see now?" he asks quietly, his pupils enlarged, nearly blending into the darkness of his irises, the sight jarringly familiar although I can't place why. There are hollows beneath his eyes, purple and black skin, sunken in. "Is this the friend you wanted, Karia?" He smiles, and it is unnerving. Teeth show, but not many. He is missing some, but he has his canines, and they are unnaturally sharp in his mouth. White, thin points, like he could puncture my skin with them. "Is this who you wished to play with, growing up?" He tilts his head and with the movement, the high collar of his shirt shifts, revealing a patch of skin along his throat.

My body grows cold.

There is something sewn inside of it. Of *him.* Something that makes his flesh lumpy and—

"No, no, I did not think so. I am truly sorry for what is about to happen, but I couldn't stay away from you. Your eyes are always inside of my head, and you did send me those pathetic letters, after all."

*He read them.*

I have one second of shameful agony, hot and bright over my fear, before I feel it.

The needle, plunging into my stomach. It is a deep, vicious sensation.

I cry out and he stares at me as I do, a small smile tipping up the corners of his lips while he holds my face in one hand and perhaps my life in the other.

The needle comes out.

I hear him toss it onto the steel table.

I can still see.

Nothing is happening yet.

*Nothing is happening.*

He is cupping my face in both hands now as he looms over me.

"What did you do to me?" I ask quietly, my eyes roving over his, my own frantic, desperate for answers. "What is going to happen?"

"Don't worry," he whispers, smoothing his thumbs up my cheekbones as he studies me as if I am a patient and he is my doctor. "When you wake up, it will only get worse."

It happens slowly.

I am sluggish.

I can't keep my eyes open.

Gray spots; white.

Then, his hands still around my face, everything slips into darkness.

# Chapter 10

## *Karia*

Cosmo is the first thing I see.

My vision blurs as I blink, thinking he'll clear when I'm fully awake, but he's still there, on the couch across from the table I recognize as the one inside Septem.

His arms are folded, his expression stern as he stares at me and heat pricks at my face, but it's *him*.

Not...

"Have you been speaking to Sullen Rule?" Those words don't come from him.

I turn my head and it is Isadora Croft.

Her hair is in braids, pulled back from her face, dark eyes locked onto mine.

I'm half-sitting, half-slumped against the leather couch and I wipe the back of my hand over my mouth, the room spinning slightly as I do. Saliva smears across my face and I swallow the dryness in the back of my throat.

I swear the faint trace of leather is on my tongue.

I drop my hand and look down, noting the destroyed black skirt, my *half-mad* crop top, white socks, white Vans.

I look to Cosmo again.

He dips his chin. "Don't look at me," he says, his tone harsh. He nods toward Isa, beside me. "Answer her."

"I think we would do well to remember she is also a victim here." Von's voice.

I turn to look over my shoulder and he's there, leaning against the wall, arms crossed in shadow as he stares at Isadora. He's dressed in black tech pants, a white T-shirt stretched over his chest, contrasting with his curly red hair.

"Sullen Rule hasn't been seen nor heard from in two years," Isadora says articulately, each word clipped from her mouth. "If he's here, it's for a reason."

"Why are you saying his name?" I can't stop blurting it out.

"You said it first," Isa answers, her tone flat. Cosmo must have told her what I whispered in the dark.

"Have you spoken to Stein?" Cosmo asks the question, and I don't know who he's speaking to. But at the name, I tense, sitting up straighter and pressing my knees together, hands atop my thighs. My heart thuds fast in my chest but I don't look away from Von. He is safer, right now, than the others.

I know he doesn't want me anymore, but Cosmo is pissed off about something, just like Isadora, and Von has a softer heart with me.

"What's going on?" I keep my voice low and Von's gray eyes flick to mine.

His expression is cold, but he speaks without anger. "Cosmo has a gash on his wrist. He was poisoned with something; whatever cut him. And the vodka you had, the bottle was spiked. Actually, all fifty bottles were. It's a good thing you didn't drink the rum; the report my dad ran said that dose could've killed you. Cosmo came to and heard you screaming. Found you on the floor in the bathroom." He jerks his head past the lounge of the bar, where I remember Sullen Rule walking me.

*But did that happen?*

"Was I naked?" I blurt it out before I can stop myself.

Von narrows his eyes. "Why would you ask that?"

"Because clearly she's been fucking the freak of Writhe and—"

"Shut up." I turn quickly, facing Isadora again as my skin heats and her eyes grow hot on mine. "Don't say that. You don't even know him. None of you do."

"But you do, don't you?" Isadora asks, arching a brow.

"Why are we discussing all of this in front of Cosmo?" I start, looking for a way out. "He's not even—"

"Because I'm going to have a scar on my fucking wrist and none of this is shit I don't know." He snarls the words as I face him and jump my eyes over the champagne flutes and bowls and books on the table. No after-party after all.

How much time has passed? Where was I? And why do I half-wish... I was still there?

*Sullen.*

"I didn't cut you," I say slowly.

"Yeah? Well what *did* you do, Karia?"

"You're the one who got me drunk. *You're*—"

"Wait. You made the drinks?" Von's cold voice to Cosmo.

"You didn't tell us that." Isadora's matches her boyfriend's tone now, and they aren't ganging up on me anymore.

Cosmo gestures toward me and his familiar grin slips back into place, but I know right now he doesn't mean it. "Are you joking? Do you even know anything about your friend here? She *wanted me to get her*—"

"Shut up. All of you, just *shut up.*" I speak then, not wanting Cosmo to expose my kinks to two people who don't *really* know them and don't need to.

I try to remember the last thing that happened before I slipped under.

My hand flies to my chest and I grope myself outside of my shirt. But aside from a little tenderness, there's nothing to prove

Sullen Rule sucked on my nipple. Or... pressed a needle into my belly.

I look down then, sliding my hand along my body to push at the waistband of my skirt.

Everything feels cold all over.

My heart pounds too fast inside of my chest.

There's a commotion along the stairwell, heavy footfalls, fast and hurried.

But I can't look up, because there's a purpling bruise as if from a needle, redness around the injection site, there on the flesh of my low abdomen.

I think I'm going to pass out.

"Karia." Cosmo doesn't sound so angry. His voice is quiet now. Scared.

More footsteps, coming into the bar.

"What happened to you?" Cosmo finishes.

Silence.

My ears are ringing.

I know everyone is looking at me.

Then Von's father, Mads Bentzen, the current leader of Writhe, speaks. "Sullen Rule is missing," he says, his voice brisk. "And we saw him on camera walking into the hotel a few hours ago." He clears his throat as I stare at the damaged skin, red and swollen and tinged with the start of a bruise.

My heart is in my throat.

*It was real.*

"He never left the building," Mads continues. "Now everyone up. We're going to search for him."

*He came back for me.*

# Chapter 11

## *Karia*

*Dear Sullen,*

*Do you remember the Night of Lies at Hotel No. 7? You weren't there, or so everyone claimed. Even your dad said you were skipping the annual party. I thought it strange; everyone wore masks for Lies and it seemed you—with your hood and your gloves and your constant disguise—would have a better time at that event than any other.*

*But then again, you rarely came to anything. The older we got, the more you hid. Initially, I believed it, that you hadn't shown up for the night.*

*It was silly, stupid—particularly after that disaster of an invitation I tried to extend to you to walk with Cosmo and I a year before, when you just turned your back on me and left—but I felt a sharp, bitter pang of disappointment at your absence. Mom and Dad were constantly hinting at the fact they wanted me to marry soon, dangling my credit cards and my clothes and my car in my face if I provided the least resistance to the idea. Of course, I'm still unwed, but I think that has more to do with their search for prospects than any change of heart on their part.*

*Regardless, at the time, nineteen and stubborn and even more spoiled than I am now, I was pouting over their decision and every time I saw them speaking to any man, I worried they would lock me up with him forever.*

*Von was a possibility, and I might have welcomed him, but everyone knew even then he thought Isadora hung the moon and dragged out the sun. Being second best for the rest of my life was not something I wanted to endure.*

*That night, I thought to myself, it would have been nice if you came. I would find a way to be alone with you in the towering hotel of Alexandria, maybe we could explore the rumored secret underground passages and climb our way to the roof where there was a pool and perhaps I could get you to do something so out of character for you, like swim with me. Fantasies, delusions, of course. Even if you showed, I knew you would do no such thing.*

*But that was my mindset that night, and as Mom and Dad got tipsy with Rig, Lora, Stein, Shella, Mads, and the others, I let Cosmo drag me to the thirteenth floor and pull me inside a suite. Wine was zipping through my system then, my head was floating, and I wore a pretty mauve gown by Maria Lucia Hohan, silk, one shoulder, drenched in tulle at the skirt. The mask over only my eyes was pink satin and lace. My hair was up, a few pieces curled around my face, nails in pastel green— the color reminds me of you, and I am never quite sure why— and Cosmo kept on his silver mask, stole all the airplane bottles of liquor from the mini fridge, and dared me to take shot after shot; three in a row. I was laughing then as he slipped off my sandals; strappy, with a heel that looked like a chandelier.*

*(Please, don't stop reading yet; I promise this is truly about you)*

51

The white duvet of the queen bed was soft on my shoulder blades and so were Cosmo's hands as he pushed up my dress, despite all of his callouses. I realized then as I lie on my back, a chandelier glittering blue overhead, his fingers working my thighs, his mouth speaking words about relaxing and letting it happen as one of my arms slipped off the bed and I didn't care enough to draw it back, that it wasn't Cosmo inside my head.

The room was dim, night arrived, and in the darkness with the lace framing my eyes, I could imagine you were touching me. Maybe you would take off your gloves for me. Perhaps you would pull back your hood. If I was really lucky, a very good girl, you might take off your hoodie, too.

And I would lie there, just like I was with Cosmo, and I would let you touch me in any way you wanted. I would get you to speak to me, tell me about your life at 44 Ritual Drive, and maybe you would let me touch you, too.

As Cosmo tipped up his mask and dipped his head between my thighs, my knees bent and manicured toes spread along the white comforter, I sensed something in the shadows to my left, where an entranceway led to a darkened living room.

My heart leapt to my throat, and I thought maybe I was just so incredibly drunk I was seeing things. Cosmo's tongue pushed into me, and my breath hitched, but I was afraid to let a moan slip from my mouth.

You were there.

A figure in a hoodie, a gleam of dark eyes.

I know it was you.

You watched me as Cosmo spread me wide with his fingers splayed into my thighs, his tongue circling my clit. You saw him bite his way up my stomach, then push inside of me without getting undressed—he always likes it best that way; maybe you already know?

He fucked me and in the dark, I could watch you, and when

*he pulled out to finish on my thigh, I imagined it was your hot cum and I thought maybe I could command you to lick it off me. Don't ask why the dirty image came into my head as I held onto the darkness I could see of your eyes; but it was hot, at the time.*

*Still is, if I'm being honest. I do not know a man who would do such a thing, but I guess I'm not extremely experienced with boys.*

*Anyway.*

*You were there that night. I know it was you. Who else?*

*But I have not been able to figure out if you were in that room before we arrived, or if you crept inside after following us to the thirteenth floor.*

*When I disentangled myself from Cosmo, I walked that way on the pretense of using the bathroom.*

*But you were gone.*

*As I write this, it's the Night of Lies again, held every September as you know, four years after that one, and I wish you were here once more, even if you stayed in the shadows again.*

*You dance inside my head in the most macabre way.*

*I hope you read these. I hope you don't.*

*I hope I see you again.*

*I hope I never do.*

*I don't know what I want or who I'm supposed to be, but I think of you often.*

*Hate me if you must,*

*K. Ven*

**I** 'm coming with you." Cosmo's voice is directly behind me in the lounge of Septem.

I clench my flashlight tighter in my fingers; Mads passed them out after my parents and the others arrived. Mom was home for this meeting, but she made her way here after the news spread.

I don't know what everyone chose to believe about Sullen two years ago; which rumor they picked to hold onto. I have no idea if the parents of Writhe truly discovered where he went; if Stein Rule contacted Mads to let him know. Allegedly, the former leader of Writhe left the country when he stepped down back in April. But in Writhe, you never know what's fact and what's only a diversion of fiction.

"Cosmo, I'm not certain you should be here." It's my mother who speaks those words.

I stiffen, my back to everyone. I was ready to go up to the thirteenth floor after the chaos that followed Mads's orders to search for Sullen. I am scared when they find him, they won't be nice to him. What, with poisoning Cosmo and I'm sure me, too. My parents always warned me away from Sullen and I knew they must really be terrified of him if they didn't want to nudge me in the direction of marrying the prince of Writhe. But he's no longer that and I'm not sure Mom and Dad would consider him a good prospect at all any longer. I'm not sure anyone in this hotel will want to keep him alive after they find him. He has no protection anymore with his father retired from Writhe.

*"He is not my dad."*

A shiver coasts down my spine remembering the words. I don't know what he did with me, where he put me, or what was in the syringe he injected into my belly, but it was real. Hours passed, according to our parents, while they met in the ballroom. It's nearly midnight now, Friday tumbling into Saturday, and I feel more alive tonight than I have any other weekend in years, even with the residual drugs in my system.

"Actis has done work for me." Mads Bentzen's voice, cold and clipped like his son's, drags me out of my excitement.

I turn, then, and see my mom, Scarletta, lift her deep blue eyes to Mads's gray ones. He is dressed in a black suit and same color tie, standing at six feet or so tall, hands in the pockets of his slacks. Mom narrows her gaze, one hand tight around a diamond-encrusted clutch that matches the dazzling colors of her dress. It's not necessary to don outfits like *these* for a meeting, particularly one Mom didn't initially come to, but the parents often do. Like peacocks, flaunting what they lie, steal, and kill for.

"That's fantastic," Mom says smoothly to Mads, never one to hide her true feelings. "But do you realize it's been two years *today* since Sully was last seen?"

I lift my chin, squeezing the heavy, black flashlight in my hand. Beyond Mads and Mom, my dad, Antwine, is speaking in a low voice to Lora, Shella, and Rig. Isadora and Von and a few others of Writhe already ascended the steps from Septem and are hunting down Sullen now.

My heart thuds frantically in my chest as I dart my gaze from Mads to Mom, ready to bolt to find Sullen first. Mads tilts his head, his lips pressed together like Von's often are. He has dirty blond hair in looping curls; the red of Von came from Lora Bentzen. But otherwise, he looks so similar to Von, I can imagine my friend easily stepping into Mads's shoes one day, or handing them off to Isa.

"It is?" I ask as Cosmo bristles at my side, waiting for a verdict as far as his presence is concerned.

Mom looks to me; she is where I get my leanness from, but she's a few inches taller and not just because of her heels. There are little lines around her eyes, and her brows furrow in a way they often do as she studies me. Her blonde hair streaked with white is pulled up into an elegant crown around her head.

She is beautiful and I always stole her clothes and makeup and hair products growing up until she got tired of it and gave me a black card to buy all my own. But sometimes when she looks at me, I see pity across her pretty face, and I don't know if she thinks I'm stupid, if she wishes I didn't live the kind of life she does, or if she wants me to be someone else. Someone stronger and sterner and more like Isadora.

Mom is like that. In my parents' marriage, she is the boss. Dad has his own command; it's not as if she walks all over him. But she is the queen and it's been that way since I can remember.

Maybe she wants me to be less of a princess and more like her. She probably doesn't love my outfit either. Anything ripped, like my skirt, or cropped like my top, is a fashion embarrassment. But she would never say that out loud; it's just conveyed in the *look* she'll give, like now.

"Yes," she says, watching me carefully, her voice strong and high. "Did you know that?" It sounds innocent, her question, but I am sure she saw how I gravitated toward Sullen when we were younger. I'm sure everyone did, even if they never really said anything.

I have always had a soft spot for monsters. *Dracula, Frankenstein,* even Scar. They are the ones my heart bleeds for.

"No," I answer her, half a lie as I push my shoulders back and try to be a little more of the daughter she wants.

"I should go with her," Cosmo says quietly at my side. "This is a big hotel." He states the obvious. "And you know the power already went out once, before we were..." He trails off because I'm not sure either of us really know *what* we were.

I glance at him by my side and see his wrist, veins along his hands but there's a pretty deep slice there on the base of his arm. Crusted blood has dried around it, and I can't help but want to smile, thinking of Sullen cutting him in the dark.

I bite it back. "I don't need a babysitter," I snap instead, sweeping my eyes up to Cosmo. His green ones look down at me. "I've been trained, too, you know?"

"You hated self-defense, Karia." Mom's haughty tone makes me clench my free hand into a tight fist, digging my pastel green nails into my skin as I cut my gaze back to her. "But I'm not sure she needs a sitter who isn't from Writhe." She glances at Mads with those words.

"I can call Von and Isa back and—"

"No." I cut off Mads, turning to stare at him. My face grows hot with my own insolence and disrespecting the leader of Writhe, but that's part of what being a member of this organization is all about. Holding your own. And I want to find Sullen before anyone else does. "Sorry," I say, not meaning it, "but really. I'll be fine on my own."

He lifts a brow, his face void of emotion otherwise. I wonder for a moment if I'll be punished for cutting him off, but I do seem to get away with a little more than the others if only because they don't take me as seriously.

He looks to Cosmo, then says in a tone dripping with finality, "Cosmo will accompany you. We're wasting time here." As he turns his back to me, Mom, and Cosmo, I want to scream at him, but I take a deep breath in and let Cosmo loop his arm through mine, his body warm as he sidles up next to me.

"Guess you're stuck with me, huh?"

Mom's gaze drops to where we're touching and there is clear disapproval written on her face. It makes me a little giddy but I know my future husband won't be of my choosing either so I can't gloat too much.

I allow Cosmo to spin me around as I grip my flashlight tight, and we walk past the gleaming bar toward the stairwell leading up to the rest of the hotel. My mind races as I think of how to get rid of him. How to ensure I find Sullen myself.

*Then what?* The question laces through my head but I ignore it. One step at a time. Absentmindedly, I press my hand to the spot over my low belly where Sullen bruised me with the needle, covered now from my skirt.

But Cosmo must notice because he stiffens at my side as we walk up the stairwell, and his arm tightens through mine. "When I find him, I'm paying him back for that," he says in a low voice.

# Chapter 12

## *Sullen*

October rain begins to fall, lashing against the windowpanes from my stolen patio. I have left the lab behind in that faraway corridor of Septem. It is through a door in the supply closet, then another three after that, all of which require a key. The problem with having so much square footage is no one could possibly examine it all each day.

But here, in the penthouse suite of the seventeenth floor, anyone could find me if they really looked, but I think I have time. The entire hotel is closed for Writhe meetings as it often is; Stein owns majority shares under the guise of a corporation, and he can do with this place what he will. I know he doesn't handle any of it himself. He has staff for that, particularly considering he is in Vancouver now for business; a different sort than Writhe's.

I told Karia he wasn't my father; he is, biologically, and I hate to understand that there are some things even I could not stop taking from his genes. Our love for grotesque curio is one of those, passed down in my tainted blood. It is why I have the lab, the animals, the wings, the disgusting and demented.

I push all of that away from the forefront of my mind and close the heavy, deep blue curtains to the patio overlooking Alexandria, blotting out most of the night. There is a light on though, inset panels in the flooring I have not yet switched off. I know more than most how easy it is for monsters to lurk in the dark, and I do not wish to be caught just yet.

It's why I had to leave Karia in the bathroom of Septem. The meeting was adjourned—a simple matter of leaving one of Stein's listening devices in the ballroom helped me glean this information—and I knew they would be up in arms about the princess of Writhe going missing. It would add an urgency to their search that could get me or her injured.

As it is, I know even though she is found, they are now looking for me.

I have to be back tonight to Haunt Muren—twenty or so hours from now; it is three minutes past midnight—and that leaves me little time to hide *and* find her. As it is, Stein will know I am here. Mads Bentzen never discovered everything I endured, but I'm not sure even if he did he would give me any leniency whatsoever. He will report to Stein just as he got his name tattooed over his chest for their bizarre initiations and disgusting proof of loyalty.

If only I were able to disfigure myself with a needle and ink to please Stein. He never gave me that courtesy.

As rain blows harder against the glass outside, I walk to the king bed and sink down onto the golden duvet, a commonality of the penthouse suites; so different from the one I watched Cosmo feast upon Karia on.

My mind flickers to her in my makeshift lab; the place I built in secret after the Night of Lies I was forbidden to attend.

I paid for that moment of sneaking out and watching as I did for all the times I was caught staring at her and dreaming when I shouldn't have.

Blood in my mouth, iron along the back of my throat, it was

another day I thought I might die from a bleed in my brain due to Stein's vicious kicks.

It was worth it, at the time.

Carefully, with her inside my head, I push back my hood. The cool air of the hotel suite grazes the back of my neck. It feels good, being momentarily free. I am so rarely without layers and layers of clothes.

I touched her, at first, with bare hands.

But if she saw the few missing nails on my fingers, the ones that won't grow back, she would hate me more.

I think of her in my mouth, sucking her pink, tight nipple and flicking my tongue against it. She was so firm and perfect and beautiful and perhaps I crossed a line, but it was really less bad than what I've seen Cosmo do to her when she is drunk and her defenses are down. It's what she likes, I think.

Maybe it's what everyone enjoys. I don't know.

Thunder rolls across the sky as I take off the black leather gloves with green stitching that have all but molded to my hands.

I don't look at my fingers; the lumps in them from bones that did not heal well. I am lucky they are all fully functional; that the worst thing is the deadened nail beds. Regardless, I still don't like to see the reminders of how I am jarringly different from the other children of Writhe.

But when lightning flashes blue-white through the drapes, I snap my head up on reflex—my body has not learned how to get off this high alert system I was born with—and see my reflection in the glittering-golden framed mirror hanging larger than I am on the wall, directly across from the bed.

It is a bad omen; having a mirror reflecting a bed this way— I read about it once, in a Writhe pamphlet—but it is a worse one when I have to stare at myself now, on accident.

My hair is deep ash brown, cut short and haphazard, another way Stein disgraces me. My eyes are dark, too, and the lines and shadows beneath them sink into hollow skin from growing up with poor nutrition and an extreme lack of sunlight. To this day, the only sun I can tolerate is *her.*

Sharpened bones along my face, stubble on my jaw—Stein will ensure this is gone as soon as he returns—and a nose which converges on a point. It is a sickening sort of torture, seeing the ways Stein never messed with my face, aside from my teeth. The other types of pamphlets he kept locked away in his study always discussed the importance of leaving the visible intact.

*Principles of Poetic Séance* was his favorite series of brochures, created in the 1800s by a mad scientist named Burbank Gates who believed taking a human life—more accurately; convoluting it in such a way it was barely human at all—led to immortality and god-like transcendence.

It became a game we played, Stein and I.

He wouldn't harm me if I did everything right, but I never knew what was *wrong.* I learned from the punishment. I think he thought himself merciful for that.

As thunder growls low outside, I can't help but smile at my reflection in the mirror and let my skin crawl as I study my missing teeth. One front top one, a few from the bottom as well. I am missing two molars and my canines have been filed into sharp points.

Sweat beads along the back of my neck and fury pounds throughout my body as I indulge in a little more self-loathing. Cosmo de Actis has all of his teeth. So does Von Bentzen. The two men she has fucked.

And what am I, compared to them?

As I grow hotter still, I wrap my arms around myself and yank off my hoodie, pulling up my high-collared shirt with it, cold air waltzing upon my spine and the burns and lacerations over my back as my necklace sways along my chest.

The fabric tugs on one of the embedded piercings up my

spinal column that I didn't want, near the middle of my back. I grind what's left of my teeth as I yank harder, pulling off the top half of my clothes. I throw the shirt and hoodie both upon the marble flooring and lift my head, my hands curled into fists as I stare at my reflection, bare chest heaving. Only it's not quite bare, but I cannot stand to read the words there, carved with an ecstatic sort of hate.

There are various objects sewn under my skin, including mangled scar tissue Stein simply covered with a patch of flesh from my thigh, right at the top of my throat. He pushed the *Principles* to their limit in that.

The lump there is what Karia saw, when I had her in my temporary lab.

Her face contorted in disgust, and I imagine she never knew a human could be so vile.

I stand to my feet dizzyingly fast as the rain turns to hail outside and I leap toward the mirror, intending to shatter it with my fists. The silver necklace and purple pendant swings with my abrupt movement. But when I am close enough to ruin the glass of the mirror, more marks visible along the line of my abs, a scar across the right side of my belly from where Stein decided he would remove my gall bladder because he could when I was a child, there is an electronic beeping sound that stops me in my tracks.

*Someone is at the door to the suite.*

I turn my head to peer down the darkened hallway at the same time a flood of light from the corridor spills into my reprieve. *They were not supposed to get here so quickly. I was supposed to find her first. Hide her. Kidnap her away. Touch her. Taste her, more.*

But she steps inside.

And she is not alone.

Cosmo is behind her, looming over her like a predator, and their eyes blink to adjust, but there is nowhere for me to run.

It takes seconds for her to spot me as Cosmo turns his head toward the dark bathroom.

Her pale hair seems to glow in the darkness, down now in haphazard waves past her shoulders, to her ribcage.

The skirt, the shirt, her frilly socks, and white Vans.

All back on because I carefully dressed her before I left her in the bathroom. I couldn't let Cosmo find her naked, even if he has already seen all of her.

She has a flashlight in one hand, but it is not on.

"I'll check in..." Cosmo's voice trails off as he turns his head and spots me, too.

Both of them stare at me, half-naked, and I remember it with a startling, visceral pain, that my body is exposed.

I wrap my arms around myself before I can think the better of it, but Cosmo's greedy green eyes are already roaming over my bare torso, and I wish I would have sliced his wrist to the bone when I poisoned him with the scalpel around my neck.

"Fuck," he says, his voice a low growl. Then he pushes past Karia, the door falling closed with a heavy thunk behind him. He does not slow as he comes closer in long, violent strides.

"Cosmo!" Karia snaps his name, but there is an undercurrent of fear within her tone. I hear her footsteps as she quickly follows him, and I take an unsure step back.

I could hurt him.

I could kill him.

I could lure him to the patio and toss him over the fucking balcony.

His eyes are narrowed, his cheeks pulled upward in his scowl.

"No," he snarls, coming toward me with balled fists. "He *drugged* you, Karia. He *scarred* me."

I want to tell him I could do so much worse but as my pulse leaps to my throat, I can say nothing at all, only squeeze myself tighter and pray his body blocks me from her view.

"You've always tried to play with the little freaks and monsters, but they aren't nice pets." He says this all as he looks at me, slowing when he is a foot from me, his gaze flicking up and down my body. "He could've raped you." He steps closer and I can smell his sweat, see the perspiration on his temple. "Why did you come back? We all wanted you to stay gone."

My knees begin to tremble.

I am not scared of him, but the words he speaks... *Does she think that, too?*

"Cosmo," she whispers behind him, but his body eclipses hers.

He shakes his head once as he stares up at me. "I'm gonna fucking hit you." I don't know why he gives me the warning, but he lifts his fist and his body twists in the way I've seen Stein's do right before he lands a blow.

I make myself stay relaxed because tensing hurts worse and I don't know yet if I should fight back because if I do, I might not stop.

And yet something...*happens,* as his body pivots to follow the direction of his fist.

There is a loud cracking sound that has nothing to do with the storm, and he seems to *still,* but his eyes widen in fear or shock or both.

The crack sounds again, followed by a feminine grunt of exertion, and Cosmo's body jolts.

I step back on some kind of strange, connective instinct.

Then Cosmo's arms drop by his sides.

His eyes flutter.

He falls to his knees with a groan, then he sways a little strangely before he collapses onto his side, curled into the fetal position. He is not unconscious because I watch as he slowly moves his hands to cup his head and he mutters *her* name.

*"Karia."*

When I lift my gaze, she meets mine, the flashlight nearly

the size of her forearm as she grips it tight in her hand. *She hit him with it. For me?*

"He'll get up soon," she says, her voice a whisper, speaking as if he is not there, like most people speak around me, not *to* me. "Let's go, okay?" She doesn't look at my body. Instead, she bends down and swipes up my clothes, then offers them to me over Cosmo's downed figure.

My chest heaves in and out, a strange, breathy sound coming from my lungs in the way they always seem to rattle.

"I promise," she says to me, her words soft, "I'll keep you safe. Everyone is looking for you though, and I just... I just want to talk to you, okay, Sullen?"

When she says my name, my pulse hammers harder against my ribcage.

I reach out for the clothes, wondering where the trick is. When she will drop her eyes over my naked torso and recoil from me.

But she holds my gaze.

Our bare fingers brush as I grab the hoodie and shirt from her.

For one second, I do not want to move.

She smiles softly, dimples indenting her cheeks, a sight I do not deserve. And I grab my clothes and quickly put them on with my head bowed as Cosmo stirs at my feet.

I snatch my gloves from the bed, but she is offering me her hand once more and Cosmo is saying her name again and I am tired of hearing it from his lips.

I take her offer without donning my gloves, my hand closing over her smaller one, then she tugs gently, and I step over his body.

This close, I can smell her. Violets and cedar; flowers and forest. I can see the vivid blue of her eyes, the white sclera, the pink in her lips as she tips her head up and stares at me.

Then she squeezes my hand.

Warmth flushes through me, hot and sticky and slightly nauseating. It would feel better if we were back in the lab. There are other rooms there too, a space with a dental chair I did not create. If I could strap her down, restrain her so she can't run... It would be easier to talk, then.

"I know where we can go," I say softly, my voice a croak.

Stein always makes fun of me for that, but she is so naive and so trusting, she only nods her head once, her eyes searching mine as she says, *"Okay."*

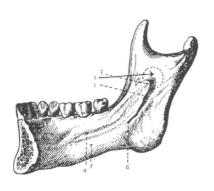

## *Principles of Poetic Séance*

The face must be avoided. It rouses
curiosity, and on the path to becoming a
god, this is unwanted. Wearing down of the
subject through brutality is necessary but
must be completed in such a way outsiders
do not pry. Transcendence can take
decades. Broken bones, lacerations,
disfigurement, and internal bleeding are
recommended on the journey, but
defilement of teeth may speed it along.

# Chapter 13

## *Karia*

He pushes his gloves into the pocket of his hoodie as we hurriedly head for the door, his hand in mine. I glance once over my shoulder at Cosmo stirring on the floor. I know I didn't really damage him, I don't think, but I do feel a little bad.

He should've listened to me though, the entire ride up the elevator after he said he wanted us to work our way from the penthouse suites down. We searched five rooms before the one we found Sullen inside of and all the while, I told Cosmo to let me do the talking.

He was silent, but I assumed he agreed.

If he didn't want to get hit in the head, he should've gone with my assumption.

As we reach the closed door to the suite, I have to let go of Sullen's hand and when I start to, I feel him grip me tighter for a heartbeat of time.

My pulse quickens and a smile curves my lips but now that I'm focused on the door, I don't look at him. I flip the automatic lock, the one Cosmo used a universal keycard to unlock, and I pull down on the silver handle and yank open the door.

Cold air greets me, along with the deadening quiet of the corridor, glittering in hues of silver and blue with a black carpet runner over marble flooring. I clench my fingers around the flashlight—I decided to keep it since it made a pretty good weapon—and press my palm to the door to keep it open for Sullen. I dart my gaze to the left, the right, seeing nothing but stillness and hearing only the torrential rains dropping over Alexandria.

"I assume we're going down?" I ask quietly, turning to look over my shoulder.

Sullen is there, the door propped open with his elbow, and I drop my hand from the wooden surface as my eyes hold his and for a moment, I'm caught.

The little sliver of amber in his deep brown irises looks unnatural in a way, like a bright crescent drawn into a digital painting. His complexion is a warm ivory tone, but the sunken circles beneath his eyes appear nearly gray, skin dipped in. He has longer lashes than me, and I take some pride in mine. He's unusually stunning and I've always thought so.

I wonder if he has any idea.

"Yes," he answers me, and he looks away a little when he does. He seems different, less sure of himself now that I'm not on the table. Now that I'm not...drugged.

For a second, I wonder if I should have listened to Cosmo. Sullen *could* have done anything he wanted to me. I think of his mouth on my nipple and I guess he kind of did and maybe I should loathe him for it but I don't. If it had been a different circumstance, I would have welcomed it, even, being delirious and at his whim.

I blink, trying to focus on what matters right now.

If Mads or my parents or Isa's find him, they won't let him go and I can't hit all of them with a flashlight.

"Okay. We'll take the stairwell. We should be able to hear anyone coming before they're on us there. Is that okay?"

He blinks slowly and says, "Yes," in the same tone he said it the first time.

"How far are we going?"

He lifts his eyes to mine. "All the way. Back to... Septem."

*All the way.*

My mouth feels dry as I think of not being able to move my limbs. But the thing is, I don't feel stupid about trusting him. I am not terrified of him, at least not this second. Perhaps because of the dream-like quality of the entire experience, or how I ended up clothed and fine after it. But I don't berate myself over saying, "It'll be hard to get there, I'm sure it's guarded. I have an idea, though. Is there somewhere to hide, inside Septem?" *Yeah, the murder room with the rabbit corpse, Karia.* I try not to think of its pink eyes as I wait for his answer.

"Yes," he finally says, watching me in a way that feels like an examination.

"Okay," I reply. "I'm trusting you." But I don't wait to see if I should regret that fact already.

We both walk out into the long corridor, doors set apart every few feet for the suites here. Briefly, for one wild second, I think of the pool on the roof and as he comes to walk beside me, his shoulder at my eye-level, I tip my head up and he glances at me as we continue moving to the end of the hall, where the stairs are.

"Do you swim?" I ask casually, trying to bite my lip to stop from smiling. Everything about this moment is slightly surreal despite my fear; Cosmo on the floor, Writhe crawling the hotel; me, beside Sullen Rule.

He lifts one dark brow, and I swear I see the ghost of a grin on his plush lips, dry from lack of water or fear or both. But he doesn't fully smile, and I decide I'm going to get him to do it somehow, eventually.

"I've never been in a pool."

"What about the ocean?"

He shakes his head once, facing away from me, and I trace the line of his cheekbones, the severity of his jaw, the way his lips are pushed out naturally.

"The bathtub? Ever swim in there?"

He flinches. It's barely perceptible, but I see his shoulders stiffen and watch as his scarred hands curl into fists. There are what looks like cigarette burns over the top, veins running rigid beneath it, and I see other marks like lacerations. His nails are hidden, even his thumb is tucked into his fist.

"No," he finally answers me when we're near the heavy black doors that lead to the stairs.

"Would you ever swim with me?" I press, feeling brave for no reason at all. I love the water. Lakes, oceans, tubs, pools. I'm most alive with little clothing as is. I like to dress up and do my hair and makeup, but I like to slip on a bikini more.

He doesn't look at me and he's silent for a long stretch of time, until we're standing in front of the fire escape stairs and I'm reaching out my hand to yank one of the doors open. I think he won't answer me, and I remember how he ignored me a lot growing up too, or said something shitty when I spoke to him, but after we slip into the dim stairwell and the door thuds closed behind us with some strange sort of finality, he answers me.

"I would...consider it."

And I want to laugh, because he said it a little funny, or maybe because I'm giddy over the answer, but I'm worried he'll think I'm laughing at him, so I bite my tongue as we hurry down the steps.

# Chapter 14

## *Sullen*

She is no longer holding my hand and I try not to fixate on it. But I see her slim fingers curled around the handrail as she descends the steps below me and I do desperately want to touch her there. Blue veins, bones flexed beneath skin, pastel green nails that clash with her red shirt... She said once in a letter the color green reminds her of me.

I suck in a breath, biting the inside of my cheek as I wonder how often she wears that color. *For me?*

Our soft footfalls echo in the corridor of stairs, from her white Vans and my black, high-top sneakers. My heart is pounding louder than our steps, it seems. I clench the gloves stuffed into the pocket of my hoodie and stay behind her, watching as her hair bounces around her low back, skimming the tanned white skin there, and her black, ripped denim skirt shifts with every step she takes. Muscles along her glutes flex and a string from the destroyed nature of her clothes grazes the spot behind her knee. I want to reach for the thread and twist it around my fingers. Break it and keep it in my pocket.

I don't touch her.

As we reach another landing and she turns to descend the

next steps, she glances up at me with her lips pushed together and her eyes intent, focused on my own.

*What are you thinking?* I want to ask it as we come to a standstill, her already on the lower staircase and me on the one above. I retract my hand from the railing, pushing into the hoodie pocket with my other. I am not ready for her to see anymore of me than she already has.

*Are you scared of where we're going?*

Her lips part marginally, like she might answer my unspoken question. But I'm worried if *I* don't say something, this moment will be gone too soon. It will break apart into cobwebs and maybe when we reach the lower level, she'll only lead me directly into the arms of Stein's former *Duo,* the name for Writhe's second-in-command.

"Is something wrong?" I ask carefully, hating the way the words seem to grind up from my throat in a coarse, offensive way.

She tilts her head and I think I see a smile start to form on her face, one corner of her pink lips pulling upward. "We *are* on the run from one of the most dangerous societies in the country." She speaks it calmly and now *I* want to smile.

"Maybe," I agree. "But I am worse." I take one step down, my body wanting to be near her. Overriding my brain in the matter.

"Are you?" she whispers, barely a sound from her soft mouth.

I tip my head, staring down at her, both of us at an angle to one another. "Do you remember it all?" *How I touched you, in those brief stolen moments? Why are you still with me now? I gave you a chance to run then.*

She glances at my mouth, and I press my lips together, not wanting her to see the dryness of them. I've always had this problem; sometimes Stein liked to dehydrate me to see how dark he could make my urine. It's as if those experiments forever left their mark.

"I remember enough," she begins, but before she can say more, we hear the creak of a door, thunderous and scratchy in the stairwell, and she drops the flashlight as she flinches. The plastic thuds all the way down the steps, loud and clanging, my body like a live wire in the way I am poised to run from the noise as it echoes.

Her spine straightens and she turns away from me, staring down at the next landing and swearing under her breath, *"Shit."*

From my spot above her, I cannot see anything.

I don't move, breathe, speak. I focus on her. Like her image can keep me here: The slight wave to her long, blonde strands. The way they glide over her shoulders, a few splaying along her arm. I see the dip of her triceps there, then the plane of her belly, and I know there may be a mark, where I pushed the needle into her skin.

I want to see it.

I want to bite over it.

*I don't want this night to end just yet.*

"Karia." A voice reverberates in the stairwell.

I inhale silently, holding the air in my lungs as I keep staring at her. I don't let my eyes roam over the gray brick walls, the dark flooring, what or who could be one floor below us.

I vaguely recognize the voice but so little of Stein's Writhe members spoke to me, it's hard to parse out who it is.

"Is he..." The voice trails off and I imagine whoever it is looking up, straining to see in the dimness, the angle, trying to find *me.*

I think I may have to run. They could easily grab the flashlight. Reveal all of me.

If I get caught like this, Stein will kill me. He will decide his transcendence has arrived and this is the moment he's been waiting for. I know I will suffer greatly before he completes the final task.

Fear balloons in my low belly, pressing on my bladder.

I want to turn and run. I am not sure where I will go but there must be hidden places on the upper levels, too. And if it came down to it, I would rather fling myself over the balcony and die in that manner than let Stein scrape me to the bone.

I lift my eyes to Karia's face.

She is not looking at me.

I wonder when she will rat me out.

It would be easiest for her. Be done with this entire thing. She has nothing to lose in giving up this game. Everything to gain in the name of her own safety. *From me.*

But slowly, she shakes her head. "No, Ms. Croft," she says. *Shella Croft.* Isadora's mom.

She has always seemed to kind to me—any soft word given to me from the others was from her—and despite the odds, a fraction of relief spreads like warmth through my body.

I still don't move.

I do not exhale.

There is a moment of jagged quiet. I wonder if Shella is deciding whether or not she believes Karia. Surely, she can't. I may even be visible from this spot; I don't know.

Then Karia adds, so softly it's a whisper, *"Please."*

I watch her chest rise, exposing more of her core. She is holding her breath now, too.

Then I hear, "Nothing here, Rig," spoken by Shella Croft in a rather loud voice, as if she is calling out to her husband.

After another second, maybe three, the door slams closed.

I watch Karia bow her head, her spine crumpling for a moment as she exhales loudly, and I do the same.

We stand there longer than we should, until she finally lifts her chin and her blue eyes flick to mine. "I don't know how much longer she'll be able to divert them. Let's go?" She asks it as a question, as if I have a choice.

But I enjoy the illusion of one.

I nod once. I think of the lab. The dental chair. If we get through all of these obstacles in our way, I will strap her down in it and we will play and maybe I will feel guilty, because of this moment in time when she saved me, and Shella did too, and neither of them had to.

*Neither of them should have.*

# Chapter 15

## *Karia*

W e are nearly to Septem.

I left the flashlight behind. I dropped it on such a high level, if it's found, it'll be a good diversion.

We keep going down.

I know we can continue on the stairs, past the lobby level, and end up at the entranceway to the bar. There will be guards there; it would be a stupid oversight to leave that area unattended and Mads is not stupid. But I know what I'll do when we are close enough. I just hope it works. The stakes seem high; not for me, but Sullen. What will they do to him? If Stein is called in... And Stein has to be the one who has marred him. For a horrifying moment as I round another set of stairs with Sullen a few steps behind me, I wonder if Stein killed Mercy Rule. If his brutality would extend to uxoricide.

If he has any limits at all, and what the lack of them has done to Sullen's head and heart.

The thought must distract me because what jerks me back to reality is the sensation of falling as my Vans slip on the topmost step and I tighten my fingers on the cool metal railing, but my palm is slick with sweat and I'm about to pitch forward and there is a lot of distance to the next landing and—

I'm yanked backward, *hard*, by a hand tight around my bicep.

I tumble a few steps, my arms windmilling before Sullen's come completely around me, holding me with my back to his chest, his chin grazing the top of my head. On some kind of instinct, I reach up and clutch his forearms over his hoodie, feeling the hard muscle beneath as my chest heaves. I stare down at the dozens of stairs in the dim lighting and try to catch my breath, my pulse racing so fast and I don't think it's entirely from almost falling.

It's from being caught.

In *his* arms. The scent of dying rose petals envelopes me. Soft grass, a cemetery in the fall.

My mouth is dry, my eyes flutter closed as he holds me, and I manage to say, "Thank you."

He doesn't reply, but he doesn't let me go, either. We are in a twisted version of a hug. I can still feel where his fingers latched onto my bicep and didn't let me trip.

And I let my eyes blink open as I drown in the sensations of the moment.

I twist my head, angling it up toward him. *How many times did I imagine he would hug me, growing up? Or let me hug him?*

He tips his chin down, his dark eyes on mine, his hood pulled over his hair, casting shadow around his temple.

He squeezes me harshly, but it's so brief.

I do the same to his forearms.

I see something flash in his eyes as he blinks.

Then, too soon, he releases me, stepping back as my arms fall to my side. He nods toward the stairs, indicating we should get moving, and it doesn't matter how much I want to stay in this moment. I know we can't.

There could be cameras in the stairwell and I'm positive

there are some on the penthouse floor. It won't be long before they find us if we aren't hidden away first.

So I compose myself, smooth a hand down my skirt in a nervous gesture, and we start our descent once more.

AT THE LAST LANDING, THERE ARE TWO DOORS AND ONE PLACE TO hide.

One door, to the left, is an exit, the sign above it lit in neon red. The other, straight ahead, is heavy and black and leads into the small foyer before Septem. It is highly likely there are people stationed outside of that one, waiting for a moment like this.

I let my hand graze the railing as I step down completely onto the dark floor of the landing, and I turn my head to look over my shoulder. At the hiding place. The spot beneath the last stairwell, clustered in darkness, flush against the wall, with just enough room for two people to crouch and stay hidden.

Sullen is silent as I work this out and I slowly lift my eyes to his. He is still on the second-to-last step, hands in his pocket, hood over his head, dark gaze watching my every move.

He looks so big in this space, tall and broad, and I want to squish him down so no one will ever find him.

I don't speak because I'm worried they could hear us even with a fireproof door keeping us hidden. But I need him to understand my intentions all the same.

Before I make any gestures, I glance at the exit door once, desperately wanting to walk through it.

We could disappear behind Hotel No. 7, vanish entirely.

But I know there are a lot of cameras on the exterior. Probably less in here; the chances of being recorded are smaller inside. And besides, where would we go once we got out? I didn't drive here and I don't have the keys to Isa's Jeep. I would assume Sullen drove except for the fact Mads mentioned nothing about his car being in the lot and he would've checked for that. If his car *is* out there, a guard will be stationed right beside it. We could flee into the streets of Alexandria but we'd either have to climb a ten-foot-tall fence or come around the front of the hotel and we would absolutely be seen that way.

Besides, Sullen said he had a spot to hide in Septem. And I think that makes a lot of sense; being in plain sight, in some ways. Eventually, they'll assume he got past detection and is no longer in the hotel.

Eventually... we'll be left alone.

So I tear my eyes away from the exit and focus instead on the fire alarm housed in a plastic case beside the entrance door to the bar.

Then I glance at Sullen to ensure he's watching me—he is —and I point toward the red and white alarm.

His dark brows lift a little. It feels good getting a reaction from him, even if it's only that.

Then he nods once.

I point again, toward the hiding spot beneath the stairs.

He tracks the gesture with his eyes, then without another word, he steps down the last two steps and heads toward the shadowy space.

Ducking low, he is able to vanish inside of it, although I can see the whites of his eyes as he stares at me and drops down into a crouch. I will have to be right in front of him for us to scooch further into the wall. We might need to close our eyes so we aren't spotted that way.

I don't care. We have to hide. I'm not ready to give him up yet, no matter what he plans to do to me.

Before I can overthink it more, I walk to the alarm, then grab the *lift here* lever.

I suck in a breath, blink once, then I yank down on the handle.

And as the blaring alarm and flashing lights scream around

me, causing me to jump even though I knew it was coming, I sprint to Sullen. Without thought, I crouch down and tuck myself against his chest.

His arms come around me, both of us on our knees, the cement floor hard and cold, but his body warms me as he holds me and again, I grip his forearms, both of us watching from the shadows.

*It feels like a nice place to be,* I think.

But his hand skims over my waist, the bare sliver of skin between my top and my skirt. I feel the leather of his gloves and wonder when he put them on; maybe as he waited here for me.

A spider of something like fear crawls up my spine with the barrier between us.

It feels like an omen.

# Chapter 16

## *Sullen*

The chaos is immediate and overwhelming.

While there are very few good things about living with Stein Rule, either at 44 Ritual Drive or Haunt Muren, silence is one of them. Aside from the moments he crashes into my room and my life, I am bubbled in quiet and drenched in loneliness and I have become accustomed to it.

So while men pour through the door leading to Septem—many heading out the exit, but one charging for the stairs, all with weapons on their hips from the calvary Mads Bentzen must have assembled—I find myself burying my head against Karia's hair as I hold her tight.

It is uncomfortable here on our knees and I know it must be more so for her, since she's wearing a skirt, but I have been in far worse positions kneeling and it's the alarms and flashing lights that jar my system most.

But *her*... With my eyes closed and her fingers curled around my forearms, her spine to my chest and my lips against her hair, I can almost imagine this is a sort of heaven. One I have certainly never experienced before.

I wonder if her shampoo is infused with violets because the

scent is stronger with my nose to her strands. Her hair is very soft, too, tickling my septum and my chin. Her body is lean, but the soft curve of her breasts is overtop my forearms and it feels... *right*. Where she holds onto me does too, her fingers tightening as the Septem door thuds open once more, then the exit, in quick succession.

Surely the members of Writhe must know the alarm is a diversion, but I don't think any hired guards want to take the risk of being burned alive for my absence.

And no one notices us, in their hurry to or away from the alleged fire.

We are monsters in the shadows, and no one ever wants to look there.

Still, we wait.

And finally, after long moments in which no more doors open and no more steps thud on the stairs above us, Karia twists in my arms.

I reluctantly lift my head and meet the vivid cerulean of her eyes in our shadowy sanctuary.

She raises her light brown brows, as if to ask if we should continue onward to *my* hiding spot.

I don't want to let her go, and I'm scared there will still be people waiting in the bar. But I don't protest, and she takes my silence for acquiescence.

Together we stand, ducking low until we step out from the shadows. My arms have fallen away from her and hers from me, but facing the bar entrance door, she reaches behind her, fingers spread wide to take mine.

I reach back, and we hold hands as she pulls me toward the door.

# Chapter 17

## *Karia*

Slipping past the bar, beyond the lounge, and toward the dark corridor near the bathroom Sullen allegedly left me in is easy. The alarm is still blaring, lights near the ceiling flashing, and *no one* is inside Septem.

*Idiots.*

But just as I think it, I hear the swift footfalls of someone running even over the shrill of the alarm, the moment before a hand latches around my wrist, jerking me apart from Sullen.

My response is immediate. I swing away from them, pivoting my stance as my heart leaps to my throat, but their fingertips dig deeper, crunching against my bones as Sullen releases my other hand.

I catch a glimpse of a man in tactical gear, his face nearly hidden from the stupid Writhe masks the guards wear, and a gun in his free hand, aimed at *me*. His eyes are narrowed, the barrel of the weapon is only a foot from my face as we stare at one another, and the only thought I have is for Sullen.

This man won't shoot me, not if he doesn't want to die himself.

But what will Writhe do to Sullen?

I don't even look at him. I can sense him, so close to me, just at my back, and I know the guard will have spotted him, but it's like I'm the hostage here. The negotiating piece. The pressure point.

I want to laugh.

Sullen won't stay for me.

*He better not stay for me.*

I jerk my arm away again, wanting to keep the focus on myself, but the man yanks me forward, closer, my feet slipping against the flooring as the lights and sirens seem to tunnel into my skull, taking away some of my panic from having a gun aimed at my head. It's like the sensory input has masked the more immediate threat, but I don't care.

Better than trembling at the thought of having my brain blown from my skull.

When the man tugs sharply on me again, pain lances up my arm and an involuntary shriek leaves my lips, lost in the cacophony around us.

A bright burning sensation travels up my forearm at the same time the shadow of Sullen moves.

His hand comes to the man's wrist, the one holding the gun, and he twists sharply in a move he has either practiced before or had done to him, because immediately, the guard releases me. I stumble back, drawing my hand to my chest, rubbing at my wrist with my fingers, and I am frozen as I watch Sullen move.

The gun falls to the floor with a clatter as the guard pivots, facing Sullen unarmed, his eyes narrowed and body center dropping a little, like he's getting into a fighting stance. But Sullen still has hold of his wrist, and he tugs him forward at the same time he swings his other arm, hand curled into a fist. He hits the guard in the face and I watch as the man's head spins to the side, and Sullen doesn't give him a moment to recover. He hits him again, this time an uppercut, his knuckles driving straight up into the man's nose. The move causes the man's chin to lift, exposing his throat, and Sullen takes the opportunity to wrap both hands around his neck.

Sullen's gloved hands are massive, they circle the guard completely.

I watch in a frozen fascination as blood trails down the man's nose, slipping into the black mask covering the rest of his face.

He brings his hands up to Sullen's forearms, trying to get him off, but Sullen stays locked on the guard's throat, pressing his thumbs into the front, against his windpipe. The guard tries to lunge forward, lifting his knee, but Sullen arches his hips back, protecting his groin.

My mouth feels dry as Sullen stares at the man while he chokes him.

He tries to go for Sullen's eyes, but Sullen turns his head and the man only scrambles at his face, but I see it. The way he's weakening. He doesn't even scratch Sullen.

My pulse races inside my head.

The sirens seem to fade away, over the sound of my own heart beating.

My breaths come in heavy pants as I cradle my wrist that no longer hurts, but it's like I can't move at all.

The man's eyes roll back, then close.

His face is nearly the same color as the blood leaking from his nose.

He staggers forward, but Sullen doesn't move and I realize it's because the man is... collapsing.

Sullen doesn't release him, but he crouches down, guiding the guy to the ground without releasing his hold on his throat. Not to set him down gently, I understand, but to keep... choking him.

And when the man's temple is pressed to Sullen's high-tops and Sullen is squatting, only then does he release him.

The guard slumps face down, arms sprawled out either side of him.

Sullen slowly stands fully again, his gaze drifting to mine.

My lips are parted and I know I need to blink and recover and we need to fucking move and *shit,* I should get the gun, but just when that last thought registers and I manage to tear my eyes from Sullen and try to find the weapon, we hear many footsteps, like someone is coming back toward the door we just entered from.

*We have to go.*

I don't spare another glance to the man lying motionless on the ground. I don't know if he's dead. I don't know if I just watched a murder. I don't know, and right now, I don't care.

I reach for Sullen.

His gaze scans the ground, no doubt looking for the gun, too, but the footfalls are louder, heavier, and after a moment, his fingers reach back for mine.

We continue deeper into the dark corridor and I wonder how long it'll take someone to find the body.

Sullen's hand is in mine.

He might have just committed a homicide with his fingers alone.

*His hand is in mine.*

He could have just killed someone for me. For us.

I try not to let my marvel over that distract me from the fact he is taking me somewhere, perhaps where he... touched me before, and although I have gotten us here with minimal discovery, I'm not sure what will happen once he is in charge.

If the potential corpse on the barroom floor is any indication, I could be in worse trouble.

We continue past the bathroom doors in total darkness—even the fire alarm does not flash here, and the ringing siren is quieter, as if muffled—with me in the lead.

But once I take five steps in, I have to stop, my heart racing at the fear of the unknown. I don't know where we're going and I'm not sure it's a good place for me to be. I've already come this far, though, and we already left a body behind, so I'm not backing down. I don't want to separate and I don't want to risk him getting hurt, but he has to show me where to go.

Without words exchanged or even me having to glance back, he walks ahead, still holding my hand, and pulls me softly onwards. I know we come through the supply closet because of the twist of the door then the vivid scent of bleach reaching my nostrils.

We shuffle through the narrow space and I glance over my shoulder, wondering if those footsteps from before were running to Septem, or elsewhere. But I sense nothing in the dark, and I close the door behind me

The deeper we go, the less I can see as we continue in blackness, and the alarm doesn't reach my ears at all. It is strange, and I wonder what this part of the hotel was originally built for because it has much more depth than a closet really needs. Perhaps it is only some place Stein and Sullen know of; in a way, I hope so, although I am terrified of the thought of Stein Rule coming here. I don't know where he is currently, if he can be found, but I really hope not.

Eventually, Sullen stops and he pulls his hand from mine.

I immediately reach out and grab the back of his hoodie, not wanting to be left here in the cold gloom. He stiffens; I feel his spine straighten as my knuckles graze against it from the way I am holding him, but he doesn't shrug me off.

I hear a soft clank of keys and I imagine they are in the pocket of his black jeans. A moment later his body shifts, then I hear the turn of a lock and the creak of a door.

Bitter cold causes me to shiver, the air crawling over my exposed thighs, along my clavicle, down my arms and across my spine. But I hold onto his hoodie and together we move through the dark. I realize he has held the door open for me and I gently nudge it closed with the sole of my shoe until I hear it click into place. Another sound follows, like the lock automatically latches shut. We continue moving deeper under the hotel and I feel claustrophobic. The walls seem to close in around me even though I can't see them and I find myself hugging my shoulders tight down my spine as I follow him along.

The scent of mildew is strong, and I think I hear water dripping from somewhere. *Don't splash on me,* I think, wrinkling my nose at the thought. *Yuck.*

Sullen says nothing and both of our footsteps are only soft whispers in the dark.

Finally, after he unlocks and I push closed three more doors, we step into a space filled with glowing lime verdant.

I recognize it immediately.

My eyes latch onto the rabbit in formaldehyde with the pink eyes, back lit green from a strip of lights around all of the shelves lining the room. It's surprisingly large for being this far beneath the hotel, square, with a sterile table and a patient bed adjacent it. The very one I was on, I'm surprised to see that although the sanitary paper is white, the bed itself is black and it looks to be made of plush leather.

But there is *the* needle, on the steel table, empty, the plunger pushed into the barrel, the metallic tip glinting in green.

The lack of liquid inside doesn't make me feel better. There are metal drawers attached to the table, and I can only imagine what lies within them.

The hum I heard before buzzes in the space, and it must be some sort of extra cooling system because I am shivering as I stand inside the last door, closed all on its own at my back.

I lift my gaze to the other shelves surrounding me. There are so many jars, some smaller like Mason jars and others so much larger with wide necks, but all are sealed with varying lids; some wooden and others much more permanent. Wet specimens, all of them, frogs and an octopus and a lizard and what looks like a fetal mouse. Formaldehyde or maybe ethanol cushions their bodies and...

I twist around suddenly, realizing there are more behind me, the shelves all in black and rising from the floor to the high ceiling above us, no lights on overhead. The sole illumination is from the green rows on each shelf. There is a bat behind me, crabs of all kinds, something that looks like pale white shrimp, and there is only a gap for the black, skinny door we entered.

My breath is coming sharply, the scent of something bitter in the air, tamped down by the cold. I swear I see little clouds as I exhale, my hands clenched into fists. When I spin again, Sullen is standing by the steel table, hands in his pockets, hood over his hair, eyes fixed on me. His posture is strange, chin jutted forward, neck slightly bent, and I don't know if he's angled this way to reach for me if I decide to bolt or if he is only watching me in fascination.

I see a cased opening behind him, leading into only darkness, another gap in all of the dead animals floating around us. I wonder what's through that entranceway. I wonder if I want to know.

If I've already made a terrible choice willingly coming down here.

I think of the potentially dead guard. Cosmo on the floor. What he said, about all the things Sullen could have done to me.

But I also remember Shella Croft letting me go, even though I *know* she knew Sullen was there. What does she understand of him? Perhaps she doesn't agree with the many shadowy corners of Writhe, or simply just of Stein Rule.

Thinking of *him,* my limbs feel shaky, and I wish I was wearing something *more*. What will he do, if he catches us?

Now I'm an accomplice. Now one of Writhe's men is injured, at best. I will share that punishment.

I flick my gaze back to Sullen, who still watches me in silence.

I remember what Mom said, about the date of his disappearance. Two years. I knew it was in October, but I spent so long after he went missing tossing and turning in my bed at night thinking certainly he would come back, show up, maybe even creep into my house and find me in my sleep, that the days blended and melded together and I hadn't quite realized it was exactly the anniversary today—or yesterday, as it were. There was something else, too, some memory of eyes I don't want to face, the day before he vanished.

"Why did you come?" I ask quietly, clouds of cold only semi-transparent as they leave my lips. It's like being inside of a walk-in freezer, this room. I wonder if whatever he spiked my drink with made me warm, because I don't remember freezing quite so much before, lying on that table as if I were his patient.

"Why did you write me?" he counters.

It's as if now that the chaos of the others has fallen away—and he must have known that's what we would need when he returned me to the bathroom no doubt after he somehow realized everyone would be looking for him—we can confront one another without distraction.

And I am no longer sedated on a gurney.

It should make me feel stronger but somehow, I am more nervous than before.

"Why not?" I give his question one of my own. "Did you... read them all?" He mentioned I sent them, called them pathetic, but maybe he grew bored with them. *I can only hope.* My neck flushes hot as I imagine every childish, desperate word I penned, trying to reach out for someone who never seemed as if they wanted to reach for me.

He lifts his chin and I note the high collar of his shirt, black around his throat, but there is the lump there underneath, hiding his disfigured skin. *What happened to you? Why do you blame me?*

"Yes," he answers me, and I don't see shame in his expression. But he gives nothing away as he watches me.

"Did you ever...think of me?"

"Yes."

"Why didn't you write back?"

"I... tried. But I never finished."

I let that and his missing words go. "Where were you, before tonight?"

"Away."

I roll my eyes. "Give me more than that."

He studies me for a long moment, tension pulled taut between us. Then, so fast I didn't anticipate it... he lunges toward me.

I react quickly, spinning out of his grasp. I dart to the right, intending to head around the table and into the darkened space that was at his back. I know the door behind me is locked and he would easily grab me as I tried to figure out how to open it. Yet even now he moves with me, and my hip bumps into the steel table, the jarring impact causing me to cry out softly. I don't stop moving though, facing him now with my back to the green-lit shelves housing the rabbit I saw when I first opened my eyes in here.

His hands are in fists at his side, his gaze darkening on mine. There are feet between us, and I am behind the gurney. I could dart to the back of the room, pray there is a place to slip away beyond the cutout.

But he isn't moving, so I don't either.

*I don't really want to run. I just want to talk.*

"What do you want to know?" I ask quickly. "Ask me anything. Unlike you, I'll give answers."

His lips press together in an unintentional pout. "I can't

talk to you this way." It sounds completely sincere coming from his pretty mouth, but I don't know what he means by that.

"What way?" I try to steady my breathing, so it doesn't sound like I am gasping as I question him. "Why can't you speak to me normally?"

It's the wrong thing to say.

He lunges toward me again, frighteningly fast, and I reach behind me, searching for a weapon in the form of a jar. I palm one, fingers closing around the cold glass. Then I hurl it at him with a small cry.

He neatly jumps back, and the glass shatters along the cement floor, causing me to flinch, the sound loud in the quiet room.

A bright, acrid scent fills the air immediately and I take several steps back as I look down, where he is staring.

The white rabbit has slithered onto the floor, surrounded by liquid and shards of glinting glass.

Its body is still curled up tight, little paws bent, fur damp and eyes facing me, pink and beady and judging.

My breaths are gasps and I take another step back.

He jerks his head up, narrowing dark eyes on me as he comes a step forward, crunching on the glass with his black high-tops, seemingly indifferent the splintered pieces could pierce through his rubber soles.

"I am not *normal,*" he says, voice low and throaty and angry.

"I'm sorry," I say, grasping for some peace between us. "I didn't mean to..." I take another step back.

He advances, toe of his shoe so close to the large body of the white rabbit.

*Fuck.*

He might step on it. Perhaps he wouldn't care at all. I remember how hard he pushed on my belly.

And I know he somehow blames me for the horrors of his

life; or at least, some of them. He said so himself. That *I* did *this* to him. Made him.

And I remember what else he said, too.

That when I woke up, everything would be so much worse.

I don't know what he meant. But I think it's this.

"Sullen." I gasp out his name.

He stops advancing.

His brows lift a little, giving him a strangely innocent expression.

"Talk to me," I whisper, wanting to reach him. Wishing for a connection between us that I perhaps invented in my head all of these years. *"Please."*

He still doesn't move.

The humming coalesces with my pulse beating inside my brain.

Then he lunges again, jumping over the glass, and I know now is not the time for talking. Maybe there never will be such a time, with him.

Grief wells up inside of me as I think it, turning my back to him at the same moment, forcing myself to run away, even though I want to stay.

I shoot through the dark cutaway in the wall, and I hear him follow, his steps hushed and quick.

He knows this space better than I do. His legs are longer. And the brief glimpse I caught of his torso in the penthouse suite, I know he's in good shape. I walk a lot and do some yoga here and there but I don't know if that's going to save me now.

I throw one hand out to sense upcoming obstacles, wishing I hadn't dropped my fucking flashlight, and keep running in the frigid dark. My lungs expand and contract rapidly, my toes hitting the cement softly, heels popping back up quickly.

I don't know where I'm going.

I don't even want to run from him.

But he isn't speaking, he's trying to attack me, he wants me back on the bed.

He wishes for me to be the patient.

Him the doctor.

He needs the power.

*He has to have the control.*

*I can't talk to you this way,* he said.

Because he needs to know I won't run? Or hurt him? I feel like I've already proven the last one. But here I am, doing the first.

Then again, he left two years ago. He ran from me, too.

I keep going, pushing deeper into the darkness, and my shoulder bumps the wall. It's like everything is narrowing around me and I can barely breathe here and there are no lights ahead and maybe this leads nowhere.

He'll trap me here. I'll die under Hotel No. 7.

The princess of Writhe, so stupid she ran with her murderer into the arms of her own death.

But as I continue onward, perspiration forming under my hairline, along the backs of my exposed thighs, I wonder if I would mind it so much. To have our story whispered in the same way only his was, before.

I want to live it, though. Even if we run away together and they talk about us, I want to live through it. I want to *know him.*

I sense him growing closer, tearing apart my darkened fairytale thoughts.

His shadow drops over mine, even here in the dark.

A cry or whimper or *something* leaves my lips, the moment before his hand slams down over my mouth.

His arm latches across my waist, jerking me forcefully into him. But we keep going, the way we had so much forward momentum. My fingers reach for his forearm, this time to pry him off, but he twists us so we pivot in the dark and I realize there is a small glow ahead.

We stumble forward into another room.

This one is far more primitive. Dirty floors, wires in the ceiling, the glow is from a macabre sort of nightlight pushed into an exposed outlet, a heavy black box beside it that looks both innocent and ominous at once.

And there's a chair, like for a dentist.

Large and imposing with so many beige straps and silver buckles, I know I couldn't fight my way out of it.

And he's going to put me there, isn't he?

He steps forward again, pushing and pulling me along both, the way he's holding me from behind, hand over my mouth so I can't scream. Not that it would help, this far underground.

I kick my feet, push back against his shin with one sole, but it doesn't seem to faze him.

Then there's a loud thud, and I realize he's slammed the door closed with his back as he jerks me a step in that direction, pulling me this time while he rests against the door.

I try to open my mouth but my lips only glide along his palm and he bends low, his breath ghosting over the tip of my ear.

"Shh," he whispers, and I freeze in his arms.

He makes me wait one second. Another.

I wonder if he can hear my heartbeat because *I can.*

Then he slides his palm down my throat, curls his fingers over my neck as he holds me, and I know he can feel my rabid pulse beating through my skin.

I think of the guard on the floor.

I stare at the chair, tears building behind my eyes.

I have never been tortured before.

"Is this what you want?" I gasp out. "To...strap me down here?"

His breath fans the skin between my ear and my shoulder.

My chest is rising and falling painfully fast as he grips me tighter.

Then he only says, *"Yes."*

"Why?" It comes out a broken gasp. I remember how he touched my teeth. The way he spoke of extraction. I imagine myself spattered with blood, nothing inside my mouth, all of my molars and canines and incisors scattered on the grimy floor.

Does he want to make me like him?

I've seen the fact he's missing teeth. I can only imagine he lost them so unnaturally.

He is still stunning, though, but I don't want him to remove my teeth. I don't want surgery. I just want to talk.

*"I just want to understand you."* It sounds jagged and weak and stupid, but I can't hold it in as he holds me.

"I think we could play a game, to make it happen," he whispers over the side of my neck.

"What game, Sullen?" I blink away the tears in my eyes as I focus on the rusted metal at the base of the chair. "What do you mean?"

He bows his head then, pressing his temple to my shoulder.

I feel his body tense. It is vibrating, the way he is so rigid.

My breath is loud and shaky. I am gripping his forearm around my waist as I feel my heartbeat in my neck, where he holds me tightly.

*"Talk to me,"* I beg. *"Please."*

He is silent.

It frightens me.

Then, he shoves me away, toward the chair, and I spin to face him, holding my hands up, dizzy with his sudden movements and release.

"Sit on the chair, Little Sun," he says quietly as he watches me. "And I will give you everything."

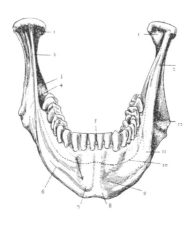

It is true, we shall be monsters, cut off from
all the world; but on that account we shall
be more attached to one another.

— *Frankenstein,* Mary Shelley

# Chapter 18

## *Sullen*

W e enter through the back door of the cathedral. *Sanctum. This is the playground of the 6, and Writhe only ever gets an invitation when there's work to be done. I won't see anyone here but the other "kids" though, as we're known, despite the fact I'm nearly twenty.*

*And maybe because of that, none of them will show. Von, Isadora,* her.

*I should've thought of this before.*

*I am so incredibly stupid.*

*As the double doors clang closed behind me, I feel hot and itchy beneath all of my clothing.* I shouldn't have come. *No one will be in the front lobby where we used to wait together. Those lighter memories are from years ago. It's been a few since the 6 summoned so many members of Writhe, and I should have known better than to get my hopes up. But when Stein asked if I wanted to get out of the house to come to Sanctum—one of the few times he offered to set me briefly free—all I thought about was* her.

*But now that I'm thinking clearly instead of holding onto warped dreams, I realize she won't be here. She'll have things to do. I've seen her with Von before, in his car. And with Cosmo, in hers.*

*She could be fucking them now and I just rode all this way in the back of Stein's armored Mercedes for nothing. I should've stayed home. I should have—*

*Stein's hand comes around my wrist, over my hoodie and the eraser burns he left on my skin, jolting me from my turmoil.*

*I snap my head up but look down at him. I have grown taller yet no more brave.*

*His eyes are light, blue and vivid under the chandelier over our heads in the empty back lobby, stone and marble and cold air coating the room. The scent of incense is strong here, but I smell the peach candy he has between his teeth as he tightens his hold on my wrist.*

*I don't wince, blink, or flinch.*

*If I do, this will be worse.*

*He smooths his other hand down the black tie he's wearing, and I see his golden wedding band. My mother's name is carved along the inside of it.* Mercy. *After she left, I had none.*

*"How are you feeling, Sully?" Stein smiles as he asks, dimples forming in his ivory skin, a pocket of his cheek pushed out from the candy in his mouth. He has a shock of black hair, darker than my own, and it contrasts sharply with his blue eyes. When I was younger, he used to marvel over how I took after my mother.*

*Brown hair, brown irises. He made those genes sound divine then.*

*It doesn't stop him from trying to rip them—me—apart, now.*

*"Good," I manage, holding his gaze as he clenches my wrist. I wish for someone to come through one of the heavy, intricately carved wooden doors spaced far apart at his back and leading into the sanctuary. To interrupt this moment where his undivided attention is once more on me.*

*But no one comes.*

*No one ever does.*

*Night is behind me, past the tinted glass of the exit doors, and it's this time I usually enjoy most. Even monsters like Stein have to sleep.*

*Tonight, though, the 6 meeting could prolong my waking misery.*

"*Great,*" *Stein says as he digs his fingertips deeper into my skin. The burn from the rectangular, pink erasers flares up with his vicious hold. Then he drags me closer, my shoes skidding over the marble floor.*

*I look down as he leans in, his mouth over my ear.* "*If you so much as speak to Karia Ven, you stupid, insolent child, I will show you what a pair of scissors can do to the web of your fingers.*" *Then he releases me and steps back like I disgust him as he straightens his tie once more while fear presses on my bladder.* "*Her parents are loyal to me,*" *he continues in a quiet tone no one could overhear.* "*But we all know you are repulsive. If you make her uncomfortable, you will cause discord for me, and you will pay for it. No one is interested in someone like you, Sully. No one but me. And if her life becomes a problem, I will ensure her death to solve it.*"

Yes, then I will have no reason not to murder you too.

*But I know Karia is safe because I will never initiate anything with her. I am not brave enough. So the sentence that rings loudest inside my head is,* no one is interested in someone like *you.*

"*I don't know why you dragged me to this,*" *Von says.*

"*Isadora dragged you,*" *Karia replies primly.*

"*Because* you *dragged* me," *Isadora counters, and Karia's pink lips turn up into a smirk, like it's true.*

*Still, she says,* "*Whatever,*" *under her breath, rolling her eyes as she glances at me.*

*I keep my head bowed and hands in my hoodie pocket across the lobby from her, sitting on the opposite benches alone. My stomach is in knots; it has been since I walked in here and discovered the three of them. I'm surprised they came; I expected to spend the night of the meeting by myself. I wish it had only been Karia here, but it sounds like she coerced the others to come with her.*

*Can she ever be alone?*

*I'd like to think she came at all to see me, but I'm positive that's not true.*

No one is interested in someone like you, Sully.

*"Let's pass the time," Karia says slyly, staring at me now.*

*I inhale and hold it, wondering what she will say next. Suggest some stupid game, like always, as if we're still kids? Maybe this time it'll be hide and seek and I can get her away from the others. Hide her in an alcove and ask her if she thinks of me like I think of her. I am nearly trembling here, trying to obey Stein, to save her life. It is a war of emotion beneath my broken skin.*

*"Truth or dare, Sullen Rule," she calls out to me, but her voice sounds a little shaky as her pink-painted nails dance in the edges of her short, mauve skirt, her legs crossed primly like she's some innocent virgin.*

*I know she isn't though.*

*I glance at Von and want to break his neck for it.*

*"He's not going to play your stupid games with you," he says without looking at me. He's slouched down on the bench, backwards hat over his red curls, chin dipped down and eyes closed like he wants to be anywhere but here.*

*She has that power, doesn't she? The ability to draw everyone into her orbit, no matter what they really want.*

*Because here I am, for the same reason.*

*It makes my skin feel itchy, knowing she can play this mind game with everyone. I am not special, to her, to anyone.*

*"Maybe we'll do 'would you rather?' instead. You only have to say a few words for that," she presses on, and I'm happy she is completely ignoring Von, but she doesn't seem to like I'm ignoring her.*

*I keep my head bowed but my eyes on her blue ones, a few feet of marble flooring the only thing between us.*

*"Would you rather have the power to be invisible or the ability to read minds?" she asks, never looking away from me.*

*Easy. Invisibility. I know what's inside people's minds; I don't want to hear that darkness all around me. And if I was invisible, I could leave. Stein would never touch me again. I could sneak into her room and hide under her bed. I could slash Von and Cosmo across the throat when they got too close to her.*

"You should make the choices correlate. Compete with each other. I don't think those are two comparable things," Von says, elbowing her as she sits up straighter, uncrossing and recrossing her long legs, frilly pink socks pulled up to her calves.

*I glance at Von Bentzen and want to carve out his eyes for touching her. For getting to see her naked. Kiss her and laugh with her and go to her house and all these things Stein would never let me do. These dreams I will never live in.*

"They're two supernatural abilities, of course they are," Isadora jumps in, on the other side of Von.

*She's right, but I'm not answering. If I give it away, Karia might pity me more than I'm sure she already does.*

"Is that too hard for you? I'll make it easier." She keeps going as she stares at me, her cheeks flushing pink like they do when she's embarrassed. *She gets mean, too. The princess unraveled. I'd love to grab her and shake it out of her, all of her attitude. I would love to put my hand over her mouth and make her stop being a brat as she looks at me. Sees me.*

"Would you rather kiss me or break your own leg?" she asks with a slight snarl.

*I almost smile. Almost.*

"Jesus, Karia," Von says under his breath.

"Look at his face, I think it's obvious," Isa adds.

*I don't know what I'm doing with my face except trying not to express anything at all, but as intelligent as I know Isadora Croft to be, she's wrong, if she thinks I don't want to kiss Karia.*

"Would you rather open your mouth to speak or pluck out your own—"

"I'd rather not kiss you and I'd prefer to break your leg," I finally say, my voice cracking. *I am a liar. I would die to kiss her. To grab her baby blonde strands and twist them around my fingers. To touch my mouth to hers. Have her cheeks pink and her eyes closed and her hands by her sides as she let me explore her.*

*But...* No one is interested in someone like me. *Especially not a girl like* her.

*Her eyes go wide as she clenches her fists in the hem of her skirt and Von's lips curve into a reluctant smile and even Isadora snorts a little.*

*But Karia seems to take it personally and she clearly cannot read minds. She stands then, the edges of her skirt skimming her thighs and her face growing red as she stares at me.*

*"You are not any fun, Sullen Rule," she says petulantly, then turns her back on all of us and heads for the corridor leading to the bathroom.*

*If I was a different person, I might follow her.*

*But I know if I do, nothing good will come from it, and Von is already glaring at me like he knows what I'm thinking and if I make a scene here and cause Stein embarrassment, I might not survive the night.*

*So I let her go and close my eyes, pretending to be completely unaffected as I wonder what it would feel like to touch her mouth.*

# Chapter 19

## *Karia*

"You never spoke to me before. When I tried to connect with you, you always shot me down. Why would you give me anything now?" I shake my head, glancing at the chair, grateful I don't see any blood on it and wondering how strange this night has become to make *that* the thing I'm appreciative of in this cold room. "Why did you come back? You tell me that, I might sit in this chair for you."

He watches me without speaking for several moments. There is no humming noise here, no fire alarm. It is dreadfully quiet aside from the beat of my own heart. I glance at the door behind him and wonder how long we have and why he is wasting it, counting down the clock in silence.

But he's always been this way, and what he said about Stein, and my teeth... No wonder he's communicating in chases and only comfortable when I'm sedated.

"Did you see me?" he asks in that peculiar voice, like every syllable scratches up his throat. A rusted tomb cracking ajar.

*I will split the coffin wide open for you.*

I don't know what he means with his question, but I hold my tongue; I don't think he's finished speaking.

"Up, at the suites. Did you... look at me?"

My mind flashes back to swinging the flashlight. The way it jarred through my wrists and forearms as it cracked against Cosmo's head.

Then his body crumpling.

And Sullen, bare from the waist up, lines of defined muscle and scars and wounds and what looked like letters and...

"You did," he continues when I don't answer him. "And I can see it in your face. You are disgusted."

I shake my head and take a step back, wanting distance between us when he's misreading me this way. "No," I insist. "That's not true at all. I think you are..." I trail off, worried flattery will sound insincere to someone unused to any.

But maybe he's not. I don't know where he's been the past two years and even before that, Sullen Rule was always gorgeous. Dark eyes, dark hair, tall and broad and with that pointed nose and full lips, the stubble along his defined jawline and even wearing his all-black, the hood flipped over his head... he is and has always been *hot*. There's no way he hasn't been with girls before—or maybe boys, or both. It's impossible he is a virgin in any way. And how he held me under the stairs, and even now, before he let me go. And before, when I was on the bed, he flicked his tongue over my nipple, and it couldn't have been the first time he did something like that.

"I'm *what?*" he asks in a low voice, his posture rigid.

"If I tell you, then you give me an answer to why you came back. Then we can talk about the chair."

His lips tip upward, but only halfway. "Do you think you could stop me, if I strapped you down?"

"I'm tougher than I look," I counter, wishing I was wearing something besides a miniskirt and crop top, but I won't go down without a fight regardless. He saw what I did to Cosmo. I want to help him, but he shouldn't underestimate me.

He flicks his gaze over my body. "Maybe," he agrees. "But

maybe not. I imagine you've spent most of your life lying on Egyptian cotton sheets and silk pillowcases, waking when you want, eating when you'd like, driving your little white BMW without a care in the world. I don't think you've ever been hit before. Have you, Karia?"

My throat grows tight but I don't blink. "Have you?" I ask quietly, knowing the answer. *Tell me your horrors. Let me ease them for you. We don't have much time here.*

His eyes seem to darken. "Tell me what you were going to say. What am I?"

"Handsome," I blurt out, feeling my cheeks heat in the cold of this strange room. "You're...gorgeous." I inhale the scent of mildew down here but also *him,* dark roses, and earth, dangerous and strangely seductive. "That's what I was going to say," I mumble when his expression doesn't change at all.

He says nothing. Does nothing.

I want to scream and force words from his pouty mouth.

He just *looks* at me, as if he loathes me for the compliment. Or maybe... as if he's never heard one before.

Seconds pass. Minutes. My face is hot in the cold room, and I can't look at him any longer when he's staring at me this way.

I take another step back, sweeping my gaze over the cement floor, littered with dirt or plaster from the half-finished ceiling. I turn for one single second to look over my shoulder at the nightlight beside the black box. It isn't macabre at all, I see now, it is only out of place, but boring and plain, emitting a pale-yellow glow, and I have no idea why it's in here. It doesn't seem like something he would've decorated with. It's covered in dust while the box seems spotless. Did he bring that here, before? What's inside?

"What is this place?" I ask when he continues to stand there in silence, and I face him once more. The room is rather small, and while there's an entryway behind me like there's a door beyond him, I am not interested right now in creeping further through this underground horror show.

As long as he doesn't try to force me into that chair, I tell myself I won't run again.

"Why is the nightlight here?" I press, crossing my arms over my body so they cover a little of my waist. I think of the bruise from the needle and can't shut up. "What's in the box? What did you inject me with?"

His expression shifts, lines around his eyes relaxed slightly, as if the thought of drugging me calms him. Instead of loathing, he looks at me like I am the most interesting person on the planet and yet he'd still like to throttle me. Or put me to sleep before he pokes at me.

I'm about to keep going, ask question after question until he chooses one to reply to, but he parts his lips and I stop, waiting.

"Stein was away," he says haltingly. "That's why I came back. He took his worst guards and left for the first time in... a long time."

I want to clap for getting some kind of answer. But I'm only more confused. "Stein has been with you? Since when? He only stepped down in April. Where were you before that?"

"Not far," he answers the last question slowly, and I take it as a win that he's responding at all.

"Does Stein live with you? Why did you leave in the first place—"

"Sit in the chair."

I grit my teeth and glance at it, the lower part angled down, the wide arms with beige straps dangling from them, metal buckles. There are more straps at the waist, over the chest, along the legs. This isn't a standard-issue chair. No dentist would get away with some shit like this.

The only plus is there's not a light above it, and no instruments of torture that I see in this nearly empty room. They could be inside that box, though.

"What will you do to me?" I ask quietly, dragging my gaze back to his.

"I have to go back tomorrow."

My heart sinks and I open my mouth to tell him that's not going to happen, but he keeps talking.

"I want to touch you. I want to let you talk to me. But I can't answer any of your questions if we're just like this."

"Why not? This is how normal people—"

"Stop using that word with me."

"So you strap me down and poke and prod at me and I get to ask you questions?"

He nods once. "Yes."

It's so simple, inside his head. And I know he is twenty-three, like me, but it's as if he's younger, in some ways. Like despite his horrors, he was sheltered, locked away as he was.

I think of his hands around the guard's throat. The way he twisted the man's wrist.

Maybe 'sheltered' isn't the right word.

"This is weird, Sullen."

His eyes flutter closed for one second. Another. He looks so vulnerable, I want to cross the space between us. Wrap my arms around his broad frame.

But I don't move as he blinks open his eyes.

"I know," he finally says. "But it seems *normal* to me."

I want to stick out my tongue at his bite, the way he throws the word back in my face. I want to refuse, too. To tell him this is insane, but... so is my entire life. Even without the constant crush on Sullen, being born into Writhe makes us all a little strange. Who else has their parents come home with bullet wounds or knife lacerations? Who else hides inside panic rooms as children, a constant alarm? Who else can't form friendships without fear of their bond being used as ransom? Or mistrusting even the best intentions, scared a simple *hello* is a precursor to blackmail? And for Sullen... even the rest of us in Writhe haven't lived what he has.

Besides that, I know Mads and my parents will find me, eventually. I won't be down here forever.

*Will I?*

I close my eyes tight as I ball my hands into fists under my ribcage. I want to trust him. I want to help him. But I don't want to die down here.

"I won't hurt you, Karia. *I promise.*" His voice is low and nearly soothing. For some reason, I trust it less.

It sends a shiver down my spine.

He can't accept my compliment, but he wants to seduce me into being strapped down for him? Like an experiment in this hotel dungeon?

I don't know if he keeps promises. I don't know if he keeps anything, aside from in jars, like the rabbit.

Before I can decide, think through *anything,* I hear him move, steps soft along the cement floor.

My eyes flash open, my entire body tense.

He stalks toward me, and fear strangles my voice for a moment. I back up, swallowing hard.

"Sullen—"

He lunges for me then, and I angle myself backward, jumping, leaping, ready to turn and slip into the darkness cut out in the wall. I spin around as my heart leaps to my throat, my thoughts a mess. *I shouldn't have saved him. A crush doesn't mean I can trust a monster. He never wrote me back. He stayed away for two years. Why would he keep me alive now? I don't mean anything to him.*

I dart to the gaping hole, ready to take my chances inside of it. But he grabs me then, jerking sharply on my hair. I cry out, my throat taut, neck wrenched backward.

The momentum of him crashes us both against the drywall, my palms up as rough plaster meets my skin. I hear a thud and something scattering, then I realize he kicked the nightlight from the wall, the way total darkness drenches us inside this tomb.

His body is pressed to mine as I try to breathe, elbows bent, forearms against the craggy wall. His gloved hand is still inside my hair, keeping my chin lifted, water blurring my eyes in the blackness.

I feel his arm glide along my shoulder, and I know he has pressed his other hand to the wall, pinning me here.

*Oh, God.*

"You said you won't hurt me," I manage to choke out, the words scratchy from fear and the angle of my throat. "You promised. I saved you."

He laughs lightly against my ear, breath warm on my skin. "You *damned* me."

"I hit my friend for you."

He wraps my hair tighter around his fist, knuckles grazing the back of my skull. *"Friend,"* he says, the word full of hoarse disdain. "What the *fuck* is that, Karia?"

The words hurt. I wish they didn't. I wish I didn't feel so much *empathy* for him. But I can't help that. I have always been intrigued with the prince of Writhe.

"Let me go. I'll get in the chair. Just... Let me go," I try to bargain.

He glides his mouth over the lobe of my ear, but it is not a kiss. "Do you know how much I will suffer for this?"

"We won't let you go back—"

*"Don't."* It's a harsh command, and I bite my bottom lip, staying quiet. "I can't live with false hope. I *will* go back, and I will pay for this. And I'm going to ensure it was all *very* worth it."

# Chapter 20

## *Sullen*

I snap the last buckle, the metallic click in the room echoing in the darkness around us. I did everything by feel alone and it was difficult, what with her thrashing and pleading, but she cannot overpower me. Not physically, anyway.

I did not strap down anything below her waist, which could prove to be disastrous but... her legs are so pretty, and I would really like to spread them, even if I cannot see.

The rolling stool I procured from the small closet at the back of the room—which leads further under the hotel, but I didn't mention that to her in case she decides to bolt—is black leather and while it squeaks a little when I shift myself toward her, hands on my thighs, gloves clinging to my fingers, it is at the perfect height for me to reach out and touch every inch of her.

The feel of wads of cash in my jeans, from the small safe by the light I destroyed, is uncomfortable and odd; the exact reason I left it here before I cut Cosmo and stole her. But I am worried I will get lost in her, in this, and when we have to run again, I won't be able to grab for the money. If there is one thing I know about Karia, it's that she likes everything it can buy.

A spoiled, soon-to-be broken little princess.

I press one hand to her chest, feeling it move rapidly in and out. I can hear her breathing, too, little gasps in the night. I trail my fingers down past the hem of her shirt, to her stomach muscles. They clench and release with every breath. She is terrified.

Lower, I caress the denim of her skirt, note by feel how it has shifted up her legs with her position, and I think I sense goosebumps along her thighs.

*So scared.*

She should be.

In my mind, I picture how she might look, wide-eyed and repulsed, staring at me as if I am her creator.

There is a strap just above her breasts, another below her belly button, several on her arms and wrists, and one smaller band over her throat. That last one I want to see most, but not now. I cannot handle her staring back at me. As it is, even the whites of her eyes and the blue of her irises is enough to strangle my thoughts.

To want to reassure her, somehow.

Being in a position like this when I was with Stein, I know how she feels. Frightened and vulnerable and maybe, sickeningly, curious.

This is the way Stein would quiz me for my homeschool lessons. Me, strapped down, and him with a scalpel he would use to dig into parts of my flesh if I got anything wrong. He once carved an *F* into my thigh, to denote my failing grade. That wound became infected; I prayed I would die from it.

My prayers, though, are forever unanswered.

I keep my eyes on hers as I grip her thigh, and with how *large* her gaze is, eye sockets round whiteness in the dark, it's as if she's looking at me like I'm God. But much like the real one, I won't be listening to her invocations, either.

I know, though, her pretty mouth is capable of sweetness, like when she called me handsome. When she lied to my face. And although I do plan to answer some of her questions in this room she may never leave, I worry she will use her ability to speak to try and... consume me. Possess me, more than she already does. She might talk me out of her own escape, convince me to watch her run.

I wish I could sedate her, but getting an anesthetic would require going to the lab and I don't want to leave her alone. There could be other monsters in the dark here. Who knows, at Stein's hotels?

I was once tormented by our family doctor, in a room several floors up. The hatred I have for Stein is only rivaled by how I feel about that man.

"Why don't you go first?" I ask quietly, caressing her thigh with my index finger and feeling immensely grateful for a thing like gloves, even in the dark. Her muscles quiver and jump beneath my touch, and I smile, unseen by her.

"I want to see you," she whispers.

"It's a shame I shattered the light." I trail my finger up higher, until I feel the edge of her skirt.

Her breath catches, but I only trace a pattern the way I came.

"I helped you," she says, as if it was altruistic. She wants to examine me like I want to her, but it doesn't mean anything. Specimens are corpses, after all.

I could remind her I strangled a man for daring to point a gun at her head, for grabbing her arm, but she will think that was selfish, too, much how I feel about her own motives.

"How would you like me to thank you?" I ask all the same, continuing my circling path along her thigh as she shakes beneath my touch. If only she could see my bare fingers; she would really fear me then.

"I don't need thanking, but forcefully strapping me down seems kind of rude, Sullen."

Ah, she is trying to be so brave with her slight attempts at humor.

This time, I push my finger under the edge of her skirt, going higher.

Her entire thigh goes rigid and stiff and she presses her knees together.

I smile to myself. She doesn't think I'm gorgeous. She knows I am disgusting.

"Relax," I say as I hold her cerulean gaze, eerie in the darkness, like the mirage of a ghost staring back at me. "Widen your knees." I keep my finger where it is, halfway up her thigh, waiting for her to comply.

"No," she says, bratty and insolent.

"I don't think you're in a position to tell me *no*," I reply calmly.

The buckles on the straps clank and I know she has shifted forward. I see her eyes loom closer, but I know that band around her throat won't let her get too close. "Do you want to hear it again? *No, Sullen.*"

I almost think her funny.

But I only have this one night to steal enough memories to last me until my death. And I know the best way to distract an animal from their lower half is to torture their upper body.

I release my grip on her thigh and shift forward on my stool, the rusty wheels creaking in the dark.

I reach for the hem of her short shirt then slip my thumbs beneath the fabric and the bra she is wearing. It is a thin strip of cotton, no wires, and I fold up both it and the shirt, all the way to the strap above her breasts, exposing her in the cold dark.

She says nothing, but I can feel her rapid pulse beneath my gloved hand as I place it over her heart, the curve of her breast. A soft whimper leaves her lips, torn unwillingly from her pretty mouth.

"Oh, dear," I say softly. "It's okay, Karia." I brush my thumb over the tight, hard bud of her nipple, remembering it in my mouth only hours ago, before I had to rearrange the pieces of this board. "But it can hurt, if you'd like it to. When I told you to relax, widen your knees, you should have listened. Now I have nowhere to go but here, do you see how this works?" I circle her nipple, marveling over the feel of firm, soft skin even beneath my gloved hand.

"Do you want me to hate you?" she whispers in the dark, eyes flashing as she stares at me, defiant.

"Isn't this what you let Cosmo do to you? Don't you want to be a doll? You let him get you drunk so he can fuck you, touch you everywhere. Or do I have it wrong?" I muse out loud, for the first time a sickening thought occurring to me. "Did he... truly take advantage of you or—"

She makes a funny noise that I don't immediately understand until I feel something warm on my face, wet and gliding down my cheek.

I still, sensing the saliva, amazed that with a foot between us, she could aim so well in the dark.

*She spit on me.*

I laugh a little, squeezing her breast and tugging softly before I let her go to swipe one finger over her fluid.

Then I push it into my mouth, savoring the light taste of *her*, mingled with the leather of my glove.

"What if he did?" she snarls, now that I am no longer touching her, even though she is exposed to me, to this room. Completely helpless like a butterfly with pinned wings. "Would you want to avenge me, Sullen? As you do the same thing?"

I swallow her spit, then drop my hand to my thigh as I

watch her. "If you are asking me if I could snap his jaw from his skull if he touched you like that, the answer is *yes.*"

She laughs. A brash sound, almost like her genuine laughter. It is braying in a way, noisy and loud, and I wish she were laughing at something else I said. I wish, for a moment, we were so far away from here. Things would be different then.

"Do you know what a hypocrite is, or did your dad not teach you that word?"

My jaw clenches, fingers curled into fists as I sit perfectly silent and still on the stool.

"What *did* he teach you, at all?" she continues, her tone haughty and biting. "The only way you can touch women is to tie them up? How many have you done this to, huh? Are there bodies buried under here from your little experiments? Do you fancy yourself a scientist? Does he? Father and son, working side by side in a lab of helpless women, thinking *that's* what makes a man? Did you both kill your mother, Sullen? Did you help your daddy as he tied up Mommy—"

I stand, then. I can't help it as my pulse races and the stool rolls somewhere behind me and my palm is slammed over her mouth and I grip her jaw in my other hand, too tight.

She is frozen as I loom over her, my eyes inches from her sickeningly gorgeous ones.

"My mother was beaten in the head with a knife block, trying to stop *him* from lighting my hair on fire to see how close I could let it get to my scalp without screaming. I was restrained then, and I closed my eyes, but I heard it all."

She goes completely still.

She is not breathing.

She does not struggle beneath me. I feel her pulse thump against her jawline.

I lean closer, the tip of my nose brushing hers. "Her screams grew quiet after a few thuds. When I stopped being a coward and opened my eyes, she was motionless. Then he shot her and claimed..." I loosen my hold on her mouth, slipping my hand down until only my thumb brushes over her parted lips. "Well, you know the rumors."

She still says nothing.

Does nothing.

Only *looks* at me as I trace the plushness of her mouth.

"Go ahead," I whisper quietly, still gripping her face tight. "Ask me what else you'd like to know. You may be my experiment, but did you know I am yours too?"

"She didn't deserve that," she says, her voice cracking. "And neither did you, Sullen."

"I think I did. Don't you see yourself now?" I smile with the teeth I have. "I guess not," I continue. "But you are at my mercy, and I have never had much of that. This is precisely what I deserve."

"Why did you disappear?" she asks in an even tone, as if she is switching tactics, taking advantage of my offer, pushing through my spilled secrets. "Two years ago. Why did you leave?"

I circle her mouth again with my thumb as I look into her eyes. Marginally, I decrease the pressure of my hand around her jaw, but I don't let her go. "Stein sent me away."

"Why?" she presses, her bones moving as she speaks.

I consider saying nothing. I think again about drugging her. Or setting her free. I don't know if I can play this game after all.

Instead, as if compelled, I answer her. Who else has ever asked me about my life? Who else has ever been brave enough to know?

"He has a very peculiar...belief system. And part of it entails that he is to hurt me, damage me, although he doesn't see it that way. Instead, he is shaping me, forming me, deconstructing me as a sort of..." I nudge my nose with hers and speak over her lips. *"Means to an end."*

Because of the blue ring of her irises, I see her pupils dilate as I speak, but she says nothing, as if she wants more. As if she is waiting.

*You stupid, gorgeous girl.*

But I have never spoken of this to someone else before. And it is strange, how I *want* to confess to her. This princess I cannot have.

I am not sure if she is familiar with any of this, but I am fairly certain none of the other children of Writhe experienced what I did. Stein kept his work and his personal beliefs strangely separate, as far as I know. Perhaps he did not want to share the secrets of immortality with the others.

"As I got older and stronger, he became more violent, and he ensured my senses were dulled with everything he fed me. Near the end, he was afraid if I stayed, he would kill me before the appropriate time."

She blinks but says nothing.

I shift my fingers from her mouth, then cradle her face gently in both hands, smoothing my thumbs over her cheekbones.

"So he sent me away, a home in the mountains. Haunt Muren." I don't know why I say it out loud. It is forbidden to give the location away. Most think Stein Rule left the country after he retired. I am supposed to keep that illusion up.

But I don't want to.

Not with her.

She may not survive the night anyway.

What do secrets matter if they are buried with bones or pushed into jars with formalin?

"And now?" she asks, her pupils wide and latched onto mine. "Now that he's around you, does he...try to kill you?" Her chin trembles; I feel it against my fingers.

I want to reassure her, and I do not know why.

I dip my head, running my mouth over hers, then abruptly, I pull back, putting inches between us.

She pities me. She doesn't want to *kiss* me.

I clear my throat, like I am dusting it of cobwebs. Still, my voice comes out shamefully coarse. "I believe this trip he is on now is supposed to give him answers to the date of my death. He is visiting a prognosticator. But in the past few months, he has slowly begun to sedate me longer, poisoning my food. Sometimes entire days will slip away." *And I grasp onto your letters inside my head. I live in the dream you create with those words.* "Not quite attempts on my life, though. Jarring anyway because I was without him for a year and a half."

"Why did you not run then?" she asks quickly, the question tumbling out of her. "Why did you stay there, waiting for him?" There is an accusation in her words. It cuts to my core.

I slide my hands down her face, to her throat, feeling the strap there. Then lower still, until I have her breasts cupped in my hands, my thumbs gliding over her flesh.

The buckles clank softly as she jerks forward, but she cannot go anywhere. She cannot do anything to stop me.

"I tried a few times to run, but Stein sent his most loyal guards with me to Haunt Muren. After a while, the pain I endured with each failed attempt wasn't worth trying again. Does this sound real to you?" I flick my eyes to hers, squeezing her softly. "While you were getting fucked by Cosmo, I was being beat by Stein? Strange, isn't it?"

"You can touch me however you want," she says, her voice a low hiss. "But you're going to answer everything I ask of you."

I smile at that. "Oh, am I?" I brush my thumbs over her hard nipples, then flick them once and I'm rewarded as the buckles clatter again when her body jolts. "What if I don't, hmm? What will you do then, Karia?"

"When did it start?" she asks, ignoring me. It is remarkable how she compartmentalizes. I have done the very same. "Your —Stein's beliefs?"

I want to torture her with silence, but again, it as if, despite the fact she is strapped down, I am tied up for her. Maybe all of these things I have been dying to vomit up for years, and she is who, in my subconscious, I wanted to tell.

"Always, but it grew worse shortly before my mother died." I swallow hard and splay my fingers over her chest, feeling her pulse beat fast. "He was forever meeting with fanatics; partly because of his job and partly because...conspiracies were his hobby. He has a ruthless fascination with serial killers. Then it became something more. A religion, discovered by so few, he believed. He really thinks I am *lucky,* being his son. That when I die—and he *will* kill me—I will earn a special place in heaven for the fact he is my god."

"He's not going to kill you." The words sound fierce.

I cannot listen to nonsense.

I drop my hands from her and step back, reaching for the stool. I grasp the plush leather seat and pull it closer, sinking down onto it once more and closing my eyes for a moment as I bow my head.

I think of seeing Cosmo touch her.

Von, too.

The way she would tilt her head back and moan their names.

How I pretended it was mine; from my hiding place, or later, at Haunt Muren, from video Stein has set up all over the houses in Ritual Drive. Sometimes I think he did that to torture me, knowing I would sneak into his surveillance room and watch her tits bounce, her legs spread, Von or Cosmo driving forcefully into her as her head lolled.

I snap open my eyes and reach for her thigh again, and despite the shakiness in my fingers, I force myself to keep my touch light.

I tap the inside of her leg. "Let's try this once more. You said I can touch you how I want. I'll keep answering your questions, but spread these for me, Karia."

She doesn't move.

I lift my gaze to hers.

She is staring back, her eyes shiny with something that could be tears. "Sullen." My name is a rasp from her lips.

A lump forms in my throat. I feel hot and itchy, but I only press my fingertips deeper into the meat of her thigh. "Spread them."

She half-shakes her head, I can sense the movement in the dark. "I'm so sorry you—"

I grab her then, forcefully as her body jolts, flinching at my touch. "Never mind," I say quietly. "You're right. That was a stupid command. I can get better access to your cunt a different way. Bend your knees instead, then let them fall to the side."

She swallows; it is audible in the quiet room, the way the buckle from the band over her throat clangs softly. I imagine what she would look like wearing my necklace. I've seen her in dainty jewelry before, but it would be nice to put a scalpel around her neck. If only I hadn't used the poison there all on stupid, silly Cosmo. If only it were enough to have killed him.

Before I can grow angrier, she does as I say.

I feel her muscles flex as she bends her knees, sliding the soles of her Vans along the bottom half of the chair, then drawing them up tight to her body.

She doesn't spread her legs, though, instead keeping them tight together as I run my hand up the inside of one, trying to put distance between her kneecaps.

She resists, never looking away from me.

"Karia," I whisper quietly, knowing Stein would have already punished me for this. And I could hit her or force her or something worse, but I have already done so much. Maybe I should just let her believe I am the worst kind of monster but there is a sickening sliver of me wanting her to think something more.

"I wanted you to touch me, did you know?" she asks quietly,

disrupting my pathetic thoughts. "Growing up, I imagined you... all the time."

I freeze with her words, my hand stalled on her thigh. The feeling of falling overtakes me, despite the fact I am sitting.

It's how I felt when she called me *handsome* and *gorgeous*.

*Liar.*

She is a beautiful little liar.

No one has ever called me those things before.

And no one has ever imagined *me* touching them.

"I wanted to kiss you. I wished you were fucking me when it was Cosmo, or Von."

My cock grows hard, hearing the words, and I try my best to ignore it. Stein would laugh at me whenever he saw me become erect, and although he never truly sexually assaulted me, the humiliation of his amusement at my body was painful enough.

"You saw me, the Night of Lies?" She swallows hard as my face grows hot. "You watched Cosmo touch me, didn't you? Lick me? Fuck me?"

*How could she know that?*

I don't answer her, unwilling to admit I stalked her the entire night to floor thirteen. I slipped inside after they did, and I crept around in the shadows while Cosmo made her another drink.

"Were you jealous? Did you want to hurt him?"

*I wanted to do more than that. Decapitate him and fuck her next to his headless body.* But I wanted to see her so badly, listen to the noises she made, I couldn't stop it. Them.

"I wanted it to be you, Sullen."

I shake my head once. *You are full of shit.* "I don't know why you're telling me this." My heart is pumping so hard in my chest it feels like it might crack my ribcage, and that is not a good feeling.

I would know.

"You think this is torture, don't you? For me?" She glances

down, presumably at my hand cupped around her thigh. Then she looks up at me through her long lashes; I have each one memorized in my mind. "I've wanted this for a long time."

"You are a fucking liar." The words are a brittle snarl. I want her to stop. *Don't give me this jagged hope. It hurts.*

"I'm not."

*"You are."* I grip her tighter.

"Bruise me," she whispers. "Do it. Go on. I want it all."

"Stop, Karia."

"Hurt me. Break my bones if you want. Peel my skin. Pull my hair. Push me so hard I throw up. I want you to, Sullen Rule. I always have."

"You are full of shit." I release her, my fingers trembling as I hold them up, like I could stop myself from doing all those things she said. "You want soft and sweet and spoiled. You don't know pain. You are fucking with my head."

"Tell me what *you've* wanted," she presses, her voice frantic and wild, *she* is the monster now. "Tell me how you've imagined me at your mercy. I can take it. *Tell me, Sullen.*"

My nostrils flare and I keep my hands up, away from her. "I have always daydreamed about kidnapping you and taking you apart since we were teenagers. Touching your hair and smearing the lipstick on your mouth. Forcing you to call out my name as I bite deep enough to scrape bone. Breaking your legs, so you couldn't run away. Keeping you under my bed so you couldn't leave me alone."

"Keep going," she challenges. "I'm not scared of you."

"Because you are spoiled and pampered, and you don't know true danger. There are many rumors about me, but there are some about you, too. Stein told me you informed your parents you would go to college to become a teacher. You said you wanted to build minds instead of break them. You are naive and hopeful and you are stupid for it, in this life."

Her eyes flash a deeper blue and she surges against the

127

straps around her arms, the clanking loud in the dark, but she gets nowhere, and I imagine the band over her throat digging into her skin. "It's because of those things that I helped *you* hide from bigger monsters than yourself. I could've given you to them, let Cosmo hurt you, but I didn't because of my *stupidity.*"

I like the way her voice breaks with her rage, her eyes narrowed into blue diamonds in the gloom. I like how she doesn't mention what I did to the guard, as if she wants to forget what I truly am. "Yes," I agree. "And perhaps that is the stupidest thing you have done, saving me."

"Do all the girls you tie up enjoy hearing you degrade them? I don't think it's a kink of mine."

I widen my eyes, my limbs rigid as I stare at her, palms still up.

"Is this the kind of thing that gets you off? How many women have you been with? What's the worst thing you ever said to them?" Then she violently lets her knees fall to the side, straps clanking. I can imagine the lines and muscles of her thighs pulled taut, but I know what she's done because the *scent* of her is thick and divine in the air.

I am trembling everywhere.

"Go on. Finger me and tell me again how stupid I am. I would hate to be a bad captive for you, Sullen."

"Every word you say makes you stupider and stupider." But I can't help it. I reach for her then and glide my palm over her thigh, other hand curled into a fist on my lap. Despite her angry tone and rushed words, her legs quake a little with my movement. I cover the spot between her thighs with my hand. It is so warm here. "What color are these?" I breathe out, feeling the scrap of her underwear.

*"Pink."* It sounds as if there is a sneer on her pretty face with the word.

I flick at the edge of what I think is silk with my gloved

thumb, then I feel short hairs there, the texture of them anyway.

My pulse pounds harder. Vicious. I have stolen moments of watching porn before, and I always preferred this to something more bare. Perhaps because Stein forced me to wax myself, growing up. The purer his experiment, he said, the closer to God. It didn't make sense to me; purity was something untouched. But it didn't stop him from giving me a cursory inspection after he locked me in my bathroom every week.

He gave that up after he sent me away. I guess when he realized my death was approaching, waxing my groin was simply unnecessary in his eyes.

I cup her tighter and listen to her shaky intake of breath as I meet her gaze once more.

She is glaring at me. I wish I could see her exposed breasts. The way she is entirely bared to me. "How am I getting stupider?" she gasps out. "Or is this what you always say to your projects when you get to this part? Push your finger inside me, feel how being brainless makes me wet for you."

It's hard to breathe, when she says that, but I manage to choke out, "I've never touched anyone before." I hinted at it, when she was sedated, but she must not have believed me. Maybe she doesn't remember.

And before she can respond, I press the heel of my gloved hand over the center of her, heat seeping toward my palm. I am unsure what to do, everything feels so soft here and I am scared to rip her apart, but she squirms a little in the chair, causing the buckles to clatter, and I take it as a good sign.

"You're lying," she whispers, some of the bite absent in her tone.

"I'm not. The only woman I ever had dance inside my head was *you.*" I feel sick admitting it, like the floor has tilted.

"Touch me more," she whispers. "Push into me." She arches her hips a little, grinding against my hand and breathing hard.

There is a surge of warmth, of slickness I can detect through my glove, the way my palm slides. "Come on, Sullen. Don't be a fucking coward."

I snatch my hand away.

I close my eyes.

I feel shaky all over as I press my fingers over my mouth, breathing in the scent of her, tasting it on my lips. Animalistic *want* wells up inside of me, straight through my chest, twisting in my gut, causing me to grow harder, so stiff it hurts. I am sweating everywhere.

But I don't know what happens next. I don't know how to touch anyone.

*What am I doing here? Why am I letting her hate me more?*

"Why did you never speak to me? Flirt with me? You said he hurt you for it, but I could've helped you. I tried to include you and you just... You never did anything with me. And why did you stop, just now? Is this not...am I not what you want any longer? What are we doing down here, Sullen? Why are we not running? What do you want from me?"

"Stop talking, Karia," I whisper, pleading as my thoughts tumble inside my head.

"No," she snarls back. "Tell me what you want. Tell me why you have this place. What is it? A tomb for me? For you? How long have you planned this? You said I could keep asking questions—"

I snap my head up and stand once more.

Turning my back to her, I lift up the stool and throw it as hard as I can across the room. It hits the wall with a violent crash, the same way my heart is thrashing in my ribcage. Then it collides with the floor, metal screeching along cement.

The silence that follows is jarring.

But she doesn't let me stand in it for long.

"Touch me," she says, a command. "I am still unafraid.

Touch me right now and answer my questions. Touch me and *let me touch you.*"

I spin toward her, then take two steps until I am crouched over her again.

I don't touch her with my hands.

I brace myself on the edge of the chair arms, then I dip my head and bite her breast, digging what I have left of my teeth into her skin.

*Half-mad.* That's what her shirt says, I remember. That's what she's made me, after all these years of being inside my brain.

I dig deeper with my teeth, hearing her gasp, and I don't stop, her skin giving way beneath my sharp canines. The hint of iron floods my mouth; it is a precursor to the blood loss she could take.

I suck her nipple, flick my tongue along it, then pull back to look up at her as she squirms, the buckles clanking.

I scraped the needle against her before, testing her sensitivity, and it was so gorgeous, watching her squirm with fear.

I don't have a needle now, but I don't need one. I can take more flesh with my teeth, as it is.

I reach for her, smoothing my hand over where I bit her, and she lets out a soft whimper, her eyes darting to mine. But she doesn't tell me to stop. *What is wrong with you, Karia? That you pretend for someone like me?*

I palm her then, grateful for the entire handful of her as I squeeze and shove her breast up, testing the elasticity, playing with her now. Before tonight, I had never touched a naked woman and I enjoy the way her skin feels so pliable here, but not quite yielding completely.

I could do this all night.

I just fucking might.

"I only told you a fraction of what he did to me, over you." I keep toying with her as she watches me, helpless to stop me.

"Stein was inventive with his experiments, and crueler with his punishment. So many stitches of things he burrowed beneath my skin. But once when he saw me watching you from my window, he quietly came up behind me and cracked my nose against the glass pane. I had Betta fish then, and afterward, blood running down my chin, he plucked up one of the mini aquariums, the size of a cup, and forced me to open my mouth. But it wasn't enough for me to swallow it down." I grin, feeling her pulse fly beneath my palm. "He would force me to chew it, lumps of scales and the soft fin squishing between my teeth." I release her only to grab her other nipple, yanking on it and dropping my gaze to strain my eyes and watch her skin flex, elastic and smooth as I twist the pink bud between my fingers. It is only outlines I can see, but her bare body is burned into my brain now.

She lurches forward to ease the sting and I push my tongue through the spot where my central incisor should be, breathing a small laugh.

"Does it hurt, Little Sun?" I ask her quietly, still gripping her tightly. "Do you want me to stop?"

"No," she says through gritted teeth.

I flick my gaze up to her. "My teeth disappeared for you, too. Watching Von carry you on his back down the street one night, Stein took one of my molars with a plier. He made me stare out onto Ritual Drive and you smiled as blood gushed in my mouth. The tooth broke into pieces, and he had to fish them out, jabbing at my gums along the way. The others were for different infractions, but never over another girl."

I see the shadow of her chin is angled down as she tries to watch me hurt her, mutilate and play with her nipple, her big blue eyes blurring with tears, and I imagine a few slipping free, clinging to her dark lashes. "I like your smile," she says softly, then she peers up at me with some kind of twisted wonder, the way the whites of her eyes shine. "And this... It doesn't hurt me. I can take worse, Sullen."

*There is no way she is real.*

*It is impossible.*

*Maybe this is some sort of trick. A more elaborate game than the kind Stein used to play. Perhaps* she *is my captor.* This *is the way my body becomes ready for Stein's ascent into godhood.*

And just as I think it, just as I realize with a slimy cold it must be true, the door to my hidden room thuds open, slamming against the opposite wall.

I release her, spinning at once to shield her with my own body. She is helpless strapped to this chair and I made her that way. *She is my responsibility.*

I see only shadows beyond the door, but I hear more footfalls follow.

Then a voice I loathe says, "Job well done, Karia Ven."

# Chapter 21

## *Sullen*

S tein's voice is unmistakable. It is quite different from my own: Eloquent, composed, audible. The sound strikes a fire in my nervous system, always. I have lived on high alert my entire life, but for one single, lost moment here with Karia, I was my own version of calm. Even when I grew angry with her. Even when I threw the stool. Those emotions were different from what I feel now as the man who helped create me steps into my sanctuary and my nerves fray again.

There is the sound of footsteps around Stein as my stomach drops and I hold out my hands to my sides to shield Karia. I know what he said to her. *Job well done.* But I don't know what he meant, and I think, even if I did, even if she stabbed me so completely in the back, I would still defend her from *him*.

He is an abyss. A darkness you cannot see out of.

And as if to contrast his true nature, a tunnel of light flickers on in the dim room and I squint, staggering back one step and holding up a hand to shield my eyes.

A guard is carrying a flashlight. I know because Constance, Stein's most loyal, steps to the side so he can pool the light on both myself, and his oh-so-beloved employer. I see Arthur and

Rex too, flanking Stein with guns in hand but the barrels are aimed at the floor. Of course Stein cannot kill me yet and I am sure a bullet is not how his subject is meant to go out, for his ascension.

Karia is silent behind me. I desperately wish I could hear her thoughts and I have never wanted such a thing from anyone else before. *Do you hate me? Did you betray me? Please don't do that to me.*

Rex, tall and lanky, in his mid-fifties, stares at her with wide eyes and I want to pluck them from his head. In the glow of the flashlight, I can't see his irises, but I know they are a dull green. He has been inches from my face when Stein ordered him to hold my head while he picked and poked at the dermal piercings along my spine. Another time before, I received those on a Halloween night; Karia has no idea what I endured but I saw her only hours afterward. She was the highlight of my day then. She has always been the only sun for me.

*Please don't rip what is left of my heart out.*

Back then, when Stein thought to tug on the piercings he had given to me years earlier, it was Constance who held down the rest of me while Arthur—shorter, broader, blond—manned the front gate to Haunt Muren, on the off chance anyone might hear my screams and come investigate.

No one ever did.

"I see you have found and entertained my wayward son." Stein sighs, then pushes his hands into the pockets of his tailored black pants. His vivid blue eyes look up at me from beneath heavy black brows, hair of the same color falling artfully over his temple. While he has disgraced and defaced me, he routinely lavishes himself with lengthy grooming appointments in which I am guaranteed an hour or two of solace inside my ugly prison.

He tilts his head as he watches me, slight amusement lifting the edges of his mouth. He is in a white dress shirt, black blazer, dark brogues. Always impeccable in his wardrobe, leaving me to wear the same thing day in and day out in order to keep hidden what he's done to nearly every inch of my body.

"Well before night fell in B.C., I received word that you left our home, Sully." He speaks slowly and carefully but with a lightness I know could fool someone good like Karia. She never spent much time around him. It was the only thing about him I didn't despise. Since he had me to abuse, he didn't go after her or the others. "I thought leaving Constance with you would be enough to keep you safe, but I'm told you have dug a tunnel far enough out, even the cameras and alarms didn't catch you?" He glances toward the bright glow of white light, seeking Constance Virgil behind it.

Constance looks similar to Stein. Dark hair, light eyes, fair white skin, lean. Their hands were just as cruel as one another too. I don't know what Stein did to stitch together loyalty from the three men around him now, but I imagine overtime they simply became frightened of him, too, then morphed themselves into his monstrous shape to keep themselves safe. They have been in my life as long as I can recall.

"Is this true, Sully?" Stein's gaze flicks neatly back to mine, the glow of light refracting off his right eye, casting the hollows of his face in deep shadow.

*Yes. When I wasn't half-dazed from your poison, I spent the last two years trying to dig my way back to* her.

It was the letters. They gave me a strangled hope I should never have entertained. But the tunnel—leading off an underground doomsday shelter Stein created himself but never visited in the many acres around the back of Haunt Muren—led just far enough out that I could slip free from it and run to the heart of the nearest town after his flight to Vancouver with Arthur and Rex, leaving me only Constance to evade.

But I don't answer him. There is no point.

I see his eyes flash with my silence, but he continues on so smoothly, putting on a show for Karia. If he and I were alone, I would pay for my quiet.

"When I touched down at the airport here, Mads told me he found you. Or rather, a glimpse of you on the hotel cameras. Of course, I knew where you would go, and the guard you strangled left a breadcrumb." He smiles coldly. "Did it feel good, having the upper hand for once?"

My breath catches. It is as close as he will come to admitting what he has done to me. My heart thunders hard in my chest as I think of his question. It *did* feel good, but not the violence for violence's sake. For... protecting Karia. Hurting someone for her. But I press my lips together. I would never tell him that. It would give him too much incentive to torture her, and even the thought of it makes me feel sick. Right now, it is my worst fear.

He lifts his gaze to the exposed ceiling with my silence and sighs. "All those times you took lumpy, oversized backpacks here, making horrible clanking sounds, you didn't think I knew what you were doing?"

My stomach twists into knots. *No. I didn't.* My lab at the house, it was in my mother's wing. I never knew he discovered it let alone had any idea what I was up to *here,* recreating my safe place. Why didn't he ever ruin it? It doesn't make sense to me; *this* is more shocking than the possibility Karia has betrayed me. I know whatever his reasons, they were not born of compassion.

"And I used to use *this* chair for suspected hostiles, torturing them in the name of Writhe." He smiles coldly, then glances past me to Karia, and I stiffen, slowly lowering my hands by my side again. "I'm so sorry he tried to do the same to you, Karia."

My breath feels tangled in my lungs, like I can't exhale properly. I don't know why, what I'm waiting for from her. Logically, it's best if she says nothing. But her absolute silence is so unnerving, I want to turn to check on her. I'm afraid perhaps

Stein will order one of his men to shoot her in the head, force me to watch only the second woman I've ever loved die right in front of me.

He looks at me again and there is an expression of sadism on his face. Lifted brows, raised cheekbones from a twisted smile, his hands still in his pockets. I've seen this look many times. It usually meant something awful was going to happen to me.

I find my body grows rigid as I brace for the blow.

But when it comes, it's not from him.

"He forced me down here. Pinned me against this chair and... and..." Karia sobs, a loud, anguished sound in the quiet room that is the soundtrack to something cracking inside my ribcage. "Strapped me down and touched me and he... he *bit* me."

I don't understand how it is that my thoughts do not immediately shatter. Instead, as my heart breaks, I remember her shirt is shoved up, she is exposed, and there are four very dangerous men facing her. And maybe I should want her to be hurt for the words she just spoke, the trap she has so carefully laid, but it doesn't stop me from reaching back, finding on touch alone the fabric of her top. I fumble with tugging it down, my fingers shaky, and she sucks in a loud, audible breath, like she is terrified of me.

*"Please,"* she rasps, and I yank on the fabric and try not to give into the desire to snap her neck. "Please, Mr. Rule." The buckles of her straps rattle as I retract my hand without looking at her, and she tries to break free. "Can you please get me out of here? I can't... I don't want him to... You saw what he was trying to do. *Please.*" Another low, guttural sob. Real tears cause her voice to tremble. She must try to lunge from the chair because the straps clank again. "Get me out of here!" Her words sound hysterical. Nothing like before. *"Let me go!"*

Her mask has slipped. She is no longer trying to survive me, so she is screaming for help and revealing just how much she loathes me.

*Touch me,* she said. *Touch me so I can manipulate you into letting me go.* That's what she left out.

Her gasps are loud, wrenching through the room, and my pulse thuds faster still. Nausea swirls in my gut and I can't move. Can't face her and scream at her and ask her how she could've almost made me believe in something like a friend.

All I can do is stare at Stein and watch as twisted, smug satisfaction curls into that smile I have come to fear.

"Constance," he says, looking right at me as Karia continues to make obnoxious, pathetic whimpering sounds, so different from when I touched her. "Can you please release Ms. Ven from her binds?"

*"Don't touch her."* I couldn't stop myself from saying it even if I tried. As it is, it doesn't matter that she betrayed me. Something far worse might happen. Stein could force me to watch them assault her; it's a punishment he would create, and quickly. And I... I *can't.*

I curl my fingers into fists, leather gloves clinging to my bones as I make myself bow my head and look up at him through my lashes, as if in submission. Karia is a brat because she doesn't know real horror, but I force myself to be docile because sometimes, it helps soften the blows.

"Please," I beg Stein as Constance steps toward Karia at my back, the flashlight's glow bouncing and jarring across the small room. "Please don't hurt her. You can... Anything you want with me, you know it's yours. But please don't hurt her."

Stein tilts his head and I hear buckles clank as Constance sets to work freeing her, presumably one handed. There is a wild, stupid part of me holding onto hope that her cries were an act. That for some ungodly reason she would still choose me over safety. Me over acceptance. Me, over anything. But I know it's a reverie, and it's proven to me when I hear the creak of the chair, then her soft footfalls following the path of the light Constance shines at my back.

Then she's there. Standing beside Stein, tugging down her shirt more, adjusting her skirt, and avoiding my gaze. Her hair is scattered around her shoulders, over her chest, and when she's finished straightening her clothes, she frantically loops her strands behind the small curve of her ears, her fingers trembling.

All the while, she doesn't look at me. She drops her gaze to the cement floor, Constance stays at my back, and Stein says to me, with one amused glance at her as her knees shake and she clenches her fists, "She will be led back upstairs to her parents. I came down with our guards as soon as we arrived, but I know they are still searching *desperately* for her."

She nods once, like she was listening. I can't stop staring at her. Pleading with her, inside my mind. *Please look at me. Tell me this was real. Tell me there was just one moment you didn't hate me. Karia. Don't leave me here like this.*

Desperation drenches my brain, trying to claw and scramble my cells to reach her.

But she says, staring at the floor, "Thank you, Mr. Rule."

A hoarse, broken, and pathetic cry leaves my lips despite the fact I try to bite it back.

And still... she doesn't so much as glance my way.

Stein's smile grows with my shameful noise. "I'm so sorry for this, Karia," he says, but he's looking at me.

She seems so small and vulnerable and *good* standing next to him, only coming to his shoulders, so much of her smooth skin exposed where he is wearing a suit. I want to cover her in me, even now. I want to protect her, despite her knife in my back. *I want you, Karia. Don't leave me like this.*

*I knew you would. Everyone good goes, don't they?*

"I will handle my son and I assure you this will not happen again. All these years so many of you thought him lost, I was only trying to protect him from the world, and everyone else from him."

Karia says nothing, her entire frame vibrating with what looks like terror. She loops one arm across her body and grabs her opposite elbow, her shoulders hunching in. So different from the girl who swung a flashlight at her friend's head. I do not know this version of her at all.

It is as if she slithers into any skin she wants to wear. Pretends for anyone around her. Perhaps she helped lead me here somehow for this shattering, treacherous moment, but maybe she only wanted to go with me to add another experience to her gilded little life.

A few hours with a monster. An exotic sort of treat.

Hatred begins to take the place of despair inside my heart.

"Constance, can you please escort Karia to her anguished parents and hand me the flashlight?" Stein glances at Karia, who doesn't look back at him. "You can step out into the hall, dear, you do not wish to see how very aggressive Sully can get. I hope he did not hurt that guard in front of you. And he must have tempered himself with you, considering you appear...whole."

As Constance begins to walk somewhere at my back to do Stein's bidding, Stein removes his hands from his pockets and pops open one lapel of his blazer, extracting something from an unseen breast pocket of his shirt. When he withdraws his hand as Constance moves beside me, focused on Karia, I see a familiar syringe.

The same I used on my backstabbing little princess.

Clear liquid in the barrel, Stein's thumb poised over the plunger. He found my supply from the drawer.

*No.*

*No, no, no.*

If he puts me under, I will never see her again. He will take me back to Haunt Muren today and I will die there. I will never know what she really thinks of me. I will never be able to ensure he doesn't come for her, too.

*Karia.*

*Help me.*

I know I can't ask it of her. I am stupid and selfish and pathetic, but as Constance steps around Karia, reaching for the door with his free hand, I don't think I can stand here and let her walk away.

*Don't do this to me.*

*Please. Don't take the sun with you.*

Stein steps toward me, syringe in hand, but then he stops.

Karia is still staring at the floor.

She hasn't yet moved.

Constance has the flashlight, aimed at the cement, everyone's face thrown in deep shadow.

My pulse ticks inside my head.

Karia lifts her chin, so slowly.

She doesn't look at me.

She is wholly focused on that exit door.

*Escape.*

*Leaving me.*

"*Do you want me to hate you?*" she asked me. I think the same thing now, but I realize as she takes a small step toward Constance without once glancing my way, she doesn't care if I do.

This was all a game to her.

*This was nothing.*

Stein turns then, extending his free hand for the flashlight. It is inches from Karia, his wrist, and my skin crawls with how close they are, because I know what he is capable of. If he hurt her, I would fracture.

"Sorry," Stein says as Constance keeps the door propped open with his shoulder and lifts his hand to give up the flashlight. "But it's only a little ways in the dark. You'll be okay, won't you, Karia?" Then he shifts his hand, running his thumb over her cheekbone, not yet taking the flashlight.

I see her back stiffen.

I take an involuntary step forward.

*Don't fucking touch her.*

*Do not.*

He strokes the curve of her face.

Her entire form is unyielding, as if she is made of stone.

"Yes," she answers him, her voice broken and slurred with her earlier tears that have quieted now.

My pulse is ricocheting throughout my body. I lean forward, hands clenched, vivid imagery of me twisting and breaking every bone in Stein's hand playing inside of my head.

"Good girl," he says to her, a smile curving his lips, and I cannot breathe. "I will meet with your parents after I am done with my son."

He stops touching her.

He reaches for the flashlight once more.

And the moment before his hand grasps it, the exact second that I see Constance loosen his fist around it, *Karia moves.*

She snatches it from the air between the two of them and flicks it off, plunging us all into darkness.

"*Sullen.*" She gasps my name, then I hear her steps.

She is running. Her soft footfalls echo over the cement. The same sound she made when she ran *from* me.

But now...*she is running* to me.

A shriek leaves her mouth, though, a loud, heart wrenching sound.

"Do *not* shoot," Stein says, his voice angry and garbled, and I know it is because of his ascension and her parents that he does not want a stray bullet flying into our bodies in this room.

But I think he has her, from that sound she made.

And he has the sedative.

*He has the fucking sedative.*

I am already there. I don't even remember moving, but I am there in the dark, and someone is wrenching at my arms from behind, but I am grabbing Stein's wrist, the first time in my life I have touched him in this way, shadows of bodies curled around us all.

He must have her in his grip because she makes a jagged, whimpering sound, and I can smell her, feel her shoulder against mine as I press down on his bones.

"You do not want to do this, Sully," he snarls as he raises his arm, trying to get the needle away from me, and someone is forcefully jerking me backward but I plant my feet and I do not let myself be moved. "*She* will pay for it, if you do."

There is a loud thud, then she gasps, as if she has been hit, and I know while a guard is on me, there were two more.

Anger is like fire in my veins as her body crashes into mine.

I reach for her, one arm wrapped around her torso as I bite down around Stein's wrist with my fingertips, as hard as I can, strong arms still attempting to force me away from both him and my princess.

Until they stop.

Until I feel Karia's body jolt, and she cries out, stiff in my hold.

I think they are jerking at her hair, and Stein is refusing to let go, but then Karia twists herself, pivoting in my grip, and I hear the impact of a flashlight cracking against Stein's skull.

I know the sound now, since this is the second time I've heard it.

A smile twists my lips as I slide my hand up Stein's wrist, and his fingers splay, dropping the syringe.

I close my hand around it, wanting to drive it into him, but before I can, Karia hits him again.

He staggers back.

There is the thud of something far away, like she threw or dropped the flashlight.

Someone moves in close, where Stein was.

They snatch the syringe from my hand even as I close my fingers around it.

"Fucking bitch," I hear Rex snarl.

A shadow of something swooping down towards her catches my sight in the dark.

I close both arms around her, yanking her away from Rex and whoever was attacking her from behind as there are footsteps from the hall, then the glow of light, and I think Constance must have retreated to get another flashlight.

We don't have time.

*We don't have time.*

Karia is breathing loud, like she is in pain, a whimper leaving her lips, then the cluttering sound of something—perhaps the needle—dropping to the ground. I glide my hand up her back, to her skull, then squeeze tightly around the bones of Arthur's wrist, his fingers jerking her hair back.

He lets out a groan as I stab his pressure point with my thumb, and I snatch her away, but the light and footfalls are nearer.

We have to run.

*"We have to run."* I say it out loud, her body pressed so close to mine.

And she just says one word. *"Go."*

The light is closer, flickering haphazardly down the hallway, but as I slide my hand down her arm and her fingers link with mine, we're moving and still hidden under the cover of darkness. A body looms in front of me—I can sense one of Stein's guards—but I shove him away with my elbow and Karia and I keep going, sprinting fast.

I know where the closet is. I am good with the dark.

And just as I hear Constance say, "Where are they?" and light gushes into the room, but not aimed our way, I pull Karia into the slip of space in the wall, the scent of bleach and must filling my nose.

We don't stop.

The space is narrow, and the walls seem to press in around us, but Karia doesn't stumble and she doesn't let go of me.

"Go. After *them.*" Stein snarls the words, and there are heavy footfalls and more light as I reach the sliver of space that leads to an underground network of tunnels I believe were created well before Stein inherited this property. It means he might not know of them, or where they lead. Then again, he knew all about my second lab—and my first—but that would involve merely following me once or twice, hidden in shadow.

Understanding the tunnels would mean more, and I can't imagine he ever took time to traverse so deep into the dark. Although he is drenched in it, he pretends to be a patron of the fucking light.

I have to angle my body to squeeze into the gap of an entrance. Karia continues after me and we slip free of the closet, into a wider, impossibly *darker* space. The ceiling is low, though, and I am crouched over as she grips my hand beside me.

And we don't look at each other, and we don't stop.

*I am so glad you are here with me.*

I don't say that, though, my lungs compressing as we run, my body stiff from all the various wounds it has housed over the years. Sprinting is not ideal for me, but I keep going, and I say something else. Something that matters as we hear voices behind us, Stein and his men—the four people who have made my life a living hell—trying to figure out the closet exit.

"There will be a fork up ahead. Go left."

"Where?" Karia gasps out, her voice thready and far-off sounding. "Where does it lead?" She doesn't stop running, though. She doesn't let go, either.

"Past the front gates. We can... I don't know," I admit,

shaking my head in the dark, my spine stiff and thighs aching. Once, Stein sliced the muscle there on both legs so deeply he had to hire a nurse to look after the wounds lest they get infected, or my muscle slip from my skin. My only solace is he didn't bring our family doctor in for that. I think even he knew what the doctor would do to me then. "But they won't know the way."

"Sullen," she whispers, her hand squeezing mine tightly.

I swallow the dry lump in my throat. I don't know if she feigned her crying when Stein entered the room or if she decided at the last minute to choose me, and I can't bear for her to tell me if it was the latter. Not right now.

But she keeps talking, and my stomach drops all the same with her words: "One of them... They...they got the syringe. In my...chest."

*Fuck.*

She is lagging now.

Her steps slow.

"I'm so sorry," she whispers, her voice weak. "I'm so sorry. You can go. Please do. Leave me here. They won't hurt me. Don't stay for me. Please go."

I don't stop moving.

I don't listen to her.

In a fluid motion, I release her hand, crouch down, and pick her up. Her body is warm and weightless in my arms.

She tries to push me away, hand on my chest, but I barely feel it with the sedative meant for me coursing through her system.

I keep running.

My hand comes to her head, pressing her skull down softly, her cheek on my shoulder, her legs wrapped around my body. I hear steps, voices.

I run faster, holding her tightly.

She whispers my name against my ear. *"Sullen."*

It's the motivation I need to keep going.

And when I hear the sound of a bullet explode from a barrel, I don't stop. I just run faster.

It doesn't hit me.

Nor her.

Another bullet.

My heart races.

She trembles in my arms. "I can't stay awake," she says, her breath soft on my skin. "I'm sorry I can't stay away."

I don't know if she meant to say that, or if she's simply drifting too quickly to speak what it is she truly means.

"I never would have left you down there, just so you know. I never would have left...you."

Another gunshot. The sound rips through my eardrums as it echoes in the tunnel.

But the fork is here.

I turn left.

We are protected by walls now, and clearly, they couldn't see us, the beam of the light wasn't strong enough to reach between the distance we gained.

I pray they go right.

I pray I never see them again.

I pray I get to hold her for so much longer than this night, even though I know that is the prayer I will never be granted.

# Chapter 22

## *Sullen*

My back feels heavy; the ache is along my low spine. I don't know the root cause of that particular pain. It's not as if Stein often gave me medical checkups for problems he directly or indirectly caused and the doctor we did have only made me... worse. But it feels as if I need to bend low, hands to the floor to relieve some of the stabbing along my lumbar. I can't, though, because Karia is in my arms, motionless as I hold her to my chest. She's not aware enough to hold onto me, and so her arms dangle along my back.

My shoulders are stiff, and my thighs are too. Everywhere along my body, even in the cold of the tunnel, I am drenched in sweat beneath my clothing and my gloves.

But I have taken every small turn possible, trying to remember how to get to the drainage tunnel just beyond the gates of the hotel, all while leading a confusing, winding path so Stein nor his guards can catch us. There have been no more gunshots, no more footsteps or flashlight beams. Only dripping water from the low ceiling and the scurry of rats or worse.

I have gone this path only a few times; I didn't run during

any of them for reasons I am ashamed to admit. It's been over two years since I've been to this hotel and back then, I still held onto the hope I might get Karia to see me in some meaningful way.

If I ran, I knew I would never be able to find her again.

And I meant what I told her. The few times I eventually gathered the courage to try and leave this life behind, the pain I suffered afterward was...immense.

I dart down another sharp left, then a right, the paths beneath this place a bizarre maze I had no hand in constructing. I could have entered Hotel No. 7 from this haunted space, but I worried the leaking water and rat feces might make me unpresentable to her.

As I grip her tighter in my arms, I slow a little in the darkness. My eyes seem to have adjusted so slightly, the way I can make out the clotted shadows of the various doorways, and when I angle my head to face her, I see the blonde of her strands in the gloom.

Her hair is spilling down over my arm, my back, sliding across my chest. Her face is turned toward me, her legs relaxed around my waist.

I have one arm across her back, my other hand cradling her head.

Slowly, in the silence, I dip my chin and let my lips linger on her nose.

I can feel her breaths along my skin, and my own racing pulse beneath it.

Warmth rushes through me that has nothing to do with the journey and my fatigued muscles. With a slow, unsteady hand, I glide my palm along her back, feeling the bones of her spine when I get past the hem of her shirt.

I shouldn't go lower.

She saved me.

Maybe this is wrong.

But in the chair, she begged me. Taunted me. And I just need to rest.

I stumble back with her in my arms, spine pressed to the damp wall. The moisture seeps through my hoodie and makes my skin crawl. I don't want to think about what happens after this. If we find a sanctuary to hide in, I have to change clothes or I'll be repulsive to her, more than I already am. Will there be a place to get something else? I can't remember the last time I walked into a store. And how do we stay hidden? I don't know how to drive; I took a train here. She does, I know, but where do we find a vehicle? I have the money I stored in the makeshift safe that was stolen from Haunt Muren in the pockets of my jeans, but not enough for a thing like a running car. And when she comes to, will she remember everything? Midazolam is for sedation, but it also muddles memory. What if she thinks I did this to her? Dragged her to this crypt for no reason? In that way I doubted her, she will do the same to me. We cannot afford to trust one another.

*So why bother preserving something that isn't there?* That is the poisoned whisper inside my brain.

I glide my hand lower, feeling my body vibrate each time my heart beats. Over the edge of her skirt, then under the slight curve of her ass. Until...my fingertips press against her bare thigh.

Her skin is frigid, soft and firm all at once. I am digging into her muscle, the way I hold her, and I could inch further center, to the warmth I felt when she was splayed out for me in the chair.

I tilt my head back, hood protecting my hair from the wall.

Every part of me wants to take more of her when she's like this. She can't stop me, or shudder from disgust, or cry at how filthy I am.

I shift my fingers slightly, inching closer to parts of her I haven't touched yet. With my other gloved hand, I massage her scalp, as if it is a consolation. I turn my head and nudge my nose to her own.

"Shh," I whisper, although she is not stirring. The sedative effect could last anywhere from an hour to six, depending on the dose Stein used. "I won't hurt you, Karia." I said that to her before, and I meant it. I even mean it now. I know hurt, and this is not it. "I promise I'll always keep you so safe, Little Sun."

I close my eyes in the tunnel. A sound like a hiss from a rat fills my ears, and I stiffen with her in my arms, my nose still pressed along her own.

I don't inch closer to where I shouldn't be.

I pretend I am not so monstrous for a moment.

I don't even know if it's all that wrong, what I wanted to do, but maybe so.

Regardless, I only hold her tighter, suspended in this limbo of good and evil. But what are those? I do not know anymore the difference between angel and demon.

I catch my breath by inhaling her scent.

This is the calmest moment I have had in... so long. And on the run as we are, I know it is fantastical, but it's true.

Water drips from somewhere.

Another hiss from a rodent.

I don't let myself be the monster to her.

*I won't.* I will not.

Another sound which I think comes from a rat.

Then a different noise.

Then...there is the sensation of falling.

I am tipping backward with Karia in my arms.

I try to find purchase as I realize the wall has given way behind me and I am stumbling.

*No.* Not the wall.

*A door.* It slams open against the wall with my weight.

I pitch back into thick, oppressive darkness, like the tunnel was freedom and this is the opposite. But I don't let Karia go and instead, I find myself cradling her closer to my chest.

The door slams shut, a loud, thundering clap in the quiet, and I turn to glance over my shoulder, my eyes scanning the space, but I can see absolutely nothing. The air is damper here, colder, too, and the scent of mildew and rot is so much stronger, even *I* wrinkle up my nose.

I want to call out, but that's a human instinct that could get Karia and I both killed. I dip my head as I press my nose to her hair, one arm still under her thighs and my other hand cradled inside her strands. Her scent is soothing, so much better than *this,* and I cling to her just as much as she depends on me right now.

As I stand in silence, I start to think I should just walk forward, find the door, get back on my pathway out of this hell. I clearly triggered a hidden entryway I was ignorant to, but there's no reason for me to stay here. As it is, I think I hear an entire pack of rats scurrying in the sludge, tiny nails clicking on the cement.

A shudder runs down my spine and I take one single step toward where I came from, when a voice speaks from some-where behind me.

"Leave her."

My throat feels tight as I hug her even closer, her limp form slipping for a moment in my grasp, but I adjust, pulling her body into mine.

I don't turn around, even as it feels like spiders crawl along the back of my neck.

My lungs constrict, squeezing against one another with each breath, and I don't know if this is someone from Writhe, if Stein could possibly have guards down here, if *that's* how he knew of my lab, or—

"Let me have her, Sullen. Lighten your load. Where you are going, it's plenty dark as is." It's a man's voice, and my mind conjures the image of someone far older than Stein, and unused to conversing, much like...me.

I still do not turn around. There would be nothing to see, as it is.

But I swallow hard, then push my tongue through the gap in my top front teeth, the space where an incisor should be, as I try to think.

*What is happening? What is this? Who is this?*

I hear liquid drip from somewhere, creating more sludge on the wasteland of these tunnels.

And although I want to leave through that door, *now,* I know nothing is ever that easy. Walking away from my own misfortune has proven impossible all of my life.

"Give her to me." The man's voice again, but it sounds like a plea rather than a command.

"No," I say, the word jagged in the darkness. I add nothing else. It's all the man needs to know.

"I know you, Sullen Bram Rule."

My lungs contract at hearing my middle name. I have not heard anyone speak it aloud since my mother died. She is the only one who ever said it to me, and it was cloaked inside of affection with her voice.

"You have always wanted to leave this place behind. The lab, the chair, your eyes watching and hoping and pleading for this girl? She will wake and she will fear you. It is not for you to have anyone in this life."

I say nothing. Do nothing.

Water continues to drip. The rats travel closer.

My skin crawls, but I cannot even blink. I am unwillingly rooted.

The weight in my arms feels strangely heavy now.

Not only can I not see the man; I can't see anything. Not the darkness, not the tunnel, not Karia's blonde hair beneath my fingers.

Loath to do so, I think of my mom once more. Glimpses and snatches of memories with her are all I have left; everything else is warped by time, and Stein. It is as if every piece of me has spent the past sixteen years without her simply...surviving. I have had no room for anything else. Only to breathe, to eat when I could, grab onto sleep when I knew I would be safe.

My only wasted dreams were spent on Karia because she is alive and whole and...*in my fucking arms.*

"I'm leaving." It's all I say next. I don't know who is speaking to me and I don't care. I learned long ago not to waste time on details that don't matter. Only those which do. Karia Ven, trusting me with her unconscious body, she is what's important now.

She saved me.

I don't know when she decided to, but what matters is she did.

I take a step forward.

There is a sound, like slithering. A snake against the flooring.

My heart squeezes, blood thudding between my ears as I twist my head one way, then the other.

I know serpents.

They are the symbol of Writhe, and so any I contained within glass jars were mutilated. Writhe damned me, in its own way. Stein may have been born cruel, but Writhe gave him access to a barbaric expansion of his coldness.

I am not afraid of snakes, but I do so loathe them.

They come closer, like scales whispering against the stone.

My body grows rigid.

I clutch Karia impossibly *more.* She is warm against me, her limbs dangling from my hold, her hair beneath my lips as I kiss her, like this is it. The end I have been searching for. The bittersweet finality to a life of longing and grief. Her and I, together dead.

I close my eyes.

The rustling grows closer.

My body trembles.

*Is this a new hell Stein has created? A serpent who speaks? Does his bidding? Did God check any limits upon him at all?*

The noise stops.

There is a moment of quiet.

Then the same man from before speaks, so close to my ear. "You are not the only one Stein Rule has cursed, Sullen Bram. But you are unlike him, are you not?"

I don't speak.

I don't move.

It does not escape me he used Stein's name instead of his biological relation to me, like people so often do.

"I warned your mother when she met him in college. I tried to tell her there was something dark inside of him, if not in so many words. I knew what his father did, the title he was passed down, the one he would never bequeath you, and truly, it is a mercy. *Anyone within Writhe is cursed, Sullen. Do not forget it.*"

I inhale. I do not breathe out.

Then I feel it. The fabric of my hood being pulled away from my hair. Air rushes against my ears.

Everything is so cold and harsh, like nails against my exposed spine, but I do not move and I couldn't even say why.

He spoke of my mother.

No one ever speaks of Mercy Rule. She did not become a ghost when Stein killed her in front of me. She became nothing. Less than ash. I could not grieve or remember or miss her.

"I know why you wear this. I did try to stop it when you were much younger. I am sorry I could not have fought harder. This was my fate, but I have made my own friends here."

I think of the sound of the serpent. I wonder if I have been wrong to hate them.

A hand comes to my shoulder.

I flinch at the touch, but it is light, and it does not hurt.

"The girl will be afraid," the man continues, touching me in a way no one has since my mother's death. "But she has looked for you too, you know?"

I squeeze my eyes tighter shut. Something builds behind them. A pressure I had grown numb to.

"Take care of her. She is used to getting what she wants, and that is good for you, because *you* are it for her."

The man moves his hand.

"Come. I will show you a quicker, quieter way."

# Chapter 23

## *Karia*

The sound of rain wakes me. But something else, too. A swaying, shifting motion. Cold drops along my temple, seeping into my hair. There is a bite of nausea in my belly, threatening to rise to my throat. Nothing is stationary and even with heavy, closed eyes, I am dizzy.

"Sullen?" The name leaves my dry lips, but I don't know who it is or why I speak it.

There is a soft breath that could be acknowledgement or simply accidental.

My limbs feel as if they have fallen asleep, and when I attempt to wiggle my fingers—dangling by my side—sharp stars dart in my veins; that painful, sandy feeling of one's body coming back to life.

I feel my eyes fluttering behind my lids, two orbs roaming under skin, but it takes long moments before I can open them, lashes thick with the sticky sensation of sleep.

Darkness lined with a strange glow greets me.

I hear something that sounds like tires on asphalt.

A mechanical voice stating, "Walk. Walk. Walk," in a way that is familiar yet far away.

I can't grasp the meaning.

And as my body is jostled and my temple dampened with cold water, I blink once more and underneath the glow of red lights, I see brown eyes staring back at me.

"Don't scream," Sullen Rule's croaky voice says in a low tone. "We're at a crosswalk in the city. If you scream, they'll find us." He keeps walking, glancing up once from beneath long, velvet-black lashes before he looks at me again. The red light and the robotic voice fades away, and all I hear is him say, "And I'm not ready for them to take you from me yet."

Everything sways in gray darkness for me, and I close my eyes and simply enjoy this fantastical dream.

"THIS IS THE PARKING GARAGE FOR MEDICI MALL." I SAY IT OUT loud after he sets me down near the entrance doors of the shopping center, everything dark inside.

*I am not dreaming.*

It is wonderful and horrifying, all at once.

I try to get my bearings, taking in the expansive parking garage accessible only by a ramp, which Sullen walked up, carrying me because I couldn't yet feel my limbs while I slowly came awake. As it is, I am dizzy and nauseous and *off,* but at least I can stand.

I feel filthy, like there's a film coating my skin, and I know it isn't from the rain still dropping from the night sky beyond the edges of the parking lot.

I assume it's from the tunnel despite the fact I can barely remember it. All of those moments beforehand, too, are so strangled with thready gaps.

What I *do* know is there's pressure building on my bladder, and I desperately need to pee. I glance back at the glass double doors leading into a boutique store I don't like—their dresses are horrendous and fit horribly; the mall will be locked, though.

As it is, I've never seen Medici Mall's parking this empty. A few quiet cars are slotted into spaces under the cement awnings and levels above us, but for the most part, it's deserted.

"Why did you come here?" I spin to take in Sullen.

He is standing with his back to the stone wall of the building, chin tilted down.

*He carried me all this way. He didn't leave me in the tunnel.*

I had a dream that he did. A nightmare he was offered so much more to abandon me. A life like he'd never known, but... *he didn't betray me.*

His hands are in the pocket of his hoodie, hood pulled over his hair, dark eyes watching me warily, like he's worried I might bolt, and he'll have to lunge for me.

"I..." he starts, then turns his head from me and I trail my gaze over the defined line of his jaw, the stubble there, dark and... *hot.*

*And he saved me.*

*Us.*

*He saved us. Maybe he loves me or maybe I'm delusional.*

*Don't think that right now. Focus, Karia. You can marvel over the fact you're on the run with your childhood crush later.*

I try to gather the facts I know inside my head. Stein... I hit at him with a flashlight. But the soreness just below my collarbone... one of his men attacked me with the syringe.

"There were the most lights here," Sullen finally says, answering my question. "Everything else is closed. I was headed this way when you started to come to. I..." He clears his throat. "I didn't want you to wake up in the dark." He doesn't look at me at all.

Immediately, I think of the green glow around the wet specimens. I don't know anything about taxidermy really, but I don't think the lighting is necessary. Does he hate the dark? Does it scare him? What happened to him there? Did Stein torment him with it?

A rush of hot anger collides under my skin like a train derailed.

I wanted to kill Stein.

Unlike with Cosmo, I didn't hold back when I hit him. But I'm not a trained fighter like Von and Isadora. Mom was right. I hated self-defense. I did the bare minimum, the requirements for a child of Writhe. And I've never regretted that fact until now.

"Thank you," I say, trying to keep the anger and regret at bay. It won't help us now.

Sullen darts his eyes toward me, then looks away again. He says nothing else. And I know no matter how much I am in awe of this moment we cannot stay here forever. We are out in the open. Too exposed.

"The doors will open around dawn. I mean, you probably know that, I just—"

"I've never been inside."

I stop short in my rambling plan, narrowing my gaze on him. "What?" I don't understand. I know I'm barely *here,* hardly awake, but his words don't make sense to me. "Aside from this crappy store," I gesture to the one in front of us, "it's Alexandria's *best* mall. They even have Gucci here." My cheeks flame as I say it, taking in his hoodie and black jeans and those circles and sunken lines beneath his eyes as he fixes a glare on me, one high-top sneaker pressing into the wall behind him.

But when he speaks, I swear he's trying to hold back a smile. "Do they? Well I certainly wish I had known. I would've definitely made a trip here if only anyone had told me *Gucci* was sold within these very walls—"

"Shut up, I get it, sorry." I roll my eyes, then fold my arms across my chest and ignore the way my heart thunders against my wrist. But just as I'm about to move on to the part about us needing to hide, needing to get clothes, too, so we aren't in the same thing we fled in, we both hear the sounds of a car driving up the entrance ramp, just out of sight, hidden by a stone column far to the left.

He moves before I do, closing the space between us and grabbing my wrist. I sprint with him, and he darts behind a black Nissan reversed in against the outer wall of the mall, the very last spot of the first row of the lot, fenced in by cement.

We crouch down as one, his gloved hand still around my bones.

Our gazes turned down the row, we watch as headlights beam through the space.

Sullen was right; this likely is the only part of downtown Alexandria lit so brightly at night, with all these overhead panels. For his thought process, it was a perfect location. But for two people hiding, right now it potentially just became more dangerous. We could be trapped in here.

Neither of us speak and in this position, tucked into a squat and the scent of oil and gasoline and mud from the parking garage overwhelming me, that nausea I had grows brighter and more urgent in my low belly. Maybe from the sedative—I can still feel the sting of the injection—or perhaps just the fear.

Maybe, though, it's something deeper.

*I do not want this night to end.*

*I do not want to let him go quite yet.*

The car's tires roll slowly over the pavement, sticky with the night rain. Their light beams reflect on the cement partition beside us, and for a moment, the low purr of the engine the only sound aside from my pulse in my head, they idle several feet from us, directly in front of Medici Mall's entrance. I can't see the vehicle itself; only the ominous blue-white headlights.

I press my hand over my mouth, careful to balance in my

squat as I try to hold back the sick feeling swishing around in my stomach.

Sullen tightens his grip on me, his fingers wrapped just over my wrist. Despite the fact leather is between our skin, it is as if every nerve in my body lights up at his touch.

I think I would catch fire if he ever let *me* touch *him.*

Slowly, I turn to look at him, my hand still on my mouth.

His eyes meet mine as my pulse races. He looms over me even in our current positions; the hood shadows half of his face, and his free hand is toward the cement, three fingers touching the ground to keep him balanced.

He says nothing as we look at one another, and I have the wild, insane urge to burst into laughter.

We are crouching down behind a Maxima in a parking garage. Hiding from Writhe at God-knows-what hour of the morning. I have been sedated twice. I am barely upright. He tried to touch me in horrible ways and yet I knocked out my friend for this boy and I would do it again. I hit the former leader of my family's criminal organization. He carried me through the streets of Alexandria in the rain. And now he is kinda, sorta holding my hand as we risk our lives for these stolen moments together.

And he is so unbelievably *hot,* with sweat glistening along his cheekbones and those deep brown eyes intent on mine, broad shoulders tense as we wait.

This could be my own twisted fairytale. *Once upon a time* at Medici Mall with the prince of Writhe. Maybe I could even get him into Gucci and we would really be living the dream—

A door slams closed.

I dig my nails into my cheekbones as he narrows his eyes on me and shakes his head so slowly in a caution.

The pressure on my bladder increases and I squeeze my eyes shut at the same time I lean in toward him. I can't help it.

It's as if I know he will protect me and right now, that's what I want.

He releases my wrist and shifts his arm silently around me, pulling me into his chest. If I didn't hear footsteps over cement right now, I might gush over how easy our connection is in this horrifying moment.

But as I inhale his dark rose scent, my cheek pressed over his heart, I hear someone coming closer.

One slow step at a time.

Our bodies are behind the tire of the Maxima now that we're together, but as one, we're too wide to hide behind it completely. And if we move to the other side of the car, whoever is here will catch the sound.

I can do nothing but tremble in his arms with my eyes closed like a baby. And he holds me tighter, like he cares what happens to both of us.

The footsteps draw closer.

There is no urgency, and that scares me more.

*Dad? Mom?* If it's them, could I talk either one into keeping Sullen safe?

But I think of the formal dinner on Halloween we had to attend at the hotel, years ago. I remember Sullen in his uniform of a hoodie and black jeans. I remember wanting to disappear with him. And I remember the way my father ensured I didn't have the chance.

They will always choose Writhe. They wouldn't even pick *me* above it, let alone Sullen.

And if it's Von, or Isa... they are the same. Maybe more reasonable, more open minded, but they would turn him in, too.

And if it's Mads or... Stein... I...

Another car door opens, breaking apart my thoughts. Then a voice says, "They were spotted near Alexandria U. Get in."

The door shuts. The steps hurriedly retreat, the person gets in the car, then it peels off loudly, engine squealing.

Relief makes me feel off balance, slightly giddy, but I don't move.

Only when the car is down the ramp and out of hearing range do I lift my head and find Sullen's eyes are closed tight, too.

He doesn't open them, his long lashes draped over his cheekbones, skin dewy from sweat.

I marvel over how beautiful he is, how he doesn't understand it.

And for a long moment, I simply stare at him and wonder what it is he sees behind his eyelids.

We find the van is unlocked. It's a dark green color, three rows of seats, and two booster seats in the middle row, crumbs from long-ago snacks littering the floorboards.

It's on the second level; we had to go up the stairs to find a car we could easily slip into without shattering a window. I watched as Sullen winced with every step, despite the fact he tried to hide it with his face ducked behind his hood.

Now, we are in the back bench seats of the older model van, doors locked and no security alarms blaring our break-in.

I don't know who was looking for us—Sullen didn't offer insight into that either—or why they thought we were at Alexandria U, but no other cars have entered the parking garage since that one. I know there must be cameras here and Writhe certainly has the resources to tap into them, but for whatever reason, they have not yet found us.

I am pressed close to the tinted back window with my

hands fisted in my skirt as I stare out the glass, watching the exit to the stairwell and elevators; worried we will be found out before we have a chance to truly run.

"Do you know how to hotwire a car?" I ask quietly, my breath fogging up the glass for a moment before the condensation retreats. It is chilly in here, but my body is hot, the sick feeling winding and turning in my gut. I still need to pee but doing it in front of Sullen... I think I'll wait.

"I took a train to the hotel. I don't even know how to drive a car." His throaty voice is deadpan, but I am smiling all the same; sometimes it feels like every serious thing he says is a joke. But I remember him looming over me when I was strapped in the dental chair; his mouth on me, his hands, too. The way he told me the horrors of his life.

I do not know when he's joking or not. And maybe right now I should be afraid of him, but it's as if, since we ran for our lives together, there is a brittle truce between us.

I swallow past the tightness of my throat; the urge I have to hold him like he held me behind the Maxima. I refuse to think of why he can't drive. The ways he has been both an experiment and a prisoner in his own life.

"We will need to change. You in *that,* me in *this,* they'll be looking for these clothes. Maybe we should split up when the mall opens so we don't attract—"

"No."

My pulse flies and I smile broader, but keep my head turned away from him. There is a sliver of a middle seat between us, and I wish there wasn't but I don't move toward him.

In the glass, though, I catch the gleam of his dark eyes and I can't help it.

I turn to look at him.

He is staring at me in silence, his hands on his thighs, head bowed as he looks up at me through his lashes. I don't think he knows how very *endearing* that is.

"Writhe has resources. Stein will tear this city apart to find us. We can't make it easy for them." I say all my worries out loud.

He is still silent, his expression stoic as he watches me. But he doesn't seem annoyed or angry; perhaps he is simply exhausted, like I am. Partly why we found this temporary solace. Even if we *could* steal a car, I don't think we would have the energy to get very far. I don't remember when I last slept, aside from being sedated, and that seems to have added to my exhaustion, not stolen from it.

"We may have to steal," I continue. "I...don't have anything on me and—"

"I have money." Three scratchy words but it's enough.

I arch a brow. "Hope it's a lot. I have expensive tastes. But I'll pay you back, I swear."

He doesn't look amused and there's something haunted around his eyes. He always looks sad and guarded but now, when I search for the signs, I see he seems frightened, too. The way his mouth is pressed together, his jaw clenched, a furrow there between his dark brows.

He has more to lose when we are caught.

I will be scolded, perhaps Mads Bentzen will visit me or punish my parents, but I will be fine.

He, though...

"I'm sorry you had to carry me so far," I tell him, meaning it, the only thing I can think to say that isn't directly about Stein. The way he winced up the parking garage stairs, I know he is sore. I don't allow myself to think of why. "I'm sorry I couldn't dodge the needle. I should've fought more, I..." I glance down at my bare knees, little goosebumps along my skin. "I wish I could have killed Stein. I wanted to when I hit him. But it wasn't enough, was it?"

There is a stretch of silence and my cheeks heat. Maybe I am silly for thinking he cares for me at all; he *did* set up a nice little torture area for me. And I need to ask about his animals and his lab. Maybe I am only a specimen to him. But before I can turn away, hide my face, he speaks.

"No one has ever hurt someone for me." His words are halting but clear. "It was...nice."

I lift my eyes to his, squinting a little with amusement. I think of what he did to the guard, and I'm sure I wouldn't use that term for it, but I do know what he means. "Nice?" I can't help the laugh that slips free.

His expression doesn't change. "Yes." Then some sort of internal cloud seems to darken his eyes. "But..." He doesn't look away. "We can't run forever, Karia."

Immediately, I want to tell him I would. We could. But I know with Writhe searching for us, we will be found. I am not yet ready to accept defeat so easily, though. I will steal as much time as I can with him, even if he does think I am only something to dissect.

"We wait here until the mall opens. We buy new clothes. Then we find a place to hide, until we can't. Okay?"

He studies me for a moment, guarded, the way his brows pull tighter together, and his lips do the same. But slowly, carefully, he nods.

I start to turn away, ready to lean my head against the window and get some sleep, despite the fact it is a risk *and* I would much rather lean against *him,* when he speaks again.

"When?" he asks quietly. "When did you decide to... run with me?" He doesn't look at me as he asks it, sitting perfectly rigid in his seat, gloved hands on his thighs as he stares at the floorboard, littered with French fries and cannibalized chicken nuggets.

For this moment in time, he seems oddly wholesome here, in this domestic scene of some family's van.

I hope whoever owns it is sleeping soundly in a bed, their children down the hall or maybe piled in with them.

I hope they are not living a life like ours; that perhaps they needed gas or an oil change or someone to drop them off in the morning, but I pray they don't feel a fraction of the heartache Sullen Rule does.

"I never made a choice," I say quietly, wanting to shift over to sit closer, but scared he doesn't want the same thing.

He lifts his head then, eyes latching onto mine.

"There wasn't one to make. I was always going to follow you, Sullen."

# Chapter 24

## *Sullen*

The Halloween storm rages outside the hotel, and I watch it from the atrium.

Blood is sticky on my skin. The hoodie doesn't help, neither does my shirt beneath it, all this heat trapped under my layers and congealing with the wounds from my fresh dermal piercings. It shouldn't have bled so much or hurt so badly. Stein taunted me that it wouldn't, that inserting titanium under my skin would simply raise me higher to God. An excessive element on earth, it was only natural I absorb it too, he said.

The six piercings along the top of my spine felt...strange. But it was a manageable pain.

The way he pulled my shirt on afterward, then ripped it up—ensuring the fabric snagged on the new jewelry—and repeated the process six times before he found the most "appropriate" thing for me to wear beneath my hoodie tonight caused the stinging sensation. The blood. And the feeling as if my back is now in flames.

And for what? All that dressing and redressing and I am not to be seen nor heard tonight, when the hundreds of members of Writhe gather together for their sporadic group orgy. The other children will be here, of course. Sixteen, we are old enough to socialize.

*But I am not part of this* we.

*I never was, even though it's been years since Stein has summoned his followers for this. But I know what he wants now. Mass energy to pray over him, whispered words to ascend him to immortality. He doesn't take blood from his members; he doesn't even take it from me. It's only a side effect. He simply steals loyalty and bites off lives. And as for what he does to my body? Desecrating me is key to his ascension.*

*My death will mark the end. My corpse isn't even necessary, he told me once. There is nothing needed the moment I take my last breath. The end of my life is sacrifice enough.*

*He seemed to relish those words to me, about how useless I really am.*

"Sullen?"

*I look up as lightning cracks across the sky, sharply visible in the glass atrium, trees spiraling to dizzying heights above my head. And as I watch the rain beat down on the peaked, transparent roof, I think I imagined her voice.*

*Of course she's here. And I assume she's with her friends. And I am not supposed to be seen so—*

"Do you want to help me decorate?"

*Frowning, I lower my gaze and turn in the direction of her voice, expecting to see nothing. Sometimes, nonsensical words from her dance inside my head and keep me company in the midst of Stein's worst torture.*

*But...there she is.*

*Standing beneath bending limbs and hanging branches of the copse of trees behind her, she is really here.*

*Black lace dress with pink nails, a pink bow tied tightly around her throat. Her hair is pulled up in a braided bun, and the style accentuates her cheekbones, dazzling with some sort of sparkle I assume is in her makeup. There are very few lights here—lamp posts scattered through the square atrium—and with the night and the storm, she is the brightest thing in the dark.*

*I blink once, pushing my gloved hands into the pocket of my hoodie, careful not to pull down on the fabric so it doesn't snag along my piercings.*

*I should be upstairs, hidden away in one of the unoccupied rooms Stein directed me to stay put in. But I couldn't help but venture down here, to the main floor. Everyone else is on the second, inside the ball-room, but I stupidly hoped I would see her, even knowing it was impossible.*

*Yet here she is. A dream.*

*"Do you?" she presses, tilting her head a little, the bow along her neck crinkling slightly with the movement. "Want to help me?"*

*Decorate, she said. I flick my gaze to her hands and note the piles of what looks like ribbons in them, black and soft, pastel pink in color, matching her nails.*

*"Decorate what?" I ask, my voice breaking. I swear I can hear the ghost of my sobs inside of it, while Stein ripped shirt after shirt on and off of my body to hurt me more.*

*But she doesn't seem to notice, or maybe she just doesn't care. "The trees." She nods toward the ones at my back. We are standing on a cobblestone pathway, and it winds throughout the high-ceilinged room, trees and flowers and a bench or two scattered around the space.*

*I do not love it here. It's usually very warm and too bright and I don't want to hide among the shrubbery to avoid guests on the occa-sions the hotel is actually operating like one.*

*But now, Halloween night, it is dark and dreary, and rain beats along the skylights above us, thunder rolling and sporadic lightning cracking.*

*"Stein only thought of making the ballroom spooky, but he left the rest of this place pretty lame, don't you think?" Her blue eyes gleam as she glances up and at that exact moment, lightning forks brilliantly across the sky, illuminating the perfect roundness of her face.*

*She flinches at the sound, but doesn't stop looking up, her fingers* tightening around the heaps of bows in her hands, some pressed to her chest so they don't spill onto the floor.

"This is the best part of the hotel," she says quietly as the rain picks up, a drumbeat soundtrack to our stolen moment. She slowly lowers her chin, staring at me. "Do you agree?"

"No." I think of the hidden space beneath the hotel I could use to create my own safe room here. Maybe another lab, a replication of my own at home, stolen in the wing my mother used to occupy in our house. The place Stein will not venture. I think he is afraid of being haunted there, by Mom.

Karia's eyes narrow. "Then what's your favorite part?"

I would like to dissect her in my lab. See what makes her scream. It is a delusion, a daydream, a fantasy I have begun to use when I have moments alone, or even when Stein is hurting me.

I say nothing to answer her question. "Why are you using those colors? Halloween isn't pink." I have never been trick-or-treating, never worn a costume for the holiday, but I know enough. I have access to limited internet, at 44 Ritual Drive.

"Anything is whatever I say it is," she says, attempting to look down her nose at me, and it kind of works, with the distance between us. She hugs the ribbons to her chest, the silk or vinyl crinkling as she does. "So do you want to help or not?"

I don't reply. I cannot imagine a world in which I work side-by-side with the girl of my dreams and nightmares both and place pink ribbons on these cursed trees.

She rolls her eyes, scoffing. "You are so boring, Sullen." But she smiles a little as she says it, turning to the tree closest to her and squinting, as if she is sizing it up in the dim light. "You know the pink looks good, doesn't it?" She glances at me with a smirk.

I can see her side profile, the way she is facing the tree, and my gaze flicks up and down her small curves in that black dress, but it's the pink ribbon around her slender throat I fixate on. Yeah. The pink does look fucking good.

But before I can say anything at all, there are footfalls, confident

173

*and quick coming down the cobblestone path, barely audible over the downpour above us, but I am attuned to always be half-listening for someone coming.*

*Karia, though she lives a pampered sort of life, turns toward the sound, too, her back to me. The lace hem of her dress stops at her mid-thigh, and I am distracted for a moment by the slope of her legs, the curve of her calves. I'm surprised to see she is wearing black socks with white bows, and black Vans. This dinner is formal; it seems rebellious.*

*A smile fights its way onto my mouth at the same time a familiar voice cuts through the atrium.*

*"Karia. What are you doing?"*

*I flick my gaze up and see Antwine Ven staring at me, despite the fact he addressed his daughter.*

*My mouth goes dry, and I am suddenly, strangely aware of the dried blood along the top of my spine, the bright and irritating pain along my dermals.*

Do you know about them, *sir?*

*Antwine's dark blue eyes seem to glow as another fork of lightning illuminates the sky above us.*

*"I'm decorating," Karia says with a pout in her words; something I imagine she uses often on her parents.*

*I sense her glance over her shoulder at me, no doubt noting that's precisely where her father is looking.*

*Antwine Ven has light brown hair, cropped close and contrasting his deep blue eyes. An angular face, wide eyes, tall and lean in an all-black suit, he both looks and doesn't look at all like Karia. She takes after her mother more, but there is something in his haughtiness I think she has absorbed into her bloodstream.*

*"I don't want to sit through the speeches," she whines, and slowly, Antwine cuts his gaze to his daughter. His eyes soften marginally, but he casts another quick, distrustful glance to me.*

*"Yes, well, we all must do things we don't want. Come along. Stein has asked where you are." Again, he is looking at me.*

Heat pours through my chest, curving around my back and flaring at the site of my wounds. Stein knows I am infatuated with her; perhaps he has told Antwine to keep an eye on me. Either way, the look in his eyes is nauseatingly familiar. It is what everyone greets me with: Wariness.

Karia clenches her fingers around the ribbons in her hands, a few black and pink tails drooping between her wrists, sagging with her annoyance. "And you've found me, so you can report back and tell him so." Then she very deliberately turns her back on her father, drops the ribbons—all but one—and begins to slide it on the nearest branch, standing on her tiptoes to do so.

I am mesmerized by the way her calves flex, the faint veins visible along the backs of her knees. What would it feel like to lick them? To dig at them with a knife? I used to have my own, a weapon I kept close until Stein realized that's precisely what it could be and that I might one day use it against him.

"Karia." Antwine's voice is harsh enough to make me flinch. It is the same tone Stein uses when I have tried to run from him.

Of course, I always fail, but... I clench my hands into fists and retract them from the pocket of my hoodie.

If Antwine even acts as if he might strike Karia in any way, I know I will choke him with one of those pink fucking ribbons.

But when I dart my gaze from her father to her, I see she is not the least bit scared of Antwine Ven.

Instead, she is plumping the ribbon, batting each loop together with her palms. It looks kind of stupid on the thin branch, pale pink set amongst the brown and green in the dim lighting of lamp posts, every other tree natural and naked, but when she takes a step back, goes down on her soles and folds her arms, she makes a noise of satisfaction. A sigh and a hum, both.

"You can't tell me this doesn't look so much better." She glances over her shoulder to meet my gaze, ignoring her father completely. "Doesn't it?"

It doesn't. Not at all. But I am marveling over this strange rela-

*tionship between them; how can she get away with so much? A part
of me even wants to punish her for it. Have her on her knees as I grip
her jaw and—*

"Either I escort you back to the ballroom or I escort Sullen back
to..." Antwine trails off, turning to face me, his eyes narrowed.
"Wherever he is supposed to be."

*I don't miss the subtle threat in his words, although none of the
other members of Writhe—aside from Stein's men—have ever
touched me. And I expect Karia will not care at all where Antwine
escorts me.*

*But shocking me, she sighs loudly, then squats down and heaves
the rest of the ribbons in her arms, scooping them all up.* "You both
are so annoying. Leave Sullen alone; at least he watched in silence."
*Then she glances at me once more, and where I expect to find amuse-
ment or annoyance etched onto her pretty face, I see something that
looks and feels a lot like sadness.*

MY NECK IS STIFF AND THERE IS SOMETHING WET ALONG THE
corner of my mouth. My legs are bent at a strange angle, and I
can't figure out how my body is occupying space. I shift one
hand, only to find bare skin beneath my fingertips, warm and
soft and certainly not mine.

I pop open my eyes.

What I see doesn't make sense at first.

Blonde hair draped over closed eyes, pink lips parted,
green-painted nails curved into my shirt.

*My shirt.*

I glance down the length of the girl lying on me and see my
bare hand over her back, on that smooth patch of skin
between the hem of her top and the waistband of her black
denim skirt.

*Karia.*

It all rushes back to me at once and I blink several times,

ignoring the way I am exposed—no hoodie, no gloves—and trying instead to *think* through precisely where I am.

In a parking garage.

Medici Mall.

There are tendrils of thin light seeping into the backseat of the van, my head is jammed against one window, my knees in a position they shouldn't be, feet on the floorboard because my entire body doesn't fit in this backseat.

And Karia Ven is sleeping on me and right now, she looks like an angel.

*This is not my life.*

I have never woken up with anyone before.

My heart races, body heating, and despite the fact I have shed my hoodie—I see it there, crumpled alongside stale fries on the floorboard, my gloves dropped on top in a semi-neat pile—I am sweating now.

Karia is breathing softly, eyes closed, long lashes splayed over top the curve of her cheekbones.

She is perched on top of me, both hands pressed into my chest, her body so warm in every place it touches mine.

My mouth is dry, I desperately wish I could brush what's left of my teeth before she wakes, and I want to cover myself prior to that, too, but... I am captivated with *staring* at her. The way her hair is threaded with gold and paler blonde, how it waves down her back, so long. The perfect pink color of her lips, plush and soft, the pale red I can see of her tongue in her mouth, the slope of her nose, how her skin is tanned, and she has the faintest freckles along her face to go with it.

Her heart, pressed to mine, but her pulse is so much softer and slower.

I wonder how long I could stay here.

I know it is forever.

I don't remember stripping off my armor in the night, and I almost feel *betrayed* that my body would complete such an action when I have these dead nail beds and this terrible haircut and scars along my hands and words written under my throat I am lucky she didn't see when I was shirtless inside the penthouse suite; so many things I want to keep hidden from her.

But...maybe there is a small corner of my brain which trusts her.

She fought for me. She fled with me. Even now, she is sleeping peacefully on top of me in the back of a van we don't own. We are risking our lives simply by being here, and she is content... And, *cuddling* with me.

Yes. I would stay here forever.

But when a car door thuds softly shut somewhere nearby and I realize we have to move soon, I know we can't stay. And I know I may never get a moment like this again. Maybe deeper than that, though, I know I need to get her off me, climb up to the front row. She is not safe with all the desires I have inside my head, the things I have twisted in my brain these long years getting hurt and hurting for her.

She is not safe, with me.

# Chapter 25

## *Karia*

"Why did you move to the front of the van? You could've been seen." I smooth down the lapels of my black trench coat, palm gliding over the matte silver buttons. My heels click on the sidewalk beneath the towering buildings of Alexandria and I'm grateful my new shoes are Jimmy Choo. More comfortable than most, even if Sullen did roll his eyes when I got them. He didn't stop me, though.

And now, he doesn't answer me. He said about the same inside the mall. I woke up alone in the backseat of our hide-away and assumed he bolted, but he was slouched down in the front passenger seat. We entered the mall as soon as it opened, took a bathroom break, bought clothes for a disguise—he opted for a deep emerald-green hoodie and gray pants instead of his usual black, and he refused to buy different shoes—then slipped out the west wing exit of the store. We have been walking ever since.

"You have to speak to me. We need to eat, we need a place to hide, and we need to talk." I mutter the words quietly as we dodge in and out of the Alexandrian morning commute—

pedestrians on the sidewalk and cars at the crosswalks. I glance at him behind my Dior cat-eye shades and find his hood up, gaze ahead, and attention definitely not on me.

"Look at me." I snap the words out as we skip over an intersection with only two seconds of the walk signal remaining. "I am in this with you but if you don't talk to me, then how the hell—"

He grabs my arm and pulls me into an alleyway, surrounding buildings high enough to block out the October sun. The temperature plummets in here and the scent of the sewer grows stronger. Damp bricks surround us, there's a puddle beneath my heel, and a cursory scan further into the side street reveals dark blue trash cans. Deep enough to hide a body. Or maybe that's just the Writhe inside me talking.

"Do you want to know why you woke up alone?" Sullen's voice drags my focus back, his gloved hand still wrapped around my forearm.

As I slowly face him, he steps forward, driving me backward until my spine presses into the rough brick exterior. I can feel it picking at my trench. He paid a lot for this and he should handle it more carefully; the wads of cash in his pockets astounded me. I'm used to buying things with a slim black card, but neither of us have any cards on us and I know they can be easily traced.

I was grateful for the money, for the fact he didn't attempt to make me buy something cheaper and spent thousands of dollars we shouldn't have, but he should really treat his purchases better.

Still, I don't say that. I swallow hard, remembering how he strapped me to the chair. And before that, when I woke up motionless in a glowing room. We formed a truce but now, his dark eyes locked onto mine, his body preventing me from running, I wonder if it's over.

I take a deep breath in, holding onto the sensual scent of

him amongst the aroma of the city. "Yes," I answer him, watching as his gaze dips down to my lips, but only for a moment before he's staring at me again.

He presses a palm to the wall next to my head, forming a cage of his body to mine. "You would already know why if you used your brain. You make the mistake of forgetting what happened the moment before Stein stepped through the doorway. Tell me where you were then."

Blood rushes into my cheeks. I feel them heating, but I don't look away from him, my chest heaving between us. "In the... chair."

"Go on." He bows his head, leaning in closer. His lips are parted, and I see his sharp canine teeth, the incisor missing next to one.

"Strapped...down."

"What else?" His voice is rough and carnal.

"You were touching me."

He lifts his brows, waiting.

"And I spit on you." I arch a brow back, even as my pulse flies painfully fast inside my chest.

He steps closer, his body brushing mine, my spine arching slightly away from the brick. "Yes," he says softly, his nose inches from mine as he leans in even closer. "And I didn't get to pay you back for that. Do you know what would have happened to me if I ever spit on Stein?"

"You're not him—"

He clamps his gloved hand softly over my lips, pressing the leather firmly to my mouth as my nostrils flare. Then he turns his head and whispers against my ear, "He would've taken my tongue from my mouth." His breath dances on my skin and I shiver, closing my eyes tight, every nerve in my body alive. "And he would've fed it to me." He takes a step forward, pressing me fully against the wall with his physicality, eclipsing mine. "I have spent too long daydreaming about wrenching you apart,

Little Sun. I am not your fucking friend. Besides," his lips brush the lobe of my ear, and my stomach tightens into knots. "I've seen how you treat those." He pulls back slowly as I look at him once more, irises of deep brown and amber edged out by the blown black rings of his pupils, jogging a faraway memory in my mind I can't hold onto. "When the pressure comes, you'll stab me in the back to save your life, and I think it's best if neither one of us forget that." He removes his hand from my mouth then, both by his sides as he stares at me and I notice his chest compressing and expanding quickly, too.

"The pressure came. From Cosmo. From Stein. Three armed men." I run my tongue over my bottom lip and watch as he traces the movement with his eyes. "I still chose you."

He doesn't reply for a moment, and it's as if he is staring into my soul. Like those daydream seconds we'd pass on Ritual Drive, when he would appear ominously while I walked the street with Cosmo.

But then he looks away, flickering his gaze upward, to the sky. I note the circles there under his lash line, how they seem to have lightened a little, since yesterday. Maybe it's impossible, perhaps it's just the angle, but maybe...

"Because you're stupid," he finally says without looking at me, voice cold. "Like I said before. Whatever you think this is inside your head, it's not that." He drops his gaze back to me as I clench my teeth, wanting to tell him to stop calling me stupid but it sounds childish in my mind, so I keep silent. "Either way, we have to disappear. Or at least, I do. If I'm found, I won't survive. Do you know Writhe often disposes of bodies in the ocean? Thrown on a semi, carted along I-40 to the sea? *That* would be merciful, and it probably won't happen to me." He turns away, toward the city streets. "I know of a place. It's a long shot, but maybe."

*You* know *of a place?* I want to say that, because he's never

182

even been inside Medici Mall, how the hell would he know of anywhere, but that's not what comes out of my mouth at all.

"I'm not stupid," I say instead, straightening from the wall, unable to keep that thought inside my head. I clench my fists as I step toward him, heels clicking on cement. "And you have no idea what the fuck I think this is. But don't forget you carried me out of the hotel. I know it hurt you. You're... injured, and you still carried me. If you thought I was so stupid, you could've left me to die or be found. And do you want to talk about the money you just spent? All of this, everything I'm wearing..." Despite the fact he isn't looking, I gesture toward my trench coat, underneath which is a black dress, new underwear. We didn't buy anything else because even I can admit spending all of the money in one very expensive place is reckless, but he said nothing about it. "*You* paid for it. Between the two of us, I'm not sure you're a shining example of intelligence, Sullen." I hiss his name, lowering my voice as traffic sounds on the street. Tires spinning, horns blaring, people on their phones and speaking to coworkers or companions. Life is rushing by and with so many eyes and potential cameras out there, we need to be going, too.

But there's a sick part of me wanting to live in this stolen moment. To stand right here and fight with him until I break through his walls and show him how unafraid I am. How I won't *let* his body end up in the Atlantic.

He doesn't turn around, but he doesn't move closer to the main street either. And when he finally speaks, he just says, "When this is all over, remember I tried to warn you, Karia."

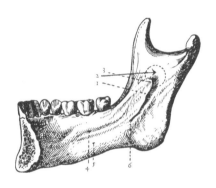

**Scully: I could meet you tonight.**

*I can't. I won't. But it is a nice fantasy.*

**MadMaude:** My parents left me to run the shop. Only for the weekend. Come over? We could... do things.

**Scully:** Things?

*After I send it, I close my eyes and see Karia. I open them and watch Maude type. If I could flee, there is only one of them I would run to. I dart my gaze to my closed bedroom door. I know I am losing precious moments of peaceful sleep, but this is my only time to... breathe. Besides, this mindless chatting takes away from the smarting sensation in my thigh; the burn of a blade dug into skin. It's a distraction from the paranoia that this might become infected, ooze through my body and end me.*

*Perhaps I want it to.*

But first, I want her.

**MadMaude:** I want to kiss you

*I grind my teeth and turn over in bed, bowing my temple to my pillow, feeling the wound shift against my mattress in a slice of agony.*

*I have seen Karia kissed by Cosmo. The saliva between their mouths. I clench my fingers tighter around my phone as I shiver in my bed and think of pouring a vat of formalin over Cosmo's head.*

# Chapter 26

## *Sullen*

The small lobby is dark. There are heavy, plum-violet curtains over the front street-facing windows. The scent of something shadowy and linen is thick in the air, and only a sliver of sunlight spills onto the rough hardwood floors.

Karia is quiet behind me as she closes the door, a too-cheerful bell chiming our arrival. We didn't speak much as we spent an hour keeping our heads down and searching for this place. *Serpents Emporium;* I knew only that it was beside a doughnut shop and had an emerald green door with the number four inked across it in black.

With no phone and no map, along with the fact I know nothing of the city due to my confinement, I'm surprised we arrived at all. But Karia, once I described the doughnut shop next door—purple signage, blue awnings—knew where to go.

Every time I have called her stupid, it has been a lie.

"May I help you?" A woman's voice spills from somewhere deep inside the shop. Past the circular lobby, there are rows and rows of...things. From where I am standing, I see books on some of the shelves, seashells cloistered along others, bags of black sand, a basket of what might be hooves. Somewhere I can't see, something bubbles viciously, and I wonder if it gives the Emporium its peculiar scent.

The shelves tower toward the ceiling, dusted in dark gold paint. The walls are black, lending the space a sinister sort of coziness that vaguely, for reasons not entirely logical, remind me of my labs.

"Where are you?" Karia asks the question with a bitterness as she steps up next to me in her heels. She still only reaches my shoulders and if I'm not careful, I'll be smiling over the fact. As it is, her question is valid. Aside from deep burgundy lounge chairs dropped with black velvet pillows and a staircase disappearing to a second level at our right, I don't see the woman who spoke.

But I hear her moving, rustling amongst the shelves, and a moment later, a shadow appears along the row with hooves, then the woman herself steps out.

I understand then what all the rustling was about.

She is wearing a red and black dress, all taffeta and lace, short, puffy sleeves, a long, elegant train covering her shoes. She has thick black hair twisted up into an intricate bun high on her head, porcelain skin, ruby red lipstick, and heavy eyeliner. I know from our brief exchange years ago she is only a couple of years older than me, and her name is Maude. Rings adorn her hands, long, black-tipped taloned nails grace her fingertips at her sides.

Karia rolls back her shoulders beside me, her arm brushing mine.

"Hello," Maude says, her gaze on me. "Are you looking for anything in particular today?" She does not look at Karia at all.

Karia Ven, of course, does not like this.

"Are we?" she echoes, nudging me with her elbow. "If so, please do tell."

I glance at her and find her cerulean eyes narrowed into catlike slits, her ridiculously expensive sunglasses pushed up onto her head, all the baby blonde strands of her hair away from her pretty face.

I do not know why she's so angry. This isn't a permanent solution, but if I'm right, it's at least one for the night.

"Yes," I answer Maude, tearing my gaze from Karia, pouting at my side. "We're looking for The Creep's Attic." My voice comes out a croak, and for a moment, Maude only blinks at me, as if she might not have heard me.

Frustration starts to swell inside my chest. I do not have any patience left.

I want a place to be alone that isn't a cramped car. I want more darkness. I want to eat Karia alive. If this is all the time I have with her, I want to pick and prod and poke at her until there is little left to dissect.

*I want cramped quarters. A room to briefly call my own. A space to think.* I am not used to all this freedom. It makes me feel itchy.

Maude's gaze flickers to my throat, which is covered by the same shirt I wore yesterday, but my heart drums a warning beat all the same. What if I've gotten this all wrong? I thought perhaps this was the one place inside the city Writhe did not reach. I could be the stupid one, though.

But then Maude says, very softly, "Scully?"

Karia makes some kind of gasping sound at my side, and I feel her eyes burning into my face.

"Yes," I say quietly, answering Maude's question, surprise flickering through me.

"I thought...the voice... Well, it is unusual. And extremely hard to forget." She says it with an inflection at the end that I don't understand.

Karia makes another choking sort of sound. I feel a little sweaty, perspiration along my brow, and I don't look at her as I clasp my gloved hands in front of me. I'm not sure what is wrong with her, but I'm trying to save our lives here.

Maude seems to recover upon seeing me in the flesh, then she nods once. "Of course. The Attic is yours. Two nights, then I have another...person, coming to take residence there." She finally glances at Karia, her dark eyes going wide as she seems to assess her, gaze flicking up and down her body in a way that makes me want to shield the Sun. But then she only turns her back to us and says, disappearing into the oddities along her shelves, "I'll be right back with the key."

"Who the fuck is that?" Karia's words shatter the brief second of solace I had after we stepped into the Attic—in name only; in reality, it's a spacious room above the Emporium, a tiny bathroom leading off the main space. The windows are covered with the same thick violet drapes as downstairs, blocking out the sunlight and lending the space a chilly, pleasant temperature. It smells of old wood and books in here, and while there is only one animal mounted on the light gray walls—a deer head —it feels better than any hotel room we could've gotten elsewhere.

And we are, momentarily, safe here.

We even have food; Maude led us here with a paper bag in her hand, set it on the dresser across from the queen bed and proclaimed it was egg and cheese bagels. I have no preference for food; I have eaten far worse than eggs, cheese, and bagels. I can consume anything when I am hungry enough, and right now, I am exhausted and ravenous both.

I close my eyes and for the first time in however long it's been since I first stalked Karia and Cosmo into Septem, I allow myself to feel the trembling in my thighs, the stiffness in my shoulders, the pain along my spine from wounds never quite healed.

It takes everything inside of me not to stumble forward and face-plant onto the burgundy silk sheets of the bed.

"Sullen." Karia bites out my name. She has not moved from her spot before the door, at my back. I would have heard her stupid heels clanking on the hardwoods if she did. "Who *is* that?" Her temper is fraying, and I know soon she will become mean.

If I wasn't so tired, so fearful of being alone with her, so *everything,* I would find it amusing.

As it is, nothing is funny right now. "Maude. She owns the shop." It's all I can manage.

"That doesn't tell me anything," Karia snaps back, too much energy inside her tone. *Where does she get it all?* "Why are we here? What is this place? How did you know to go here? *I'm sorry,*" she says in a way that implies she isn't, "the lock on our door might be a deadbolt, but it's not going to keep Writhe out."

I say nothing.

I keep my eyes closed and think of the man beneath the hotel. The one I foolishly told I wouldn't give Karia up to. I don't know if that was all a dream, the way things are so delirious inside my head, memories slipping away. I don't know how much sleep we got last night in the van, but it wasn't enough. My body is in pain. My mind is muddled. I cannot stay with Karia. I will have to part with her. I do not know what the *fuck* I am doing. This is starting to feel like a bad dream.

I should not have come.

"Sullen! Answer me! You can't just expect me to trust this witch in a taffeta gown and give me *nothing*—"

I spin around then, eyes flashing open, hands in fists at my side.

Karia's lips are parted, arms crossed over her chest, and she sucks in a breath and stops talking at my sudden movement.

Why did I think it would be a good idea to get her alone in a room where no one can check me? No one will interrupt us? No one will hear her scream if I push a pillow over her face until she passes out? And there are more innocuous things here that aren't actually, at all.

A minifridge, Maude said. I glance past the old, cherry wood dresser where she set down the paper bags, and there it is, gray and short, but it could have alcohol. Karia is a big fan of that, which means this room has everything I need to shut her up.

I should not have done this.

All of it was so incredibly stupid.

"Say something," Karia pushes.

I cut my gaze to her. "I know this will not make sense to you," I whisper, not wanting anyone to hear anything I am about to say. "But I did speak to other people sometimes, growing up. Not in person. But I had limited internet access. Years ago, I connected with Maude on a forum. We exchanged voice messages."

Karia's brows dig in, her bottom lip pushing out. She has the same look she did downstairs when Maude first appeared and stared at me, and I cannot decipher it at all.

"I pretended I might meet her one day. She told me about this place. The Creep's Attic, as it's called. A safe haven to hide in the city."

Karia half-turns her head, her nose lifted in the air. "Excuse me? *What?* Wait a second. You *met* someone online who you... planned to run away with?" She is spitting out the words like they are poison.

My face grows hot, thinking of her mocking me for a dismal thread of hope I held onto in my teenage years that one day I could be free.

"And if it's known as a *safe haven,*" she mimics the way I said the words and my pulse trips, "won't Writhe find it immediately?"

"No. It's...not connected to that world."

"If you know of this place, if you used the internet from 44 Ritual fucking Drive, won't Stein know of it too? He barely let you breathe. He only allowed you outside of the house when you were like, eighteen. What the fuck, *Scully?*" She says the name like it's a contagious disease; the one Maude used because it was my username when I escaped into the forum at night while Stein slept.

I never truly planned anything. Karia is right. Stein would not have given me that much freedom. Just like the labs he apparently knew about. I think he loosened the leash to gift me an illusion of hope I never really had.

"I don't trust her," Karia continues on. "I don't—"

"I don't trust anyone," I say evenly, holding her gaze.

Her eyes flicker, a moment of shadow creeping across them, and her body grows stiff, as if I hit her. "This is true stupidity," she says with a vicious little snarl, her top lip curling up. She gestures around the room, then folds her arms over the trench coat again, tapered at her waist, fitting her figure so gorgeously. I shouldn't have spent so much of our money on it, but I can't refuse her anything. It's disgusting. "We can't stay here. They'll be on their way in minutes, if they're not already."

"Then leave."

She lifts her brows. "Are you kidding me right now?"

*No?* I roll my eyes and turn my back to her, crossing past the bed, heading toward the door that leads to the bathroom. I glance at the paper bag but I don't feel like stopping and pulling out the food. I don't feel like doing anything except being *alone.* Sometimes I would steal minutes of sitting on the cool tiles of the bathroom floor back on Ritual Drive; the only place aside from my lab I had a semblance of privacy.

Yet, before I can walk into the dark checkered tile bathroom, Karia spits something else out at my back.

"Was she like, your internet *girlfriend?*" she hisses.

I stop, furrowing my brow. *What?* I don't look back and I don't say anything, but the question is so hilarious, I don't continue my retreat.

"Did you ever exchange nudes? Did you fantasize about strapping her down in a chair too? Or biting her? Or—"

"What?" I can't keep it in as I turn to face her. "What are you talking about?"

She looks angry, jaw clenched, still rooted in the same spot she's been in this entire interrogation. "Do you *like* her?" She jerks her chin toward the black door at her back, the one we all walked through.

I glance at it, thinking of Maude. She is pretty, and kind, and I did not believe this would actually work out. That years later, this place would exist, if it even existed in the first place. I meant what I said to Karia; I do not trust anyone, and this is not a safe haven forever. But we have no other options right at this moment. It's the best I could do, and it's *free.*

But *like* her?

"I don't understand you," I say through clenched teeth as I stare at Karia. "Do you mean do I like her in the way you like Cosmo and Von? How you let them fuck you? Cosmo's head between your thighs and you drunk out of your mind? Do I like her that way, is that what you're asking?" As I imagine it, as I speak it, my voice hardens in my own anger. I am nearly vibrating, thinking of watching her with them, and I do not know how I held myself back all these years. If Von Bentzen or Cosmo de Actis walked through that door right now, I would not hesitate to disembowel both of them. It is as if now I've had a taste of Karia, however unwilling it might've been given from her, I can't imagine anyone else ever having the same. Despite the fact I know this is a temporary fantasy, I can't help my feelings.

"Yes," she says, no remorse in her answer. "That's what I mean."

And it's only then, right now as we stare at one another in a strange room above a strange shop, that I understand what she's feeling.

*Jealousy.* I have lived with it my entire life, watching her smiling, happy face, surrounded by all of her friends, while I cloaked myself in bruises and worse, hiding in the dark.

She is *jealous* of Maude. Over...me?

"Why are you *smiling?*" she snaps, her face flushing pink as she stomps her foot, a harsh clack against the hardwoods.

The smallest laugh leaves my lips at her reaction. "Karia," I manage to say, very calmly as she glares at me. "You should be very upset that she is *not* the object of my affection." Then I turn away from her and disappear into the bathroom.

# Chapter 27

## *Karia*

I get deliriously, gloriously drunk.

It is what I always do when I do not want to be in control anymore. And while Sullen was in the bathroom, I rooted around in the minifridge of this odd room and found a full bottle of wine. Something dark red with a black label that only said, *XxX.*

The bottle is nearly empty, perched precariously atop the black painted dresser on my side of the bed. There were too many pillows—gold-threaded decorative ones—and I tossed all of those onto the floor. I took off my trench coat, my heels, my sunglasses, pulled back the heavy duvet and slid into the white sheets, my back propped up against the fluffy white pillows along the ornately carved red headboard.

It feels like night in here, despite the day. And although beyond the hum of the minifridge I can hear the traffic of Alexandria down below, all of it is far away in this moment.

Or perhaps that's just the alcohol zooming through my veins.

I know I need to brush my teeth—our *host* told us there were both toothbrushes and paste under the sink in the bathroom, and that we could wear any of the clothes in the many drawers of the dresser with a wide, spacious mirror perched atop it across from the bed—and wash my face, but Sullen is still hiding in the bathroom and right now, for this moment only, I do not care what I look like.

In fact, as I meet my reflection in the mirror, displaying the high ceiling overhead and the chandelier—turned off—just above the center of the bed, I think I'm hot.

My hair is a mess, slightly oily, and there is eyeliner smeared beneath my eyes, but I have this sad, dirty look and although it isn't like Maude's Goth Queen appearance, it's sexy, too.

I hiccup, grabbing the wine bottle by the neck and bringing it up to my lips, tipping it backward, swallowing down the rest of the red. My legs are parted and extended in front of me in an unladylike pose—considering I'm wearing a dress—but the sheets are so soft on my skin and I am warm and languid and... I just don't care.

"What are you doing?" Sullen's throaty voice makes me flinch.

I drop the bottle down to my lap, clamping my thighs around it and drawing up my knees slightly as I place my hands over my shins, leaning forward and meeting his gaze, alcohol burning down my throat. Everything is hazy, soft, and he looks so beautiful, hood pulled over his head, eyes piercing on mine.

For the first time, this feels like a playground. An adult escape. I am not thinking of Writhe, or running, or what trouble I will be in when I am caught. I'm not even thinking of *Maude,* and the way she stared at Sullen like she wanted to drop to her knees and suck his dick right in front of me.

"I am drunk," I announce, laughing at the end as I hiccup again.

Sullen glances at the bottle between my thighs, then drags

his gaze back up. "Karia." It's all he says, but there is some sort of warning in the word.

"Why did you keep animals in jars?" It comes tumbling out of me as I stare at him. I scooch down on the pillows, resting my head and letting one knee fall to the side, the wine bottle tilting with it.

Sullen's gaze drops to my legs, but he is perfectly still.

"I'm not scared of you," I add, out of nowhere.

"So you keep saying," he whispers, the words jagged.

"So? Why the jars?"

"You don't want to talk about that right now."

"Would you tell Maude, if she asked you?" I smile at my own joke, feeling flushed and entirely too comfortable. Some sober part of my brain reminds me of the hotel. The horror I should have felt.

But all I can think of is what I told him even then: *Touch me. I am not afraid.* We have spent what feels like twenty-four straight hours running.

I am allowed to have fun.

"No," Sullen answers me so seriously, his dark eyes on mine again.

"Then tell me."

"We are not friends."

"That hurts my feelings." I mean it when I say it.

"I am sorry." He doesn't sound like he means that, at all.

"Tell me anyway. I'm going to die soon, so—"

"You're not." His voice is vicious.

"Humor me anyway."

"We shouldn't do this."

"You are so fucking boring." I yawn, stretching my arms over my head and elongating my body. "I would have better luck fucking this wine bottle." I slowly reach a hand down to wrap my fingers around the neck of it, then slide it close to my body, the center of my thighs. I press the roundness of it against

The Monster of Hotel No. 7

me, my dress dragging up with the movement, a feigned moan leaving my lips. Sullen appears shimmery, but everything else is blurry, and he is all I focus on.

My vision is swimming, my breathing is shallow, and I am doing things I would not do sober, which is how I know I am perfectly content to play in this dreamscape.

I slide the bottle along the outside of my black underwear, letting my eyes flutter closed and blocking out the dark room as I put on a silly show for Sullen.

But he says nothing, and despite my intoxication, I start to feel what he called me. *Stupid.*

I swallow hard, then blink open my eyes.

I almost scream, but he clamps his gloved hand over my mouth.

He is *right there.*

Looming over me, his upper body leaned down into my own, his dark irises the only thing I see.

He tugs the bottle away from me with his other hand, wrenching it from my grip.

My pulse pounds painfully inside my chest, and I am not breathing at all as I stare up at him.

"You wrote to me almost every month, Karia Ven. Is that what you do to every man you think is boring?"

I can't speak, my teeth clenched together as he stares at me, his hand firmly pressing into my mouth, fingers digging into my jawline.

"Every fucking month. You told me about letting Cosmo fuck you. You taunted me. You had no idea what kind of freak I really was, did you?"

"You're not a freak. You're still a *virgin,*" I manage to snarl beneath his hand on my mouth. "Unless that's something you say to all the girls who pity you."

His eyes flash and he throws the bottle further along the bed. I feel it land softly in the sheets, but the next second, his hand is gripping my thigh, sliding high up as he pulls me down the bed. "Pity me? If you got yourself into this position because of *pity,* you are really going to regret the rest of your fucking life, Karia. You should know better than to feel sorry for monsters."

"You're not a—"

"You don't know what I am," he snarls, his eyes livid as he leans in so close, his nose is touching mine. "You have no fucking clue. Do you want to know about the animals in jars?" he asks, mimicking me.

I slowly nod my head, my body tense, but I don't want to move away.

"Let's play our game. I'll answer you if I can touch you." He slides his hand down from my mouth, grabbing my face instead.

"Without your gloves," I whisper. He starts to protest, I can see it in his eyes, but I glance down, where his hand is on my thigh. "At least, there. I want you to... *feel* me."

"Karia." Another warning, like a snarl.

I swallow hard, my face hot. "Please. I'll listen to you. You can do whatever you want to me. Just... I want to feel you."

"You don't," he says, like a promise. "You really don't want that." His grip along my jaw tightens.

"I do," I say, even as my tongue feels clumsy inside my mouth, everything about this moment dreamlike. Perhaps none of it is even real. A side effect of the sedatives I had. "If I'm the first girl you've touched, I want you to feel everything. Think of it. How warm I'll be. How *wet,* just for you. I'm like your own specimen, Sullen. I'll be your doll."

His eyes press tight closed.

I want to smooth the crease between his brows. Lick it, even. Lick him. But I know, even in my hazy mind, that's too far for him.

*Please touch me.*

I shift a little on the bed, inching his hand closer to where I want him, and his eyes flash open.

Then he says, "My doll?" in a rough sort of voice.

"*Yes.*"

He shakes his head once and his eyes look sad as he stares at me. "You will regret this."

# Chapter 28

## *Sullen*

*nd so will I.* It's what I don't say.

I tug off one glove with my teeth, turned away from her so she can't see what she's inviting in, then stroke my fingers along her inner thigh as I study her once more.

I am half-sitting on the bed, my hip next to hers, her face in my gloved hand, and I watch as her body trembles with my featherlight touch.

There is a part of me scared to touch her *there,* because I don't know what I'm doing. It would be better if she was bound to the bed in some way, like she was in the chair, but her intoxication will have to be enough.

I squeeze the inside of her thigh, hard, and watch as her pupils dilate. Her arms are once more above her head, her entire body laid out for me, but I focus on her face as I drag my hand up her bare leg, in awe once more over the softness of her skin.

Unintentionally, my touch has changed from aggressive to... soothing, maybe. Like a massage. I've never had one of those, but once a nurse had to check the piercings on my spine and perhaps she felt bad for me because she squeezed my shoulder blades a few times in some semblance of reassurance. I had never been touched like that; not that I could recall. It made pleasant shivers dance along my spine.

I wonder if it's the same now...for her. There is a furrow between her brow as she looks up at me, but perhaps it is our positions. I know what it's like in some ways; Stein ordered me naked many times while he lectured me, solely for the humiliation.

"At first," I tell her as I touch her, still gripping her face in my hand in case she looks down to see my bare one— "the specimens were a punishment. I..." Trailing off, I close my eyes for one second.

Two.

She will hate me after she knows everything I have ever done, forced or not. It is impossible to stare this type of freak-show in the face and not feel revulsion.

But a deal is a deal, and I do not want to stop touching her, even if it is only her leg I'm brave enough to graze now.

"The Betta fish? They were...like that. I had to create them, of course. Fill them with formalin—"

She widens her blue eyes, staring at me so immediately it's like we are... magnets. I loosen my grip on her face, trail my palm down to her chest, and feel her heart race.

I begin to massage her there. Kneading her in this way soothes me in my own.

"Formaldehyde," I say softly, understanding her confusion. "It's dangerous, you know. I should've worn a respirator but..." I glance down at the outline of her body beneath her dress, the way her abdomen contracts in and out as she breathes. I roam my eyes up higher, to her pebbled nipples, and I want to bite apart the fabric keeping her from me, but I clench my teeth and hold the compulsion back. I wonder, despite our deal, if I should tell her these things at all. It feels...acidic somehow.

Corrosive. Peeling back layers of me so she can examine the burnt soul beneath.

"Tell me," she whispers, making the decision for me.

"But I was not allowed. I injected each creature with a needle, placed them in the jar and sealed them. Some smaller creatures I kept in test tubes, like worms. After a few weeks, they were ready for ethanol instead. The final step. They began to...keep me company, in a way. Eyes and mouths and bodies. It was freezing in my room, always, some sort of strange draft in the house. They became a familiar presence to me, but when I did something wrong... I had to... consume pieces of them."

She trembles as I touch her, gliding my fingertips up and down her thigh, and I cannot bear to look at her face. I keep my gaze on her chest.

But as fear and anxiety storm through me, I need something more than what I'm touching.

I slide my hand up further, then feel the silken edge of her underwear.

A low breath leaves her lips, audible between us, but I still don't meet her gaze.

Slowly, I inch one finger beneath the side of the silk fabric, feeling her short hair there.

It feels so good, just this, that it's hard to breathe, let alone speak. Discomfort blooms inside of me, but *desire* is thicker.

"It made me sick. Always. But I still...liked them around me. *Company,*" I reiterate. "I never had that, after my mother..." I lift my gaze and stare at the lightest blonde, thinnest hairs just along her upper arm. She is made of light. "When Stein realized that, caught me speaking to them one night, he forced me to destroy each sample, watched as I broke every jar along the pavement behind our home." My chest tightens. It felt like killing friends, that night. "Eventually I...recreated everything. Our house is big, and he never went near the little office upstairs my mother claimed for her own in her wing. Nor the small, secret space beneath it. I'm sure he knew it existed, but maybe once he loved, before. My mother. He stayed away, and over time—years—I made my own lab. I grew my friends again." I don't mention the fact it seems he knew about that, and the lab at the hotel. It still doesn't make sense to me that he let me keep it at all. I don't mention either the way I hurt the snakes a little bit, taking out my anger against Writhe and Stein on them. She might despise me for that, but they were the only punching bags I had.

"When you left? Who looked after them?"

Slowly, I lift my chin to look at her. Surely she is mocking me. I understand, logically, wet specimens are not friends. Not even pets. I do know the difference between a beating heart and a lifeless one. And I feel the familiar despair and rage and anger twisting under my skin with her questions, but when I stare into her eyes, she is not smiling or cruel.

I don't understand it. Or her.

"I don't know." I feel compelled to answer, like the blue of her eyes is this ocean she wanted me to swim in with her and I am being pulled under the sea. "I... They are still there, alone. Stein retained ownership of the house."

"Did you create them again, at... Haunt Muren?" She says the name of Stein's estate like it is unfamiliar, and I suppose it is, but the fact she remembered it makes me feel strangely, comfortably *warm.*

"I wanted to," I tell her honestly, and I can't shake the feeling she is still mocking me in some way that I don't understand, like who would actually want to hear about this? About *my* life? Yet I can't stop sharing tiny scraps of information with her. "But I was just so... tired, then, of everything I liked being ruined." *Like you,* I don't say. *They will ruin you for me too.*

My heart squeezes inside my chest and I desperately wish it wasn't true. That this one thing, this beautiful creature I could have for myself.

"I'm sorry, Sullen," she says quietly. "I wish I had known."

I don't know what to say to that. The kindness is so unfamiliar as to feel like a lie.

She searches my gaze as I run my finger along her labia. I know the term; I know every word. But I have never... touched anything like this. I am not worthy, and I know that I have to steal each of these moments. It is the only way someone like me should have them at all.

Her pulse races under my hand over her chest, but she doesn't shy away from me.

"I can... take off my dress. If you want." She whispers the words, and I smell the wine on her breath. "You can see where you bruised me, with the needle." There is nothing of anger in her words. It's like a true offer, and I feel myself growing harder when she says it. Thinking of her skin, blooming yellow and red and purple from me.

I swallow hard, but I don't agree with her, or move. This moment already feels impossibly delicate as is.

"Or maybe I could...touch you?" She tilts her chin, as if in waiting, but she doesn't move her arms from above her head.

I lift my gaze and stare at the beige-pink of her palms. The beautiful underside of her nails.

I flex my fingers in my gloves. My hand is clammy, and I have the sudden, vicious urge to yank this outer shell off, too. But the places where my nails won't grow, then the strange color beneath the others, alongside the lumps and angles of my fingers... she can't... see that.

And I... I've told her too much.

I've given all of me away. I told her I was forced to drink wet specimens and I left out the way my throat burned and I vomited and worse and was dizzy in bed for days, puking on myself. And no one cared and when Stein came, it was only to command me to clean myself up. And some nights I thought I might die and sometimes I simply wanted to.

I could've killed myself. Drank too much. Finished what Stein always started. But *she* would cross my mind and I... couldn't. Wouldn't.

I am pathetic. She does not love me. She's *drunk*. And before, she was held captive. Maybe she pretended to be jealous over Maude, but as it is, I think it would be much easier to flirt and touch *her* then continue to expose myself to Karia. What am I doing, giving these pieces away? If I let her live, she will mock me to Von. Cosmo. The men she has given herself to and will again. And I...

I cover her eyes with my hand.

I can't look at her.

Not like this.

Not when I am so exposed, in more ways than she is.

She goes entirely still.

She does not even breathe.

I shift slightly, so I can see her legs, her thighs rigid now that she is once again remembering she doesn't really know me at all.

And as I stare at the smoothness of her flesh, my hand beneath her dress, I know I should've never told her anything. How did she get me to speak so much? My mouth is dry with regret, my throat aching, and I just realize it all now. That those are the most words I've spoken in... perhaps ever. Glimmers of laughter with my mother echo in distant memories but I cannot hold onto those.

*No one is interested in someone like me. No one.*

"Sullen?" she whispers, and I hate that I love she has never once called me Sully and I hate that I would love it if she ever did.

In a world of loneliness, it wasn't the animals who kept me company. It was the sun of her.

But I am the night.

We can never exist at the same time. I will blot out all of her goodness.

"Keep touching me," she moans out, her lips pale pink and so perfect I want to bite them.

She slowly bends her knees, distracting me from her mouth, and plants her bare feet on the sheets. I notice her toes, slender and beautiful, painted with a pastel shade of pink. Carefully, her legs trembling, she spreads her knees wide, her dress slipping up higher, revealing the black of her underwear, and my jagged finger beneath the scrap of fabric.

I smell her, clean and earthy, the scent enough to make my body light with *need*.

"Look at me, at least," she whispers. "I want to be the first girl you really see."

My chest heaves and I don't remove my hand from her eyes, but I can't help it.

I pinch the fabric of her underwear and shift it over to the side, revealing short, brown-blonde hair, the curve of *her*, the inner crease of her thighs. My pulse is wicked inside my head as she lets her knees fall to the side in a way I think must be painful for her, stretching so impossibly far, but it's enough to open up her labia, to show me the soft pink-red of her and I cannot breathe.

I want to...explore her. I will steal the memories of her flesh upon my fingertips and before I am dragged back, maybe I will let her go.

But perhaps not.

"Touch me, Sullen." Her back arches off the bed despite the fact I am *not* touching her, not aside from my hand over her beautiful eyes.

My heart races. She seems so eager, writhing below me. She is ready to give herself to me, but I know a ruse. I have been tricked by Stein so many times before. Nothing feels real here.

If she wasn't stupidly drunk, she wouldn't offer herself to me like this.

"I'm going to kill you if you keep…doing this to me," I whisper, and I mean it. Things would be so much easier if I did. "I don't like when you mess with me this way, Karia."

"Sullen." Her nostrils flare. She inhales so deeply, it is audible between us. "This isn't a joke. I'm not teasing, *I'm offering*. I'm so wet for you. *Touch me and see.*"

"I might…hurt you. I don't know how to do this." My voice is choked, the words barely pushing their way out.

"I'd like it if you hurt me."

"Stop saying that."

"Do anything you've dreamt about."

"You don't want that."

She reaches down when I don't and splays herself with her fingers, exposing so much *more* of her to me, glistening and swollen pink flesh, so gorgeous, delicate, and the *scent* of her drives me insane.

"Touch me." She brushes aside the fabric of her underwear with the side of her hand, so I don't have to. "Please, Sullen. Cosmo has. Von, too. They've put their—"

I slide my finger down the center of her, my breath catching at how wet she is. So soft and delicate and *soaked*. I really could rip her apart. "Don't talk about them when you're with me," I warn her, brushing my index finger over her clit. It is puffy, and she squirms when I touch her there.

"Why?" she gasps out as I try not to focus on my missing fingernail, there, on my index finger. All the monstrous parts of me infecting the angel of her.

My skin crawls despite my lust.

I want to bite her.

I want to drive my filed canines into her here, make her bleed.

She arches her back more, circling her hips around my

finger. If only she knew what was really touching her. If only she could see how gross I am.

"You don't like thinking of other men pushing inside me?" She keeps her fingers hooked into her underwear but glides her hand down until she is spreading herself once more, and this time, I see her tight hole.

I am shaking as I stare at my fingers. Broken and distorted, ripped cuticles and yellowed nails, of those still attached. She wouldn't want *that* inside of her.

*No one will want you.*

*No one.*

"Then *you* do it," she urges, ignorant to my internal battle. "You touch me. Replace them. Their fingers, their tongues, their cocks. *I want you, Sullen.*"

No one will want me.

*You don't know what you're asking for.*

"I want *you*," she repeats, more urgent in her fervor.

"Shut up."

I watch as she teases her manicured nail around her entrance. So pretty and perfect and nothing like me.

"Please," she whines. "Please finger me."

*You are such a stupid girl.*

"Please, Sullen." She is gasping now, begging for me.

But she will pretend I am someone else. She will imagine Von or Cosmo or another man of Writhe. Someone I can never be.

*"Sullen."*

*Fuck you.* I drive my finger lower, pushing into her cunt, watching as the juxtaposition of my repulsiveness dives into her perfection.

She moans, a sigh leaving her lips right after, like she has been longing for this. If only she could see how defiled she is now.

Tight and wet and soft around me, I marvel over it before I

move my finger out, but not all the way, then back in. Her clit grows puffier, her hand grazes my bare one, and she says, "Add another," with a whine.

I glance at the yellow tip of my middle finger and feel a sick sense of satisfaction knowing I am fucking her up this way with my disgrace.

But my satisfaction morphs with anger. Glee turns to wrath. Desire to please her commingles with an overwhelming sensation to press on her thigh and break her leg so she can never run when she truly sees me for what I am.

"If you knew what I looked like, you would hate me." I speak as I stare at her, at the glistening wetness along my fingers every time I push in and out of her, her walls gripping me tight while she writhes beneath me. "If you could see how vile you are now, you wouldn't let me touch you. Von won't want you anymore. Neither will Cosmo. You're tainted now, Karia."

She grabs my wrist, bare skin on my scarred flesh. Her other hand pulls down at the one covering her eyes and I lift my gaze to her, then curl my fingers around her throat. If she talks about *them,* if she calls me by *their* names, I will strangle her.

But she says none of that.

She lets me live in this dream.

"Let me see you," she says, her face flushed, but just as she averts her eyes to look at my hands, I shift on the bed, looming over her on my knees, my palm pressed to her windpipe as I finger fuck her faster as she gasps, her eyes wide with fear at me above her.

"Pull down my shirt," I whisper, feeling her throat roll beneath my hand. How tight her walls close in around my fingers as I fuck her with them. I think she is contracting so much because now she is scared again. "You want to see? Pull it down."

Her nostrils flare as she breathes, but she lifts her hand,

grasping the high collar of my shirt beneath my hoodie. Her fingers graze my skin and I flinch, hand still between her thighs but I leave my fingers inside, unmoving. If she screams or tries to run, I will ruin her.

Her blue eyes lock on mine and she tugs at the fabric there, just below my chin.

Then, not slow at all, she yanks it down, exposing the lumpy, sewn flesh. "Lower," I snarl, because there are so many more delights for her to see.

She is trembling beneath me, clenched around my disfigured fingers. But she does as I say, tugging down the fabric.

Her eyes go wide.

I know when she's seen it.

He did it with an Exacto knife. I had to spell out each word.

"More," I say, spreading my fingers inside of her and she flinches. But she doesn't disobey me.

She keeps drawing down the collar, pushing on my hoodie, too, when she gets there. Her face is pale, her eyes glistening.

"You can't see it all unless I take this off, but you'll never get that part of me." I lean down close, then grab her jaw and twist her head so she isn't looking at me anymore. "What it says is true," I whisper into her ear.

I can't touch her anymore.

I remove my fingers from her and push them into her mouth.

Obediently, scared, she parts her lips and I shove my fingers to the very back of her throat. I feel her gag, my hand splayed along her jawline, over the top of her neck.

She is nothing but a body to me right now, having physical, bodily reactions. I feel nothing, making her convulse. I feel nothing, speaking horror into her ear.

"I *am* fucking pathetic," I whisper, speaking the words Stein carved into my chest, starting just below the lump of flesh on my throat. There are worse things, too, written onto my torso, over my kidneys along my back. But *I am pathetic* hurt the most. I was thirteen and Stein caught me watching porn, hand around my cock as I saw other girls but dreamt of her.

I was naked when he punished me for it and his reaction was only laughter as I spelled each letter out for him, Rex and Arthur and Constance drinking beer as they watched my misery with smirks on their faces.

"And now, so are you." Then I lower my head and I bite the side of her throat, hard enough she finally, *finally* starts to scream around my fingers inside her mouth, teeth gnashing against my skin. I laugh as I taste iron on my tongue and give her enough air to suck in a breath. *"Do you want to leave me now?"*

# Chapter 29

## *Karia*

He pushes his fingers further down my throat and saliva edges around the corners of my mouth. A desperate sound wrenches free from my lips, strangled with his hand in the way. My neck stings where he bit me, and my stomach starts to hurt as my head spins. From the wine, from him; I don't know, but either way, I am grotesquely intoxicated.

Yet I *want* to speak. I want to answer him. *No, I don't want to leave, you stupid boy. I am not scared. You are not frightening. You are not the monster you believe yourself to be.*

I bite down on his hand then because I can't say a word when he's gagging me with his fingers.

But he doesn't remove them.

I clamp my teeth harder, feeling the bones beneath and tasting myself on him as I remember how he commanded me to do just *this* before, when I was sedated for him.

*He likes to be bitten. He probably never knew that until me.*

A groan leaves his lips, and my body grows hotter, my fingers fisting the sheets because despite the drool around my face and his punishing position, he isn't hurting me and he doesn't scare me and I will repeat it inside my head a million times until it's true.

I dig my incisors deep into the knuckles of his fingers, my pulse pounding inside my temple, but he only pushes himself further down my throat until bile burns up from my stomach and I'm forced to widen my jaw.

Then he abruptly pulls back.

I gasp for breath, my lungs squeezing together as I dig my nails into my palms with the padding of the white sheets buffering the sting.

He is straddling me with his body weight as he jerks my head to face him. His damp fingers tremble as he strokes my hair back from my face in the strangest, most tender gesture, a paradox of what he did only seconds before. His eyes follow the path of his bare fingertips along my cheekbone, his chest heaving beneath his hoodie, eyes wild and dark as he studies my facial structure like it is the most fascinating thing to him.

Like he didn't just bite me, or gag me, or try to scare me.

Like I didn't just bite him back.

Or maybe like he wants to break apart every bone beneath my skin.

I tuck my elbows tighter to my body but resist the wild urge to push him off as the wine swirls too fast inside my head and I am trying to catch up with everything that just happened in only a matter of heartbeats.

Through it all, not once did I try to fight him off. I pulled down the collar of his shirt, but I did not push him away. Surely he noticed?

*I am pathetic, it's true, just for* you.

My mind stumbles over the scars under his throat, the jagged words, the inches of flesh desecrated with some sort of blade, dug deep into his beautiful skin.

*How dare he?*

It's what comes from my mouth first as he calms, pinning

me down with his knees splayed over my hips, our bodies so close and yet his mind is out of reach.

"How dare you?" I whisper, trying to catch my breath as I stare up at him, resisting the compulsion to wipe my own saliva from my face.

I take in the sharp line of his jaw, the lump of flesh beneath his collar, now pulled up to cover him again. His long lashes, that pointed nose, and the bitterness inside his brown eyes.

"Did you do that to yourself?" My voice is thready, and the room has that spinning sensation again, but I focus on the stillness of him. "Did you hurt yourself?"

He continues to trace the shape of my cheek with shaky fingers, over and over, like he is mapping the bones beneath. His gloved hand holds my face, as if he is afraid I will turn away from him.

He cannot see I never would.

There is the faintest trace of red on his bottom lip, where he bit me, and I feel my pulse along the wound over my throat, but it is oddly more intimate than painful. Like a bitten secret I can always keep.

"Tell me," I whisper, never looking away from him. "Did you write that yourself?" He would've had to look into a mirror; the pain would've been immense to scar that deeply. Permanently. The letters did not have the pearly pink of a fresh wound. I wonder which year of his life he felt he needed to carve so wickedly with such vicious words. I wonder if I could have ever stopped him in any of our adolescent encounters. *Why wouldn't you let me save you?*

He stills his index and middle finger over the ridge of my cheekbone. Then his eyes slowly slide to mine. With the emerald-green hood pulled over his face, casting it in partial shadow inside the dark room, I cannot see all of his hair, but there are thick brown strands of it peeking beneath the fabric, and I want to run my fingers through them. I want to stroke his scalp. Tell him he is so much more than *pathetic.*

He looks down at my neck, eyeing the spot where he dug his sharp canines into me. His expression doesn't change.

"No," he finally answers me, his voice low, gaze focused on my bite. "That will bruise," he whispers, slowly spreading his fingers to cover the side of my cheek, two others close to my eyes, his large palm spans the entirety of my face. It is like he is cradling me. "It could get infected."

"It's shallow," I say quietly, my heart hurting at his confession that he didn't do it to himself. There is a prick of sweetness inside it, though. That he did not get that low. Or, if he did, he did not act on it, at least not there. But so much of his body is always covered, I am almost terrified to know what he could've done to the landscape of his precious flesh. "It'll be fine."

He swallows hard. I see his jaw work as he does, but he won't lift his gaze to mine. "You'd be surprised, sometimes. How the most trivial wounds can rot." He closes his eyes a moment, as if he is in some kind of inner turmoil. "I will clean it for you. I'm...sorry." Then he starts to move. He was never fully seated on me in a way that would compress my body and constrict my airway, and I find I don't want his warmth to leave me just yet.

As he lowers his hands from my face, I reach out and grab the bare one, awkwardly gripping his fingers, still wet from my mouth and...something lower.

I feel how taut he becomes with my touch, like a corpse. And he doesn't look at me, only stares at some space between us. I note the bones of his fingers, jagged and bumpy, but I don't glance down.

I am not sure I'm ready for everything he has been through, despite the fact I will adore him regardless of his trauma. The story of the wet specimens rolls through my head, but instead of simply grief at his past, I feel oddly proud of him, that he learned to do so much, so young. Even if it was on cruel command. How many teenagers can create such creatures?

"Please don't be sorry." The nausea inside of my belly rolls and turns like a strong wave, and the drunkenness is unpleasant, but I still want to try and communicate what is inside my brain for him. *I'm obsessed with you, I think.* But what comes out instead is, "Don't leave me here yet." I don't know exactly what I mean. Right now, because I feel sick and exhausted from stupidly drinking so much wine after being sedated twice? For the rest of our nights here, because I don't want to be alone? *Ever, because I am enamored by you?*

But he doesn't ask for clarification. Instead, a crease forms between his brows then he lifts his eyes to me. And slowly, carefully, he nods.

# Chapter 30

## *Karia*

There is the unmistakable sound of a serpent's slither. I hear it, but when I force my eyes open, I see nothing but darkness. Night has fallen, or perhaps I am buried alive, the way it is as if a ceiling of ink is cloistered around my body.

The snake grows closer, the creeping sensation of its movements transferring to a physical reaction inside me. Little hairs stand up on the end of my neck, along my arms, down my legs.

My limbs are bare. The realization comes to me in an abrupt rush and I try to sit up, drawing in a ragged breath and contracting my core muscles, but I cannot move. As the snake draws closer, the rustling of its belly over the same hard surface I am lying on growing louder, I realize I can only blink up at the gloom over my head. A chill sets in that has nothing to do with the stagnant air of this tomb and my teeth clack together. It is unfair, how my body reacts but my brain is in a prison, unable to unlock any mechanism of its own.

*Something is coming.*

*Someone is after me.*

*The snake is here.*

It doesn't stop moving when I sense it by my head. I cannot tilt my chin to look up, and even if I could, there is nothing to see in this hell. But the cold scales of its body slide up my bare arm and I open my mouth to scream.

Silence comes out.

The frigid creature curves itself over my eyes and I cannot breathe.

I am trapped inside my own human form.

It crawls lower, along my nose.

I am useless. I cannot get it off.

The serpent glides across my bare chest and tears prick and press behind my eyes. The creature slithers over my belly, its weight immense, body so long I still feel more scales unspooling over my shoulder cap, brushing beneath my eye. Across my ribs, the planes of my abs, then lower still, against my hip bones, and I—

"*Karia.*"

His voice calls out to me in the dark. Pain pricks beneath my eye, at the corner, blinding when I blink open my lids only to see nothing. I am trembling, tears tracking down my cheek stinging the sharp hurt beneath my lash line.

"*Stop.*" Sullen's croaky voice is followed swiftly by a hand along my wrist, pinning it back to the bed alongside my other, an immense shadow over my body.

My heart is racing, and I start to thrash, confused, drenched in a cold sweat.

My breaths are loud, audible, *terrible* noises inside the darkened tomb, and I do not know if we are both buried here, where the snake is, what is wrong with my eye, or why Sullen Rule is pinning me to a...bed.

This must be a bed. It's soft beneath me, and before, I was lying on something colder, harder.

I blink again and there is a blur along the inner corner of

my vision. It's a sensation more than a sight since it is so dark around me.

"Shh," Sullen whispers, his mouth along my cheekbone, his presence closer. His heart is pressed to mine. He is lying on top of me.

He is the weight, where the snake was.

I can feel my pulse rise up to pound with his, but his own is slower. The scent of darkened roses and earth surrounds me. *Soothes* me. I remember the wine, Sullen pushing his fingers into me before putting them in my mouth, the way he bit me, how he wanted me to be afraid.

His childhood horrors, which keep unspooling like a scattered roll of black thread.

I try to clear the film over my eye, Sullen's face so close I wouldn't be able to see anything even if it was light in here. The sharp sting is still there beneath my lash line; it was not just a part of my strange serpent slumber.

There is a loud, horrible whispering noise inside the room but just as I hold my breath to understand what it is, it quiets.

*It was me.*

My hands shake violently in Sullen's tight grip around my wrists, his body arching into mine as I shiver beneath him, the back of my neck damp with what I think is sweat.

"I am right here, Little Sun. It was only a dream."

I blink again, licking my dry lips, trying to think of a question to ask. Something to say. But with Sullen's mouth on my cheek, his hands pinning me to the bed, I find I don't want to say very much at all.

"I am going to turn on the light now." He says it cautiously, almost as if *he* is afraid of *me*.

I don't know why, just as I don't know how long I've slept. I vaguely remember stumbling into the bathroom, brushing my teeth, changing into a white pajama set I found in the drawers, then crawling into the bed, all as Sullen watched me silently after our fight.

I don't think I did anything terrifying.

But he slowly uncurls each finger from my wrist, then pushes away from me, his body weight dipping along the bed but never leaving me completely. Still, he shifts positions, his hip brushing mine as he sits beside me. Then I hear a faint click and dim, pale-yellow light floods the room.

I bring my fingers beneath my eye where it stings, my vision still strange, but as I do, Sullen turns from the nightstand to face me and I watch his jaw clench the moment before he captures my hand again, his bare fingers biting into my skin.

I freeze, blinking rapidly, trying to clear the smudge in my sight so I can see what has changed him.

"Do you want to hurt me, too?" he asks, his voice low and bitten with an edge I don't understand.

I swallow hard as I try to sit up, but he lowers his arm, still gripping my wrist and using his forearm to press on my chest, forcing me to stay down.

Irritation flares through me at the same time my mind snags on the snake keeping me restrained in my dream. *Serpent's Emporium.* The name of this store echoes through my head too, like a warning, but I can't hold onto the connection as Sullen twists his body to face me, leaning more weight against my chest.

"If you did this on purpose, I might take your eyes for it."

I blink rapidly, wanting to clear the spot from my vision, but before I can ask him what the *fuck* he's talking about, he reaches for me with his free hand and gently swipes his bare finger along my lash line.

I hiss between my teeth as he lifts his hand between us, drawing my focus.

Surprise jolts through me, waking me more, like cocaine paste injected into my veins.

*Blood.*

Viscous and red, seeping into the swirl of his fingerprint.

Oh, god.

*I'm bleeding.* That's why I can't see properly.

Panic lurches through me and I am no longer half-awake. I scramble upright, kicking at the damp sheets around my body. Sullen releases me and I dive over him, sliding along his lap before my bare soles hit the cool hardwoods of the Attic. I move so quickly I'm dizzy, my limbs tingling with a warning as my body feels faint, like I am on the verge of blacking out. More spots pop in front of my eyes as I get to the dresser, slamming my hands down on the wooden surface and leaning in, afraid to look but compelled to see.

I suck in a breath at the sight of a thick line of blood smeared at the corner of my eye, oozing a slow red path down the line of my nose.

"What the fuck?" I whisper it at the same time I catch sight of my throat, a purple and green bruise where Sullen bit me, but the skin there glistens, like it is coated in ointment. I remember his words, about wounds becoming infected, and for one brief moment I am not panicking. A flood of warmth surges through me, thinking of him doing what he said and taking care of me while I slept, probably finding a first aid kit somewhere in the Attic. *Maude* seems to have thought of everything.

But when I lift my eyes back to my reflection, blue irises edged out by blown pupils, I see the blood crawling along my face again and a tang of iron is bright on my tongue, and I am positive I am going to collapse.

My knees tremble beneath me, a dizziness flooding through my bloodstream and causing my chin to tilt downward, lolling toward my chest. Fuck, *fuck*. I'm going to faint.

I can no longer see and it isn't the blood; it's my blood pressure dropping. My palms are clammy and the blood is blurring my gaze and now that I know why, I feel worse, sick and waning, and—

Sullen's arm bands around my waist.

I didn't even notice him move, the way everything dims around me. But I do notice when his hand grips my throat, thumb pressing against the side of my neck as he lifts my head.

I blink, my body resting into his own, so much bigger than me, comforting, too, in this moment when I feel like I'm holding onto consciousness with a single thread.

I catch my gaze in the mirror, him looming over me, but only for a second before he dips his chin, and he forces me to arch mine. We are staring at one another upside down, his hand keeping my head tilted back, his arm wrapped tight around me and pulling me into his warmth.

Then he leans closer, bending over me, and I feel his tongue along my skin, just beneath my eye. He is cleaning the blood from my face.

A surge of adrenaline keeps me awake as I reach up with shaky fingers, curving them around his forearm, the one threaded over my chest, his hand still gripping my throat.

He licks me again, my eyes closed, skin warm where his tongue is, then cold as the air hits my flesh. A soft moan leaves his lips when he pulls back, only to press his mouth to the tip of my ear.

"You were whimpering in your sleep. I thought it was because I was trying to...touch you."

My legs feel boneless with those words; my deepest fantasy. My longed-for dream; Sullen taking advantage of me when I'm dreaming, lost in reverie, coming awake to him buried inside me, his hand over my mouth so I don't scream.

"But you started shaking. I thought I was doing something wrong. I wasn't inside you, but I was trying to make you... feel good." His mouth dances along my skin, his arm barred hard around my body, the other clamped over my throat.

I feel him growing hard behind me, his erection pressing into my back. He feels so *big,* and suddenly, I don't care I was apparently digging at my eye in my sleep. I don't care he just tasted my blood. I am *alive* again, no longer on the verge of fainting.

I want him more.

I want him now.

"You were dreaming, though, weren't you?" There is a marveling sort of tenderness in his throaty voice, and he must have seen from my reaction in the mirror I didn't intentionally hurt myself. "What was it, Little Sun?"

But before I can answer him, he pulls back and spins me around so easily, like I am his doll. My eyes flash open and I can see perfectly again as my back hits the dresser and he catches me with both of his hands wrapped around each of my wrists.

He lifts my right hand between us, my fingers slightly curled as he twists my wrist, my palms up.

There it is.

Blood beneath my index and middle fingers.

His gaze shoots up to mine as my heart thunders hard in my chest. I've never picked at myself in my sleep before. I don't know what happened. Maybe it was the dream, the serpent's tail near my eye.

Again, I think of the name of this store. The symbol of Writhe. It all feels too coincidental to be that at all. It's obvious, in our faces, and maybe that's why Sullen thought there was no connection. That, and his online girlfriend from years back drawing him in.

But I feel as if any moment we might be found. He will be dragged away from me.

He doesn't seem to be thinking the same thing as he runs his thumb along the underside of my nails. Despite my fears about being trapped inside a store of traitors, I want to examine his hands, trace all the scars, suck on his bare fingertips, particularly those without nails of his own, but he swallows hard, the sound audible between us, and my eyes lift to his as if I couldn't help it even if I tried.

He is focused on me. Intent as he traces his thumb along my fingertips, back and forth.

"If you ever hurt yourself intentionally with these," he whispers, squeezing my fingers tight in his grip, "I will bite them off."

I narrow my gaze even as my heart races, but before I can say anything back, there is a knock at our bedroom door.

# Chapter 31

## *Sullen*

"Like Maude said, you definitely don't want to leave tonight, man. Not if you've got anything to hide." The blond boy looks like a yellow lab in a brown polo shirt and khaki pants. But his eyes are red, his shaggy mane of blond hair flopped over one. He speaks slowly, giving me the impression he is in an altered state of mind. "Cops are crawling all over the place. I only live five blocks from here and I got stopped three times." His mouth falls open in what I think might be horror but instead an outlandish laugh leaves his lips and I smell it, then. Marijuana.

Stein and his guests used to get high sometimes in the parlor of our home. I was only drawn out to prove I was alive, every now and then. I often got the distinct feeling even Stein's kept company wished I wasn't.

"Besides, if you're here at the Emporium, well, we all got shit to hide, don't we, bro?" The blond boy leans forward, and I stiffen as he nudges his shoulder to mine. He is skinny and shorter than I am, perhaps my age, and I think briefly about breaking his scapula but instead I take a small step back on the first floor of the store.

There's a creak at the stairway leading up to the Attic and both the boy—I think he said his name was Fleet, but I don't know nor do I care—and myself look up.

Karia is clutching the handles of an old, velvet green bag for travel in her hand, and it seems fully packed, nearly bursting at the seams. She's dressed in black, high-waisted jeans and a cropped pink T-shirt that says *horror* in an oozing, bloody font of white across the front.

I know she had to have found it in the drawers and I am suspiciously amazed over how this building had something that suits her so perfectly.

Her blonde hair is up in a messy bun, tendrils framing her face, her cerulean eyes locked on mine as she descends the stairs in her white Vans. But beside me, *Fleet* or whatever method of transportation his name is, has his eyes on her.

Briefly, I think of when I lapped up her blood with my tongue. The taste of iron and metal made me strangely want her more; perhaps after years of being forced to eat the worst sort of creatures, she is divinity in comparison.

Regardless, I don't want Fleet gawking at her. I don't want her around anyone else at all. If it were up to me, she would stay locked upstairs.

Maude was at the door earlier, interrupting my hand around Karia's throat after the last two days of watching her sleep off the bottle of wine and the two sedative doses she should not have had. If they had been any closer together, or if Stein had used more, he could have put her permanently to sleep. But when I realized she was constantly still breathing, I couldn't keep my hands off her, touching her over her clothes in ways I have seen Cosmo de Actis do before.

It never got very far; guilt is foreign to me and yet feeling her nudge her body into mine when I would run my hand down her breasts made me nearly choke with lust and self-loathing both. For the fact I was taking advantage of her, *and* that I couldn't bring myself to do so much worse.

I knew it was time for us to leave tonight, though, and I thought of where we could go next as she slept. I also thought of simply leaving her; she will be okay if Writhe catches her, I tried to convince myself. But she hit Stein Rule over the head with a flashlight.

If *he* had any say in her punishment... I can't leave her. Not yet.

I assumed Maude was going to tell us it was time to "check out," but instead, she told us we should reconsider leaving tonight, because of the police activity in Alexandria.

She has no idea it must be all for us.

The Emporium is hosting a dinner, she said, and she invited us to it, mentioning a couch in a lounge room we could sleep on if necessary.

We are *not* staying here tonight but waiting a few more hours until Writhe gives up for sleep seems like a sensible idea. Then again, Stein keeps odd hours. Either way, I don't feel comfortable being in this place much longer.

Karia packed our things, took a few from the Attic at Maude's offer—Karia didn't speak to her at all—and I came down to ensure no one from Writhe came to the door.

It's where I ran into Fleet, who won't stop languidly speaking to me despite the fact I do not talk back. He's to show us the way to the basement dinner when Karia has joined us.

And a few more stairs and steps later, she has.

The cut beneath her eye from her fingernails is still there, but I see she must have found makeup in some of the Attic's drawers because it is barely visible now and she has eyeliner along her top lash line, flicking out into a sharp point at the corner of her eyes.

I want to drag my thumb across her lids and smear it all, but instead I stay where I am and take the bag from her hands. It is startlingly heavy; I hope Maude does not mind we took so much, but I'm not going to tell Karia to put anything back.

"Yo, you must be Karia. Maude told me about you before everyone else arrived." Fleet's voice is full of a smirk I can *hear* in his words.

*Everyone else.* I do not know who else is here, and I do not like the sound of those words.

Karia glances at him as I clench my gloved hands tighter around the bag. "And you are?" she asks, her voice polite but groggy.

My heart beats fast in my chest with her attention diverted away from me. I do not know when I started to believe she is *mine,* but the word seems to echo in every beat of my heart.

"Fleet." He extends his hand to her, and I glance at his trim nails, smooth skin. Not a single wound or even a callous to be found.

Karia starts to accept his offer, but I dart my own hand out and grab her wrist, pulling her toward me.

"We can find our way to the basement," I say quietly, turning to glare at Fleet's dopey blue eyes as he flicks his brows up, looking from me, to Karia, his hand still awkwardly extended.

"Are you sure? It's kinda creepy, the steps, you gotta be careful because there's no light and—"

I smile fully at him, revealing my teeth.

He stops talking, trailing off as he takes a single step backward. His gaze flicks to Karia once more and I can see his confusion. *Why are you with him? He is disgusting. You are beautiful. Come with me. I wear fucking polo shirts.*

I want to choke him with his polo but finally, he turns his back on us and heads deeper into the shop, giving only one last glance before he disappears into the darkness of the store.

Karia's pulse is beating quickly beneath my fingers on her wrist, even through the leather of my gloves.

I slowly turn to her and find she is staring up at me.

"You scared him."

It feels as if she kicked me in the stomach with those words, despite the fact that was my intention. I clench my teeth and release her, taking a step back in my high-tops. I glance at the locked door of the shop; Maude said everyone was already gathered at this fucking dinner. I hear sirens beyond the walls, and I know we cannot leave just yet but I desperately want to.

Karia will not like my interactions with others.

*I* don't like interacting with others at all. But holing away upstairs will seem more suspicious, Karia told me, and the room isn't ours any longer. Maude gave us enough, as is. I drop the bag by the door where it lands on the hardwoods with a heavy thud, and I don't say anything.

In my head, Karia is pressed up against me back in bed. In my head, I am a coward for not doing what I have wanted with her for so fucking long. But the horrible ideas in my brain over the years seem so difficult to enact with the truth of her. Soft and strangely sweet and running, *with me.*

It was easier to drug her at the hotel. To caress her nipple with a needle. Bite her skin. Because I hadn't seen what she would do for me then. But even with her loyalty briefly proven, I am afraid this is all a ruse, and I have just not discovered the twist yet. She cannot actually want me.

"Sullen."

I lift my gaze to hers.

She takes a step forward, lifting her bare hand to my chest, fingers softly curled along my emerald hoodie. Her cheekbones rise as she smiles slightly, her gaze dropping to my throat.

"I like this," she says, nodding toward the white bandana I tied around my neck. "A lot."

I put on a white T-shirt I found in the drawers, the same gray pants I bought from the mall, but there was nothing to hide my throat. A curious collection of bandanas was in one of the smaller drawers though, and it seems to work well enough.

But I cannot tell if she is mocking me now. My throat feels dry, my pulse pounding too hard where her fingers are along my hoodie.

Her smile falters with my silence and she slowly drops her hand, glancing at the floor. "We can't trust any of them," she says quietly, her tone harder now. She flicks her gaze up to mine, peering at me from beneath her lashes. "Not even your girlfriend."

At this, a warmth spreads through me that is hard to explain. Something light and overwhelming all at once.

"She isn't my girlfriend." *I've never had one of those.* "And I don't trust her."

"Yes, I know," she says softly, her pink lips articulating each word carefully as she arches a brow. "You don't trust anyone." Then she turns from me, heading deeper into the store. I glance at her ass, the perfect, slender roundness of it, the mass of her hair piled haphazardly on her head, the beauty of her cervical spine peeking beneath her pink shirt.

But just as she is about to slip past the welcome lounge into the shop, I stride forward, then grab onto her wrist, jerking her backward.

She spins around with a glare, pulling her arm away from me.

Reluctantly, I let her go.

"Promise me you won't...laugh with him," I say quietly, my voice hoarse in the darkness and quiet of the store. It's not really what I want to say, but I don't know how to articulate what I'm feeling.

Her brows wrinkle together, eyes narrowed, the faint cut at the corner of one starker with this expression. "What?" she asks, shaking her head once. "Laugh? With whom?"

I glance past her, into the darkness of Emporium. "Fleet." Saying his name is annoying.

Something softens in her features, her lips parting, brow smoothing out. Then she just says, with a small smirk, "I'll be on my best behavior if you are on yours."

# Chapter 32

## *Karia*

The stairwell is frightening. Pitch dark, the scent of wet cement and some sort of wicked incense both fill my nose and each step creaks as I slowly descend into what looks like a deeper well of darkness. There is no handrail and while Sullen is behind me, he does not reach out to help me keep my balance. Maybe he thinks I don't want him to touch me since I pulled away from his grip earlier. I wish he would, and yet... I cannot stop thinking of my dream. My nails against my eye. The blood streaming down my face.

Sullen, telling me he touched me in my sleep.

I do not remember it; I don't know how far he went.

Not far enough, but I don't think I should tell him that.

There was blood beneath my nails, and he seemed angry when he thought I hurt myself, but with Maude's words on the police searching for someone, the name of this store, and the strange turn of events leading us to a fucking *dinner* with a gangly blond boy named *Fleet,* everything feels...suspicious.

Even my hot childhood crush, at my back.

We continue down in silence, but as I reach a landing, I can see a faint red glow through a thick pane of frosted glass. There is the sound of music beyond, mainly bass as I can't make out lyrics or beats.

I reach out my hand for the doorknob, thinking of Sullen warning me not to laugh with Fleet. I think he meant *flirt,* and if it were anyone else—Cosmo, Von—I would've told them to fuck themselves. But there was something strangely endearing about the way Sullen tries to be possessive.

I push the thought aside and mentally prepare myself for who might be down here. Maude, Fleet, I don't know any of them by sight or name, but... what if this is some sort of elaborate trap, and I am walking right into it?

I'll run, if it is. We'll both run again.

I twist the ridged knob, cold beneath my fingers.

Then I push open the door and step inside a low-ceilinged, dark room.

The chatter that was taking place the second before I walked in falls silent, only the music playing in the background. I recognize the song. "Antichrist," by The 1975. For some reason, hearing it in this room with dark red lights strung along the ceiling, a burnished red, rectangular dining table taking up most of the space, a bar cart pulled close to the table, and snake spines pressed into glass hung up along the black walls, it feels oddly... creepy.

As I cast my eyes around the red velvet chairs set at the table, seeing Fleet, Maude, a pretty girl with pink hair, and a guy that looks eighteen with a baby face and black, tight curls, my unease grows, despite the fact I don't understand why. I am still standing in the doorway, preventing Sullen from fully stepping into the room. I check out the corners of the space and see a hallway that leads somewhere dark. Just as I start to spin around to scope out the walls to my right, there is a quiet, familiar voice in my ear.

"What the *fuck* are you doing here, Karia?"

235

# Chapter 33

## *Karia*

I startle, turning around to find Cosmo standing in the shadows beyond the door, too close to me.

Panic lodges itself in my throat, my chest rising up sharply, but I can't seem to get a breath. I release the handle of the door, glancing at the stairwell. At Sullen, watching me. But he can't see Cosmo because of the fact the door opens inward.

"Do you know the entire city is looking for you?" Cosmo says quietly, his voice smooth, brow raised, but there is wrath in his features. He's dressed casually; gray sweats and a black T-shirt, hands in his pockets. But his shoulders are rigid and for one crazed second, I wonder how much the back of his head is still swollen from where I hit him.

He steps closer, reaching out to wrench the door open further.

And I look to Sullen once more and notice the second he sees Cosmo.

And the heartbeat after, when Cosmo's eyes lift to Sullen.

For one moment, nothing happens.

There is only silence in the room.

I don't know if music is playing anymore.

I can feel everyone staring at us.

And I know I have to fix this.

So I step forward, grabbing Cosmo's arm, feeling his warm skin beneath my fingers as his eyes cut back to me.

"Hi," I say quietly, forcing myself to smile even though I am trembling all over.

His gaze dips to below my eye and his olive complexion pales, his lean jaw clenched.

"Can I...speak to you?" I keep my voice soft, but my pulse is pounding so hard, it's making my entire body shake.

"You are," Cosmo says, the words threatening. I can feel heat radiating off him, the bones in his arm stark against his skin with how tightly coiled he is.

I flash him a smile with teeth. "Alone?"

But a shadow falls over me, and I feel Sullen's body brush up against mine before Cosmo can reply.

Slowly, Cosmo turns his head, regarding the man he knows drugged him. His eyes flash as he says, very softly, "I'm going to fucking kill you."

It feels like there's cotton in my ears and my mouth is so dry, but I know I have to salvage this. With an audience, with cops crawling the streets, with Cosmo here, we can't run. Not right now. Not yet.

So when Cosmo takes a step toward Sullen, I squeeze myself between them. I feel Sullen against my spine, but I don't release Cosmo.

"Please," I whisper, searching my friend's eyes. "Can we please talk?"

Sullen's hand comes to the back of my neck as I'm caught between them in this red-tinted room. He curls his gloved fingers around my bones.

Cosmo's expression shifts to disgust.

Sullen's voice comes to my ear. "Stop. Touching. Him."

I drop Cosmo's arm immediately, and I reach back,

brushing my fingers over Sullen's core, trying to reassure him without words.

"We need to talk," I reiterate to Cosmo. "You know we do." I try not to beg, but I am not beneath it, if it means saving Sullen.

Cosmo drags his gaze back to mine. I think, for a moment, he is going to disagree. He is going to lunge for Sullen, or maybe just me.

But after a second, he nods once, then says, "We can talk, but I am not letting you walk out of this building with *him.*"

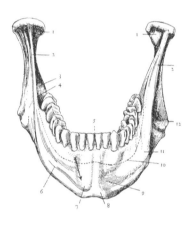

*but I am rather the fallen angel, whom thou*
*divest from joy for no misdeed.*

— *Frankenstein*, Mary Shelley

# Chapter 34

## *Karia*

I climb the winding steps up the hotel with a Poco Grande glass in hand as I cast my eyes around the chandeliers overhead, then the darkened hallways before me, unnerved by the quiet of such a vast space.

I glance down at my piña colada like it is a companion, then lower my head and sip from the paper straw. The icy blend of pineapple juice and coconut milk alongside the rum spills down my throat and it doesn't fit the season, but this has always been a favorite of mine. Perks of having a bartender mostly to yourself; I can coerce him to create anything, anytime.

October first, and despite my drink, it feels like Halloween here, even if Writhe has no taste and has decorated nothing. As it is, my parents are in Septem with Mads Bentzen and others, waiting for Stein Rule to emerge from some part of the hotel, and neither Cosmo, Von, nor Isadora are here. All three of them are working, even if they're doing different jobs.

I am twenty-one, alone, too sober, and very fucking bored.

My mind drifts to Sullen Rule as it always does when I am this way, and as I reach the second floor of the hotel, turning to drift aimlessly down the darkened, silent halls in my black lace dress that *drips off my shoulders and reaches the floor, I wonder if he is somewhere in No. 7.*

*I wonder, if now that we are older and I have fucked two men, giving me a little experience, I could coerce him to kiss me.*

*My cheeks heat at just the thought, imagining his dark eyes and brown hair, the intensity in which he stares at me, with his hood pulled over his head. Hot. I would get to my knees just to see him without his shirt on because his signature sweatshirt is hiding a broad, muscular body. Even all the extra clothes he wears cannot fully conceal that.*

*As I'm lost in thoughts of daydreaming about a boy I know I will never have, a thump sounds to my left and I jump, skittering away from the door, my heart thumping too fast in my chest.*

*For something to do and maybe for liquid courage, I take a huge gulp of my drink, flexing my cold fingers around the icy glass and letting the sweetness explode on my tongue as I stare at the room in front of me.*

*Number 234.*

*The hotel is closed to the public as it often is, since Stein called this meeting.*

*No one should be here.*

*I suppose the cleaning staff could be in, tidying up, but... Maybe I didn't hear a thing. Perhaps it's the spooky season and the rum getting to me, or maybe the desire I have to feel* something.

*Life is passing me by and I'm standing still, and I don't know what I want, who I should be, and I am very rich and very bored and too spoiled and it feels like I am waiting around for my parents to marry me off because I'm that pathetic.*

*I glance at the space between the door and the marble floor, and at first, I see nothing. I'm about to continue my aimless stroll, my yearning for Sullen, when* there.

Right there.

*A shadow.*

*Footfalls.*

*I suck in air, flattening myself against the door at my back which might be a terrible idea because if 234 is occupied, perhaps this one behind me is too and some serial killer will open the door and slice my throat and I'll bleed out all over the hallway and Sullen will find me too late.*

*But before I can move to avoid such a fate, I hear a whimper.*

*Like... sniffling.*

*Someone... crying.*

*The shadow grows closer to the door.*

*My heart is erratic, and I have to tighten my grip on the drink in my hand lest I drop it and give myself away.*

*I glance down at my black boots, the baby pink laces suddenly seeming so very much like a dead giveaway. No one else in Writhe wears shit like this. Not even my mother.*

*Whoever is in there will know I'm here.*

*Unless... My parents were waiting for Stein. They all were. Maybe he has some sort of little experiment happening behind these doors? A torture session?*

*Stein gives me the creeps, but I couldn't say why.*

*As it is, I don't move.*

*I don't breathe.*

*The shadow falls closer, blocking any hint of light beneath the door.*

*Then I see something that makes my stomach turn, but I'm not even quite sure what I'm looking at.*

*It seems to be...an eye.*

*The pupil is so large, there is no iris to be found.*

*Only blackness and the whites, swiveling around frantically as if searching for something. Someone.*

*Fingertips tap against the base of the door.*

*It must be a person, but it looks so disembodied, this single eye visible under the crack.*

*The whimper sounds again, strange and distorted, like maybe their mouth is sewn shut or...*

Get the fuck out of here, Karia. Fuck this. Run.

*For some reason, I don't want to. Especially as that swiveling eye with the blown pupil looks onto me, and I swear I hear them pleading inside my head.*

Save me.

Just open the door.

I'm right here.

*But I am pathetic.*

*I don't stay.*

I fucking run.


"Here." Cosmo thrusts a black plastic cup toward me, full of blood-red punch from a bowl set upon a dark table topped with platters of hors d'oeuvre in skeleton-painted black serving trays. Chocolate-covered pretzels and shrimp cocktail and black bean dip and ghost-shaped marshmallow dessert. Despite my nerves, my stomach grumbles and I think about grabbing a handful of all of it and stuffing it in my mouth just so I don't have to carefully talk my way out of this predicament with Cosmo.

I reach for the cup, our fingers brushing for a moment and his green gaze catches mine as the music changes in the dining room. *This* space is off to the side of the main basement. It must have once been or is still partially used as a cold storage room. It's freezing in here and I don't think it's meant to host eclectic dinner parties that play sultry bass beats, but Serpent's Emporium has a lot of fucking surprises.

Including Cosmo de Actis's presence.

He quickly explained to Maude we all knew each other but were meeting tonight by surprise, and he didn't elaborate on our *friendships*. No one in the strange group seemed too inclined to ask further questions as Sullen reluctantly left me to speak alone with Cosmo.

I think everyone here tonight is keeping their own secret.

I bring the punch to my lips, catching the scent of cherries and bourbon. I only take a small sip, knowing it's been a long time since I had food and soon, Sullen and I will need to fucking run again.

As the ice-cold punch freezes my throat while warming my belly, I turn to glance into the main dining room, just past the entranceway to this dim space, red lights the only glow in here, too.

Sullen is between Maude and the pink-haired girl, his chin tipped down, hands in his lap. The women lean in close to him with dizzying smiles. I think I even see a corner of Sullen's mouth tip upward as Maude says something I can't hear, and I clench my fingers tight around the black cup in my hand.

Just then, as my heart races and I try to fight back my own jealousy, Sullen's dark eyes lift to mine and our gazes lock.

The half-smile on his full mouth disappears.

I lift my chin, take another drink as I keep my eyes on his, then wink at him before I turn away without waiting for his reaction.

A giddiness runs through me that is out of place tonight, but I can't help it. This new bond between us makes me feel...dizzy.

"What the fuck is wrong with you, Karia?" Cosmo's tone is ice. He finishes off his own punch, then crumples the cup in his hand. The plastic breaks, a jagged piece pushing into his palm, but he doesn't seem to notice or care.

Cosmo and I went to the same private high school. I've known him for years, and he's usually easygoing and relaxed, always with a smile on his face.

But I suppose nearly knocking him out with a flashlight and running away with a guy who drugged him might have shifted his attitude toward me a little.

"You do understand the entirety of Writhe is looking for

244

you. Cops are *crawling* the streets. Even if I were inclined to *let you* leave, you'd be found in seconds." He stares down at me with hard eyes, his back to the small table of food. For a brief moment, I want to upturn the entire thing. Dump the bowl of punch on his fucking head and run with Sullen from the chaos.

But although I have no desire to rule Writhe or even work within it, being raised by parents profiting from underground crime taught me a lot of things, including how to negotiate. *Weapons come last,* I've heard my mom say more than a few times.

"Say something," Cosmo snarls, his gaze narrowed as he takes a step toward me, veins in his hands bulging under his skin. "You *hit me* with a fucking *flashlight,* Karia. For that freak." He jerks his chin toward the dining room, and I pray Sullen can't hear a word he just said.

As it is, *I* heard it.

I step closer too until I'm forced to look up higher to meet his eye. "Don't call him that," I say quietly, my teeth clenched. I squeeze my fingers around the cold drink in my hand, a shiver running down my spine and not just from the punch or the cold temperature of the room. Anger is hot in my blood, but I'm sweating, the contrast between it all freezing me to the bone.

"*What?*" Cosmo's mouth falls open, and he genuinely looks shocked. "You don't think you should say *sorry?* You don't think you owe me a fucking *explanation,* Karia?" He hisses my name, dipping his chin so he's closer to me, both of us leaned in toward one another like two snakes coiled up and ready to strike. "What did he do to you, huh?" He glances at my eye and I know he sees the cut I tried to hide with new makeup samples I found in the Attic. His jaw clenches as he studies it, then he says, "I'm going to kill him, you get that, right?"

"Why are you even here? How do you know about this place?" Maybe I've answered none of his questions, but I don't care. This all feels very distinctly like a setup, save for the fact Cosmo doesn't work for Writhe.

The thought occurs to me that perhaps it's not a trick for Sullen, but for me. My muscles tense and I squeeze the cup in my hand, hearing the plastic crinkle. Maybe I should be running for an entirely different reason than protecting Sullen. After all, he might have carried me out of the hotel but before that, it's not as if he treated me kindly. Then again... *Kind* is not what I want.

"Nah," Cosmo says bitterly, clenching his jaw. "I'm not giving you shit until you tell me why you chose him over me *and* say you're sorry."

"I'm not sorry." The words are tangled in my chest, but I push them out as I watch Cosmo's brows lift, his complexion flushing with the same anger I feel. "You were going to hit him. You don't know him at all. You don't know half the shit he's been through—"

"So a little sob story got him in your pants? I didn't know you were so fucking easy, Karia." He steps closer, his chest heaving, hands by his sides, the cup still splintered in one. "He's fucked up, yeah, but you know what?" He flicks his gaze up and down my body. "So are you, if you'd trust him before me. He might be in your parents' little cult club, and I might not belong there, but that doesn't make the two of you fucking friends. *I'm* your goddamn friend." He lifts his hand, the one holding the cup, and points to himself, his index finger against his chest. I see a shallow well of blood along his middle finger from the plastic of the cup, sliding down toward the web of his fingers, but I say nothing about it as I lift my eyes back to his.

"Then you'll let me go. And you'll trust I know what I'm doing."

"Karia." He says my name on a sigh as he shakes his head, rolling his eyes for a second before he focuses on me again. "Even though you fucking *hit me,* I mean this respectfully; you don't know *shit* about the real world. You can't run from the cops, your parents, all of Writhe. Von, Isadora, you know, your *other* friends? You're not gonna get away from them. You're spoiled and pampered, and you've never had a job in your fucking life. You spend your days shopping and painting your nails and watching movies in your home fucking theater and driving aimlessly in your BMW and moping around while Von and Isadora actually do something with their lives. You let me get you drunk and *fuck* you and you don't care what I do to you as long as you can't fight back. You're kind of pathetic and you're just waiting around for Mommy and Daddy to find some asshole cult member to sell you off to so you can suck his dick while he does the important shit."

For a moment, I have no control over my facial expression. I'm not entirely sure what I do, if I'm even breathing.

All of that vitriol cut to the quick of my worst fears. That I'm not valuable, that I'm nobody, useless, weak, pathetic, disposable, *unseen.*

The same way my mother looks at me. How my father coddles me because he knows I'm not a real threat to anyone, or anything. Once upon a time, I told him I wanted to be a teacher, thinking it was important because *my* teachers were important to me. I glowed with pride when I got something right in class and I became a favorite. I thought the goal might give my parents some honor to place in me. But Dad only smiled and clamped his hand gently on my shoulder, his fingers lightly tapping my back in a patronizing way every child experiences at least once in their life and he said, *"We'll see, honey. Writhe might have a better use for you."*

I was twelve.

And I knew then what *use* I might one day have.

Bows in my hair, ballet slippers on my feet because I liked how they looked, braces on my teeth, and still... I knew my worth then, to Writhe. To my own parents. Turns out, I'm not worth anything more to my friends.

"Shit, Karia, I didn't—" Cosmo starts.

*"Don't."* It doesn't even sound like me saying the word. It's my voice, I'm looking at Cosmo's shadowed eyes, red glinting off the whites of them from the lighting, but mentally, it's as if I am far away from this moment.

I don't even know what the hell it is I'm supposed to do here anymore. Convince my *friend* to let me and Sullen escape? To where? For what? I don't know how to run; Cosmo was right about that. I don't know anything. I will only hold Sullen down. He really could survive on his own; he has already lived through so much. He's intelligent and crafty and cunning and terrible and he deserves to have a life without the threat of Stein Rule or Writhe hovering over his head.

I will drag him down.

I am like a child; someone who needs to be taken care of.

I am not for him.

"Karia, I just... You *hurt* me, and I don't mean physically. I thought... Despite what your parents have insinuated, those talks we've had about it, I thought maybe you could choose *me,* and..." Cosmo pauses, glancing down.

I am still frozen. I don't know what I feel. What I think.

I take another drink.

Another.

I feel suddenly so incredibly *stupid* for being here. For dragging all of Writhe upon Sullen. If I had let him escape alone, maybe Stein would have tried to hush it up and look for him more quietly. Maybe he would have already been so far away, he would be out of reach.

I drink more.

Icy sludge slides down my throat.

"Fuck it," Cosmo says quietly, then he drops his empty cup to the ground, the one that cut him, and he reaches for me, the girl who hurt him. He grabs my wrist, then jerks me forward, punch sloshing from my cup and running icy rivulets down my hand. Before I can think or breathe or get my bearings, Cosmo's fingers tangle in my hair and he leans down, then presses his cold lips to mine.

I am aware of one thing.

The volume of the dining room.

Aside from the sensual music playing in the background, there is no light chatter. No hushed laughter. No sounds of utensils on plates.

There is nothing.

"Open your mouth for me," Cosmo says against my lips. His own mouth is so familiar. He has traced every inch of my body with his tongue, his fingers. We have been fucking one another casually for years, and he is the only person who knows my darkest fantasies. I joked about it once to Von and Isadora, but I don't think they believed me, the way I like to be violated when I'm intoxicated or sleeping, maybe both.

But Cosmo knows.

*"You're kind of pathetic and you're just waiting around for Mommy and Daddy to find some asshole cult member to sell you off to so you can suck his dick while he does the important shit."*

No matter what he fucking knows, *that's* what he said to me.

That I'm *kind of* pathetic.

"Open for me, Karia." His fingers are in my hair and his hand is still around my arm.

*Go fuck yourself for me, Cosmo.* I twist my arm free, lift my cup up, then dump it down his back, wiping the knuckles of my hand along his shirt the second after, from where punch got on my skin after he grabbed me.

He sucks in a breath as he pulls back immediately, letting me go. He yanks at his shirt, his brows dug in, eyes narrowed into slits on me, jaw clenched.

But before he can say a word as he glares at me with my

empty cup in hand by my side, dripping punch onto the cement floor, someone else speaks at my back before stepping closer, their arm brushing my shoulder.

"What did he just say to you?"

My pulse slams harder inside my chest. Sullen is standing beside me but he is looking at Cosmo so blankly, I'm frightened for my friend.

Only... I'm not so sure he is that anymore. Is he?

I glance at Cosmo's hand by his side, the one with blood along his middle finger. More of it snakes across his nail now, then drops off to the dark cement floor.

I take a breath in, icy air from the cold room frosting my lungs. Sullen is so still beside me and when I turn my head to look at him, I see his lips are curved upward into some strange sort of smile.

"He said a lot of stupid things," I answer Sullen, trying to grasp his attention again. "But mostly he said he's going to let us leave quietly." I cut my gaze to Cosmo. "Didn't you?" I ask, arching my brow.

But Cosmo is grinning at Sullen, and it isn't a nice smile. "No. That's not what I said at all. But you're right. I did say a lot of stupid things. What I really meant was, *leave the freak alone, and let me fuck you again.*"

I drop my cup and grab for Sullen's arm. It seems the wisest thing to do, my hand wrapped over his hard bicep, his muscles tense beneath my fingers. My heart is galloping inside my chest, so fast it's hard to breathe.

I open my mouth, wanting to cut at Cosmo, the way he just tore Sullen down, but before anything comes out, I see Sullen's face.

And he's looking at me now.

I suddenly feel incredibly stupid I'm holding onto his arm like I thought... What? That he would attack Cosmo for kissing me? Punch him for the words he just spoke about fucking me?

My face flushes hot and I wish I hadn't poured my drink down Cosmo's back because the alcohol might help ease the embarrassment flaring warm in my cheeks.

Sullen is *smiling* at me. Lips closed but eyes shining, dark brows lifted from under his brown hair and that hood over his head.

"You can let go of me now, Karia," he says, and I feel a small stab of pain somewhere near my heart that he didn't call me *Little Sun*.

Slowly though, I unfurl my fingers from his taut muscles, then I retract my hand.

"Maude insists we stay for her dinner." Sullen speaks in his beautiful croaky voice but his tone throws me. Incredibly even and steady and...mildly pleasant.

His pupils are wide, edging out the brown and amber of his irises, and the red lights cast a demonic sheen along the sharp curve of his cheekbones but otherwise... he looks strangely happy.

"Oh?" I manage to choke out. When I run my tongue over my bottom lip because my mouth is so very dry, Sullen traces the movement with his gaze but then he's looking back at my eyes. "Does she?" I try to hide the confusion and irritation—about his reference to Maude—from my voice, but I fail miserably.

He seems to notice, the way he tilts his head, and his smile widens, almost revealing his teeth. "She does," he says carefully. Then he turns to face Cosmo, and nothing in his expression changes as he adds, "I'll meet you two back at the table?" He glances at me once more. "And I brought our bag down to the bottom of the stairs. Just in case one of us needs to leave in a hurry." The way he says it, I feel as if he means...*me*.

Then he walks away without once looking back, taking his seat beside Maude once more.

"Fuck this. Fuck all of this," I say, the confusion threaded through my tone, forcing sporadic words out. I turn back to Cosmo, who is watching me with the same skepticism in his gaze. "I don't care if he wants to stay. I'm leaving." I don't mean it. I won't leave without Sullen. But... I expected him to react so differently. And I am crushingly disappointed he didn't. Am I just *a* girl to him? He said himself he's never been with anyone. Perhaps since I was the first girl he was close to, he unintentionally made me feel special when all I really am is something new. Now he's chatting with Maude and the pink-haired girl. He has options. And perhaps I'm no longer one. As long as he doesn't have to be found, maybe he doesn't care who he gets lost with.

"No." Cosmo shakes his head once and I glance at the blood still slowly streaking down his finger. "You're not. You're going to sit your ass down at that table, you're going to drink with me, and you're going to tell me right now if he did that, to your eye. If he hurt you, in any way. Because he doesn't seem to care I just tried to kiss you so I'm wondering what else he doesn't care about with you." He steps close, looking down at me. "You know, like your safety."

"You're so fucking concerned about me, so angry, and yet here you are playing tea party. Tell me now, why the fuck are you even here, huh?" I deflect from everything else he said about Sullen not caring for me. I don't want to think of all the things I let happen to me with him and yet I still ran away by his side.

Fucking. Stupid.

"The entire hotel was searched. We found Stein Rule. Then, they sent me home." Cosmo glares at me. "Your parents and Mads Bentzen. Obviously I still looked for you. I found your phone—it's dead, by the way—and searched our usual places. Coffee shop, that little luxury store you like with all the fucking ribbons and bows, the theater. Obviously, you weren't there. I stopped by here for word on you, not really expecting I'd find it.

But I know this is one of the only places in the city you could hide in plain sight."

I furrow my brow. "How do *you* know of this place? Who even are these people?"

"The girl with pink hair?" He jerks his chin toward the table. "That's Alivia. She has the same job as I do. She—"

"Performance artist. Yes. I know what you do, Cosmo. And Fleet? And the other guy? *Maude?*"

Cosmo smiles cruelly. He can sense my jealousy. "This is my life apart from you. You have Writhe, I have my work. They all have helped in some of my acts here and there. Fleet is a wild-card. His parents are rich as fuck, both lawyers, and he's caught somewhere in between. Elliot is set to head to Harvard next fall but he's rebelling a little in his gap years until that happens."

"You know all of these people and I've never even heard of them." The feeling of being tricked is back, slithering down my spine like the snake did across my torso. I just don't understand who is deceiving me.

"When's the last time you came to watch me perform?" he shoots back.

It's been years. Most of his performances are around NYC, but if I really wanted to go, I could.

"Exactly," he says in a low tone. "While you were fucking around with Von in a past life and going to all this Writhe shit you don't even like, I've come here."

"But... They don't know about Writhe, do they?"

Cosmo shakes his head. Behind me, I hear Maude laugh and there's a sinking feeling in my stomach. "Nor you. Writhe is against everything Maude stands for. She's an artist, through and through. I imagine you've been staying in the Attic. It's for people in trouble. Anyone, no questions asked."

"That still doesn't explain why you're here when allegedly, you've been worried about me. You said it yourself. You didn't expect to find me here."

He steps closer, his nostrils flaring. I see red punch just under his black shirt, along his shoulder and I know it's growing sticky on his skin, but I don't say a word, definitely not to apologize.

"I get the best of both worlds in some ways," he says quietly, watching me. "I hear what you want to whisper about Writhe, and I hear everything everyone else wants to whisper *around* them. Maude may not know them by name, but everyone understands it's the corrupt who own this city." Cosmo tilts his head. "And it's Stein Rule who owns Hotel Number Seven, hiding his name behind a corporation. But there was another Number Seven, before the one you hit me at, did you know that? The *original* hotel, before the company built multiples, maybe to deflect from their sordid little history?"

*No. I didn't know that.*

He leans even closer, his mouth going to my ear. "Word is the worst sorts of people flocked to that one for dinners not too different from these. A think tank of serial killers, rapists, murderers, thieves. It was *Maude* who told me about the original, years ago. Of course, she has no idea Stein Rule is the owner, or that I know him. And she has no idea *Scully* is his abominable son. I came here to see if you had found the city's safe place, or if Maude knew what exactly happened to that sick little club that used to meet at the original Number Seven before we were ever born, thinking maybe Sullen took you there for some kind of torture fest. She hadn't gotten around to telling me any details when *you* showed up, and I think it must be divine fucking timing. You're going to sit down at this dinner, and you're going to listen. And when it's over, you'll see Sullen Rule is just as fucked up as his father and the rest of the family that came before them. And I promise you, I won't break his neck for drugging me or you, not yet, not now, because I think the worst thing would be for you to see how bad he is yourself."

His lips graze my ear and my spine crawls, but I don't move. "Then you can *thank me* for saving your life."

I jerk back from him, narrowing my gaze. I curl my hand into a fist and have the vicious urge to launch it into his face. "So all you've really been doing is looking for more dirt on Sullen? That's extremely helpful in finding me, Cosmo. What a fantastic friend. Excellent search party, asshole."

"You *hit me* with a flashlight, Karia."

I step forward, getting in his face as I stand on my tiptoes. "And I would do it again," I snarl. "Why did you bother with this? Why do you even care at all, after that shit you just said about me, huh?"

His eyes flick over my body, and I'm very aware my nipples are two tight points from the chill of the cold room. A salacious, cruel smile curves his lips. "That's why."

I launch my fist toward him but turn it into an open palm at the last second, slamming my hand against his sternum so hard his body jolts and brushes against the snack table, punch sloshing precariously up the sides of the bowl.

I know I can't full-on fight him because I still need him to let us escape, but whether I knocked him out before or not, he deserved that.

"I'm going to sit down at this stupid dinner not because you told me to, but because I know you'll stab me in the back if I don't. Just to be clear, you are *never* fucking me again." Then I put my back to him and head toward the table.

# Chapter 35

## *Karia*

"Burbank is dead," Maude says in the dark red room, a glass of blood-colored wine in her manicured hand. Her nails are black talons, eyeshadow smoky gray, lashes false. And she looks like an ethereal dream with her pale white skin in a black silk gown looped with blood-red crystals. Everyone here is dressed in the strangest way, nothing coordinating or indicating what kind of attire is expected at this *dinner.*

The pink-haired girl, Alivia—brown skin, red lips, golden eyes—is dressed in expensive denim and a white baby doll tank top. Elliot, sitting to my right, has on basketball shorts and a yellow T-shirt that says *No* in a dark academia-type font. My baby pink crop top and high-rise jeans fit in, but I almost wish I wore the dress Sullen bought me from Saks because I don't seem to be stealing his attention like *Maude* does.

If anyone suspects the tension between me, Cosmo, and Sullen is wound so tightly it might strangle all of us, no one acts like it. Perhaps it has to do with the wine flowing freely, bottles scattered now in the center of the table, all plates put away as everyone finished eating while Cosmo and I argued. Or it could be the heavy cloud of marijuana coming from Fleet, on the other side of Elliot, his only contribution to the conversation a few too-loud guffaws of laughter. Or even the tab I saw Alivia discreetly place on her tongue as Maude sloshed everyone another glass of wine. I wouldn't mind some LSD myself; it feels like I'm tripping as is.

I grip my Riesling glass tightly, glancing at the silver skeleton hand wrapped around it beneath my fingers, part of the decoration. I've drank little since Cosmo excused himself to mop up the punch I poured on him and I came back to sit awkwardly at the table across from Sullen, who barely glanced at me.

Maude is delighted he's here. Beside her. I can see it in the way her eyes shift to him every few heartbeats, her hands waving dramatically as she speaks, the poised goth queen morphing into someone more open and friendly as she drinks, but she still remains incredibly eloquent. She owns this shop. Hosts these dinners. Knows this history of some dead guy named Burbank Gates—a guest at the original No. 7; someone I've never heard of—and Sullen seems to be holding onto her every word. He can't stop staring at her, his posture a little rigid, hands in his lap, dark eyes enraptured as she speaks.

"Cosmo wanted to discuss all the notorious criminals the original Hotel has hosted over the past hundred and fifty years or so, but Burbank Gates was one of the most loyal and still, in my opinion, the most fascinating. He cultivated enough of a following that many people still believe in his promises. He was a man of science, you know, and that holds weight." Maude winks at us like she doesn't think it should, then she takes another drink, glancing up through her lashes at Sullen. "Since the current owner of the small chain of Number Seven hotels is shrouded in mystery, we have no way of knowing if *they* know this unsavory past." She sounds like she's narrating a podcast as she speaks so dramatically. "But some say his ghost prowls the original location, and his followers still stalk the streets of Alexandria, snatching up unsuspecting victims found in dark alleys."

Cosmo snorts beside me. He leans back in the red velvet chair, cocking his head as he watches Maude. "Do you think his *followers*—must be only like, two, give or take—are responsible for the heavy number of missing persons in Alexandria?"

I stiffen but say nothing. I don't know if Cosmo is trying to hint that perhaps *Sullen* is intending to make *me* go missing for this Burbank Gates's religion, but I wouldn't ever believe that. Besides, the fact Cosmo is keeping a secret on Sullen's connection to the hotel is enough for me to keep quiet, for now.

Maude sets down her glass, eyes bright with wine as she looks to Cosmo with a smile on her red lips. "It was you who thought we should chat about the hotels. Maybe you should tell me what you think since this is your unexpected contribution to tonight's dinner."

Sullen cuts his eyes to Cosmo, who glances at me. He lifts one shoulder in the mock display of a lazy shrug, holding my gaze even as he speaks to Maude. "I don't know a fucking thing. I was just...feeling *curious* tonight. Tell me more about this *Burbank Gates.*"

"Feeling curious?" Her eyes linger for a moment on Cosmo, and a chill glides down my spine in the red-tinted room. What if we've been found out? Cosmo knows too much, and now I realize I should've never let him in so close. My parents often remarked upon it with disapproval, how much he knew about Writhe. But I'm positive he's done some work with lower-level organizations before—Mads said he did a job for him specifically—and I assumed he understood how to keep a secret because of all of his own.

It's too late to take any of it back now, though.

"Okay, Mr. Cryptic," Maude continues, and I'm relieved there's true amusement in her words. "Well, Burbank Gates believed if you tortured a human being long enough, physically made them appear *inhuman,* you would have immortality."

I stiffen, my gaze going to Sullen.

He isn't looking at me, that placid smile on his face as he stares at Maude. But I remember what he said. That Stein was deconstructing him. Visiting a prognosticator to find out the best date for his death. That he had peculiar belief systems. For *this?* Immortality? Is this the man Stein Rule worships?

"That... makes no fucking sense," Cosmo says, his tone light but his eyes serious as he looks at Maude. "Transmutation? Is that what Burbank was getting at? Some sort of alchemy?"

"The devil buys souls," Elliot says from beside me, voice casual but the words make me shiver. "Maybe he takes other people as payment, too?"

"You're very close. But it's not the soul," Maude presses on. "It's not the body, the blood. It's not transmutation." She glances at Cosmo. "Not exactly. It's the idea that you can be so corrupt, so heinous, so godawful as to reduce a human to nothing but the body, essentially obliterating the soul, that you rise above the empathy innate in most human beings and therefore shed the constraints of humanity, and mortality. Burbank believed sadistic serial killers who toyed with their victims achieved this rather easily. In other words, they didn't become immortal *because* they murdered; they weren't offering sacrifices to Satan for some mythological longevity. They were creating it for themselves by stripping the morality from their core. Now, Burbank's followers differed on what came next. Some believed you let the body die its natural death, or in the case of murderers, *unnatural* death. Others, who didn't like the idea of serial killers outdoing them, that you needed the subject to see *you* as their creator. Burbank called his major manifesto *The Scientist,* which supported that idea. You created the experiment. The mind fuck of breaking someone down so much that they worship you, that's what gave you true power.

Then you could stitch them back together in your own making and dispose of them when you chose. Then, you are God. And God never dies."

Something like thunder seems to roll above our heads, in the shop.

I flinch, my gaze once more going to Sullen.

And this time, he's looking back at me.

"Truthfully, you're right, Cosmo. His work made little sense," Maude continues as Sullen holds my gaze. "He contradicted himself at every turn. In his haste to find god-like life, he wasted his own going down random rabbit holes and killing off his family to chase his high. I think he was little more than a serial killer himself and the science of dismembering people got him off."

"What do you think, *Scully?*" Cosmo drawls, using the name he first heard Maude say, pretending for everyone else that Sullen didn't drug him, or me, and that I didn't hit him over the head to run away. We're all holding onto our secrets in tight fists, and I have a feeling before the night is over with, they're going to come out in ways we don't want. "You buy any of this shit?"

I glare at Cosmo, but he still doesn't mention Stein or Writhe, and for that, I'm glad.

Yet before Sullen is put on the spot, someone else speaks up.

"I don't think any of this is true," Fleet says with amusement in his words. "I don't understand how Burbank's bullshit is still being touted as truth to *anyone,* but obviously it's all garbage. And I don't think that's why anyone is going missing *here.* We're only talking about this because Cosmo wanted to, but what the fuck does Burbank have to do with our city now? Homelessness, the housing shortage, drug addiction, mental illness, those types of things? You know, real problems? That's the issue Alexandria is dealing with."

"He's right," Elliot chimes in, glancing at his wine. "This city is crazy, but Burbank Gates had no traction. I know a little about him. He was raised by militant Christian parents, became a scientist who really wanted to be a cult leader and realized Christianity wasn't the way to go for it."

"Then why do we still talk about him?" Alivia asks, leaning in toward Sullen in a way that makes me want to scream. There is a strange smile curling her lips that I think has everything to do with the acid she dropped. "And why hide the information?" I don't know what she means by that, but no one interrupts her. "He's not supremely influential but here we are, discussing him."

Elliot shakes his head. "Yeah, only because we're *us.*"

"Where did you learn of him?" Sullen asks, his voice so much more jagged than everyone else's. Each person's eyes flick to him at the sound and I grip the stem of my wine glass tighter, wanting them to back off, even with their gazes. "Why the personal interest? How do you know so much?" he continues, and he's staring directly at Maude as if she holds all the answers to even his unspoken questions.

Maude spins her own wine glass on the table, smiling as she glances up at Sullen, like she's so fucking delighted he asked. But he is silent, and she pivots a little in her chair, leaning over and plucking up a large leather bag from the floor, studded with metal in places. She thunks it on the table and pulls out a manila envelope, then drops the bag to the ground once more. Flicking open the envelope, she retrieves a few papers and spreads them on the table, pushing one over to Sullen.

"When Cosmo told me what he was so *curious* to learn about tonight, I retrieved these files from the back room of the Emporium. They're not freely accessible. But Alivia is affiliated with someone who can fetch locked away history in the library at Alexandria U."

261

I glance at Alivia as she looks down at the table, her eyes strangely darkening. I wonder if she knows someone in Writhe, or maybe higher up.

Maude is still looking at Sullen, and when she speaks next, it's with unexpected gentleness. "I remember you were always so averse to religion and any kind of ensuing cult talk, Scully," she continues. "I wondered if you might hate our topic tonight."

I bite the inside of my cheek to keep from speaking.

"Wait," Cosmo says, nudging me with his elbow.

I want to break it.

"You two know each other?" He flicks his fingers between Sullen and Maude as he laughs a little and I want to strangle him.

"From years back," Maude says primly, a secretive smile on her lips. "I'm fascinated that you two are friends as well." She glances between Cosmo and Sullen.

"Did I suddenly become invisible?" I bite out, annoyed she's acting as if I'm not even fucking here.

Every eye at the table turns to me, except Sullen's.

He doesn't seem at all alarmed that these two people in his life are catching on to one another. Instead, he's staring down at the paper Maude passed his way, a printed page I can't see from this angle.

"I'm sorry," Maude says carefully, "I didn't mean to offend you. It's just, well, I don't know *you,* but I know them—"

"Yeah?" I demand, lifting my chin as I grip the stem of my wine glass tighter. "How well, huh? You fuck both of them?"

Sullen shoots his eyes to me.

It feels like a victory.

Beside me, Elliot clears his throat. "I didn't know we were getting down to the orgy so quickly," he says wryly.

I glance at him, meeting his amber eyes as he looks at me with a slight smile. My heart hammers hard in my chest and I lift my glass to my lips, downing all the red, relishing in the soft, tangy burn on my tongue. "Orgies? Are you even old enough to be having sex?"

Alivia laughs loudly at this and despite my annoyance with the turn this night has taken, I feel strangely lighter with her amusement. It seems Maude takes my outburst in stride too because she doesn't cuss me out.

Elliot lifts a brow. "I'm twenty-one," he says, flicking his gaze up and down my body. "How old are *you?*"

"And how many orgies have *you* had?" Fleet drawls, leaning in toward the table, his elbows atop it, hazy eyes on me, a joint between two fingers.

I tilt my head and beside me, Cosmo's arm brushes mine. A second later and I hear wine glugging into my glass as he refills it.

And I can *feel* Sullen staring at me now.

"I'm twenty-three," I say to Elliot. "And none," I answer Fleet honestly. "But there's always a first for everything." I turn my head and stare right back at Sullen. "Isn't there, *Scully?*"

Maude's pale cheeks flush red and she takes a sip of her own wine while Alivia looks at me with shining eyes, a smile hooking her lips.

But Sullen turns to Maude, almost as if he is dismissing me. He lifts one corner of the paper he's been studying.

"Is this photo..." He trails off, his peculiar voice silencing everyone once more as he ignores me completely.

"The original Hotel Number Seven," Maude says with a smile, her eyes batting from the paper and back up to Sullen. "Located by Lake V, outside of the city. Much more natural location than what they have now in Alexandria. Anyway, Burbank was a guest at this hotel all those years ago but it's not even a footnote on Wikipedia, although they do mention criminals, they just leave out which ones, and all the scientists that flocked there, too."

Sullen is still staring down once more at the paper before

him like he's found God. "The original. It's still...around?"

Maude nods once. "Absolutely. Allegedly it's taken care of by the same owners of the new location."

Sullen's gaze lifts to mine.

Maude looks at him curiously, her hand sliding over the table to the paper, then moving a little closer, her fingers grazing his gloved ones. "Do you have an interest in this particular hotel, Scully?" she asks quietly.

Alivia is speaking to Fleet and Elliot now, the three of them talking about murders and buildings and things I don't care about. My pulse pounds hard in my ears and I want to make a fucking scene again, just to grab Sullen's attention.

"No," he says, his tone distracted.

Maude laughs, like he's told a joke.

Cosmo leans in close to me as I watch her say something to Sullen, her eyes brightening, but I can't hear the words as hard as my heartbeat is clanging in my head.

"He's fucked up," Cosmo says so quietly no one else can hear him. "Just like his father. See how much he loves this shit? So while your *family* are busy raiding the city, I was actually trying to find out why this little fuck wanted you. And who knows? Maybe I've saved your life tonight since Maude is trying to fuck your little boyfriend over there. Maybe he'll take her instead. I could let it happen, Karia. After all, she has no idea who the hell he is. Why would she? Sullen Rule is a ghost. Always meant to be a victim. But the thing about having psychotic fathers is the sons usually turn out fucking worse."

"Yeah, you never do want to talk about *your* daddy, Cosmo. Let's hear how horrific you're going to turn out." But even as I say it, I watch Maude put her hand over top Sullen's and he does nothing to stop her.

But when Cosmo brings his fingers to my cheek, curving a strand of hair behind my ear as I flinch, Sullen's dark eyes lift to my own.

Then Maude's hand is below the table and I'm certain she's touching his thigh.

I down another glass of wine. The one Cosmo refilled.

His shoulder bumps mine as Elliot and Fleet speak on my other side, the music dulling my senses alongside the alcohol.

"You can try to deflect all you want but I would never drug you without you asking nicely. Besides, I always knew you wanted to fuck him," Cosmo says softly, but his voice is harsh. "The way you looked at him on Ritual Drive when he'd come sulking out of his house anytime I was near you..." There's a self-satisfied smirk in his words. "But he never did get to taste you, did he? Then the first opportunity he has to do just that, he's got to drug us to get it done?" He snorts softly and Alivia is staring at Sullen as Maude keeps talking, her false lashes batting with every other word.

She's gorgeous and I hate that.

"But he doesn't really want you, does he? He was too sheltered for too long. He just wanted any pussy he could get."

I clench my teeth and narrow my eyes into slits, but I don't look away from Sullen as Maude leans her head on his shoulder briefly before pulling away and laughing in some mock display of closeness.

"And right now he might get a two-for-one deal. Shit, Karia, I don't even think I need to ruin this party after all. He's content to be fucked by anyone. I can get you drunk, take you home, violate you, and sleep with you beside me in my bed. I'll even let him keep running from Writhe; I don't give a fuck." Then his hand comes to my thigh, squeezing hard.

And right at that moment, impossibly as if he feels it, Sullen lifts his eyes to me once more.

Cosmo isn't paying attention. I can feel him staring at me as he comes in closer, his mouth inches from the side of my face as he slides his palm up higher. "Tell me yes, and I'll leave him alone for you." He squeezes my thigh tightly as I watch Alivia speaking to Sullen now, her eyes bright with acid as she gestures with her wine glass. "Tell me yes, we'll let him have his own fun."

Sullen's dark gaze is latched tightly onto mine like Cosmo's hand is on my thigh. I don't know if Cosmo lied to me about why he really came here and I don't understand how Sullen didn't know any of this information about the original hotel— even though I didn't either—or why he cares at all about it, but I feel as if I'm entirely on the outside of a game I don't remember agreeing to play.

*I let Sullen touch me.* Maybe not the first time, but each time after. I agreed to it while I questioned him. Then I went up against *Stein* himself, ran through an underground hotel tunnel into utter darkness and slept in the back of a family van, all for what?

Did I just want some fun in my life? Am I really as pathetic as Cosmo said I was? Did I go through all of that to watch Sullen be groped by two women we can't trust?

Cosmo's hand reaches the center of my thighs. He flexes his fingertips, pressing against me. "What did he do to your eye, Karia?" he asks quietly. "Why did you run with him? What's going through your pretty blonde head?" His lips graze my cheek and the hairs on the back of my neck stand on end as I remember the serpent dream. The snake slithering over my body as I lay in darkness. "Come back to me."

Maude is leaning into Sullen. Alivia has shifted closer too, although she seems a little out of it and still slightly less intent on invading his space. Elliot and Fleet are laughing softly together beside me, and Sullen's eyes burn into mine.

He hasn't said a word in so long. *Does anyone even notice?* It's like he's a creature for them to toy with.

Cosmo's lips are at my ear. "Come home with me and I'll leave him alone. You've always had a soft heart beneath that bitchy princess facade." He runs his mouth over my lobe. "Come home and we'll make sure he's never found."

Sullen doesn't blink as he stares at me. The white bandana around his throat draws my eye, and I think for a moment of the words in his skin.

*If Stein gets his hands on him again...*

As the thought strikes through me so sharply I flinch, Maude lifts her arm and cups the side of Sullen's jaw with her fingertips.

I don't breathe.

Her thumb is close to his mouth. Full and soft and hiding his beautiful smile; but he isn't smiling now.

"See?" Cosmo whispers against me. "Let her touch him. Let her kiss him. It's only fair he should get all this attention. He never got out much, did he, Karia?" His teeth prick my ear. "Let him feel good."

Sullen's eyes narrow. Maude's finger sweeps over his bottom lip. She isn't laughing anymore, staring up at him as if she's going to touch him everywhere.

Cosmo bites my ear again, tugging gently on my lobe.

Sullen grabs Maude's wrist then, his eyes flashing as he looks at me and slowly brings Maude's arm forcibly down to the table with a soft thud.

She winces, and he releases her, but he still doesn't say anything. To her, to me, to Alivia. It's almost as if he is trapped inside himself.

"You two good over there?" At the sound of Fleet's voice, I flinch, turning my head to see him squatting down between the two red velvet chairs Elliot and I are currently occupying. He's holding something out to me, white paper rolled around marijuana, the end lit, a soft smile on his face.

He's cute. Not hot like Sullen, but cute.

Fleet glances under the table, at Cosmo's hand on my thigh. "Here," he says softly, gesturing with the joint as he slowly rakes his gaze over my body and meets my eye again. "This will help you relax. You seem tense."

I don't think about it as Cosmo laughs softly and Elliot says, "Oh, boy." I reach for the joint, bring it to my lips, and inhale.

The cherry flares bright and the smoke fills my lungs. I've smoked many times before and I don't take too much, only coughing a little as I pass the joint back to a smiling Fleet and exhale through my mouth.

My head feels lighter already. Cosmo is still touching me, Fleet is staring at me like he wants to fuck me, and even Elliot's presence is soothing.

Then I hear Maude giggle.

I clench my teeth and cut my eyes to her and Sullen and Alivia. Everything feels a little hazy, including my vision, but they are definitely closer than they were, all three of them pressed together, Sullen in the middle.

He's watching me with a scowl, and I see Maude reach for him again, not having learned her lesson the first time. Her fingers drop down to the bandana around his throat and he visibly tenses, his eyes widening.

And he finally speaks. Just one word.

Just my name.

*"Karia."*

It sounds broken and rough but angry, too, and I watch as he cuts his gaze to Fleet, then Cosmo, all while Maude toys with the bandana at his throat.

I stand then.

I don't know what I'm going to do, but I feel as if he's paralyzed for some reason, like he doesn't know how to navigate this, tell people to fuck right off and stop touching him. Or maybe that's what *I* want to say.

I don't, though.

I stay quiet, but I turn and wind my way past Fleet, whose fingers graze my calf over my black pants, and I can feel his eyes on my ass as I saunter around the table. I brush past Alivia, who watches me with a small smile, then I step in the sliver of space between Maude's chair and Sullen's, forcing her to stop touching his bandana, my back to her.

He slowly looks up at me from beneath his dark lashes, then he shifts his chair back a few inches.

And I straddle him, my head floating from the punch, the wine, the weed.

*Him.*

Everyone is looking at us. The music thuds, pulsing in time to my heart, a storm is thundering outside these walls, but all I see is him.

His body is so warm, solid beneath me. I loop my arms around his neck, leaning forward and pressing my nose to his.

He isn't touching me, not at first, but slowly, his hands come to my hips, fingers splayed over my ass. I shift forward a little, grinding against him, and I feel him growing hard beneath me as his dark eyes stay locked on mine.

"What do you need?" I whisper to him, my mouth inches from his own. My pulse is pounding, I am hot all over, and when his fingers slide up a little to touch the exposed skin along my back, I can't help but imagine fucking him, just like this, in front of everyone here.

I arch my spine, giving Cosmo, Fleet, and Elliot a good view of my ass as I brush my breasts against Sullen's chest.

He swallows, his full lips pressed together as he stares down at me in his lap, his expression unreadable.

Then he says it again. My name. "Karia," he whispers, his breath over my lips. He smells so good, clean and without a hint of alcohol. He hasn't been drinking at all. He is perfectly sober, and I am wasted; this is exactly what I always want.

I know we should think about leaving this place. I know there is an entire city waiting to devour us. But for this moment only, I don't care.

His fingertips press against my spine, and he jerks me closer, a small gasp leaving my lips as I tilt my head, angling our mouths. I feel how much he wants this, his cock bulging beneath my pelvis.

*God, your dick is big.* The thought explodes inside my head, because if I can feel this much when it's buried beneath his clothes, *fuck.*

A small smile curves his lips and he looks down at my mouth, then back up. "What?" he asks quietly, as if no one else is around to hear us. "What are you thinking right now?"

I shift against him, a fluttering in my low belly as my body ignites at this small amount of sensual contact. "Your dick," I say with a small laugh. "How big is it?" I know I shouldn't ask something like that in front of all these people, but I don't care. I couldn't have stopped it if I tried.

Sullen's dark brows lift in surprise, and he flexes his fingers along my waistline, but he shakes his head once. "You do not have any manners."

"You drugged me," I say against his mouth, brushing my lips over his. "I think we're even."

I bite at his bottom lip and his eyes flutter closed. The need welling up inside me is nearly all-consuming. My legs feel shaky, my feet don't touch the ground as big as Sullen is beneath me, and it's like I am floating in all this *want* for him.

"Kiss me back," I whisper, shifting over his erection again. I run my lips over his open mouth, listening as he draws a sharp intake of breath.

His eyes are still closed, all those thick lashes making me envious. He is gorgeous, perfect, and he has no idea.

"Please kiss me," I say quietly. *"Please."*

Then I hear a voice that isn't his, right by my ear. "Kiss her," Maude says, and I smell the alcohol on her breath. A second later, I feel her hand on my back, over top Sullen's.

He snaps his eyes open, turning to stare at her. Then he

says, the word articulate and focused, *"No."*

Maude nudges her nose against the side of my face. I think she's drunker than I am. "Why?" she whines, dancing her fingertips along my spine. "I want to watch you touch her, Scully."

I glide my mouth over Sullen's cheekbone, his stubble under my lips, alongside his smooth skin. "She can watch," I whisper close to his ear, although the hood of his sweatshirt blocks my way. "Let her watch."

But Sullen tightens his hold on me, squeezing me to his chest, and he says, *"No.* And get your hand off her." I know that part is to Maude.

A soft moan escapes my mouth at his possessive tone, and I'm shifting against him again, tightening my arms around his neck, wanting him so much it hurts as Maude moves her hand away from me.

"Stop, Little Sun," Sullen whispers, his tone less harsh, but firm all the same as I dry fuck him right here. "I don't want them to see any of you, any of this."

I don't stop though, my eyes drifting closed, feeling his cock between my thighs, wanting more, wanting *him.*

Then his hand is at my throat, pushing me roughly back, gripping alongside my jaw as I lock eyes with him and his index finger presses vertically, right into my windpipe.

*"You're mine,"* he says in his rough voice, eyes flashing. "You are not entertainment for *them."*

"Nah, she sure as fuck isn't, because this is kind of boring." Cosmo's cocky words spread through the room, penetrating my haze.

I turn to look at him as I hear chair legs scraping against the floor, but Sullen holds me tighter, gripping me harder and not letting me see.

"I've gotta make a call, but you all have fun without me," Cosmo says.

*Fuck no.*

All at once, I push away sharply from Sullen, as if I'm suddenly awake after living in the haze of him. He releases me and I stumble into the table.

I hear Cosmo laughs as he asks, "You good, Karia? You need me to *take care of you,* fucked up as you are?"

I rub my fist against my eyes, turning to glare at him across the table.

Sullen's hand comes to the back of my thigh, squeezing hard, like a warning. But Cosmo has his phone out, and I know what he's going to do. His green gaze on mine as everyone stares at us, there's a glint of cruelty in his eyes.

"I'll... I'll be right back." I stumble over the words as I twist out of Sullen's grip, then I'm rounding the table, crashing into the side of it, Fleet's hands darting out to steady me.

Music plays through the speakers, pounding inside my head. "I Hate Everything About You," but it's distorted and garbled. The bass seems to pound in time with my heart as I reach Cosmo.

He's grinning at me, holding his phone close to his chest. "You want me to do what he wouldn't?" he asks, arching a brow.

*Fuck you.*

But before I can say anything, something louder, *deeper,* rolls over our head.

The storm raging aboveground seems to shake the entire Emporium, rattling down through the basement. The lights flicker, but only for a moment.

That rolling thunder rumbles again.

The lights flick once more.

It's like I've done this before.

*Duplicity.* Doubleness.

I turn to look at Sullen.

Maude's mouth is too close to his face, even though she's not touching him.

I want to leap back across the table. I want to break a wine glass and cut her with the shards.

"You want me to invite Isa over after I tell her who's here and we get rid of the trash?" Cosmo asks softly, his voice a low drawl.

"You?" I counter, turning to stare at him.

He smiles down at me, phone still cradled to his chest. "Actually, I was thinking *you.*" He flicks his gaze up and down my body. "You're looking a little messy right now, baby." He jerks his chin, indicating the storage room. "Let me clean you up. You can call Isa with me. You should be happy I'm not breaking his neck myself. I thought the little princess of Writhe had a heart, unlike the rest of them."

I ignore that. I feel a little heartless at the moment. Like I wouldn't mind if Sullen pulled both Cosmo's and Maude's spines from their backs.

As it is, no one is watching us anymore. No one but Sullen.

"If they come, they *will* take me. If you call Isa, you're fucking me over too." I speak lowly as my chest grows tight when I glance across the table and see Maude lean in to whisper against Sullen's ear. The way Sullen stiffens, I can only imagine what she's saying.

"No," Cosmo stupidly insists. "I won't let that happen."

"You can't stop them." I speak the words to Cosmo but I'm staring at Sullen. That same strange sense of déjà vu rolls over me again, despite the fact nothing is anything I've ever experienced before.

But Cosmo laughs beside me, and I know what he's going to do.

He's going to ruin us all. Sullen most.

I turn to him, tearing my eyes from Sullen as I dart out a hand to grab Cosmo's own, my fingers threading through his.

His jaw clenches. I know he doesn't forgive me for betraying him and I'm not even sorry.

But I won't let him send Sullen back to hell.

"Don't," I whisper. "It'll hurt me, too."

Cosmo narrows his gaze. "I think he's already done that enough." He glances at my eye. Then he tries to pull away, but I hold onto him tighter.

"No," I say, my voice low as my heart races. "You can't do this."

"The fuck I can't. Let go of me, Karia. You don't usually make yourself seem so pathetic." He jerks his hand from me once more.

That's the second time he's used that word on me.

The thunder grows deeper, louder above our heads. I think I hear the rain, too.

I lunge after Cosmo, grabbing onto his shirt and bunching the fabric in my hand. I'll physically restrain him if I have to. He is not going to ruin Sullen's chance at freedom.

"No," I snarl the word. "You're not going to—"

He spins around and grabs my wrist, leaning in so close I can smell the cherries from the punch on his breath. "Then kiss me right now in front of him, like you dry fucked him in front of me, and maybe I'll consider your begging."

I want to spit on him. I want to slap him. But I don't get to do either before the red lights all flicker out as one. The music skips, too. For a moment, we're in dark silence.

Then the lights flare bright once more, the audio rising to a hair-raising volume before it falls back to normal.

Cosmo's fingers latch tighter around my bones. My breath catches and in my mind, I'm thinking the same word as before: *duplicity*.

Sullen cutting the power at the hotel. Putting me to sleep to be his own little experiment.

Something disgusting like hope wells up inside of me, wanting it to happen again. Sullen's hands all over me, his teeth against my skin. Him, not holding back.

But the lights flicker twice more, then stay on.

Disappointment washes over me. I'm still at this stupid fucking dinner, watching Sullen get hit on by two women who aren't me even after I tried to claim him, all while I attempt to save our lives.

*Stand the fuck up.*

*Come and get me, Sullen Rule.*

Cosmo turns but tries to drag me with him, my white Vans sliding along the floor. I reach for him, digging my nails into his skin, trying to plant my feet.

"You're not stronger than me," he snarls without looking at me. "But you want to stop me, you try to fucking stop me then."

The thunder cracks again.

What sounds like the high-pitched whisper of wind floods through the house, down the stairs, into the basement.

The lights cut, but the distorted version of a Three Days Grace song still plays.

A hush falls over the dinner, but I hear Fleet laughing.

Then...

"I think that's enough talking to Cosmo." Sullen's hoarse voice is in my ear, and I suck in a breath.

The lights flicker back on, red drenching Cosmo's green irises as his eyes widen and he looks at Sullen, over my shoulder.

"And I think you should let go of her now." Sullen's arm bands around my waist and he tugs me backward, my spine flush with the broadness of his body.

Cosmo's fingertips dig deeper into my wrist. He doesn't release me. "I can make you disappear again, in seconds," Cosmo says in a low voice, not letting me go. I don't think the others can hear us, but I'm suddenly worried Maude is going to discover exactly who Sullen is and either turn him in or become more obsessed with him, like I am.

Sullen's arm is a vice around my waist, his fingertips

splaying over my bare skin beneath my crop top. He leans in closer to Cosmo, curling around my body, dominating me and casting Cosmo's face in shadow.

"Yeah?" Sullen asks quietly. "And I suppose in the time you make your call, and we wait for someone to capture me, you think I'll let you keep breathing?"

"Hey." Maude's voice has me turning my head, my pulse leaping to my throat. She's standing right beside us now and I don't like her this close. I can smell the wine on her breath, the dark melancholy of her perfume. "What's going on?" Her eyes flicker from Sullen's arm around me to Cosmo gripping my wrist. A frown mars her brow.

No one speaks.

Maude brings her manicured nails to her throat, her red lips parted as she watches us. "Scully?" *His name is Sullen you fucking*— "Do you and Cosmo not...get along? Is this about..." She looks to me. "Her?" she asks quietly, and I swear her lip curls even though she was touching me only moments ago, but I know that was to get close to Sullen.

"I have a name," I say through gritted teeth, my pulse thumping in my jaw. "It's Karia."

"Yes but quite frankly, you slept two days straight and every time he's around you, he seems uncomfortable. I'm not so sure you two are a good—"

"Don't," Sullen says, voice dangerous. He's squeezing my waist so hard I feel nauseous, but I don't want him to stop. "Don't speak about her. About things you don't understand."

A pleasurable warmth floats inside my chest, burning up to my cheeks. I feel as if I'm spinning, my face flushing hot.

Maude blinks, taken aback. I don't know why Sullen acted so completely fascinated with her at dinner but the relief I feel knowing he just chose my side in this is enough to wash away any negative feelings.

But Cosmo snorts, bursting through my bubble. All at once,

he releases me and I snatch my hand back, curling it around Sullen's forearm over my waist.

"If you all will excuse me," Cosmo says with gleaming eyes. "I have a call to make."

Then he turns his back on us.

*No.*

I press down on Sullen's arm, intending to sprint after Cosmo. But as my friend disappears into the small alcove of the cold room, Sullen doesn't release me. Instead, he slides his arm down, across my back, then threads his fingers through mine, his hand engulfing my own.

I glance at him, at Maude staring at us, but he says nothing as we stride across the room, following Cosmo. *Stalking* Cosmo, it feels like.

I don't want him dead. I do feel a little bad about hurting him, even if I don't regret it. But as we step through the entranceway into the cold room—it's darker in here, as if the red string of lights dulled when the power flickered—I worry what Sullen will do.

And I worry I won't stop him.

Cosmo's back is to the dark gray wall, his phone to his ear, eyes on us, lips tipped upward into a smirk.

He opens his mouth to say something, but whether it's to us or someone on the line, I don't find out. Sullen releases me, then he steps forward quietly.

"I really wish you hadn't put your mouth on her," he says in a low tone. But he doesn't make a threat. He simply begins to quietly strangle the boy I almost kissed. His hands are around Cosmo's throat in a blink, his thumbs digging into his windpipe as he tips Cosmo's head back, knocking it into the wall. I can't see Cosmo's expression over the height of Sullen, but I hear his phone drop to the floor with a clatter.

I react on instinct. Crouching low, I swipe up the phone and see the line is connected to Isadora. I hear her voice calling

Cosmo's name. I end the call, then push the phone into my back pocket.

Cosmo is fighting back, trying to knee Sullen, but Sullen presses his body into Cosmo, until they're flush together, and he doesn't stop strangling him.

There's a knot in my throat as I step forward, right behind Sullen. So close I can smell him; darkened roses and the musk of his sweat.

I glance over my shoulder, ensuring no one has followed us. And no one is there.

When I turn back, Cosmo has his hands fisted in the hem of Sullen's hoodie and my breath catches as he lifts it up, the fabric of Sullen's white T-shirt beneath too.

I step closer, pivoting to the side of both of them, and I see horror in Sullen's gaze, but when I look to Cosmo's, it's reflected on his as he stares down at Sullen's abs.

As if in slow motion, my gaze cuts there, to the ridged muscle of his broad body that I refused to look at in detail back at the hotel. His abs are tight and thick, and staring at his flesh, I don't even understand how his core is in such good shape.

There are so many scars there.

So many jagged, distorted-shaped wounds that look half-healed, poorly treated.

I hear Cosmo's breath, a wheezing sound, and I know Sullen has released his grip on his throat. The next second, when I lift my eyes up, Sullen's fingers are wrapped around Cosmo's wrists and he twists his own grip sharply outward, as if snapping a limb.

And I hear it, a pop in Cosmo's bones.

He cries out, leaning against the wall, and I don't know what Sullen did—if he really broke something or only popped his wrists—but Cosmo's face turns a pale shade of white.

Sullen is glaring, but not at Cosmo.

His dark eyes are locked onto mine, gloved hands by his

side now, his hoodie hem pulled back down. He's breathing hard, chest rising and falling sharply, and I see a new darkness beneath his lash lines, the hollows under his eyes worse somehow than they were before. Or maybe it's only the way he's looking at me, like he wants to peel my own eyes from their sockets.

Thunder rumbles, as if far away, then something else follows, quicker and lighter.

And I hear Maude the second before I see her. "What the hell happened?" For some reason, her gaze comes to *me,* and she's reaching into the low neckline of her dress, her fingers slipping beneath the silk of the gown.

She produces her phone, taloned nails clenched tight around it as she looks to Cosmo, then me again.

"It's her," Cosmo snarls, taking advantage of Maude's hostility toward me. "This is the woman the police are looking for tonight."

In shock, I turn my head and meet Cosmo's green gaze. He is *smiling* at me, but he's still got his hands clutched toward his chest, and I can tell he's in pain, a vein straining in his temple.

When I look back at Maude, I see she's staring down at her phone, even though she hasn't made a move to call anyone yet. She seems...frozen.

*Fuck this.* I'm not going to rat Sullen out, but if the cops come here, they'll get him, too.

I lunge forward, swiping the phone from her hand before she can make any bad choices. With her fingers splayed, she looks down at me in horror. Without a word, I push forward, elbowing Sullen out of my way, then I dunk Maude's cell in the punch bowl, pressing it down flat with my hand, icy rivulets of melting slush coating all the way up to my forearm, as deep as the bowl is.

Then, confusion and hurt and rage sliding under my skin, alongside anxiety and panic and *fear* and *wrath* at Sullen's scars along *his* skin, I retract my hand, grab the bowl with both hands, and spin around. I grip the edges with my fingertips and slosh the entire contents toward Maude, drenching her chest, her dress, her phone clattering to the floor in a pile of punch as she gasps.

I turn quickly to Cosmo.

Then I throw the bowl at his fucking head.

*"Fuck you,"* I snarl.

The dish knocks against his temple and he winces, head popping back, his eyes full of the same anger I feel before the plastic container thuds to the ground, spins a little on its side, then lands flat on the floor.

Maude is sputtering, I hear footsteps, more thunder, the lights flicker. But there's a louder sound, heavy knocks upstairs, no doubt against the front door of the fucking Emporium.

I think of my dream. The snake.

I hold Cosmo's gaze.

He shakes his head once, a red mark on his temple from my attack. "You're too late," he says quietly, still cradling his wrists to his chest. "You're stuck with me. And they're going to ruin the rest of him." He glances at Sullen.

Panic crawls up my back and I follow his gaze, ignoring the appearance of Fleet, Elliot, and Alivia in the cold storage area as they try to understand what the fuck just happened.

Sullen's gaze meets mine.

He's no longer trying to catch his breath from the shock of being exposed. All of his hurt revealed to Cosmo.

Instead, a wicked smile curves his full lips.

The knocks upstairs grow louder. They're going to tear the door down.

"You are beautiful," he says quietly, in front of everyone, and it's as if we are the only two people on the entire planet right now. "I'm going to take you away from here." His voice grows softer as the storm rages on, the red lights flaring dark, then bright, casting his face in an eerie shadow, giving the illusion that everyone around us has disappeared. "I'm going to take you where no one can find you. I'm going to kill you, Karia Ven. After I destroy everything good about you."

I clench my teeth, my nostrils flaring as I try to keep breathing while voices yell on the opposite side of the door and everyone else inside the shop is silent.

"Because you can never leave me. I won't let you go now."

The floor seems to tilt, and I realize it's not from his words. At least, not solely. The thunder shakes the room, the lights go out and don't come back, everyone plunged into blackness. Upstairs, the sound of a door slamming against a wall ricochets throughout the shop, footsteps pounding inside, the sound of heavy rain like sprays of rapid gunfire.

But even in the blackness, I see the amber glint in Sullen's gaze.

And he reaches for me, his gloved hand coming to my wrist, jerking me forward. I fall into his arms, my cheek against his chest. His body is trembling, mine, too, but I know we can't just stand here in this twisted embrace.

I push up onto my tiptoes as people move around us, but strangely, no one speaks, no one rats us out, and I put my lips to Sullen's cheek.

"We have to go," I say. "So you can debase me." I paraphrase his words, then lick his skin, right beside the corner of his mouth.

He holds me so tight I can't breathe, let alone move.

Then Maude speaks, her voice a hushed whisper. "You two are fucking psychotic," she says, her drunken words slurring near my ear.

"Don't give her to them." Cosmo's words in the dark, contradicting his earlier blame on me about who the people upstairs are looking for. I don't know if it's police or soldiers from Writhe; tonight, they all serve the same purpose, but one will be worse than the other. They haven't said a word to announce their presence though, so I assume it's that one; *Writhe.*

"He's the danger. You heard what he said." Cosmo is speaking rapidly in the darkness.

"I'm high as fuck," Fleet drawls slowly, but there's no amusement in his tone anymore. "What the hell is happening?"

"Elliot." Alivia's voice. "I'm tripping." There is panic in her words, and I feel someone—probably Elliot—moving towards her voice in the dark.

"Our dinners can never end peacefully, can they?" Elliot says quietly, as if he is all out of patience. But none of them seem as freaked out as I feel. Maybe they have this kind of drama every week. But they have no idea Writhe shouldn't be fucked with.

"Cosmo." It's Maude's voice, and I know that tonight, in this shop, she's going to be making all the decisions on whether to give us away or not.

I shouldn't have thrown that punch on her or drowned her phone, but too late for regrets now.

"You have a lot of explaining to do before you are invited to the Emporium again. We don't want interference, and we *do not* give up fugitives."

I roll my eyes in the dark; it sure as hell seemed like she was going to make a call to give me up, but then again, she didn't, even before I dunked her phone.

My body is still pressed to Sullen, and he grips me tighter as we wait. We are both silent now, listening as footsteps sound up above. It's as if we are waiting for a verdict from the rest of the misfits here. Cosmo's fellow performance artists.

"I hear voices. Down here!" someone yells from the first floor, and we all grow silent.

The power stays off, though, but I see a needle of blinding white light tilting down the stairs and several people head for us here, following the path of the flashlight.

Sullen clutches me so hard it hurts; he is shaking all over.

He has lived the horrors. He knows what he might go back to. In some ways, I think that's worse. I have no idea what will happen to me, but Sullen will not survive for long after Stein gets his hands on him again.

I bury my face in the crook of his neck, standing on my tiptoes, and I breathe in the scent of him, dark and sensual. In another life, we would be doing this in the light. He wouldn't be shaking from fear. I might have him trembling for something completely different.

But now, as the footfalls grow closer, I do not know what to do.

It feels impossible, escaping.

The light sweeps across the main dining room, illuminating our scattered chairs and empty glasses, the wine bottles on the table. There is quiet now from our hunters, and Sullen dips his head, his lips brushing the shell of my ear in some semblance of a kiss.

I squeeze my eyes shut tight and curl my fingers into the fabric of his soft hoodie.

For long moments, no one moves. No one breathes. I don't know why Cosmo changed his mind and is keeping silent but perhaps now he's felt the fear of Writhe, he can't bring himself to give me up.

I blink open my eyes and wonder if I will awake back in the bed up in the Attic, like I did from the dream of the snake.

*Duplicity.*

But it's not on my side tonight.

"Where the fuck are they?" the same deep voice from before growls.

Then Fleet, bless his high little heart, streaks across the dining room in the darkness, inserting himself into the glow of the light and drawing attention away from us. At the same time,

Maude leans in toward me, the sweet scent of the punch filling my nose.

She says, very quietly as chaos descends on chasing Fleet, "There's another stairwell, it leads further down, then ascends up, to the back street. I know you're both here for a reason, and I know he isn't really going to kill you. I saw the scars on his throat, at the table." She sounds as if she's speaking through tears with those words, and I realize I have severely misjudged her. "Get past them, past the door you entered through down here. It's in the corner, flush with the wall. *Get the fuck out of my shop.*"

She doesn't have to tell us twice.

As the flashlight swipes across the room in a haphazard arc, trying to catch sight of Fleet, who is now jumping up onto the table and sprinting across it, dishes crashing and shattering to the floor in his chaos, I pull away from Maude, Elliot, Alivia, and Cosmo.

I don't say goodbye to any of them. Especially not my *friend.*

My hand is in Sullen's, and I tug him along, toward the stairwell that leads *up,* as the shadows of men and women from Writhe—I catch a glimpse of them dressed in tactical gear, all in black—try to reach for Fleet.

We'll have to run behind them.

It's the only way.

And as we draw nearer, a random spear of light illuminates the green travel bag I packed. My heart lurches; my nice dress is in there and I want to reach for it, but I know we don't have much time.

I keep running, Sullen behind me as I move forward unseeing in the darkness. Something crunches under my Vans and I almost trip; glass, from the wine glasses Fleet and the tact team have destroyed. But Sullen's hand grips mine tightly, his body a solid force to take my haphazard weight as I right myself.

Despite all of this shit we're in, I can't help the smile on my face.

Fleet is still flailing around on the table, a sacrifice for all of us as he laughs hysterically, and I want to kiss his blond head, but there's no time for that.

We're passing the stairwell entrance, I'm lunging toward the corner of the dining room, my right hand grazing the wall, feeling for the exit, my left hand in Sullen's gloved one.

But all at once, a body slams into mine, slamming me forcefully into the wall.

I bite down to keep from crying out as a masculine voice says, *"Gotcha,"* in my ear, and hands come around my shoulder cap, jerking me out of Sullen's grip. Whoever it is smells like the rain outside mingled with sweat, and they don't have a flashlight, because they aren't illuminating anything of me or them.

I dig my fingers against the wall, as if I could hold on that way, but my nails flex and several break instead, sending a searing pain along the tops of my fingertips. I ignore it, attempting to lunge ahead, clawing with both hands now.

"I've got one!" the man who is trying to haul me backward says. He wrenches hard on my shoulder blade and *that* is a pain that's not so easy to disregard. The ache is deep, throbbing, like something has been twisted the wrong way, and a sharp scream tears unwillingly from my lips.

The man *laughs.*

Rage and shame and pain all collide inside my body as I scramble at the wall and another hand fists my hair, jerking my head backward, tendrils of my bun yanked from the hairband.

The bright agony tears at my scalp, then the man presses *down,* forcing me to my knees.

I drop my hands on instinct, to keep my balance.

I feel the haphazard shards of glass beneath my palms the moment before I register the sting in my skin. *Fuck.*

But I can't lift my hands because the man is pressing his

knee into my back, keeping me down. I'm scrambling over the ground, trying to push up to my feet, but with his hand in my hair and the weight of his body concentrated on my spine, I can't get up. My palms slide over more glass and tears sting the back of my eyes. I can feel blood warm on my skin and I don't know where Sullen is and I don't—

I hear a *thud,* like a fist colliding with someone's face.

I'm released, all at once as my attacker grunts and stumbles away from me. Then someone is yanking me to my feet, hand around my upper arm, the injured one. I don't cry out, though. I know it's Sullen and he doesn't know I'm hurt.

I get to my feet as he shoves me along while still gripping me tightly.

I don't let myself marvel over it or think about my bleeding nails or skin or aching shoulder.

I keep running, my fingertips at last gliding over the outline of a frame. I slide my palm along the wood until I feel a round, cold knob. I twist it, hoping it's unlocked, and as my heart thunders inside my chest and Sullen keeps pressing his palm to me, it opens up.

The scent of alcohol fills my nose, and I don't understand why as I jog down the steps, Sullen at my back, a lot of commotion further behind us—laughter from Fleet, silence from the others, and frustrated yells from Writhe because they can't see where we went in the dark and I think Sullen closed the door back. But as we keep going, the noises grow further away, my eyes adjust, and I see a dim thread of light over top of a glass case.

A smile curves my lips as I realize what's inside of it.

*Maude. You really are better than I gave you credit for.*

Row and rows of liquor. Bourbon, vodka, rum, tequila.

This is like my own personal heaven. But when I glance over my shoulder and my eyes collide with Sullen's, I see my hell.

# Chapter 36

## *Sullen*

I t's pouring.

The wind whips rain up into our faces. Police sirens wail around the darkness of the city but the crack of lightning is sharper, fear slicing down my spine as I flinch, then reach for Karia with my free hand, our overnight bag I grabbed slung around my other arm. I draw her close and she leans into me, her head ducked against my chest as we scan the messy street.

When I look down, I see her blue eyes gazing up at mine, and there's a bottle of Jameson dangling between her fingers.

I didn't see her take it, but I don't question her.

She's trouble. She's always been that to me.

"What did they do to you?" I ask quietly as we move down the street, sticking close to the unlit shops. My high-tops sink into puddles of rain, but I don't stop looking at Karia. Her scream is lodged into my head, and although she's here, under my arm in the October storm, her tanned complexion has gone pale, and I see from the orange glow of the streetlight the hand she has around the Jameson is trembling.

I glance up and catch blue lights flaring ahead, likely not

close enough to spot us yet but we can't take chances. I pivot into the next alleyway, Karia's body following my lead. We step into utter darkness, no streetlights reaching here. The scent of the sewer and something fouler like death reaches my nose and I think of what Maude said to me. *Revealed* to me. Stein never told me much of his beliefs, his circle either within or outside of Writhe. But my thoughts flicker to the Gothic building of the original Hotel No. 7 and inside my head, I see blood along the carpets, staining the halls.

Still kept up by the same owners of the newer hotels, Maude believed. It doesn't change anything, it doesn't help me run, and I should want nothing to do with it. But it reminds me of my duplicate labs, my safe spaces at home and in the newer No. 7.

It could be a place to hide. In the end, Maude helped us despite the fact Karia was a horrible guest. A beautifully possessive one, but horrible nonetheless.

When she sat on my lap... It's impossible to describe how I felt. Like everything I ever wanted but couldn't articulate was coming for me all at once.

"I'm fine," she bites out over the roar of the rain. The sirens sound as if they're coming closer and I wrap both arms around her from behind then turn, so my back is to the street as we step deeper into the alley, the rainfall lessened here but the puddles beneath our feet worse. The bag along my arm is heavy and sodden with water but for now, it's all we have.

I tug Karia into me when we're deeper in the alley, my shoulder against the rough brick exterior of one wall. The sirens abruptly fade, and I think they've turned down another street.

"Where did they hurt you?" I ask quietly, my mouth near her ear.

"I said I'm fine." She snarls the words and I hear the petulance in her voice but I think it's only to cover her pain. "We need a plan, Sullen. The sun will rise soon. The city is crawling with people looking for us."

"It won't be for long," I whisper, my lips brushing the shell of her ear.

"What if Maude sells us out? Or... Cosmo?" She says his name quietly and I know she doesn't want to think of him betraying her again.

I bite down on the inside of my cheek as my fingers splay over her bare skin beneath her shirt, biting in against her ribs. I remember his face when he pulled my hoodie up. I don't even know why he did it.

But a thought occurs to me, and I curve my nails deeper into Karia's flesh, the leather of my gloves the only thing sparing her.

"What have the two of you whispered about me, Karia Ven?" I ask her in the dark as the storm rages around the city. "What have you laughed about, at my expense?"

She doesn't move, going perfectly still. I'm very aware she has a liquor bottle in her hand and no problem using strange objects as weapons. But I do not feel fear. Instead, a horrible, sickly shame wells up inside of me, thinking of Cosmo fucking her while they laughed at all the things so incredibly wrong with me.

"I don't have time for your insecurities right now, Sullen. What makes you think Writhe will stop looking for us in the morning?" She tries to turn in my grip, but I hold her still, one hand shooting up to her throat as I tip her chin up and stare down at her, curving over her body with my own.

I can see the gleam of blue in her irises even here, in the depths of darkness. "Was that what Cosmo was picking at? Insecurities? When you looked as if you were going to cry moments before you nearly let him kiss you?" I am drenched in rain, and I'd like to say it's discomfort that drags a shiver over my body, but I have lived through so much worse, so often.

"You didn't care about that," Karia retorts, her voice rising. "You didn't care because you left us there and went to Maude. You laughed with her and flirted with her, and I know you wish you could've stayed there and—"

I slip my hand up her throat, pressing it across her mouth. "I told you not to touch him." I wrap my arm tighter around her waist.

"But you let Maude touch you," she says under my palm over her lips, the words garbled.

"I hated every second of it. And that's all it was. Seconds." I dip my chin and glide my nose up her jawline and I tell her the truth. "I wanted to jump across the table and hurt you both for taunting me. When you came to sit in my lap..." I trail off, remembering her pleas to me to kiss her. How very hard it is to keep any self-control when I'm with her. "You are mine, Karia Ven, and she is nothing to me."

"You didn't want her instead of me? Or maybe both of them? To kiss you and fuck you and get on their knees for you—"

I pull back and grab her face once more, fingertips splayed along her cheekbones. "Don't be stupid." I press my temple to the side of hers. "There is no one I want to hurt instead of you."

"Then why didn't you do anything, when you saw him try to kiss me the first time?"

Because Maude was talking to me about something I have wanted to understand my entire life. About Burbank Gates and why Stein hates me so fucking much.

But I don't say that to her. I can't say that.

Instead, I whisper against her skin, "I'm going to take you far enough away they will never be able to get near you again. No one else will kiss you. No one else will touch you. No one will hear your screams."

She makes a wretched snorting sound. "I'm not screaming for you. I'm not afraid of you. And what if the truth of you is something so much simpler than your threats? What if it's you..." She angles her head back to stare at me. "Who is afraid of me?"

"What did he say?" I press, refusing to entertain her question. "What did he say to you to bring you to the verge of tears?" Maybe I'm envious he did it instead of me. Perhaps I want to know how to cut her that deeply.

She twists her body out of my grip and glares up at me. Vaguely I register there is less thunder, no wind. I don't hear sirens either.

Writhe won't look for us in the light because it'll draw too much attention. They've already caused a stir as is. A false police report will have to be issued to explain their presence tonight. It's a lot of coverup and Writhe will want to tiptoe during the day.

"Nothing," Karia says, her teeth clenched as she flicks her eyes up and down my body in a way that makes me feel self-conscious. "Nothing but the truth." Then she starts to twist off the cap for the Jameson with her free hand, but I watch as she winces, her lips pushed into a pout and again, I think of her scream in the basement.

I lean against the brick wall, satisfied she won't be running from the alley without going past me first. "What did they do to you?" I ask again, my voice quiet.

She brings the bottle up to her mouth, using her teeth to bite down and twist the cap loose. Then she plucks it off with her fingers and drinks straight from the bottle for three entire seconds.

And I see it then.

Blood along her palms.

It's hardly visible in the low light here with the night and the fading storm around us, but I see it.

I clench my teeth and reach for her hand, the one holding the cap, jerking her wrist to me.

She keeps drinking as she eyes me and I flip her palm, coaxing her fingers softly to unfurl for me. I take the cap from her and push it into the pocket of my hoodie as I see the glass glinting beneath her skin, a small, jagged sliver, blood welling up in other shallow cuts.

She slowly lowers the bottle as my entire body goes rigid, seeing her cut open and not from me.

Catching her breath as I circle her wrist with one hand and keep her fingers spread with my other, she stares up at me with a heart wrenching openness, her in all her own self-destruction, and I don't mean her blood. She is a fucking mess. Far less polished than I ever thought, and all I want is more of her.

"Is this why you screamed?" I ask quietly, staring at the blood pooling along the lines of her palm. Perhaps she is more delicate than I imagined.

"No," she says, like I've offended her. "He grabbed my shoulder and nearly twisted it out of socket."

I know that feeling. Literally. Imagining *her* experiencing it...my own hands start to shake.

She shrugs. "But I'm fine." Then she takes another drink.

"I don't think you are," I say quietly. "And if I had known that, I would have broken his fucking arm instead of only hitting him."

"You don't think I'm fine?" she asks quietly, ignoring every-thing else I said, and meant. "Well excuse me if we aren't all strapping women down in dental chairs and poking their nipples with needles. I suppose not everyone can achieve that level of sanity, Sullen."

I jerk her closer with my hand on her wrist, her Vans sliding over the slick cement of the alleyway. Then I dip my head, flicking my tongue along her bloody palm, tasting the iron-metal of it to show her just how goddamn *sane* I am. I feel the brittle prick of the shard of glass, too. I tilt my chin and use the unnatural sharpness of my canine tooth to scrape it from her skin.

I have to bite down with my fingers on her wrist to stop her trembling. My eyes lift to hers as I raise my tongue to the edge of my tooth, feeling the aculeate glass there. I flick it back in my mouth and swallow it as I stare at her.

Her lips are parted, the bottle still in her hand.

"I suppose not," I say quietly, then press my lips to her palm and watch her shiver in the dark.

Slowly, I lower her hand, the taste of her bright on my tongue.

"Sullen," she whispers. "That's...dangerous."

I smile coldly at her. *I have survived worse.* "You can say *thank you*, Karia." Or you can say *thank you, God.* I know she would never call me that but perhaps I did take something from Stein's delusions of grandeur.

She doesn't look away from me as she takes another drink and this time, I grab the bottle from her hand.

"Hey!" She steps forward, lunging toward me, but I step back. "I stole that. It's fucking mine. Give it back." Her voice is shaky, but she swipes her hand out to grab the Jameson and I snatch her wrist in my free hand, stopping her.

For a moment, neither of us move, eyes locked in the alleyway as I realize the storm is completely gone, leaving only damp, dreary fall air behind.

"Give it back."

"Just because you believe I am fucked up," I say carefully, never looking away from her. "Doesn't mean I'll let the same thing happen to you."

"I think you need to worry about your own daddy issues, Sullen, before you tackle any of mine."

I flinch with those words, but she doesn't stop.

"You threaten to kill me one minute then you want to save my soul the next, swallow the glass from my skin. Like I said.

I'm not scared of you, and you don't own me, and my shoulder really hurts," here, her voice breaks a little, "and I don't know what the fuck we're supposed to do. I want to protect you, but I don't even know if you like me and I..." She trails off, snatching her hand from my grip and wiping her fist over her eyes.

*Of course I like you. I'm obsessed with you. I don't swallow fucking glass for just anyone.* But I don't say that. I keep quiet.

She drops her arm by her side and lifts her chin as she stares at me, taking a deep breath. "You want to go to the original hotel," she says steadily, changing topics and tone so completely, I feel momentarily dizzy, as if I've consumed the liquor from the Jameson bottle in my hand. "I could tell. That's why you pretended to be interested in Maude. You're just like everyone else, it's almost fucking hilarious. You want to go, and I don't know why, or what we'll find, but we'll go there. Maybe they'll keep our secret and Writhe won't think to look there, especially if Stein never told you about it. If there's cameras—"

"There may not be. If it's still in operation for anything, it's criminal. Even Stein didn't put them up everywhere, so he could hide his own misdeeds." And catch everyone else's. Including Karia's, with Cosmo and Von.

"So we'll go there, and we'll find whatever you're looking for and maybe along the way, I'll find something too. Something that makes me not so fucking pathetic." She wraps her arms around herself. She is drunk and belligerent and still so beautiful.

"Pathetic?" I ask softly, thinking of the word along my sternum. "Who said you were pathetic?" But I'm sure I know.

"Oh, fuck off. *You* said the same thing, remember?" She abruptly gestures toward the bottle in my hand. "Put the cap on," she snaps. "Don't let it spill."

I almost want to laugh, but I twist the cap on and hold the bottle by the neck instead. With my other arm, I adjust the bag of our clothes on my shoulder. She sees the movement and swipes the Jameson from me before I can even react.

"To lighten your load," she says dryly. "Now somehow we need to get into a fucking cab and hope we can find the address to this *original* hotel." She walks past me, toward the entrance of the alley.

I turn to track her movement, imagining threading my fingers through the messy bun in her hair and jerking her back to my side. But then I'm thinking of me and Cosmo de Actis calling her pathetic, and why she would ever believe it to be true.

# Chapter 37

## *Karia*

I lean away from Sullen in the back of the cab. Drinking the Jameson straight was a bad idea, but I know I'd feel even worse if I was sober. My shoulder is aching, my palm stings, my temples throb, I need to eat, and I have zero answers about Sullen and far more questions.

The cab driver glances up at me once and our eyes meet as he drives through downtown Alexandria, the sun starting its deep amber ascent over the city.

Sullen was right. The cops are out of sight, and no one is stopping any of the morning commute that I can see.

Still, with the driver's blue gaze on me, I slink down a little in the cracked seats, despite the fact the windows are tinted.

The Jameson bottle is between my thighs, the bag I packed and Sullen saved in the floorboard between him and I. He takes up so much space in here with his far bigger build, his head is tipped forward, so it doesn't touch the headliner. I'm extremely aware of him but act as if I'm not.

I rest my head against the door, the potholes we roll over jostling me every few feet, but I just close my eyes and deal with it.

Sullen found a place near the original hotel we're going to walk from, so the driver doesn't know our exact drop-off location in case he's questioned later. Sullen used Cosmo's phone I'd stolen to check, then I threw the thing in the alleyway where I heard it clatter against the bricks before dropping to the pavement.

I don't feel bad. Cosmo pissed me off, too, and I do know he had a right to be angry at me for betraying him, but I don't care about examining any of this fairly right now. I think our friendship has disintegrated.

"How long?" Sullen asks, his jagged voice sharp in the quiet of the car.

When I snap open my eyes, I see the cabbie's gaze shifting from me, to Sullen, then quickly toward the road like he's frightened. We're currently stopped at a red light and his fingers tap dance on the steering wheel out of what I think are nerves.

"GPS says half an hour. On the outskirts of the city." The cabbie swallows hard after he speaks. Everyone seems a little scared of Sullen Rule. *I'm not.* I suppose he is intimidating. But to me, he's everything I ever wanted, wrapped up in barbed wire.

I glance at him. "What? You don't have enough money?" I joke, knowing I personally put the fat wad of cash he stole in a sock of mine at the bottom of our green bag.

He slants his eyes to mine, turning his head a little, hood still up, fabric of his sweatshirt soaked from the storm and clinging to his body much like my shirt is doing with me. I realize my nipples are hard at the same moment he does, his gaze dipping. I remember Cosmo dismissing me as nothing more than a body to fuck.

I cross my arms over my chest and Sullen looks at me once more.

"I don't think you should worry about my money, Karia. But

you *should* hide while you can," he says softly, glancing at my chest again. "There will be no one there to save you."

"You don't know that," I counter, keeping my voice low. "And we've been saving each other's lives for days now. Drop the monstrous act. I'm unafraid." Then, in a brave bit of daring bolstered by the Jameson in my veins, I carefully set the bottle down, tuck it between the base of the middle seat and our bag, then shift over closer to him. I never put my seatbelt on and it makes maneuvering easier. I pull my knees to my chest and lean in toward him, hooking one arm through his bigger one as I smile up at him, watching him glower. "Tell me why you threaten me," I whisper, keeping my voice down. "Tell me what you don't want me to see."

The driver must not be too keen on overhearing my words because he turns on the music as the light shifts to green, "Slow Down" by Chase Atlantic, and it's at such a high volume I know he won't be able to hear anything happening in his backseat.

I rest my head on Sullen's arm, just to feel his body stiffen like I disgust him. He even shifts in his seat, turning slightly to glance out the tinted window.

"You didn't act like this at the Emporium. I felt how hard you were," I whisper, murmuring against the soft fabric of his hoodie.

"Karia," he says through his teeth.

"You touched me then. You touch me when I'm strapped down. Why do you act like I repulse you now?"

He's quiet a moment, every muscle in his body tense. Then, still looking away from me, he gives me one of his very first truths. Not his father's, not Writhe's, but *his*. "I am not used to anyone touching me in want. Of course I desire you." He scoffs, like anything less than that is unthinkable, and he still isn't looking at me. "But I do not know what it means to be wanted back." He says it quietly, without a trace of self-pity. Then he slowly turns to look down at me. "I don't know how to handle you, when you are like *this*."

This? All over him? "You seemed to handle it fine at the Emporium."

"Yes," he says, gaze dropping to my mouth. "Because they all needed to know the truth. You're fucking mine."

I feel my cheeks flush with those words, and the pain along my palm, in my shoulder, it all fades away as I hold his eyes with mine. "Tell me why you said you would murder me, in front of everyone else." My thoughts flicker to Maude, to Sullen between her and Alivia and I feel that strange flush of heat well up in my belly.

*You're mine, too, you sensitive asshole.*

But until that single second of truth moments ago, he won't speak of anything except what Stein has done to him and only that when I can't run away. When he has some physical or medical hold over me. And he doesn't answer me this time either, locking up again.

"Yeah," I say bitterly, hiccupping a little and not caring as his eyes flicker to mine and he lifts his brows as if to call me out on it. "You're shutting down now, aren't you? You can't speak to me at all without your gadgets or your strength. You don't scare me, Monster Boy." I hug his arm tighter anyway, a false smile stretching my lips. "And good luck next time, getting me strapped down to a table or a chair. I won't make it so easy for you anymore." I start to slide away from him, unthreading my arm from his, but he reaches out and yanks me closer, his fingers biting into my upper arm.

I'm half-sitting in his lap, my hips atop his thigh, the way he has me pulled in so near to him, and his grip is painful, strong and unyielding.

I don't try to get away as he stares at me with narrowed eyes, his brows furrowed, those swollen lips pushed together.

For a moment, he just looks at me.

Then he only says, "I think I'll like it even better when it isn't easy, Little Sun."

I shrug out of his grip, and he actually laughs, a low, rough sound that sends that warmth flaring lower in my belly. But I don't move away from him as he mocks me. I just reach down, grabbing the Jameson, and without looking at the cabbie or thinking it through, I screw off the top and take another drink, letting it burn down my throat.

Sullen isn't the only one with problems, even if most of mine are self-inflicted.

As I drink, I note the fact we've left the downtown core of Alexandria and now we're taking a curving road lined with orange and yellow leafed trees towering over us on either side of the street, the sight of fall making me feel alive.

Or maybe that's Jameson doing its job.

Either way, I start to take another drink, but Sullen grabs the bottle and cap roughly from my hands, sloshing alcohol over us both, the scent strong in the car.

The cab driver says nothing as I turn to Sullen and watch him screw the red lid back on, his eyes still on me.

"What the fuck are you doing?" I hiss, clenching my fingers into fists. My nails are aching, I don't even want to *look* at how ruined my manicure is, and my shoulders still hurt. "That's the second time you've taken that from me and that's two times too many."

"You've had enough." There's something rough in his voice as he turns to look out the window, black leather gloves curved around the handle of the bottle, held tightly in his fist.

"I've had enough when I say I've had enough." I reach for the bottle but I can't tug it from his hold. "Give me this back." The snarl leaving my lips isn't feigned. I will slap him if he doesn't let go. It's not even the alcohol that I'm fighting for. I don't *need* it, but I think I deserve it and either way, he shouldn't be the one to take things from me. Maybe that's the drunk me talking, maybe I wouldn't mind if he took other things from my body but not this.

I attempt to twist the bottle in his hand, pulling and tugging, but he doesn't look my way and he doesn't appear to be under any stress keeping the Jameson easily away from me.

"Let. *Go.*" I reach up and grab at his bandana, curling the white fabric in my fist as I jerk his head around, forcing him to look at me.

His eyes narrow and he glances down at my hand around his disguise.

"I've been naked in front of you and you've bitten me, put a needle in me, and licked my blood from my face. You ate glass from my skin. Yet you can't even take *this* off when you're around me. You're not used to anyone wanting you back? Well here I am. *Get fucking used to it.*" I tug at the soft fabric of his bandana. A belligerent feeling of hopelessness is welling up inside of me and I don't want to face it.

He only talks to me in sporadic bursts. He won't open up unless I'm splayed out for him. He won't communicate, and we just keep running. Even if we get to this hotel, what then? They'll look eventually, if they're not waiting for us already. And we got lucky with Maude; she must be a good person, like Cosmo and Sullen both believe her to be. But I'm not, and pretty soon, my luck is going to run out.

I crawl my fingers down to one triangular edge of the white bandana. If I pulled just *here*, I might unravel the entire thing.

Sullen's nostrils flare.

"Give it to me, or I'm taking this as payment."

"Why?" he asks quietly.

"What do you mean *why*?" I'm practically shrieking, and I don't care who hears me now. "Because I want to *see you*. I.

Want. *You,* Sullen. Not Cosmo. Not Fleet." He flinches when I say his name, then wrinkles his nose. "Not Von. *You.*"

He studies me carefully. Then he says, "Just when I start to believe you are smarter than I gave you credit for."

I lift up my middle finger. I don't care if it's childish. Fuck him.

He glances at my hand, and I swear I see him bite back a smile before I drop it.

"This isn't fair. *You* aren't fair. I have crushed on you for *years,* and now I've finally got you here, stuck with me, and you are just as closed off as you always were. Your father isn't here to punish you for speaking to me—"

"He is not my father," he says coldly, his eyes locked on mine.

"And yet you *still* won't talk. You threaten me and hurt me and fight for me, but you won't speak to me and if that's how you're going to be, *I* am going to level the playing field." I twist the scrap of fabric between my fingers to indicate precisely what I mean as I hold his gaze, giving him another chance.

"Careful, Karia," he says quietly, never looking away from me. "There are some things you can never unsee."

"I've already *seen* your throat!" I explode, twisting fully to face him, my knee pressing over top of his thigh. I know I am drunk and erratic and losing it, but I mean every word I'm saying. "I've seen the words in your skin and the scars on your abs and I want to see all of you. I want to see *more.* I want you without all of this *shit* you put in the way of us and I want—"

"I don't give a *fuck* what you want, Karia." He turns to me then, grabbing my wrist and twisting, yanking my fingers from his bandana. "This is all a delusion in your head. A nice little vacation from your regular life. This isn't high stakes for you. This isn't something you've had to live with for twenty-three years. You were interested in me because I was an oddity. Because I *did* scare you." His voice is lower than I've ever heard it. He yanks my hand closer, and I lean toward him in the seat, completely involuntary.

His gaze drops to my nails again, and I follow the path.

There's blood crusted on the outside of one, another was bent clearly in half, a line cracked through it from the way I scrabbled for the wall back at the Emporium. Two more are jagged edges, broken off from my fight. I've never had nails this bad probably in my entire life, most of the polish chipped and flaked away.

His chest is heaving but he doesn't look back up at me, his thick, dark lashes grazing his cheekbones.

"Don't make the mistake of thinking this is real, Karia." He still keeps his gaze on my nails, his grip tight on the base of my hand. "You will crave your old life soon. But don't blame me for it when it happens. It's like you said to me before. There was no decision to be made. I was always going to follow you." He flicks his tongue out along the crusted blood of my ring finger, lifting his gaze to me as he does, the warmth of him causing me to shiver. "But the only way I can keep you is through your death." His teeth scrape against my finger, and he glides his canine up to my middle knuckle, never looking away. "And maybe the threats feel like love to me. Maybe that's why I give them to you. I know you will eventually fight me off, you won't like what's underneath everything you want to strip away." He bites at my finger and I stiffen, refusing to make a sound. His teeth dig deeper, canine against bone, but I still don't pull back.

I can take it.

I can take worse.

He smiles, but it isn't nice, and it doesn't meet those dark eyes as he pulls back, huffing a small laugh. There are indents from his teeth in my skin, deep and red. "You will want to run when you know everything. But remember what I said?" He throws my hand back at me, turning his gaze to the window as we pass through the never-ending forest. "I don't give a fuck what you want."

I stare at his reflection in the window, his pupils distorted by the tinted glass. They seem inhumanly large, black edging out any brown. My mind flickers back to two years ago. The hotel in October, just before Sullen Rule went missing. The eye under the doorway. *And how I ran.*

# Chapter 38

## *Sullen*

"You're drunk. You have to eat. We're not leaving here until you do."

She tilts her head, her fingers laced together under her chin as she bats her lashes while we sit at a secluded bench in a desolate park.

The princess of Writhe went with me into the drug store I had the cabbie drop us off at and secured *pounds* of makeup and "self-care" products instead of the food I told her we needed. Scooped it all up in her arms and tossed it into the store's red basket I carried, jostling my shoulder with the weight of everything she got while I browsed the snack aisle, our clothes and her Jameson in the heavy duffle on my other arm.

*"These are necessities. Don't look at me like that."*

I roll my eyes now as I did then, an hour or so ago before we walked from the shopping center to this location under a cluster of thick, looming trees.

"Eat it." I glance down at the lemon-flavored protein bar in her lap. It isn't much in the way of food, but we cannot risk going into a restaurant and we have nowhere to cook anything.

As it is, I've already consumed six protein bars, so I've done my share of suffering. My jaw hurts from chewing it all, and I don't have all my teeth.

It's her turn now.

She sighs but picks up the shiny yellow package and begins to tear it open, a small smile on her lips as she lifts her gorgeous eyes to mine.

I turn away from her before she sees too much of what I'm thinking.

The sky is still gray from the morning storm, and I glance up at the stern bruise-colored clouds, marveling for one moment over what my life has become. I am sitting on an iron bench with a girl I have watched for decades, *yearned for,* believed to be so far out of reach I was disgusting for ever hoping.

And she has left a trail of pain behind her; hurting Cosmo, Maude, *Stein.* All for me.

It is unbelievable.

It is unfortunate, knowing what comes next.

The wind sweeps through our sanctuary, and I shiver. I am grateful for the cooler temperature today—I always am with all of my excess clothing—and even more so for the bite of the breeze.

I'm not so sure that's the only reason I am trembling, though.

"What's your favorite color?" she asks me while chewing her food.

I dart out a hand and grab onto the large reusable shopping tote beside me as the wind picks up again, putting it in my lap and glancing inside to see the bananas and Band-Aids, topical ointment and rubbing alcohol on top. I got those things so I can clean her wounds. She let me apply one of the bandages to her palm outside of the store, but she said my tongue probably had healing properties so nothing else was necessary.

I didn't miss the mischievous smile on her face with that quip, or the way it made lust well up inside of me, so hard to control now around her.

I push those thoughts aside and turn away from the sky, the forest littered with yellow, red, and orange leaves, North Carolina coming alive in the dying season. Her eyes connect with mine as she pops the last bite of the protein bar into her mouth and chews with her lips closed, crinkling the wrapper in her fist.

I don't answer her question as she stares at me expectantly.

Then she swallows, throws up her hand in impatience, but slides closer to me on the bench. I smell the lemon of the bar and the Jameson, too, but I don't think much about any of it as she slowly rests her head against my arm.

I am completely still, lest I scare her or ruin this.

I don't know how to do any of these things she seems to want from me. I don't know how to handle the jealousy I feel when *anyone* else captures her attention—Cosmo I loathe of course, but even Fleet or Elliot or *Maude* touching her or talking to her... Where we are going now, I never want us to leave, and yet even then, I'm not so sure I'll learn how to do anything right.

"Mine is pink. Pastel pink, hot pink, mauve pink. Also pale green. Like the soothing kind." She speaks quietly but quickly, her words tripping a little in her mouth and I know she is still feeling the effects of everything she had last night, or this morning, or both, it seems, since time passed so quickly at the Emporium, in the worst sort of dramatic, chaotic way.

When we were running in that basement, I thought of turning myself in. I wanted to let her escape, particularly when I heard her scream.

But imagining Stein getting his hands on her, envisioning the next day without her—if I survived it—I couldn't.

I can't let her go.

I know this now.

It's horrible news for her, but there is nothing that will change my mind.

She stifles a yawn, bringing the back of her hand up to her mouth as she cuddles closer to me.

I release one strap on the grocery bag, then hold out my hand, resting the back of it on her thigh. "Give me the wrapper," I say quietly.

She breathes a small little laugh, but obediently places the trash in my palm. She doesn't move her hand back, though.

She threads her fingers through my gloved ones, the trash crinkling between us. The top of her hand is so beautiful; smooth, delicate skin over her blue veins. Her nails are hidden, fingers laced as they are with mine curved over her knuckles, but I saw the cracked nails, the chipped green polish (she bought more of that too at the drugstore). All the ways she has been desecrated, for me.

"Does your shoulder still hurt?" I ask quietly. She seemed protective of it as we walked here, about a mile from the drugstore; we saw a sign for this place there and she grabbed onto her arm as she nodded to it, noticing it first. *Treefall Park.* I know from staring at Maude's papers that Treefall is two miles from the original Hotel No. 7. If it's cloistered like this place, it's no wonder no one finds it unless they're looking for it. I had never heard of an original building; but it's not as if Stein kept me in his confidence or I spent my free time looking online for information about a group of hotels he owned.

I do not know what to expect when we get there, but I hope for a few days at least, Karia and I can catch our breath.

"Answer me first, then I'll tell you." She sounds suddenly exhausted, and I am not surprised it's all catching up to her. She's done so much in the past few days.

With me.

*Because* of me.

"Your favorite color," she presses, as if I've forgotten, which I haven't. "Tell me, Sullen." She whispers the last bit and I close my eyes a moment, relishing her hand in mine, her head on my arm, and our aloneness.

I think of taxidermy. My own little touch, with the green lights keeping them company when I could not. But I think, too, of Karia's penchant for pink over the years. She wore many other colors, mostly seemed to prefer black, actually, but pink is there in a lot of those memories of her I would hold onto when Stein hurt me.

"I like yours," I tell her. "Pink." I smile around the word as she jerks her head up, turning to me as I open my eyes and her own light up. "And green," I add.

"You like pink?" she asks, her voice full of doubt.

Despite the fact she insisted on going into the bathroom at the drugstore and making use of some of her makeup products and wipes, there is eyeliner scrubbed beneath her blue eyes, mascara flecked below her brow. She looks as tired as she sounds too, gaze bleary. Her hair is resettled up in its bun, piled on her head with a pink hair scrunchie, a few paler blonde strands framing her face.

I have a sudden, vicious urge to pull her to me and tell her to sleep. To let her rest. To whisper in her ear she is *not* pathetic, nor stupid, nor anything else shitty that anyone in her life has ever called her, including me.

But I also want to knock her out, tie her down, never let her go.

"Yes," I say, glancing down at her hand in mine. "It reminds me of you."

"Are you trying to get in my pants, Sullen Rule?"

I flick my gaze back to hers. "Is it working?" I ask, arching a brow.

She bites her bottom lip as she stares at me. "You don't have to work very hard," she says, almost shyly.

My heart squeezes inside my chest. Part of me doesn't believe her. That she is as captivated with me as she seems to be. What I said in the back of the cab, about me being a vacation from her real life, I still think that's partly true. But there's so much of some emotion I haven't really had directed my way, shining through her eyes when she stares at me like this from beneath her lashes. It's strange. I can't reconcile the truth of it inside my head.

"Are you like this for everyone?" I ask quietly. Maybe unfairly.

A blush stains her cheeks, pink and round, but she doesn't pull away from me. "No." She glances at our hands, the trash between them. "I've been like this for no one, Sullen."

I desperately want to believe her.

But I've seen her with Von and Cosmo. And while I don't know Von Bentzen very well, I know enough about Cosmo. I know he wouldn't have tried very hard with her—not as hard as she deserved for him to try—and she still gave him everything. I don't want her to do that with anyone else, anymore.

I think about walking into an old hotel, hearing only the creak of the doors before us and silence around us.

I think of putting my hand over her mouth.

I don't have any syringes, any medication, but there is the Jameson, and there's my palm on her face, stopping her breath.

I could make her sleep for me.

I could make sure she really never is like this, for anyone else, ever again. But for now, I stay nice.

# Chapter 39

## *Karia*

"What if we just took a train?" I ask quietly, staring up at the looming building ahead of us. "What if we really disappeared?"

The very first Hotel No. 7 is smaller—but taller—than I imagined. Inside my head it was a fortress, a castle, complete with high stone gates and nearly impossible for us to get to.

But as the hotel emerges on the path ahead of us—a dirt road lined with thick trees, blocking out what little sun there is —I see I was partly incorrect about most of my assumptions.

Sullen doesn't answer me. He just stares ahead, like he's enraptured.

There is a high fence around the building and it is made of iron, but the entrance gate is rusted near the top spire—several feet over my head—and it's ajar, giving us no obstacle to walk inside. The building itself is old dark brick, a dozen or so stories tall with rows of windows along each floor, an archway for the black double doors lined with silver trim. Curtains are drawn in each window, a few panes look worse for wear, dark silver shutters line the first few floors. There is not outright damage to anything I can see, and I crane my neck up, staring at the silver trim lining the roof. A few turrets spaced out along the roofline give it a Gothic feel, but it isn't a castle. Maybe a cross between a miniature version, and a haunted house.

It's taller than I expected, and I imagine it took a long time to build, being so far away from the city center.

A simple, circular fountain is beyond the gate, no water running from the stone plinth in the center that's shaped like a gravestone. Powerful, thick trees flank each side of the building, obscuring any view of the backyard, although it seems this place is set directly in the middle of a forest, and I imagine more woods line the property.

Maude said a *Lake V* was nearby, but aside from a feeling of humidity in the air, I can't tell there is a body of water close, and I certainly can't see it.

A black placard affixed to a stone post by the gate declares this is *Hotel No. 7, Alexandria, NC. Welcome to your new night.*

"What the fuck does that mean?" I ask quietly, unease prickling at my scalp, but again, Sullen stays quiet.

I turn to glance over my shoulder, wincing in pain as I do, but I still scan the long, meandering drive behind us that Sullen would not give up on even amongst all of my questions of, *are you sure this is it?*

But there is nothing there save for a whisper of wind floating through the many trees. We cannot see the road from here, and I wonder how much traffic this hotel got whenever it was still operational.

I remember Maude saying it was under custody of the new owners, but when I look once more at the place, I am not sure Stein Rule has visited here in years, which is probably for the best. As it is, I lift my eyes to scan the spires, the corners of the home, even the trees closing in on Sullen and I, but I do not see any cameras.

My heart doesn't slow down in my chest though, and I don't

think it's all from the ridiculous amount of walking we did today.

"What is it, exactly, you hope to find here?" I press quietly, thinking of Maude's stories that serial killers gathered within these walls for dinners. A shiver runs through me and I shift closer to Sullen, my shoulder brushing his elbow.

He is still staring at this place much like he was looking at Maude when she was giving the history of it. Like he will find answers to questions that have tortured him for years on end.

"We can't take a train. Not yet. They'll be watching. They know it's how I got to Alexandria in the first place." His voice sounds faraway as he speaks.

"How long are we staying, then? What are you looking for?" I reiterate my question.

"I don't know," he answers carefully, and it sounds like a lie. He slowly turns to look at me, shouldering the bag of our clothes, clenching his fingers around our shopping tote. "You never told me. If you're still in pain." He glances at my shoulder as he speaks.

It seems a strange thing to say right now.

My heart thuds a little faster. "I'm fine," I lie. It aches. I don't think the guy dislocated it but if a shoulder sprain is possible, that's what happened.

Sullen frowns, his dark brows pulling together. "Don't lie to me, Little Sun. I don't... like it."

I pull my bottom lip between my teeth and watch as he studies the motion. "I don't want to be weak for you," I finally say, giving him a deeper truth than maybe I should have. Perhaps from my nerves, or the alcohol still in my veins, or maybe the honesty he gave me back in the cab. "I don't want you to think you have to take care of me."

He tilts his head, and a single ray of sunlight penetrates the cloud coverage and trees enough to light up the amber in his irises. He is breathtakingly beautiful, but I know if I said that, he would think I'm lying again.

"I like taking care of you," he finally says, glancing at my shoulder. "Stop trying to be someone you aren't. I don't mind the weaker version of you." He turns away from me, staring at the house. "That one won't run from me."

"THIS LOOKS EXACTLY LIKE A PLACE THAT HELD CONVENTIONS FOR serial killers." I twirl in a circle, staring around at the black and silver in the room, different from the blue-tones of the downtown hotel. There are silver armchairs, silver rugs over black marble floors, chandeliers dripping in silver set among the high ceiling of the first floor.

The lobby is enormous, a double staircase beyond it, leading up and around to heights I can't see from here.

The scent of an old building locked up for years and the hint of bleach is what greeted us after Sullen managed to pop open one of the doorknobs. It was locked, but pathetically so, as if no one is too interested in keeping all of this secret.

That bothers me. Despite the fact it seems deserted, everything is neat and clean and there is no visible damage to the building's interior that I can see.

Someone has been checking in, tending to this place. I just don't know if it's Stein or Writhe, or someone else.

The door creaks closed at my back and I glance over my shoulder, watching Sullen throw a large deadbolt that wasn't engaged when we arrived.

*Why?* Is it abandoned? Forgotten? Or simply so hidden the owners feel comfortable being lax in security? Aside from Treefall, we saw nothing as we walked here along the side of the road. No traffic passed us, either.

Sullen's eyes lift to mine, his gloved hand still on the lock, and I turn away, my pulse pounding hard for reasons I don't understand.

Now we are shut in together.

I'm not so sure that makes me any safer.

I turn away from him, then dart over to the long counter that would have been used for checking in. I quickly run my finger over the marble top, the feel of it cold on my skin. Then I raise my hand, glancing at my fingerprint.

"No dust," I announce, lifting my gaze to Sullen as he stands inside the door, on the silver carpet at the entrance. He says nothing; he's only studying me in silence, and it unnerves me. I drop my hand and wince, my shoulder throbbing, and I see Sullen's expression change.

His eyes narrow, a muscle in his jaw jumping. Then he drops our bags—the shopping tote and duffle—before he slowly starts to prowl toward me. And that's what he looks like; a hunter stalking his prey. But even as he moves so preternaturally, I see the stiffness in his gait, and I know I am not the only one in pain.

The urge to run to him is strong, throw my arms around him, kiss him everywhere. Beg him to let me make him feel better.

But I know he won't want that.

I drop my gaze from his and turn my back to him, walking around the lobby counter slowly, trying to move as if my heart is not nearly beating its way through my ribcage, anticipating him reaching me.

Golden phones are lined under the lip of the countertop, curly black cords attaching the handsets to the receivers. I've never actually seen phones like this, and I smile a little, pressing my fingertips to the counter as I study them. There aren't wires connecting them to any source of power or phone line though, and that makes me feel marginally better about being here.

"My mother had one of those, on her wing in the Ritual Drive house." Sullen's low voice startles me and when I look up, he's right beside me.

I tense, watching him study the phones. My nostrils flare and I inhale his sensual scent combined with sweat from our walk. I want to lick it off him. I want to throw myself at him.

I bite the inside of my cheek and don't move.

"I think I tried to order a new father once." He smiles, but it's so cold. "Mom was watching me. She didn't stop me."

My lower lip trembles and the urge to reach for him grows so much stronger. But again, he recounts these memories with such a flatness in his tone, I know he doesn't want me to pity him. To touch him.

To combat the desire, I reach for the nearest phone cord instead, curling it around my finger, watching it press into my skin, blanching it white.

"Karia."

I blink and find him staring down at me.

"We should shower, find a room, and you can let me take care of your shoulder."

My throat rolls as I swallow. I don't want him to have to worry about me. "I'm fine."

His gaze searches my face and I know he can see the circles beneath my lash line, the redness in the whites of my eyes, the pinched look about me; all the things I saw in the mirror at the drugstore. All the things I tried to hide with my new makeup. He can probably smell the alcohol on me, too, and I agree with him, about showering.

Even so, I lift my chin and don't look away. *I am fine, Sullen. I can take you. I can take this.*

"Okay," he says softly. "That's nice. But we can't just hang out in the lobby. If someone has been coming to clean, we never know when they might come back. I don't think we should make it easy for them to find us. This building has a dozen or so floors. Let's not stay on the first one."

"I feel like I'm being lectured," I shoot back, my brows furrowed. "Excuse me for wanting to have five minutes of joy. I know the concept is foreign to you, but it's been a long weekend."

He glances at my mouth, and I swear he's imagining biting it. But then his gaze stalls on my eye and after a blink, my face heating, I know he's studying the cut there. The concealer wasn't thick enough to hide it completely.

"I know danger is not something you're often in," he counters softly, "but this is me, trying to protect us both." He gestures between us with his gloved fingers.

I try to fight back a smile and his eyes seem to brighten, like he enjoys that. Me, finding him funny.

"Do I need to tie you down while *I* shower, so I can ensure you don't do something stupid?"

"I'm not stupid, Sullen Rule."

He closes his eyes for a moment, inhaling deeply. I swear I see regret furrow his brow and I wish I hadn't said that. He's going to think I can't let anything go. But that's true, isn't it? It's why I'm still obsessed with him after all these years, including two where he was absent completely. He never got out of my head.

"But if you let me watch you shower," I say quickly, "I promise I will be on my best behavior."

He snaps open his eyes at that and my heart races once more inside my chest. Before I can take the words back, knowing he's self-conscious and always hiding, he moves in front of me, pinning me to the countertop with his body, his hands on either side of me, caging me in.

I press my palms to his chest, curling my fingers into the fabric of his hoodie, willing myself not to look away. To apologize or backtrack or flinch or show fear.

And I realize his face is flushed as I stare back carefully, the pink color on his cheeks drenching him in humiliation. He is so ashamed of his own body, even a joke hurts him.

*I would want you anyway. I will want you always.*

"I told you before," he says, leaning down into my space, the lemon on his breath from the protein bars gliding over my lips. "You don't want to see me."

"And I told you I do," I counter, gripping his hoodie tighter in my fists. "I told you I want all of you."

He drops his head then, his lips coming to my shoulder, the injured one. He presses his mouth to me gently, then scraps his canines against the fabric of my shirt, as if in warning.

Chills crawl down my spine, my nipples hardening into sharp points. I arch my back, pressing into him, sliding my arms around him in some semblance of a hug.

"You don't scare me," I whisper. I won't ever stop saying it until he believes it. I glide my hands up his back, feeling the firm muscle there. Then I reach higher, my fingertips grasping at the hood of his sweatshirt.

But when he notices, he reacts almost violently, jerking back from me and snatching my wrist between us, off of him. I drop my other hand, pressing it firmly behind me to steady my balance. Something rattles under my palm, causing me to flinch as I touch more marble, but I don't look away from him.

"That's the problem," he says quietly. "In this place? Until we're caught? You should be fucking afraid."

I narrow my gaze even as my nerves coil tight in my low belly. "We're doing this again? The boy who can't remove his hoodie is telling the girl whose been strapped down that she should be scared?" I roll my eyes, forcing myself to appear far braver than I feel.

The intensity leaves his gaze then, his lips curving upward into a smile. But with his hand still gripping tightly to my wrist and his body so close to mine, I know he doesn't think I'm funny. "Open the drawer, Karia." He glances at my hand, pressed to cool marble beneath the lip of the counter.

Frowning, I slowly turn and realize it is exactly what he said. A drawer. There's a curved silver handle on it, and I circle my fingers around the cool metal and pull.

The rattling sound from before grows louder, and Sullen releases my other wrist. I put my back to him and stare down at hundreds of skeleton keys in the shallow drawer, randomly tossed inside in no order whatsoever. They're mostly silver but a few are rusted, too.

I glance over my shoulder to find him looking back at me, silent, so close I can feel his body heat.

*Did he know these were here? Did he guess?*

"Which one?" I ask quietly, lifting my bandaged hand to graze along the keys, hearing them rustle in the drawer. This place hasn't been used as a hotel in a while; it's too disorganized, everything thrown in here haphazardly. And nowadays, don't hotels all use cards, or even wireless entry?

I see numbers etched onto the space between the bow and the stem of the keys and wonder how many rooms are in this building.

"Pick one," Sullen whispers quietly behind me, and I can feel his gaze still on my body, like fingertips crawling along the back of my neck.

As if compelled to do what he says, I pluck one up at random, my heart thrumming fast in my chest.

I don't know why the decision feels monumental, but it does. I close my hand around the cold key, noting it's more rusted than the rest, silver turning into reddish brown along the pin.

And when I unfurl my fingers and see the number, I almost want to throw it back and choose again, but I take a steady breath and keep my decision.

Even if it is room 234.

# Chapter 40

## *Karia*

I sit gingerly on the edge of the queen bed in 234, listening to the shower running from beyond the closed bathroom door behind me. The air in here is thick with humidity and the scent of cloistered rooms and unread pages of a book.

In fact, on the wall beside the locked entrance door that my skeleton key opened, there's a small bookshelf sagging with the weight of leatherbound volumes I have yet to open up.

I'm not quite sure I want to know what they say.

In fact, all I really want is to lie back on the cream-colored duvet in this surprisingly large room, close my eyes, and sleep.

It's a little hard to do though, knowing Sullen is naked only a few feet at my back.

I glance over my shoulder, seeing the glowing yellow light from beneath the crack under the white door, warmth pooling in my low belly. I tear my focus away to the dark curtains collecting dust over the windows adjacent the bathroom, noting slivers of gray-blue sky beyond.

This room has a view of the side of the hotel, revealing only thick forest around the grounds. I already looked, trying to resist the temptation to peek at something else much more appealing. A boy I desperately want but can't quite have.

Sighing, I run my fingers through the damp ends of my own hair.

Sullen told me to shower first and he stood guard here, barely giving me a cursory glance when I emerged from the bathroom, steam billowing around me, before he went in himself, closing the door sharply behind him.

It doesn't have a lock on it, though. So there's that.

I smile to myself and turn toward the ornately carved night-stand beside the mounds of pillows on this springy bed. It's devoid of anything but a lamp, turned off, and the skeleton key to this room.

*How long has it been since someone has stepped foot in here?*

Logically, I know it can't be that long. The tub basin was yellowed, the shower curtain the same, but there was no mold, no bugs. Everything seemed relatively clean, if unused. The power works, and the water too. So someone is caring for this place. Someone has been here.

At the thought, I swear I hear a creak outside, in the hall.

Flinching, I wrap my arms around myself and sit up straighter in the bed, staring at the sliver of space beneath the door, the dim light beyond it.

Little hairs all over my body stand on end. I'm dressed in the only skirt I found in the Attic; black and short, just how I like them, a red, silky bra top, soft against my skin, and white lacy socks, my white Vans pushed off by the door.

And that's where I keep my focus now, holding my breath, straining my ears.

But I don't see any shadows or hear anything more beyond the running water behind me.

I shift on the bed, hearing the springs squeak beneath me.

I almost laugh at the sound, but I think that's just my paranoia causing me to become a little unraveled.

I flick my gaze to the wooden bookcase again, skinny and small, and wonder if I should see if any of these volumes discuss Burbank Gates, or Stein Rule's plan for this place.

But I hear it again.

Something in the hall.

My breath catches in my throat and I stand this time, legs shaky.

I want to run to Sullen, but I need to protect him, too. He's at his most vulnerable right now, and he must trust me a little to even shower at all, knowing there's only an unlocked door between us.

I swallow hard, taking one step forward on the soft gray carpeting, blinking as I focus on the light beneath the door, waiting to see if any movement occurs in the hallway.

They'll find us here eventually, but I didn't think it would be just yet.

I wait a minute, maybe more.

There's no one out there. No more sounds.

But the flimsy lock set in the door suddenly doesn't seem enough.

*Fuck this.*

I dart for the bookshelf, pivot to the side of it, then plant my palms against the wood, my soggy bandage catching on the hard surface. I dig my socked feet into the carpet and *push,* my shoulder lancing in pain, but the narrow bookcase moves, sliding along the floor. Relief spears through me and I keep shifting it even as my shoulder throbs. I don't stop until it's directly in front of the door, covering the knob.

It won't stop someone hellbent on murdering us, but it will slow them down. Besides, we're only on the second floor. If we had to, we could open the window and... jump.

I step back, admiring my work and feeling kind of proud.

I can still see a sliver of space beneath the door since the bookcase doesn't cover it completely. And I swear the lights in the hall flicker for a moment, plunging everything out there into darkness.

I step back, limbs shaky.

There are no lights on in here, but when I twist my head, I see the yellow glow is still there in the bathroom.

*I'm drunk, I'm paranoid, I'm horny.*

That's all.

No one has found us yet.

Sullen didn't know this place existed, so why would Stein come here so immediately? And I trust Maude and Cosmo and the rest to keep our secret, even if I shouldn't.

Still... I don't want to be in this space alone anymore.

Adrenaline is pumping too fast through my body, and I'm freaked out and I want to be near *him.*

I turn away from the door and stare at the bathroom instead, trying to imagine his broad, muscular body beneath the stream. How hot and fit he is, all those scars and injuries making him more beautiful as they map out the horrors of his life.

I curl my fingers into loose fists, holding onto the fantasy, attempting to calm myself and protect his boundaries both.

But I hear it again.

A creak from the hallway.

This time, when I dart a glance behind me, *the lights in the hall are completely off.* Pain lances down my shoulder with the sudden movement and I grit my teeth, but fuck this.

The lights don't come back on.

I need to tell Sullen.

I stride over to the off-white bathroom door, the scent of soap reaching my nose. I take a deep breath, my chest rising and falling too fast. I think of the glowing green room. The rabbit slithering to the floor when I shattered the jar. The way Sullen pinned me down. How he injected a needle into my skin.

I shouldn't go in here. He's been warning me all along.

But I am shaking, especially as I look one more time, praying in my head the lights will be back on.

Nothing.

There's nothing but blackness in the hall.

I reach out my hand for the cool knob of the bathroom and twist it slowly, closing my eyes tight for a moment before I tell myself to stop being a baby. *This is important. He would want to know.*

I spring open my eyes.

I open my mouth to call to him. To warn him I'm coming in.

But the word dies in my throat.

The first thing I see is the white tile of the floor, the door only opened a sliver, humidity rushing out and warming my skin, causing me to shiver with the contrast of cold and heat.

It's not that which has his name refusing to leave my mouth, though.

It's the second thing I see.

*Blood.*

Along the floor, thick and smeared haphazardly, a few drops leading out of sight, toward where I know the shower is, the water still running.

It wasn't there before.

The floor was clean.

My heartbeat thrashes in my ears and I glance up to see steam clouding the rectangular mirror above the sink, my makeup and face products set along it, but nothing else.

My own shadow hovering here in the doorway like a specter reflects back to me, too.

I realize Sullen is...too quiet. Not that I would expect him to be talking to himself; he barely talks to anyone else as is. But it's like he's not even moving under the stream of water. There is no jump or dissonance in the flow, just a steady rush of it.

Dread wells up inside of me.

I twist around to stare at the sliver beneath the room door again.

And this time, the lights are back on.

I should feel relief. Power outages are probably common here if this place isn't taken care of daily, but for some reason, I'm only more unnerved.

I tighten my fingers on the bathroom knob.

The shower is still a steady, continuous stream.

He isn't moving in there.

Blood is on the floor.

*Something has happened to him.*

Or maybe... Maybe it's not even *him* in the shower.

My limbs feel strangely cold as I turn once more to look at the bright red blood, vivid against the white tile.

*What if he isn't there?*

It doesn't make any sense, but the thought bubbles up in my brain and I can't reel it back. Panic causes my heart to beat faster, stronger, sweat pricking beneath the dampness of my hair, unfurled down my back, grazing my exposed skin from the bra top.

*Sullen.*

I step fully into the bathroom, inhaling the steam, dropping my hand from the knob.

My white socks are inches from the red blood, streaked and vibrant.

*No.*

We should have searched all of this place. We should have been more cautious. We shouldn't have come here at all.

That feeling of being tricked sneaks up on me again, like it did at the Emporium. I swallow hard, and it's as if I am walking into a trap with each slow step I take, but I can't stay away from him. Even if he's baiting me.

*Duplicity.* Doubleness, but also *deceit.*

I slowly take another step, glancing at the clean toilet to the left, beyond the door. I inhale the damp air and refuse to look at the blur of my reflection in the fogged-up mirror.

I'm scared of what else I might see.

Sullen still hasn't moved under the spray of water.

I am trembling, my knees weak, my head swimming.

I slowly turn my head toward the off-white curtain. It's opaque, and I can see nothing behind it, only the white tiles curving around it before it disappears behind the vinyl.

I look down and note the drug store bag just outside of the tub. A lot of my stuff is gone from it, placed along the sink, so it's half-empty. But I spot a tube of topical medication I hadn't noticed before, then the bananas and protein bars.

He must have taken out his soap.

I glance at the silver towel rack and see the bleached-white towel *I* used hanging to dry from it. More are beneath the sink, but maybe he didn't know that. Maybe he wanted to use mine. Have *me* all over him.

I should say his name.

I don't want to scare him, but incomprehensible fear lights through me.

I wish he would move. Maybe say my name, even in anger. I want to catch a glimpse of him.

But I don't see anything.

Not even over the metal bar high above my head.

And all at once, I realize his clothes are gone. I glance to the tote, then over my shoulder at the floor, but there's nothing. The green travel bag is in the room; I picked my outfit from it before I took my own shower.

*Sullen? Is it really you in here?*

Maybe he's wearing his clothes now, though. Maybe he showers with them.

I feel as if I'm falling when I cut my gaze to the white tiles enclosing the space. I can't see him. His feet, his legs, even a shadow of him, and the stream is still flowing, uninterrupted.

It's hard to breathe. I want to grab at the curtain, but I don't want to humiliate him if he is in there, or make him hate me. I should say something, but what if it's someone else? What if it isn't Sullen at all?

*That's not possible.* I know that to be true.

But I think of the tunnels beneath the newer hotel. The secret rooms no one knows about.

I glance back at the blood on the floor. It's not a lot; maybe the amount I would have smeared back at the Emporium, crawling through glass. But I don't remember seeing Sullen injured. He didn't act like he was hurt, but then again, I don't think he ever would.

Fear pulls tight under my skin like cement in my veins.

I can't turn back to the shower. If after all this, something has happened to him, I don't know what I would do.

*Please be okay, Sullen. Please be okay.*

Yet before I can look to ensure he is, I hear the metallic screech of the rings from the curtain sliding against the metal pole, the vinyl being snatched away. My entire body flinches and a second later, a hand grabs the back of my neck, jerking me backward. My calves collide with the sides of the tub but I lift my feet to keep myself upright and a moment later, I'm inside the shower.

A cry leaves my lips, but a palm slams over my mouth, and for a second, as my attacker closes the curtain again, drenching us in darkness, I don't think it's Sullen. Because it's *bare fingers* over my skin.

Fear squeezes through me and my bladder feels tight and full and I'm not even just afraid for myself. If Sullen is caught by Writhe, Stein will kill him.

Something warm trickles down my thigh, soaking my underwear, and when I inhale through my nose, my nostrils flaring wide with fear as I try to breathe, I smell my pee.

And I know *he* does too, but I'm too relieved to be embarrassed when I hear Sullen in my ear. "Oh dear," he says quietly, his throaty voice a balm to the terror in my veins. "You had an accident."

I close my eyes in the dark, damp space, marveling over the fact the stream of water hasn't gotten me soaked yet. My body is so close to the curtain and maybe Sullen adjusted the shower-head so it doesn't reach us here. Either way, I don't care.

Despite how his hand is pressed tightly to my mouth, other arm wrapped around my waist like a snake crushing its victim, I still feel giddy with solace.

My legs tremble, though, the water rushing behind me not enough to drown out my heartbeat in my head. "Sullen." I manage to mumble the word beneath his palm. I don't open my eyes. "Are you okay?"

He tugs me closer to his body, and I feel the water on him pressing into my clothes, drenching me. My socks are soaked, clinging to my feet, and it's an icky sensation, yet I can't find it in me to care enough to remove them.

Slowly, Sullen slides his arm down my waist until his bare fingers grip my thigh, just under the short hem of my skirt. He slides them up higher, making my muscles jump, then he laughs against my ear.

"I feel it," he says quietly, and my face flushes hot as I realize what he means. I peed on myself. My body burns with the fact, and I am trembling, but I don't try to hide away. "Did I scare you so badly, Little Sun?"

I open my eyes then and twist my head to stare up at him. His gaze meets mine, lashes wet and thick.

He *is* dressed, I realize, bandana still around his throat. He is drenched, and I wonder if he showered just like this, or if he got dressed afterward and kept the water running for some reason. Maybe to see if I was going to betray him by slicing through his boundaries.

"Sullen," I whisper again, and he slides his hand down to

my throat, curling his fingers softly around my neck so I can speak. "I'm sorry. I just... I saw the power went out, in the hallway."

"It's an old hotel," he muses quietly, watching me. "This isn't the luxury you're used to."

I narrow my eyes, feeling braver with his taunt. "And I saw...blood."

A twisted smile curves his full lips. Water glides down the line of his jaw, the tip of his nose, a drop on his mouth, right at the corner. I have the sudden, vicious urge to lick it off.

"Did you?" he asks quietly. Then he drags me toward the showerhead and the hot water sprays all over me, oozing through my scalp, dripping down my shirt, over my stomach, my skirt, lower still. I shiver despite the warmth. The feeling of clothing sticking to my skin makes me feel dirty, even though I know it's also washing away the urine on my thighs, his hand still gripping one tightly.

I feel his erection as he crushes me to him, and I don't look away from him even through the water drenching me. He's now behind the spray of it and he looks at me with cruel amusement as he debases me.

He doesn't understand this is exactly what I want.

But I can't let go of the blood on the tile. The nerves I felt thinking he wasn't in here.

I try to twist in his arms, to see the rest of him, make sure he is whole, but he only squeezes me tighter, both with his hand around my throat and his arm over my waist.

I shiver in his grasp, the water blurring my vision, drenching me entirely as he only stares at me. "It's your blood," I gasp out. "It wasn't here before."

He tilts his head, staring at my mouth. "You are very observant."

"What happened? Are you...hurt?"

His dark eyes slowly slide back up to mine. "I'm always

hurt." He says it so flatly, no emotion in his words. It chills me more. But before I can say anything to that, he releases me, only to turn, putting his back to the shower curtain, to the *escape*. He pushes me, pressing my spine against the tile as he pins me there with one hand pressed over my chest.

Slowly, he reaches up with his bare fingers and brushes back his hood, water dripping now over his face. But it's his hair I'm staring at as he studies me carefully, as if waiting for a reaction.

I couldn't hide it even if I wanted to.

His strands are thick, a dark, chocolatey shade of brown, cool in tone. It's cut in a haphazard style, tufts longer in places, strands above his brow, but overall, very short. And despite the sporadic lengths, being able to take him in like this, without his hood, it feels... sacred. His cheekbones appear even higher, his nose sharper, lips fuller, the line of his jaw more severe, especially with water gliding along his face and the stubble there.

He is breathtaking.

But before I can try to vocalize any of what I'm feeling, he turns from me, swiping back the shower curtain. He doesn't release me though and I don't try to move as he crouches down, grabbing something from the drugstore bag.

When he stands again, pulling the curtain closed once more and trapping us in here, I see he has the topical medicine in his hand, a cream for sore muscles.

As he faces me, he is seemingly indifferent to the water saturating his hoodie, his bandana, causing it to cling to his skin. He looks at my thighs, the tiles, then he says, very quietly, his gaze coming to mine, "Turn around."

I glance at the white and red tube of cream in his hand. "Tell me about the blood," I say quietly, meeting his gaze again. "Tell me what happened to you." I scan his body, but with all of his clothes on, even his high-tops, I can see nothing.

"Turn around, and I'll tell you." He curls his fingers in the top I'm wearing, pulling at the silk fabric, and exposing one breast. I feel the water streaming over my bare skin and glance down, watching my pink nipple harden into a tight ball.

He runs his bare thumb over it softly and every nerve in my body is alight. "Turn around," he says again, his voice rougher. "You're safe with me, Karia." The exact opposite of what he's said all along, and yet I feel it.

My paranoia washing away.

The hotel is old, like he said.

No one is here.

Not yet.

And I want to listen to him. To obey.

But when I glance at his pants, I see how hard he is for me, his erection bulging.

And I decide I won't turn around.

I know what he intends to do; he wants to take care of me, put the cream on my shoulder.

But I want to take care of him, too.

No one ever has. *I want to be the first.*

And maybe if he's not so sexually frustrated, he'll answer some of my damn questions.

Before I can think it through, I step forward suddenly, and he doesn't try to pin me back against the wall before I drop to my knees in the tub, the water cascading down my arm as I slowly reach my hands to his thighs, gripping them firmly.

His body is tense, but he says nothing. When I lift my head up to stare at him through my lashes, water swirling around my knees toward the silver drain, he's staring back at me, his lips pressed together.

"My shoulder hurts," I tell him softly. "But my mouth doesn't." And before he can think I mean something more than I do, I palm his erection, feeling how hard and thick he is beneath my hand.

His jaw clenches, but he doesn't stop me.

"Take care of me," I whisper, knowing I'm pushing my luck. "And I'll take care of you."

"Karia—"

"I won't take your pants off. I won't...*really* touch you. Just... this." I glide my hand up and down the length of him, wondering if I could possibly make him come like this. *"Let me, Sullen."* And before he can say anything, I press my face to him, running my cheek over how hard he is.

A low groan leaves the back of his throat and his fingers tangle in my hair, but instead of pushing me away like I expect, he only holds me closer.

Something knots tight and warm in my chest, and I keep running my cheek over him, wishing desperately for more but contenting myself with *this*.

A moment later and I feel the cream on my skin. Then he drops the tube with a soft splash in the water around my knees and starts to massage me. He draws aside the thin strap of my bra top, pushing it down my arm before he slides his palm back up.

The touch makes the tiny, damp hairs all over my body stand on end.

It feels *divine*. I groan as I continue rubbing him with my face, and his fingers splay around my back, curving over my shoulder blade. His hand is so big, he touches all of me easily. He curves his fingertips into my skin, massaging deep in a way that's borderline painful but the cream is icy-hot, tingling and soothing at once.

I pull back a little to mouth at him over his pants, running my bottom lip over the length of him, and when I look up through my lashes, I see his eyes locked on mine and his lips are parted in a way that is so fucking *hot*.

He glides his fingertips over my clavicle, pressing softly, then his entire palm brushes down my top before he grabs my breast roughly.

I gasp over his erection and his pupils seem to darken, a flashback of the eye under the hotel door causing me to shiver, but I'm not afraid.

It was him.

I know it was.

It had to be.

And I should have helped him then.

Instead, he watched me walk away like a coward.

But I'm not leaving him again.

I bite softly at him through his pants, the fabric wet and rough in my mouth, but I don't care. I would do anything for a taste of him, and if this is all I can get, it's what I'll take.

He twists my nipple as he stares at me, as if he wants me to flinch. To tell him to stop.

But I don't say that.

I only dig my teeth into the fabric of his pants, wondering if after all the pain he's experienced in his life, he's gotten a taste for it. I know he likes to be bitten.

His eyes flutter closed, answering my question, and he releases my nipple only to slap my breast softly, his hand striking down and making me flinch, but a warmth lights up through me, too.

I curl my fingers tighter against his solid muscles as I slide my open mouth over as much of his cock as I can get with the fabric in the way. I want to take him bare, but I know he won't let me. Not yet. Still, his fingers tightening in my hair, tugging at my scalp, his eyes half closed, I know he's into this, too.

And as the cream that was on his hand starts to sink into the skin around my breast, I gasp, the icy sensation chilling me at the same time heat begins to swell and it's unlike anything I've ever experienced before.

His eyes flash as he stares at me, a small smile curling his lips when he realizes it, too. He grips me harder, and I lick the solid ridge of him through his pants.

333

His smile disappears as his lips part and he groans again, a delicious, rough sound that feels almost as good as his touch.

He tilts his head back, exposing some of his throat, the bandana wrapped around the rest. "Fuck, Karia," he whispers, squeezing my breast hard. But then his eyes flash open and he dips his chin.

Something changes in his face that I don't understand.

He grabs my arm, jerking me violently to my feet before he pushes me against the shower wall, hand on my breast. *"Karia."* He whispers my name like he's in pain.

"Sullen?" Now, I'm scared again.

His chest is rising fast, falling faster. I don't understand what I did wrong.

But the moment before he parts his gorgeous lips to speak, to say something that seems to be getting under his skin, the lights in the room flicker.

The stream of water from the showerhead stalls, gurgling to a jerky spray.

Then everything is dark.

The water stops, only the sounds of uneven dripping and the rumble of the drain reaching my ears.

Sullen still has his hand on me and my fingers curl in the damp fabric of his hoodie.

"Tell me this is normal," I whisper quietly, my voice shaky. "Tell me it's because I'm not used to luxury." I repeat his words, wanting to hear his condescending tone say that again.

But I think he stopped me for a different reason.

He heard something before I did. He's always on alert, isn't he? Even when I was lost in him.

The gleam of his brown eyes meets mine.

And I hear it then, too.

A slithering sound, like something in the pipes over our head.

His hand comes to my mouth, the other cupping the back

of my damp hair, and I am grateful for his touch as I shake in the tub, my legs trembling.

Something clanks and shifts, just above us.

I think of my dream.

The snake over my body.

I swear I hear a hiss of laughter.

Water drips from the showerhead.

A whimper leaves my lips.

We are staring at one another in the dark.

I am trembling everywhere, and my heart sinks when I realize... *he is too.*

My nostrils flare and I smell soap, him, *fear.*

He presses his temple to mine. Then he nudges his nose against the side of my face, lower, over my jawline, down my throat. His teeth scrape my neck and I close my eyes tight, feeling as if he is saying goodbye.

There's a thud from somewhere outside of the bathroom.

Tears prick behind my eyes.

"Sullen," I whisper, wanting him to tell me this is nothing. We're safe. We can still make it.

But all he says, his mouth on my throat, is, *"Someone is here."*

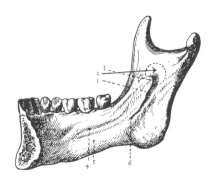

*if I cannot inspire love, I will cause fear;*

— ***Frankenstein*, Mary Shelley**

Sullen & Karia's story continues in *The Scientist of Haunt Muren.*

# Do you desire more?

*If so, you have a few options.*

- **Sign up for my newsletter:** authorkvrose.com/newsletter
- **Join my Patreon** for bonus scenes, character art, and more: patreon.com/kvrose
- **Start the Unsainted series** to dig deeper into the organization that is above Writhe
- **Join my Facebook reader's group, Order of KV,** to chat about all KV characters

# About K.V.

I explore the darkly romantic side of humanity.

If you're into that, you can find me:
instagram.com/kvrosedarling
facebook.com/authorkvrose
authorkvrose.com
And on Spotify, where I spend most of my time

# Also by K.V. Rose

**Ecstasy Series**

Ecstasy

Ominous Book I

Ominous Book II

**Unsainted Series**

These Monstrous Ties

Pray for Scars

The Cruelest Chaos

Boy of Ruin

Like Grim Death: Part One

Like Grim Death: Part Two

**Unsainted Novella**

Ambition

**Sick Love Duet**

Unorthodox

**Razer Rabbits Series**

Verglas

The Fells

**Stitches & Teeth Duet**

The Scientist of Haunt Muren

Made in the USA
Monee, IL
10 January 2024

51521799R00213